PRAISE FOR THE VERONICA SPEEDWELL MYST

A TREACHEROUS CUR

"The relationship between Veronica and Stoker is [illegible] will really snag you. She's a refreshingly un-missish historical heroine and he clearly enjoys her intelligence—so you'll be left wondering when they'll get together already (in other words, you'll be eagerly awaiting the next book in the series)."

—NPR

"If you haven't started this series yet, now's a perfect time to get caught up!"

—Book Riot

"The third adventure for the attractively eccentric duo is a clever and witty follow-up to *A Perilous Undertaking*." —*Kirkus Reviews*

"While readers of Elizabeth Peters's Amelia Peabody mysteries will enjoy this title, it is fans of *Jane Eyre* who will truly appreciate the third volume in Raybourn's historical series. Her intricately plotted and dramatic story features a strong-willed, independent woman who is the intellectual equal of the brooding Stoker." —*Library Journal*

A PERILOUS UNDERTAKING

"A fine combination of detective story and character study, *A Perilous Undertaking* is sure to interest mystery lovers and Anglophiles alike. . . . Clever plotting and explorations in the relationship between Veronica and her equally mysterious and passionate partner, Stoker, are always a source of delight." —*The Historical Novels Review*

"Raybourn is the queen of Victorian mysteries, an author who manages to write stories with historical characters and settings without ever allowing them to feel old-fashioned or stale." —Culturefly

"Smart individuals trying to make their way in a world that they don't quite fit into, while at the same time satisfying their intellectual curiosity and refusing to apologize for who they are—hello, there, my catnip. . . . The Veronica Speedwell series is excellent and intelligent fun."

—Smart Bitches Trashy Books

"Full of innuendo and amusing repartee, Deanna Raybourn's sly wit will be appreciated by readers of romance and historical fiction alike, especially those who enjoy her Lady Julia Grey series. The sexual tension between Veronica and Stoker is intense, and Veronica's antics will keep the reader laughing. . . . A fun read, reminiscent of Elizabeth Peters's novels, whose cross-genre charm is sure to appeal to readers." —Shelf Awareness

A CURIOUS BEGINNING

"Sparkling. . . . The intrepid Veronica's witty narration and the sexual tension she shares with the equally eccentric and articulate Stoker deliver a fun read with promises of more to come." —*Publishers Weekly*

"A fantastic read, both wickedly clever and devilishly amusing. . . . Veronica Speedwell is a joy—unflappable, unrepentant, and thoroughly delightful."

—Susan Elia MacNeal,
New York Times bestselling author of the Maggie Hope series

"With wicked intelligence, Deanna Raybourn has created a fresh and fascinating sleuth. Veronica Speedwell is sure to join the greats of mystery fiction."

—Alan Bradley,
New York Times bestselling author of the Flavia de Luce series

"A treat. One of the few writers who can make history feel immediate and exciting without losing a feel for the period."

—Rhys Bowen,
New York Times bestselling author of the Royal Spyness series

"Raybourn introduces her latest feisty heroine, deftly twining together suspense, romance, and cracking good dialogue . . . a thrilling—and hilarious—beginning to a promising new series." —*Kirkus Reviews*

"A smart, plucky, way-ahead-of-her time heroine. . . . The plot moves swiftly and surely with the expected delightful twists, and the ending left me looking forward to Veronica's next exploits." —*Fort Worth Star-Telegram*

ALSO BY DEANNA RAYBOURN

Veronica Speedwell Mystery Series

A Curious Beginning

A Perilous Undertaking

A Dangerous Collaboration

Lady Julia Grey Series

NOVELS

Silent in the Grave

Silent in the Sanctuary

Silent on the Moor

Dark Road to Darjeeling

The Dark Enquiry

NOVELLAS

Silent Night

Midsummer Night

Twelfth Night

Bonfire Night

Other Works

NOVELS

The Dead Travel Fast

A Spear of Summer Grass

City of Jasmine

Night of a Thousand Stars

NOVELLAS

Far in the Wilds (prequel to *A Spear of Summer Grass*)

Whisper of Jasmine (prequel to *City of Jasmine*)

A TREACHEROUS CURSE

A VERONICA SPEEDWELL MYSTERY

Deanna Raybourn

BERKLEY
NEW YORK

BERKLEY
An imprint of Penguin Random House LLC
1745 Broadway, New York, NY 10019

ISBN: 9780451476180

The Library of Congress has cataloged the hardcover edition as follows:

Names: Raybourn, Deanna, author.
Title: A treacherous curse: a Veronica Speedwell mystery/Deanna Raybourn.
Description: First edition. | New York: Berkley, 2018.
Identifiers: LCCN 2017013413 (print) | LCCN 2017018530 (ebook) |
ISBN 9780698198401 (ebook) | ISBN 9780451476173
Subjects: | GSAFD: Mystery fiction.
Classification: LCC PS3618.A983 (ebook) | LCC PS3618.A983 T74 2018 (print) |
DDC 813/.6—dc23
LC record available at https://lccn.loc.gov/2017013413

Berkley hardcover edition / January 2018
Berkley trade paperback edition / February 2019

Printed in the United States of America

Cover art and design by Leo Nickolls
Book design by Kristin del Rosario

To Danielle Perez,
for befriending Veronica
and taking her farther than I ever
imagined she could go . . .

CHAPTER 1

London, 1888

"I assure you, I am perfectly capable of identifying a phallus when I see one," Stoker informed me, clipping the words sharply. "And that is no such thing."

He pointed to the artifact I had just extracted from a packing crate. It was perhaps three feet in length, carved of some sort of exotic hardwood, and buffed to a smooth sheen. Bits of excelsior dangled from it like so much whimsical decoration. It was oddly festive.

"Of course it is," I said. I brandished the item in question at him. "Just look at the knobby bit on the end."

Stoker folded his arms over the breadth of his chest and looked down his nose at me.

"Consider, if you will, the length. Improbable, you must admit. *Most* improbable." He was doing his best to avoid the appearance of embarrassment, but a touch of rose still bloomed in his cheeks. I found it winsome that such a hardened man of the world could have gained so much experience as scientist, explorer, natural historian, naval surgeon, and taxidermist and still manage a maidenly blush when confronted with a fertility icon.

"Stoker," I said patiently, "both male and female genitalia have been celebrated in ritualized art since the beginning of time. And frequently their proportions are exaggerated in order to convey their importance to the peoples in question."

He curled a handsome lip. "Do not invoke ethnography, Veronica. You know how I feel about the social sciences."

I shrugged. "There are those who maintain the study of culture is just as important as the examination of a bit of bone or a fossilized snail. And do not pretend that you are immune to the seductive siren call of the humanities. I have seen you mooning over journal articles about the role of religious ritual in the decreasing populations of certain South Sea turtles."

"I do not moon," he retorted. "And furthermore, those journal entries—"

He proceeded to lecture me for the next quarter of an hour, about what I cannot say, for I turned my attention to the contents of the packing crate. I had long since discovered upon my travels that men are largely the same no matter where one encounters them. And if one is prepared to let them discourse on their pet topics of conversation, one can generally get on with things quite handily without any interference.

The packing crate was the newest arrival at the Belvedere, the budding museum Stoker and I had been commissioned to organize under the aegis of our friend and benefactor, the Earl of Rosemorran. Situated on the grounds of his lordship's Marylebone estate, Bishop's Folly, the Belvedere was either a glorious trove of undiscovered treasures or the storehouse of a family of madmen, depending upon one's perspective. The earls of Rosemorran had been an acquisitive lot, haring around Europe to amass a collection of art, artifacts, zoological specimens, books, manuscripts, jewels, armor, and a thousand other things that defied description. How we came to live amongst such treasures is a story that merits its own volume.*

To investigate one murder is a curiosity. To investigate two is a habit. Stoker and I had fallen into the practice of murder when our mutual friend, the Baron von Stauffenbach, had been slain the previous summer. We had uncovered some difficult truths and made a cautious alliance with Sir Hugo Montgomerie, the head of Special Branch, Scotland Yard's most prestigious division. When, at the end of that investigation, Fate had proven to be an unkind hussy and left us without home or employment, the current Lord Rosemorran had graciously invited Stoker and me to work for him, living on the grounds of Bishop's Folly and cataloging his collection with an eye to one day opening the Belvedere as a public museum. It was arduous work, consisting of unpacking, inspecting, reviewing provenance, cleaning, and registering each item—the beetles alone could take years—but it was enchanting. Every day offered its own surprises, and as word spread of our undertaking, donations to the collection began to arrive. It seemed that Lord Rosemorran's project was the perfect opportunity for his friends to rid themselves of items they no longer wanted. They would never send anything truly valuable—the English aristocracy are nothing if not sharply attentive to financial advantage—so we received instead a steady stream of decrepit hunting trophies and wretched oil paintings. They were of no use to us, so Stoker regularly burnt the moth-eaten trophies in the garden whilst I arranged the portraits into a grim sort of family, giving each a pet name and taking particular delight in each baleful new addition.

But the shipment that arrived that morning had been the most peculiar yet. The large packing crate had been stuffed with excelsior to cradle an array of phalluses, each more impressive than the last. Clay,

* *A Curious Beginning*

leather, marble, wood—the materials were nearly as varied as the objects themselves, and the assortment of sizes was frankly extraordinary. From a modest little fellow about the width of my handspan to the enormity I brought to Stoker's attention, they represented a thorough study of that particular piece of anatomy. At the bottom of the crate nestled a leather box with a piece of card affixed to the lid.

> *Personal gift to Miss Veronica Speedwell. I have not forgot my obligation. With my compliments and heartfelt gratitude. Miles Ramsforth*

Suddenly, the mysterious collection made perfect sense. Our second investigation* had saved Miles Ramsforth from the hangman's noose, and I was not surprised he had chosen to repay the debt with part of his extraordinary array of erotic art.

Understandably, Ramsforth had quitted England immediately upon his release from prison and we had never met in person, but he had sent an effusive letter of thanks with a splendid silver watch chain for Stoker and a promise to remember me with something even more noteworthy.

My curiosity piqued, I extracted the box carefully and opened it with a rush of anticipation. I was not disappointed. Wrapped lovingly in cotton wool was yet another phallus, this one a masterpiece of the Venetian glassmaker's art. Of clear blown glass, it was striped with luscious violet color that gleamed like a boiled sweet as I held it to the light. I remembered it well. I had admired it when Stoker and I first studied the collection, although how Ramsforth happened to know of my appreciation was a mystery. It was a testimony to both his gratitude and his puckish sense of humor that he would present me with the costliest specimen from such a deliciously lurid collection.

---

* *A Perilous Undertaking*

I brandished it at Stoker. "I was quite right about the hardwood piece," I told him. "This was at the bottom of the crate. It is the doing of Miles Ramsforth. A personal gift," I added with a waggle of my brows.

Stoker blushed furiously. "For the love of God, put that thing away."

"I cannot imagine why you are so bashful on the subject of the male genitalia of *Homo sapiens* when you are the only one of us who can boast of owning it," I muttered as I replaced the offending item carefully into its box with a mental note to examine it more thoroughly in private.

"I heard that," he said as he returned to the task at hand—hollowing out the remains of a badly mounted platypus. The task was messy but not arduous, so he had kept on his shirt, a rare occurrence given his penchant for working stripped to the waist. I regretted the fact that he was fully clothed, but I contented myself with the occasional appreciative glance at his muscular forearms, bared to the elbow. His shirt was open at the neck, and he seldom wore a waistcoat and never a coat if he could help it. His hair, black and waving and badly in need of a barber's attentions, was punctuated by a slender streak of silvery white, a souvenir of our most recent foray into detective pursuits. It had ended when he had been shot in the temple in a ridiculous attempt to shield me from a murderer, and the result was a single snowy lock where the bullet had struck him. Gold rings glinted at his earlobes, and one of his many tattoos, relics of his days as a surgeon's mate in Her Majesty's Navy, peeped from the edge of his rolled sleeve. He wore a patch over his left eye, a habit since an accident in the Amazon had nearly taken it from him, leaving him with slim pale ribbons of scars that marked him from brow to collarbone and beyond. He looked like precisely what he was: a man in his prime with a good deal of experience and precious little regard for Society's expectations.

"Stop scrutinizing me as if I were one of your damned butterflies," he said in a conversational tone.

I sighed. "It has been a year since my last indulgence in physical congress," I reminded him in a wistful tone. "Admiring your physique is my only consolation."

He snorted by way of reply. I had made no secret of my perfectly sensible approach to relationships between the sexes—namely that marriage was a ridiculously outmoded institution and that sexual exercise was both health-giving and revivifying to the spirits. In the interest of respectability, I never indulged whilst in England, preferring to satisfy my urges during my trips abroad, a discreet and wholly efficient arrangement. The fact that it had been more than a year since my last expedition had begun to try my resolve. Stoker did not judge my predilections any more than I judged him for living as chastely as any medieval monk. A brief and hellish marriage followed by a period of Bacchanalian overindulgence had soured him on romance, although I regularly recommended to him a restorative bout of coitus, preferably with a strapping dairymaid—a course he had yet to embrace.

I considered the various phalluses, uncertain of where to begin. "Ought I to arrange them by size? Or shall they be grouped according to geographical region of origin? Or material?" I asked. Stoker and I frequently quarreled about various methods of organization within the collection. I preferred a chronological approach whilst he maintained a firm preference for theme.

This time he merely flapped a hand, clearly finished with the subject of phalluses. I hefted the largest, the hardwood piece from the Pacific, scrutinizing it with a practiced eye. "You know, I am rather reminded of a charming American fellow I met in Costa Rica," I said with a nostalgic sigh. I made a point of never keeping in contact with my paramours once I had finished with them, but I had very nearly made an exception for the American . . .

I did not pursue the conversation. Stoker was in a good mood for once, something that had been sorely lacking of late. February had been thoroughly nasty, with snowfall of apocalyptic proportions and temperatures that would have caused a polar bear to shiver. We had made the best of the situation, applying ourselves diligently to our work, but both of us had suffered bouts of ennui, longing for balmy climes and sea-scented winds. Our planned expedition with Lord Rosemorran to the South Pacific to search for new specimens had been thwarted by accident—namely his lordship's unfortunate collision with his Galápagos tortoise, Patricia. She lumbered around the estate with all the grace and speed of a boulder, so how the earl managed to fall over her was a matter never fully explained to my satisfaction. But the result had been a broken femur and months of recuperation. We sympathized with his lordship and told him we did not mind in the least, but I drank a significant amount of strong spirits as I unpacked my bag, and I suspected Stoker sniffed back a manful tear or two as he put away his maps and charts.

Saving Miles Ramsforth from the noose had been a diverting occupation, but a Christmas spent with Lord Rosemorran's unruly brood of children underfoot and the rigors of a perilously long winter had nearly undone us both. Stoker had amused himself by unearthing the most ludicrous of the taxidermy mounts while I had taken to reading sensationalist newspapers. One, *The Daily Harbinger*, had proven useful during the Ramsforth case, and I had resorted to bribing the hall boy, George, to bring me the copy each morning before his lordship had a chance to read it.

This morning he skipped in, bearing the newspaper and the first post, whistling a merry tune. George broke off as he caught sight of the object in my hand, his eyes round with interest and his errand forgotten.

"Here, now, miss, that looks like—"

"We know what it looks like," Stoker cut in ruthlessly.

George peered into the packing crate. "Where are these from, miss?"

"All around the world," I told him. "They were amassed by a gentleman named Miles Ramsforth, a famous patron of the arts and a suspected murderer."

He blinked. "Imagine that."

I put out my hand. "*Harbinger*, please."

He gave me the newspaper before wandering to where Stoker was bent over his trophy. "That's a funny old stoat."

"It isn't a stoat," Stoker corrected. "It is a platypus."

"Why has it got a duck on its face?" George put out a tentative finger and Stoker flicked it aside.

"This is *Ornithorhynchus anatinus*, the duck-billed platypus, native to Australia."

"But why has it got a duck on its face?" George persisted.

"It hasn't got a duck on its face. That is just its face."

"Are you taking the duck off its face?"

Stoker's nostrils flared slightly and I knew he was about to say something unpleasant.

"George," I called as I skimmed the front page of the newspaper. "What is the latest news of the Tiverton Expedition?"

George trotted over, his face bright with interest. He had a penchant for the most outrageous stories in the *Harbinger*—and the *Harbinger*'s stories were already more outrageous than most. But he was a good lad and took great pride in his budding literacy, so I encouraged him.

"Oh, miss, you ought to read it. They say the expedition is cursed," he said with an unholy gleam in his eye.

From behind his platypus, Stoker gave a snort.

"You don't believe in curses, sir?" the boy asked.

Stoker opened his mouth—no doubt to hold forth on the subject of superstition—but I anticipated him. "Curses are not rational, George. There is no scientific basis for them. However, there is good reason to think that the belief itself in a curse can create deleterious effects."

"Dele—what?" the boy asked.

"Deleterious. It means bad. I was saying that the mere belief in a curse can give it power."

"Hogwash," Stoker said succinctly.

"It most certainly is not. There are well-documented cases of individuals—"

"Exactly that. Individuals. There has been no empirical study done on the subject."

"And how, precisely, would one conduct such a study?" I asked in an acid tone. He did not bother to reply, and I turned back to George. "Tell me about the curse."

George and I had become fascinated by the exploits of the Tiverton Expedition in Egypt. Led by Sir Leicester Tiverton, an excitable baronet of middle years, the group had found a cache from the Eighteenth Dynasty. The burial was incomplete, but the sarcophagus of a princess and an assortment of grave goods were enough to ignite a furor of international interest. Sir Leicester had become something of an instant celebrity. A series of calamities had forced the early return of the expedition, and stories of their misfortunes had kept the reading public enthralled.

"It is said that the site of the dig was visited by one of the Egyptian gods. Can't remember his name, but he wears a dog on his head," George said, gesturing to the lurid illustration in the newspaper. I skimmed the article quickly.

"Anubis," I told him. "God of the underworld, and that is not a dog on his head. It is a jackal."

I pointed him to the Greco-Roman sarcophagus Stoker and I used as a sideboard for our meals. Incised on its side was a parade of ancient gods. George had little trouble spotting Anubis.

"Is this cursed too?" he asked.

"I doubt it. The thing is a late Greco-Roman copy of a much older piece."

"Is there a mummy inside?"

"I'm afraid not," I said absently as I studied the drawings in the newspaper. "Just a collection of early prosthetics."

"Pros—what's that, miss?"

"Prosthetics, George. Fake arms and legs meant to replace those that have been lopped off."

"Blimey! But no mummy?"

"No mummy," I assured him. "And don't say 'blimey.' It's common."

"I'm common, miss," he returned cheerfully.

Of that I had no doubt. For all I knew, Lord Rosemorran's butler, Lumley, had found him squatting in a gutter under a cabbage leaf. But the boy was bright, nimble in understanding, and blessed with a solid ear and a head for figures. If he could curb his tendency to slang and the dropping of 'h's,' he might well make something of himself.

George turned back to the illustration. "They say that this Anubis fellow came into the workers' camp at night, looking for a soul to take."

"Rubbish," Stoker said succinctly.

"No, sir, it's true," George maintained stubbornly.

I held up a hand. "The boy is right. The director of the excavation died a few weeks ago, and now the expedition photographer has disappeared along with a diadem belonging to the mummified princess. Apparently, the Egyptian workers blamed their troubles on a curse inscribed on the princess' sarcophagus."

"Horsefeathers," Stoker replied.

"George, you'd better get on before you learn any new words of which Mr. Lumley wouldn't approve," I told the boy. He grinned and went on his way as I finished the article.

"You oughtn't to encourage him," Stoker said as he returned to his platypus. "The boy already has a febrile imagination."

"No more than this reporter," I said absently. "I do not recall seeing his name before, but J. J. Butterworth has made quite a reputation for himself writing about the Tiverton Expedition."

"'Our man in Cairo'?" Stoker asked.

"More like 'our man in London.' This was filed here in town. Apparently the Tivertons have returned to England after John de Morgan's disappearance." I would have said more, but I broke off as soon as I caught sight of Stoker's face. Still bent over his platypus, his features had frozen into an expression so thoroughly devoid of emotion, it was impossible to interpret. His complexion had gone perfectly white, then flushed a quick and violent red. I feared he was well on his way to an apoplexy. "Stoker, what is it?"

"Nothing," he answered after a long moment and a visible effort. "Afraid I was woolgathering. What did you say?"

I pressed my lips together, holding back the question that rose to them. Whatever had caused him to react so strongly, he had no wish to share it, and I had no wish to pry.

(I have pledged myself to honesty in these pages, gentle reader, so I will admit that in point of fact I had a rather ferocious wish to pry, but I had learnt through painful experience that Stoker responded far better to the oblique approach than to more direct methods. Considering my extensive experience in hunting butterflies—notoriously skittish and elusive creatures—Stoker was less trouble than a Chimaera Birdwing.)

I went on. "I said that the Tivertons, Sir Leicester and Lady Tiverton, have returned to England. The death of their excavation director loaned credence to the idea of the curse. The local workers have refused to reenter the tomb, and the director of antiquities in Egypt has agreed that it is best they seal it back up and leave things to settle until next season."

"And there is no sign of the photographer?"

"John de Morgan? No. Apparently he disappeared from the dig site with his wife. At the same time, the jewel of Sir Leicester's find, a diadem belonging to the dead Princess Ankheset, went missing, and no one knows if de Morgan and his wife stole it or if they met with foul play."

Stoker said nothing. His color slowly returned to normal, and his hands resumed their work. I turned to the post, sorting the various envelopes into pigeonholes. Bills to Pay. Bills to Pretend I Have Not

RECEIVED. LETTERS TO ANSWER. LETTERS TO IGNORE. LETTERS FROM TEDIOUS PEOPLE. The rest I consigned to the wastepaper basket.

But the last demanded my immediate attention. I will admit to a small groan as I recognized the imperious hand of our sometime friend and occasional sparring partner at Scotland Yard.

"Sir Hugo?" Stoker guessed as I took up the lion's tooth I used as a paper knife.

"Sir Hugo," I confirmed. "How did you guess?"

"He is the only person of our acquaintance who could excite such a reaction. We are invited to call?"

I skimmed the brief message. "We are not invited. We are instructed. He wishes to see us, but he is ill at home, and he summons us to his sick-bed. Gird yourself, Stoker. We are about to meet Sir Hugo in his nightshirt."

Sir Hugo Montgomerie, head of Special Branch, loyal watchdog of the royal family, and our sometime ally, was tucked up in bed when we arrived. His house stood in one of the quieter, leafier corners of Belgravia, so elegantly nondescript that one might easily pass it by without a second glance. I suspected that was a deliberate choice on Sir Hugo's part. Whenever possible, he opted for understatement, and I was not surprised when the door was answered by a very correct parlormaid rather than a butler.

"Miss Speedwell and Mr. Templeton-Vane to see Sir Hugo," I told her. "We are expected."

She did not wait for a calling card. Cap ribbons starched and snapping, she led us to the stairs, past the public rooms, and up two flights, going directly into Sir Hugo's bedchamber without pausing. The room was well proportioned and tastefully furnished with Regency fruitwood pieces and a very fine Aubusson. The draperies were the color of crushed mint leaves, and the counterpane a darker green. Against the soft apricot walls, the result was soothing elegance, but the effect was slightly ruined by the tropical temperature. The windows had been firmly sealed and the fire stoked high, so that the entire room was hot as Satan's boudoir.

A pair of small tables stood next to the bed and were crowded with bottles and bowls, various medicaments, stacks of handkerchiefs, and a spirit lamp. The smell of camphor hung heavily in the warm, damp air.

Sir Hugo was sitting up in bed, surrounded by newspapers and holding a handkerchief to his streaming nose. Atop his head perched a nightcap with a lavish tassel of blue silk.

"Mith Thpeedwell, Templeton-Vane," he said with a brusque nod. (For the duration of our visit, he proceeded to lisp as he breathed stentoriously through his mouth, but I will make no attempt to reproduce the ghastly noises he made.) He waved us to a pair of chairs next to the bed as the parlormaid waited at the door.

"What is it, Carter?" Sir Hugo demanded.

"Time for your tonic, sir. Lady Montgomerie is most particular," she told him.

He pulled a face. "Lady Montgomerie is not my mother. Get out," he grumbled.

The maid grinned as she left, and I suspected she was as amused by Sir Hugo's pettishness as we were. I could feel Stoker suppressing a laugh as he stared in rapt fascination at the tasseled nightcap.

"We are very sorry to find you unwell," I told Sir Hugo.

"At least you have some sympathy," he said sullenly. "My wife fusses, the maid bullies, and Mornaday gloats. I'll wager a guinea the little flea is sitting in my chair right now."

The fact that Inspector Mornaday longed for his superior's job was one of the worst-kept secrets at Scotland Yard. No doubt he was relishing every moment of freedom from Sir Hugo's watchful eye. But it would not do to upset the patient any more than necessary, I decided, so I ignored the mention of Mornaday altogether.

"We should not keep you longer than necessary," I said, setting a bright smile on my lips. "You need your rest."

"I need occupation," he retorted, stabbing at the newspapers. "Do you know what is happening in my city? Murder! Mayhem! Misanthropy! And where am I? Stuck in bed waiting for Helen to dose me with Dr. Brightlung's Pulmonary Tonic and force-feed me a blancmange."

"Heaven forbid we stand between a man and his wife's blancmange," Stoker murmured.

Sir Hugo reached for a pillow to heave at him, but I lifted a hand. "Do not distress yourself, Sir Hugo. Stoker is merely teasing. I will drop something into his tea later to revenge you."

"Make it arsenic." Sir Hugo fell to coughing then, a hideous bout that left him gasping for breath. Without a word, Stoker went to the windows and wrenched one open just a little. Fresh cold air rushed into the room, lightening the heavy atmosphere. While Sir Hugo regained his composure, Stoker busied himself with the spirit lamp and various bottles. After a few moments, he approached the bed, carrying a steaming bowl and a towel.

"What's that?" Sir Hugo demanded.

"A remedy," Stoker said. He put the bowl onto a bed tray and set the whole affair onto Sir Hugo's lap. He draped the towel over the ailing man's head. "Now, slow deep breaths and hold the steam in your lungs for as long as you can."

I sniffed the air. "Sage?"

"And thyme with a little peppermint oil. I would have preferred white eucalyptus, but the stuff is devilishly hard to find outside of Australia."

We chatted for a few minutes, comparing herbal remedies we had collected on our travels, until Sir Hugo emerged, snuffling and red of face, but with markedly easier breathing.

"That works," he said in some astonishment.

Stoker sighed. "I *am* a surgeon," he reminded Sir Hugo.

"Yes, I just didn't know you were a good one." Sir Hugo settled back against his pillows, still wreathed in fragrant steam. "Ah, that is better." He drew in a deep breath and let it out again. "I haven't been able to do that for almost a fortnight."

"A little fresh air and regular herbal steam baths," Stoker instructed. "And pour out that tonic. It's poisonous stuff."

"I will," Sir Hugo promised, clearly in better spirits. He looked to me. "You may be wondering why I asked you to call today."

"We are entirely at a loss," I told him truthfully. "We haven't meddled in so much as the theft of a tea towel since last autumn." Our amateur investigative efforts were a thorn in Sir Hugo's side. He veered between reluctant tolerance and frothy rage when we found ourselves at the business end of a murder. I could not resist the urge to tweak Sir Hugo's nose a bit. "I presume it has something to do with my unwelcome connection to the royal family?" I suggested. My status as a semilegitimate member of that august group both rankled Sir Hugo and elicited his most protective instincts. "Is this my periodic harangue that anything I do might reflect badly upon them?"

Sir Hugo looked hurt. "I do not harangue."

"You have upon numerous occasions. Shall I list them?"

"I did not summon you to harangue you now," he corrected. "In fact, I mean to offer you help."

Stoker and I turned to each other, blinking. "Stoker, is there anything in those herbs that might cause Sir Hugo to suffer hallucinations? It is the only explanation."

"I am entirely serious," Sir Hugo protested. "I know I have been strict with you in the past—"

"You had me arrested," Stoker pointed out coldly.

"Yes, well—"

"Your men put me into a Black Maria and hauled me to Scotland Yard like a common pickpocket," Stoker went on.

"Be that as it may—"

"My person was searched. My *entire* person," Stoker finished.

Sir Hugo fidgeted. "Perhaps I let the lads go a bit too far," he admitted.

I turned to Stoker. "They disrobed you?"

"They stripped me mother-naked," he affirmed.

"Well, that must have intimidated them," I mused. I had had the pleasure of seeing Stoker's undraped form on multiple, if innocent, occasions. Any man who stripped him would doubtless suffer by comparison.

Sir Hugo was still gaping at my last remark when I pressed on. "What do you mean, you intend to help us?"

"I mean exactly that. Something has come to my attention that might prove . . . difficult," he said, seemingly at a loss. "I don't know how best to begin."

"Sir Hugo! I have seen you at your bellowing worst, and I must say, I am far more discomfited by this avuncular consideration for our feelings. Spit it out, man."

"Very well." He pushed himself higher up on the pillows. "I am sorry to bring to light things you have no doubt buried," he began.

I opened my mouth to ask what in the world he was wittering on about, but in that instant I realized Sir Hugo's gaze was not resting upon me. He was staring at Stoker.

I snapped my mouth shut. Stoker's expression was as imperturbable as usual.

"What things?" I demanded.

"Things that might cause Stoker to be a person of interest in a man's disappearance."

"Whose?" I asked, but Stoker did not stir. He knew already, I realized, for there was a bleakness in his face I had never seen before.

Sir Hugo went on. "A fellow by the name of John de Morgan. He was most recently employed as a photographer with the Tiverton Expedition in Egypt."

At that I did burst out laughing. "What nonsense! Stoker has no connection to John de Morgan."

"Veronica—" Stoker began softly.

I flapped a hand. "Hush, Stoker. I am berating Sir Hugo." I went on in the same vein, poking fun at Sir Hugo for the sheer ridiculousness of the notion that Stoker might be involved in de Morgan's disappearance. After a minute or two, I realized Stoker and Sir Hugo had been suspiciously quiet, the silence between them hanging heavy in the room.

I whirled on Stoker. "You mean it is true? You have a connection to John de Morgan. Why didn't you say?"

"As Sir Hugo said, I buried my dead," he told me simply. I waited, but he said nothing more. I turned back to Sir Hugo.

"Very well, they have a connection. But you cannot seriously suspect Stoker of harming the fellow. Might I remind you that you are speaking of Revelstoke Templeton-Vane? The *Honourable* Revelstoke Templeton-Vane? His father was a viscount and his maternal grandfather was the Duke of Keswick."

"I am aware of his antecedents, Miss Speedwell. That will not immunize him from suspicion if certain facts become public knowledge."

I took a deep breath. "Very well. We must have a clear understanding of these facts. Proceed."

Sir Hugo looked a trifle relieved, as if he had expected hysterics. He should have known better. I was a scientist, after all. I had learnt early in life that facts were the only things one could truly rely upon in this world.

Stoker said nothing. He merely sat and waited for Sir Hugo to speak.

"John de Morgan was hired at the beginning of this Egyptological season to act as photographer for Sir Leicester Tiverton's expedition. He traveled to Egypt with the Tivertons in November and was permitted to bring his wife, as Lady Tiverton and Miss Iphigenia Tiverton were expected to join the party after Christmas. As you have no doubt read in the newspapers," he said with a twist of the lips, "a discovery was made. The Tivertons located the partial burial of a princess. Two weeks ago, de Morgan departed Egypt abruptly, accompanied by Mrs. de Morgan. They left without a word to the Tivertons, taking only a single carpetbag each."

"Curious," I murmured.

"At the same time, a priceless diadem belonging to the dead princess went missing. It is the most significant piece in the collection, and it was regretfully presumed that de Morgan had stolen it."

"Presumed by whom?"

"The Tivertons. They did not like to point fingers, but as the collection must be cataloged for the benefit of the Egyptian authorities, they had to report its theft." He cleared his throat, resuming his narrative. "De Morgan and his wife traveled by a fast steamer as far as Marseilles, where they boarded the train for Paris and then to Calais. From there they took a Channel steamer, arriving in Dover at just about midnight. They proceeded to a small private hotel in Dover, where they took separate rooms, as de Morgan was suffering from ill health and did not wish to disturb his wife."

I pursed my lips but said nothing. What sort of woman accepted a separate room for her own comfort when her husband was ailing and in need of attention?

Sir Hugo picked up the thread of his tale. "They slept apart. In the morning de Morgan had vanished without a trace. At the insistence of his wife, the local police investigated and there was no sign of him to be found in Dover or in London. Notices have been placed in newspapers around the country. Passenger lists, ticket offices, railway porters—all avenues have been pursued, with no result. John de Morgan has simply disappeared."

I curled a scornful lip. "I am surprised at you, Sir Hugo, for making such a mountain out of a particularly sordid little molehill. Clearly the fellow wished to be rid of his wife. He saw her safely onto English soil, which was the gentlemanly thing to do, but at the first opportunity he absconded with his purloined diadem to start life afresh somewhere else. No doubt he pawned the crown to fund his escape from England. You above anyone must know that it *is* possible to elude the police with a bit of luck and proper care. It seems perfectly simple."

Sir Hugo said nothing.

"There is more," Stoker guessed shrewdly.

Sir Hugo nodded, the tassel of his nightcap swinging like a pendulum. "Yes. You see, John de Morgan was not the only disappearance. When his wife came to wake him the next morning, his entire hotel room had vanished as well."

A damp little finger of horror crept up my spine. "What do you mean, his hotel room had *vanished*?"

"Mrs. de Morgan insists that when they checked in, de Morgan's room was blue with a rose-print wallpaper and walnut furniture. Mrs. de Morgan tucked her husband up into bed and sat with him for some time as he fell asleep. She amused herself by counting the rosebuds in each section of the wallpaper. The next morning, when she went to see how he had fared in the night, the room was empty. And the wallpaper—"

"Was different," I finished.

"Forget-me-nots," Sir Hugo informed us. "Rather a grim joke under the circumstances. The carpet had been changed to green, and the bedstead replaced with one of iron. The hard chair she had sat upon the night before was now a plush affair of striped yellow velvet."

"It sounds dreadful," I remarked.

"And nothing at all like the room John de Morgan had taken."

"What of the hotel proprietor?" I demanded. "Surely he must have some explanation."

Sir Hugo shrugged. "Proprietress, actually. According to Mrs. de Morgan, she checked them in upon their arrival the previous night, but when questioned by the Dover police, she said Mrs. de Morgan arrived alone."

"The hotel ledger," Stoker said quickly. "John would have signed the hotel ledger upon checking in."

Sir Hugo shook his head. "Mrs. de Morgan signed for them both, as her husband was feeling ill upon their arrival. The only entry in the ledger bears her handwriting."

"If there is no proof John de Morgan ever set foot in this country, how can you possibly suspect Stoker of having anything to do with his vanishing?" I asked.

Sir Hugo's expression was pained. "In point of fact, I do not suspect Stoker. But with no clear answers as to de Morgan's disappearance, naturally it became necessary to consider the possibility of foul play. And once the idea of murder was mooted, the next step was to determine if John de Morgan had any mortal enemies. As it happens, he has just one."

He raised his eyes to Stoker, who did not flinch from the scrutiny. "Yes," he said calmly. "I hated him. But if I wanted to kill him, I would have done it openly and let you put the noose around my neck with your own two hands."

I stared at him. In the months we had known one another, I had come to understand him better than most. Some stories he told me; others I guessed. But there were secrets within him, dark and spiny things that scuttled from the light of day.

"Who is John de Morgan to you?" I asked him softly.

He said nothing. He simply sat, so still, so silent, I could almost imagine he was not there. It was Sir Hugo who spoke.

"John de Morgan was the supporting partner of the Templeton-Vane Expedition to Amazonia in 1882."

I felt a jolt of something electric pass through my body. "He was your friend," I said, forcing the words out through lips suddenly cold and stiff. "He left you there when you were about to die."

Stoker's smile was a thin and mirthless thing. "He did more than that. He married my wife."

CHAPTER 3

A surge of laughter, exquisitely balanced on the knife edge of disbelief, rose within me. I smothered it as Sir Hugo gave a solemn nod of assent. "Mrs. John de Morgan was, before her marriage to him, Caroline Templeton-Vane."

My thoughts spun and tumbled. It appeared another shard of Stoker's past was coming to light to add to the slender collection I had hoarded. I knew that he had led a failed expedition to the jungles of the Amazon, an expedition that had cost him his marriage and his honor as well as his career as a rising star in the firmament of natural history. I had never learnt the details; he seldom mentioned that period of his life and never without obvious pain.

That Caroline Templeton-Vane had left him in Brazil and returned to England to petition for divorce on the grounds of cruelty was public record. Reporters had scented blood in the water and gathered for a feeding frenzy with Stoker's reputation the casualty. If he had returned at once, he might have mitigated the damage, mounted some defense that could have turned the tide at least a little. But instead he had lingered in Brazil, healing from wounds sustained in a jaguar attack, not bothering to book passage home for three long years.

By then the damage was beyond repair. He had sunk into obscurity and poverty, and only the efforts of our mutual and much-mourned friend, the Baron von Stauffenbach, had kept him from complete degradation. The baron had sent him taxidermy commissions and provided a workspace, and since his death I had taken it upon myself to be Stoker's prop and support. There was a spark of genius in him, but sparks are fragile things, and they need careful attention. I had seen progress in the past months, a reviving of the spirits and the confidence that had been broken to splinters by his experiences. A surge of dislike for Caroline de Morgan threatened to choke me. I had kept Stoker hard at work, coaxing and bullying him into the best state he had known since she had annihilated him, and now her name was spoken once more, like a terrible incantation summoning a ghost that had never been entirely laid.

"I believe I require fortification," I said succinctly. I rose and went to the bedside table, where I helped myself to a glass to accommodate the measure of aguardiente I poured from the flask I always carried on my person. I drank it down in one swift motion, capping the flask and wiping my mouth carefully. When I had cleaned the glass and resumed my seat, I looked at Sir Hugo.

"You can prove motive. You cannot prove murder. You have no body."

"How many times must I say that I do not wish to prove murder?" he asked in some exasperation, throwing his hands heavenwards. "I do not believe he was murdered."

"What do you think happened?" Stoker asked in a voice rather unlike his own.

Sir Hugo passed a hand over his fevered brow. "I am inclined to agree with Miss Speedwell. I think the fellow saw an eye to helping himself to a fortune and ridding himself of a wife at the same time. For these reasons, he took the jewel and slipped away. A rotten thing to do, but apparently the fellow had money troubles and a tempestuous marriage."

I perked up a little at this last snippet of information. "Did he indeed?"

"The members of the expedition indicated that the de Morgan marriage was not always a cordial one. They were frequently cross with one another—money being a constant source of friction."

"It would be," Stoker said quietly. "John could never keep two shillings together in his pocket. His wife wouldn't like that."

The mention of the woman caused something green and slimy to slither in my belly. "What does Mrs. de Morgan have to say about the state of her marriage?" I asked.

"Mrs. de Morgan is not answering questions. She spoke with the Dover police, but has refused all efforts to reach her since. The chaps there were not as tactful as they ought to have been, and the whole ordeal was too much for her. Her father came and took charge of her and has made it perfectly clear that we are not to trouble her again. Our hands are tied."

"Mrs. de Morgan cannot cope with difficult realities," Stoker said. "If John left her, it would shatter her entirely."

"Perhaps she killed him," I offered pleasantly.

Sir Hugo huffed into a handkerchief. "Unlikely. I am told she is of middling height but slim and fine-boned. She might be able to kill a man, but she could never dispose of the body."

Stoker rose and went to the window, staring out as Sir Hugo and I continued to talk.

"Why are Special Branch involved? This sounds like a matter for the Dover police. Ought it not to have begun and ended with them?"

"Initially, we were not part of this investigation. The disappearance of one insignificant man is not enough to involve us," Sir Hugo said, a trifle loftily. "But as he was connected with Sir Leicester Tiverton's expedition, and since de Morgan may have absconded with a priceless piece of historical significance, we have been kept informed."

"Not our history," I corrected.

Sir Hugo smoothed his moustaches. "The expedition was funded and undertaken by Englishmen. If it were left to the Egyptians, the artifacts would still be moldering in the ground." Seeing that I was about to argue, he held up a quelling hand. "But that is beside the point. Sir Leicester's name is a prominent one, and we were obliged to take note. I should perhaps mention, there is another party who is quite enthusiastic about all things Egyptological and encouraged our involvement," he said with a significant twitch of the lips.

"My father," I guessed.

Sir Hugo did not like to acknowledge the relationship so openly, but he gave a short nod. "His Royal Highness sailed up the Nile in the spring of sixty-two." He paused, knowing I would seize upon the significance of the date.

"When in the spring?"

"March. Two months before your birth and some three months after the death of his father. Prince Albert had planned the trip as a sort of royal tour, and in spite of her grief, Her Majesty thought it best that her son carry out his duties. It was a quiet affair, with no official entertainments. His Royal Highness spent most of his time smoking cigars and reading sensational novels and having himself tattooed," he finished, his lips tightening in disapproval.

"You seem to know quite a bit about it," I said, attempting a casual tone I did not feel. Two months before my birth. My mother would have been heavy with child and expectation of a future with my father—an expectation that died with her before my first birthday.

"I accompanied His Royal Highness," Sir Hugo explained. "Special Branch did not yet exist, of course, but it was considered advisable for the prince to have companions of a sober and discreet nature who could encourage him to take an interest in the people and politics of the region as well as its history."

"And did he?"

He pulled a face. "I regret to say, His Royal Highness was more interested in shooting crocodiles than in learning the intricacies of foreign policy. But he did bestir himself to ignore his mother's dictates regarding invitations on at least one occasion. He met with the local authority, Said Pasha, and developed rather a remarkable rapport with the fellow. There are few men as personable as the Prince of Wales when he exerts himself," he finished.

"What was he like on the trip?" I asked in a small voice.

"There are photographs," Stoker said, not turning his head from the window. "A fellow named Francis Bedford took them and published them in two folios."

Sir Hugo said nothing, but I knew he must have been aware of the photographs. I had glimpsed my father once, in passing and at a distance. It was not enough. The prince I had seen was middle-aged and corpulent, exquisite tailoring not quite concealing his avoirdupois. But he had not always been so. He must have been handsome once, I knew, in order to turn my mother's head. She had been the rarest beauty of the age.

"You have seen these folios?" I asked Stoker.

Still he did not turn. "Briefly. One of the gentlemen on the tour, Arthur Stanley, brought along a manservant named Waters who had a talent for stuffing birds. I can mount anything with feathers, thanks to him. He showed me the folios once. It should be a trifling matter to find other copies."

Sir Hugo gave a little cough. "I suppose I could hunt up my own set," he said, not ungraciously.

"Thank you. I presume his travels in that country sparked an interest in Egyptology?"

He nodded. "He has been a keen observer ever since that trip, although it was Lady Tiverton's writings which really kindled his interest. He found her to be quite knowledgeable on the subject."

"And knowing his reputation, I would hazard a guess that Lady Tiverton is an attractive woman," I said in an acid tone. Every fact I gleaned about my father always seemed to come back to sex.

"Most attractive," Sir Hugo admitted. "She was the foundress of the Tiverton Expeditions, funding them through her private fortune and encouraging her husband to excavate in previously unexplored regions of the Valley of the Kings."

"She must be immensely gratified to have discovered a royal burial," I mused.

"She would be," Sir Hugo agreed. "If she were alive. Regrettably, the first Lady Tiverton died some years ago. She was an invalid in poor health and made her home in Egypt. Consumption," he said with a shudder. "Her widower, Sir Leicester, has made the find with his second wife, the current Lady Tiverton."

"That hardly seems fair," I protested. "The poor woman spends her money and what little health she has pursuing a dream, and no sooner is she dead than her husband and his new wife see that dream realized."

"Fate ith a cruel mithtreth," Sir Hugo said, ending on a heavy sneeze.

"Stoker, Sir Hugo is becoming unintelligible again. Have you no remedy?" Stoker did not reply, and after a few minutes' work with a handkerchief, Sir Hugo managed to retrieve the conversation.

"As you say, Miss Speedwell. It is a sad irony that Lady Tiverton did not live long enough to see her life's ambition fulfilled. One can only hope that her spirit is consoled. She did her very best during her short time on earth to create interest in Egypt and its history. She wrote a number of scholarly articles and published several volumes of her own essays. It is thanks to these books that the prince is keenly aware of the developments in the field of Egyptology.

"He has read Sir Leicester's reports as well, and naturally he became all the more interested in John de Morgan's disappearance when he understood the fellow's history with someone who is a close connection of yours. There is your safety to consider." He flicked a meaningful glance at Stoker's broad back. The implication was only too clear.

"You cannot be serious," I told him, my temper rising. "My father is not worried that I am partnered with a potential murderer. He is worried that if Stoker becomes notorious again, reporters will dig too deeply into his connections—specifically, his connection to me. And then what? They investigate my past? They uncover the truth about who I really am? The Prince of Wales is not concerned with my safety. He is worried that some stroke of misfortune will see all his sordid secrets come pouring out in the newspapers."

"His Royal Highness expressed no such sentiment," he replied with unusual sternness. "His Royal Highness doesn't even *know* what Stoker is capable of."

I fixed him with a cold stare. "What precisely is Stoker capable of?" I demanded.

Sir Hugo had the grace to look uncomfortable. "Shall you tell her or shall I?"

Stoker did not turn from the window. "It was a long time ago."

"A year," Sir Hugo corrected. "Not so very long."

"I am hardly the same man." Stoker's protest was halfhearted.

"What did you do?" I put the question gently, as if a soft tone would make the lash sting less.

Stoker turned very slightly so that his face was in profile to me. "Our paths crossed last year, mine and John's. I saw him in the street. I daresay if I had expected it, I might have behaved better, but I had no idea he was in London. I simply looked up and there he was, coming at me. I did not think. I did not consider. I acted."

"What did you do?" I repeated.

He said nothing for a long moment, and Sir Hugo broke in. "He thrashed John de Morgan within an inch of his life."

I smiled. "Good."

"What a savage young woman you are!" Sir Hugo protested. But there was no condemnation in his voice, and it was apparent from his expression that he did not entirely disapprove either of Stoker's action or my feelings.

"I have seen Stoker fight," I told Sir Hugo. "'Savage' is an understatement. De Morgan is lucky he escaped with his life, and Stoker is telling the truth. If he had meant to kill him, he would have." I turned back to Stoker. "Out of curiosity, why didn't you? I mean, I would have at least been *tempted*."

"I was," he replied, still keeping his face in profile. "But after I knocked him down, he refused to get back up. I won't kill a man on his knees."

"There," I said with some satisfaction to Sir Hugo. "You see? Stoker has standards. He won't kill a man on his knees, and I can promise you he also will not spirit away a man under the ridiculously Gothic circumstances you have described. Whoever is responsible for the disappearance of John de Morgan has clearly been reading too much Mrs. Radcliffe."

Sir Hugo did not disagree. "It does indeed bear the hallmarks of a ghoulish imagination. But the fact is, a man has gone missing, no matter how outlandish the circumstances."

"And you think that since Stoker publicly whipped the fellow last year, his name will be bandied as a potential villain in the piece?"

"It is only a matter of time," Sir Hugo said. "De Morgan was apparently a very likable fellow. No known enemies apart from Stoker. A few small outstanding debts of honor, one or two tradesmen's bills, but nothing worth killing a man for. There is no one in de Morgan's life who bore him the sort of grudge Stoker did."

"Then why hasn't his name come up before now? Why hasn't he been interrogated or arrested?"

"Because no one else at Scotland Yard knows what I know," Sir Hugo replied with obvious satisfaction. "The disputation last year was not a matter of public record, but the facts are to be found in a rather singular file in my collection at Special Branch."

I gaped at him. "You have had him investigated. Because of me!"

He did not even have the grace to look embarrassed. "Naturally. If a person is going to spend as much time as Stoker does with a member of the royal family in such an intimate situation as the two of you enjoy—"

"I am *not* a member of the royal family, and it is the grossest violation of his privacy—" I was just warming to my theme when Stoker turned back from the window.

"The newspapers," he said flatly. "How long do we have before they discover de Morgan's connection to me and rake it all up again?"

Sir Hugo's expression was apologetic. "A few days if we are lucky. The file is in my personal collection, but there are men in my employ who gathered the information and we must be prepared in case a tongue should wag. That is why I asked you here. I wanted to advise you that this scandal was about to break. There is not a newspaper in England that will fail to print your history with the de Morgans—in the most lurid detail. They will throttle every fact, twist every truth for a good story. Whatever you thought they did to your name the last time, it will be trebled. You must get right away. I know Lord Rosemorran has a shooting box in Scotland that he would be more than happy to put at your disposal—"

"No." Stoker and I spoke in unison.

Sir Hugo blinked his puffy, streaming eyes. "What do you mean, 'no'?"

Stoker gripped the back of his chair, his knuckles white. "I mean that I was not here the last time. I did not fight. I made no effort to save my good name. That has been lost to me forever, but I have clawed back some shreds of decency and dignity and I will not have them taken from me again."

Sir Hugo started forwards, but Stoker flung up his hand in a gesture of dismissal. "I will not flee. I will not hide. I am not a murderer, and I do not care who says that I am. I will keep my name."

With that, he turned on his heel and strode from the room. After a long moment, we heard the bang of the front door as he quitted the house. I clucked my tongue at Sir Hugo.

"Really, Sir Hugo, that was badly done. You ought to have known better. If you wanted him to go away, you should have ordered him to stay."

Sir Hugo tipped his head. "He said almost exactly the same about you one time. What is it about the pair of you that you must be so contrary?"

"What is it about the rest of the world that it cannot take us as we are?" I asked.

I rose, and Sir Hugo caught at my hand. "You will be careful, Miss Speedwell?"

"With him? There is no need," I promised him. "He is changeable as the sea but solid as the earth."

"What will you do?" he asked almost plaintively.

I shrugged. "What we must, Sir Hugo. We will find John de Morgan."

Stoker was waiting for me when I emerged from the house, his expression thoughtful. "I ought not to have left you. It was rude."

"That is the least of your offenses," I told him, not breaking stride as I passed. "What kind of impossible moron have you become? Do you really intend to find John de Morgan?"

"Certainly," he said, falling into step beside me. "Don't you?"

"It is the logical course of action, and it is the one I told Sir Hugo we would pursue, but you must admit it is madness."

"How so?"

"How so? How so? You cannot be so dull-witted. In the first place, we have employment. We have been engaged by Lord Rosemorran to catalog his collection, not hare off after possible murderers. In the second, we do not know if it is even possible to find John de Morgan. I would direct you to Occam's razor—the simplest explanation is the likeliest. A man has a wife with whom he does not always get on amiably and a fortune in stolen gems. Any fool could draw a line between those two points. He ran away," I pronounced, crossing the street in the wake of a hansom.

"Furthermore," I said, increasing my pace, "there is the matter of publicity. You heard Sir Hugo. Once the newspapers get their teeth into this story, they will not turn loose of it. They will tear you to pieces, and there is nothing we can do to stop it. And," I added with a touch of malice, "it will displease the royal family if they get wind of what we are about."

Stoker's long stride kept up easily. "To answer your objections," he said with maddening calm, "we have been involved in newspaper-worthy exploits before and never yet seen our names in print. This matter has no direct connection to the royal family, so they should not care in the slightest what we do. If anything, they should be grateful if our efforts cause John de Morgan to be found and the mystery solved. As far as the work in the Belvedere, we have a century's worth of cataloging. A few days will hardly matter, and I didn't notice you raising an objection when we flitted off to investigate the Miles Ramsforth case at your instigation."

I stopped so suddenly that Stoker carried on several steps before he realized I had not kept pace. He turned and I gave him a long, level look. "They will hunt you, you know. They will hunt you like a pack of feral dogs. And they will break you."

Something cold touched his smile. "Let them try."

CHAPTER 4

Stoker was in an unaccountably foul mood for the rest of the day. Rather than attend to his jaunty little platypus, he instead tore into the hide of a white rhinoceros that had been afflicted with mildew, cutting into it with a savage satisfaction. I tidied up a *gonerilla*—a New Zealand Red Admiral, a brownish black butterfly with chic red slashes—took the dogs for a run, and wrote an article for the *Surrey and Home Counties Aurelian Society Semi-Quarterly Folio* on the subject of *Satyrium w-album*, the White-Letter Hairstreak, an unprepossessing and surprisingly elusive little butterfly with a fondness for elms.

At last, as teatime beckoned, the dogs and I settled down in the upstairs snuggery. Stoker's bulldog, Thomas Henry Huxley, had formed a fast friendship with his lordship's immense Caucasian shepherd, Betony. Well, perhaps not so much a friendship as a torrid affair that had already resulted in one litter of extremely unfortunate-looking puppies. They were an inseparable though comical pair, and I gave them each a pat as I passed out horse tibias for them to gnaw on. (The bones, I should note, came from an obliging fellow who sent them to us believing them to be the leg bones of tiny dinosaurs.)

As the dogs settled happily to their treat, Stoker flung down his tools and shook the moldering sawdust from his person.

"Have a rock cake," I suggested, proffering the plate. "Cook has outdone herself. This batch is actually edible." One of the perquisites of living and working at Bishop's Folly was that our meals were provided by the earl's cook. While her roasts were unsurpassed and her puddings were Stoker's greatest joy in life, her rock cakes inevitably lived up to their name, thanks to her habit of taking an afternoon tipple of cream sherry followed by a nap. The scullery maid left in charge of the cakes was usually to be found hanging over the shrubbery, watching the gardener's boy wield his hoe, with the result that the cakes invariably suffered.

But nothing could keep Stoker from cake, and he applied himself with vigor as I poured the tea.

"I know you do not wish to discuss it," I began.

"Then why are you introducing the subject?" he countered through a mouthful of crumbs.

"Because we must develop a strategy. No good general goes into battle without a plan," I said stoutly. "Caesar wouldn't have done so."

"Caesar was murdered by his friends," he reminded me.

"Because he didn't listen to the woman in his life," I countered.

"Touché." He helped himself to another rock cake, slathering this one with jam and cream.

"You have the table manners of a Visigoth."

"I am hungry," he protested. "You try excavating the insides of a rhinoceros on an empty stomach. He was full of rubbish. I found a litter of dead kitten skeletons in there and newspapers from the passing of the Corn Laws. And a snakeskin."

"I know," I told him with a fond glance. "There are bits of it in your hair."

He brushed most of them away, then shrugged and went back to his cake whilst I reboarded my train of thought. "Now, to proceed logically, we must begin at the beginning. In Egypt."

"Yes," he said with a twist of the lips. "It all began in Egypt, didn't it? But not the Egypt you think."

I blinked. "Not the Tiverton Expedition?"

"No. The Egypt of 1882. When John and I were in Egypt together, when we first encountered her." He sat back in his chair, the rest of his cake untouched on the plate. Tendrils of steam rose from the cup in his hands, sinuous ribbons that twisted in the air. "John and I were both assigned to HMS *Luna*. That is how we met."

"What was his position?"

"Master-at-arms—a position to which he was distinctly unsuited. John was not the most disciplined of souls. But he managed. He ran afoul of the captain on our first voyage, and I was tasked with stitching him up afterwards. We became friends—the best of friends."

His voice trailed off as he gazed into the depths of his cup.

"What was his situation? Who were his people?"

Stoker shrugged. "His father was a vicar, the younger son of a younger son. John's great-uncle inherited the family home and the baronetcy that went with it. John had no prospects, save what he made of himself in the navy. He had already tried the church and reading law. The navy was his father's last attempt at sorting him out."

"Was he troubled?"

"No more than I," he said. "Naval life suited us. There were months of excruciating boredom. God, you cannot imagine the tedium of life at sea." He must have remembered my own travels then, because he smiled a little. "Or perhaps you can. But that's when you really get to know another man. I liked John. He was the closest thing I had to a brother."

"You have three brothers," I reminded him.

"And they are the closest thing I have to acquaintances. Tiberius and Rupert were at school before I took much notice of them, and Merryweather was barely out of the nursery when I left. John was my first real experience of camaraderie. I trusted him."

He broke off and swallowed a quick draft of his tea.

"And then Egypt," I prompted.

"The Bombardment of Alexandria. July of 1882." He cocked his head. "Where were you then?"

I counted backwards, reckoning the dates. "Let's see. I would have just turned twenty. Ah, that was my South Seas and Indian Ocean trip. In July of 1882, I was floating on a raft in the middle of the Coral Sea with a Chinese gentleman. We were shipwrecked off the New Hebrides."

"One of your lovers?"

"Certainly not. He was four times my age, although that was not the reason for my restraint. As it happened, he was a religious and had taken a strict vow of chastity. He was also most informative on the subject of the defensive arts. We passed the time by practicing holds and spearing sharks."

"I ought to have known." He took another drink of his tea, then shook his head. "This needs something."

I poured a measure of aguardiente into his cup and he stirred it with a finger. "Better," he pronounced after a taste. "Where was I?"

"Heaving bombs at civilians in Alexandria."

"Otherwise known as the reason I left the navy. Ironic, isn't it? I managed to get myself mentioned in despatches for the very engagement that persuaded me I could not kill for a living."

"You were the surgeon's mate. You ought to have been saving people."

"I did a fair bit of that as well. But I had no taste for the business of war. I left the navy, as did John."

"But that was to have been his career," I pointed out. "What plan had he formed?"

His mouth twisted again. "One doesn't speak of John de Morgan and plans in the same breath. He wanted to go where I went. He thought adventure would follow and we would manage somehow. We spent the last of our pay in Cairo, living like lords as long as the money lasted."

"And that is where you met . . . her."

"Yes. At a dance given at the consulate. It was just before we resigned our posts, so we were both in uniform, looking quite dashing in our blue coats. All the naval lads were the toast of Cairo, at least for the moment. We went everywhere—dances, polo fields, sailing up the Nile. The consul-general held a grand party for us, and a family called Marshwood came. The husband was attached to the consulate in some minor capacity. The wife was one of those overbearing Englishwomen who sustain themselves on gossip and complaint while the sons gambled away their prospects. But the daughter. She was unlike the rest of them. They got up a tableau that night as part of the amateur theatricals to entertain us. She was robed as the incarnation of Justice, all golden hair and long white gown, so ethereal I could not imagine even touching the hem of her gown. I do not know where I got the courage to approach her. I only remember it was more terrifying than the bombardment had been. I did not even ask to be presented properly. I simply walked up and asked her to dance, and when she put her hand in mine, it trembled. And I thought myself the most fortunate man alive."

I crumbled a piece of cake with my fingers. "She must have been beautiful."

"Like an angel," he said slowly. "And I have never been religious. But if you had asked me in that moment if seraphim existed, I would have pointed you to her and you would have believed."

My tea had gone cold and scummy, and I put the cup aside, careful not to let it rattle in the saucer.

"And so you married her."

"I married her." He fell silent again, and that silence encompassed the whole of their time together, for when he spoke again, he said nothing of the marriage itself. "After the divorce, she married John. I have heard the odd bit of news here and there. He has attempted to attach himself to numerous expeditions, but his reputation was rather blackened by the scandal of marrying a divorced woman. Nothing to the scorching my own name took," he added with a grim smile.

"Do you think he abandoned her?"

He shrugged. "It is possible. John left everything else in his life when he found it dull or it lost its charm for him. He is not a steady sort of man."

"And do you think him capable of stealing the diadem?"

He gave me a curious look. "I sometimes thought John de Morgan would steal the miter off the pope's head if he thought he could make use of it. He was a prankish boy. I cannot tell you what sort of man he has become."

"I rather wonder that you were friends with him," I said lightly.

"Then you have a kinder opinion of me than I deserve." He drank off his tea and motioned for the flask again.

"It is empty," I lied.

"Veronica."

I sighed and handed it over. He did not bother with tea this time, merely tipped his head back and emptied a considerable amount of the liquor straight into his mouth. He gave a shudder of satisfaction.

As he drank, my mind whipped back some months to a night I had not entirely forgot. I held only pieces of it in my memory. The rest were lost to opium and cocaine, thanks to an ill-advised foray into intoxicants during our previous investigation. But I remembered the feeling of his lips on mine, the broad sweep of his back muscles under my palms. And I remembered the name he had whispered into my mouth before I shoved him away. *Caroline.*

I gave him a tight smile. "I pity her. She must be in a terrible state, not knowing what has become of her husband. Perhaps we should pay a call upon her."

He did not flinch, but something caused his hand to flex and his mouth to draw back for an instant. "I think not."

"As you wish," I said silkily. He gave me a sharp look, but I evaded his gaze as I emptied my cold tea into the slops bowl and poured a fresh cup.

"But you are quite correct that we must discover what happened to John de Morgan," I said. "I see that now. And if you intend to investigate, I mean to help you. After all, we have sleuthed out two murderers already at my behest. One might even say I *owed* you," I concluded, deepening the smile.

He said nothing, but his brows drew together and a line etched itself between them.

"However"—I smoothed my skirts over my lap—"if we are not going to call upon Mrs. de Morgan, we ought to gather the facts as clearly as we can, and I can think of one person right under our noses who is bound to know everything about Sir Leicester Tiverton's expedition."

Stoker had fallen into a brown study but roused himself. "Oh. Who might that be?"

"Lady Wellingtonia, of course," I said. The aunt of our benefactor, Lord Rosemorran, Lady Wellingtonia was a formidable woman with her fingers in more pies than a baker's son. She knew everyone and, more importantly, she was up-to-date on the latest gossip. If there was anything of interest to be discovered about the Tiverton Expedition, Lady Wellie would know it. She hoarded information like diamonds, and she was not averse to sharing it—within reason.

Stoker looked doubtful. "We have hardly spoken to her since the Ramsforth affair."

"That's because she was away," I said. Lady Wellie had taken her leave of Bishop's Folly soon after the conclusion of the Ramsforth case and had returned only at the end of January. At one point she had been holidaying at her shooting box in Scotland, but for the rest of the time her whereabouts had been a mystery. Lady Wellie liked to know everything about everyone, but prying into her affairs was not encouraged.

"No," he corrected. "It is because you didn't want her meddling again."

On that count he was not mistaken. Lady Wellie had proven herself to be an ally with the great and powerful—specifically with Sir Hugo Montgomerie, her godson and partner in protecting the royal family.

"If we apply to Lady Wellie for information, she will only confirm to Sir Hugo that we are investigating."

"Good," I said, smiling like a cream-covered cat. "Good."

The next morning we followed the sounds of strenuous work and found Lady Wellie in the enormous glasshouse on the grounds of Bishop's Folly, supervising the final arrangements of the newly installed heating system. Once a tumbledown wreck, the glasshouse had been completely refitted with fresh glazing, and I looked it over with a rush of possessive pride. Lord Rosemorran had ordered it refurbished and overhauled with an eye to creating a vivarium, a butterfly habitat where I could raise Lepidoptera to my heart's content. The fact that he had done so at Stoker's urging was something I should not quickly forget.

We opened the door to the vivarium and reeled backwards. Steam billowed forth in great foggy gusts, draping rags of veiled mist over the gardens.

"Who the devil is that?" called Lady Wellie. "Come in and shut the door before you let out all the heat."

We did as we were ordered, pushing through the thick atmosphere of the glasshouse to where Lady Wellie stood, hands wrapped firmly around the knob of her walking stick, staring upwards at the network of steam pipes lacing the ceiling of the structure. Standing beside her was Lord Rosemorran in an identical posture. Her walking stick was due to the extremities of old age, but his lordship's was due to the torturous recovery from his shattered femur. It had been a bad break and he had only been on his feet again since the New Year.

"Good afternoon, your lordship," I said. "I am glad to see you up and around again."

He smiled his wistful scholar's smile. "You are too kind, Miss Speedwell."

Lady Wellie gave a snort. "She only says that because she is ready to hare off to the South Pacific. You would be somewhere around Fiji right now if it were not for that leg of yours," she added with a poke of her walking stick in the direction of his lordship's thigh.

"Lady Wellingtonia maligns me," I said coolly. "Nothing could be further from the truth." Actually, it was exactly the truth. I had deeply regretted his lordship's accident—certainly for his sake, but far more for my own. I had been anticipating that expedition with fervor, organizing it to the last detail until Patricia the tortoise's great lumbering body and his lordship's slow reflexes put paid to my plans. Stoker and I had been frank with one another about our disappointment, but it was not consoling to realize Lady Wellie guessed it as well.

Remembering we had come to ask a favor of her, I bared my teeth in a cordial smile. "Stoker," I said, turning to him with an expression of angelic sweetness, "it's very warm. Take off your coat."

Sweat had already begun to stream down his face, so he obliged. Lady Wellie never could resist a handsome man, and Stoker was one of the most attractive of her acquaintance. She did not leer—she was too well brought up for that—but she gave an appreciative little sigh as the humidity soaked through his shirt, plastering the fabric to his biceps and pectorals.

"How go the repairs?" I asked the earl.

He nodded. "Capital. The heating system I designed is quite effective," he told us with a vague gesture to our surroundings. Moisture poured like rain down the insides of the windows, and a bit of cloud floated just overhead. Through the mist, a few score of men—estate workers and builders—moved here and there, clearing away building debris and bringing in the first of the potted trees which would form the botanical infrastructure of my little jungle.

"Effective?" Lady Wellie interjected. "We shall be boiled like Christmas puddings if you cannot regulate it."

There was a *halloa* and the sound of banging on pipes from somewhere in the fog, and his lordship hurried off to confer with his men. He reappeared almost immediately. "Stoker, the valve is broken, and it happens to be in rather an inaccessible spot. I don't suppose you could oblige?" he asked hopefully. "Only I remember you have some experience as a climber."

Stoker did not bother to reply. He was already moving towards the lacework of metal, stripping off his boots. He swarmed up the armature, moving loosely, hand over hand, with the ease of a large primate. The earl stood just below, rubbing his hands together. "Splendid effort!" he called by way of encouragement.

Lady Wellie shook her head as she gazed after the earl with a fond expression. "He was ever thus, man and boy. Always tinkering, always thinking, our Rosemorran. Now, what brings you here? Fancy being roasted like a chestnut?"

I might have pretended I was on hand simply to inspect my vivarium, but there was no point. Lady Wellie had as keen a nose for prevarication as a hound does for a vixen. I came to the point instead.

"I have been reading of late about the Tiverton Expedition, and Stoker and I are curious about Sir Leicester Tiverton."

"Tiverton! Messy Lessy, the boys at Eton used to call him," she said fondly. "He was at school with another of my nephews, on the Fothergill side, one of the duke's boys." Anyone else might have spoken of ducal connections boastfully; with Lady Wellie, it was a mere statement of fact. Lady Wellie was connected through blood or marriage to half the noble families in England. The Beauclerks, besides producing a line of earls, had run strongly to daughters, marrying them carefully into the cream of the aristocracy and creating a network of cousins that Lady Wellie exploited ruthlessly for favors and information. Her sister had married the Duke of Wrexham, producing five sons in seven years before quietly expiring in the Royal Enclosure at Ascot. It had been an unusually exciting day for the races, and apparently no one had noticed the dead duchess slumped in her little gilt chair until it was time to leave.

Lady Wellie went on in a thoughtful voice. "Leicester was a younger son and not expected to inherit the baronetcy, but his elder brother died in the Crimea just before his thirtieth birthday. Poor lad, cut down in his prime, like so many others."

Her face took on a melancholy cast, and I wondered how many dashing young men she had known, lost before their time, thanks to the depredations of war. But Lady Wellingtonia Beauclerk was not a sentimental creature. She recalled herself and favored me with a particularly hideous smile, revealing an array of bad teeth.

"But I daresay he would have turned out to be a pervert or a cheat at cards, so perhaps it is for the best he died young."

I choked a little. "Why do you say that?"

She twitched her stooped shoulders in a semblance of a shrug. "Firstborn Tivertons have always had a streak of recklessness in the blood. It leads them into stupidity. Their father broke his neck when he was steeplechasing. Tried to hurdle a vicar." Lady Wellie gave herself a little shake, banishing the nostalgic mood. "But you want to know about Leicester. Dashing boy, lots of bottom." I did the arithmetic. Assuming his elder brother was not very many years older, Sir Leicester must have been courting sixty, hardly a boy. But then, Lady Wellie was old enough to be Methuselah's wife, so I supposed anyone might seem young to her. She went on, her sharp black eyes focused upwards as she recalled what she knew.

"He was a bit of a daredevil in his youth. He too fought in the Crimea, but he didn't care much for coming straight home when it was finished. He cashiered his commission and did a bit of exploring along the Silk

Road, then carried on climbing mountains in some godforsaken country I have forgot the name of. Spent the better part of a decade surrounded by heathens and donkeys. He stopped off in Egypt on his travels and that was where he seemed to find his life's purpose. Bit by the archaeology bug, as it were," she added with a merry twinkle. "By which I mean, he met Miss Lucie Ward, who had already made a name for herself as an Egyptologist. They married and he settled down to studying properly. She taught him history and methodology, and he provided the stamina and strength for the actual excavations. They were well suited."

"I understand Lady Tiverton passed away a few years ago," I said, rolling back my cuffs as perspiration began to pearl my hairline. Lady Wellie was not the sort to be offended at the sight of a bare wrist.

"Lucie was never going to make old bones," she said, shaking her head. "Consumption. All the Wards have weakness in the lungs. Arresting looks with great dark eyes and very pale skin. They seem like faeries until you hear them wheeze and hack like miners," she added with a shudder. "I made my debut with Lucie's grandmother. She shivered so badly, I had to loan her my swansdown cape just to keep her teeth from chattering like castanets during the presentation at court."

She had a faraway look in her eyes, and I was just opening my mouth to speak when she pressed on, her manner brisk.

"No, the Wards never make old bones, but Lucie had a better run than most. I was her godmother, you know."

"Were you indeed?"

She flapped a hand. "I have stood as godmother to half of England, child. Everyone knew that the Duke of Wellington was *my* godfather, and if they couldn't get him to sponsor their brat, they would ask me. They thought the Wellesley shine might rub off a little, I suppose. Thank heaven the Church of England is not *religious.* I don't think I could have borne actually teaching them about Jesus or listening to them lisp a catechism. No, I sent along an apostle spoon to each and that was the end of it. But

Lucie was a lively thing, for all her ailments. She used to send me letters from Egypt, long, chatty efforts full of interesting bits. She visited once or twice, when she came back to England. She always hoped that she had grown stronger and could stand the climate, but invariably the fogs and damp drove her back to Egypt again. She was very happy with Leicester for all his tempers and gnashes. Pity they hadn't longer together. She left a girl behind, if I remember correctly. Leicester's only offspring, an unfortunate-looking girl called Figgy."

"Figgy? No one calls a child Figgy," I protested. "It's indecent."

"She's Iphigenia," Lady Wellie explained, "but the name was too much for a wee mite, so she was called Figgy instead. I should have thought Prune would have suited her better. Mouth like a sour apple, that girl. However, I have not seen her in some years. She might have improved." But Lady Wellie's expression was doubtful. Like Mr. Darcy, if she lost her good opinion of someone, it was gone forever.

"How old is Figgy now?"

She shrugged again. "Thirteen? Fifteen? It's only a guess, mind. I do not get about these days as much as I used to."

I looked at the bright beady eyes and tried not to laugh. Lady Wellie gave a good impression of an infirm old lady when she wished, but the truth was, she had more vigor than people a fifth her age.

"What of the present Lady Tiverton?" I inquired.

Her thin brows lifted. "A bit of a *mésalliance*, that marriage. It caused some gossip in certain circles when Leicester married her."

"Is there something objectionable about the lady?"

"Nothing whatsoever," Lady Wellie said roundly. "She is as respectable and virtuous a wife as any man could ask. She also happens to be Anglo-Egyptian."

"Indeed?"

Lady Wellie nodded. "British father—a Scots merchant, if memory serves. I cannot remember much about her mother's family except that they were native Egyptian. Such marriages are always difficult, particularly with regard to the children. They are neither fish nor fowl, one foot on dry land, one in the sea."

Her metaphors were appallingly mixed, but I took her meaning.

"She seems to have done rather well for herself if she married a baronet," I mused.

"Oh, yes. She was very quietly brought up and given a thorough education. Scots are usually reliable about such things. When her parents died, she was obliged to take up genteel employment, and she became a sort of secretary companion to the first Lady Tiverton. She nursed Lucie quite devotedly through her final illness. I suppose it was natural that she and Leicester would turn to one another in their grief. She stayed on for some time as his amanuensis. She was reluctant to accept his proposal of marriage, which I think speaks well of her. But in the end she relented, and she has proven a good wife to him. She's knowledgeable about Egyptology, speaks the local languages. And I'm told she has never left off wearing mourning for the lady whose place she now occupies."

Her expression had grown a little vague as she recalled what she had heard about the Tivertons, but suddenly her eyes sharpened. "This is more than a passing curiosity. Why the interest in Leicester Tiverton?"

I saw no reason to lie. "We are interested in the disappearance of his expedition photographer, a man named John de Morgan."

Lady Wellie's brows—wisps of sternly silver hair—rose swiftly. "Are you indeed? Well, well," she said.

"I know what you are thinking and the answer is no," I told her firmly. "This will have no possible bearing on the royal family and cannot bring them embarrassment."

She scrutinized me for a long, careful minute. "You would be surprised at what involves them," she said mildly. "The newspapers have made quite a fuss over this story. Some ridiculous palaver about a mummy's curse."

"Palaver indeed. I don't believe that any more than you do. But we had an interesting interview with Sir Hugo this morning," I said, watching her closely.

She pursed her lips. "Bloody fool. He ought not to have troubled you. Stoker's past is his past and it ought to be buried. Just because he knew de Morgan, it has no bearing on the fellow's disappearance."

I was not surprised that Lady Wellie knew of the connection, nor that she took Stoker's side. She was, when it suited her, a stalwart champion. "I could not agree more," I told her. "But Stoker had an unfortunate altercation with de Morgan last year. Sir Hugo is afraid if word of it got out, it would cast Stoker in the role of likeliest villain. We mean to clear his name of any suspicion," I warned her.

"Of course you do. Any man would do so under the circumstances, and you will go haring off with him because you're cut from the same cloth. Ridiculous, the pair of you, always tilting at windmills. You are reckless devils," she said sourly. She looked up to where Stoker was balanced upon a slender beam of iron some forty feet above the stone floor.

"Hardly that," I said, ignoring Stoker's exploits. "As soon as the newspapers get wind of this, Stoker's reputation will be torn to pieces once more. I am not certain he could stand that. And there is the question of my father," I added significantly.

She turned on me with a stern look. "Your father is an unmitigated ass at times." She broke off, chewing furiously on her lower lip. Her gnarled hands tightened on her walking stick. "I told His Royal Highness there was nothing to fear from Stoker, that he was pure British bedrock, but did he listen? No, the stubborn goat."

"Why should the prince take against Stoker now?" I demanded. "We have been working partners for some months, we live in unorthodox circumstances, and we have been involved in two criminal investigations. No objections have been raised from that quarter in all this time. Why now?"

Lady Wellie looked uncomfortable. "When we first discussed your friendship with Stoker, I was not entirely forthright with His Royal Highness about Stoker's past. Bertie has a profound horror of divorce. He thinks it un-English, says that it flies in the face of everything he holds dear."

"The story of the Templeton-Vane divorce was in every newspaper in London. How did he not know of it?" I demanded.

She shrugged. "The respectable newspapers were more concerned with the eruption of Krakatoa than a sordid divorce case. When speaking to Bertie, I stressed Stoker's connection to the titled Templeton-Vanes and omitted any mention of the more colorful elements of his history. I am sorry to say that this has led His Royal Highness to view me as a less-than-reliable source where Stoker is concerned," she said with a twist of the lips. "He thinks I am overly fond of the boy and declines to take my word for Stoker's character. He naturally now views him with a somewhat jaundiced eye."

"Then we must ensure that the truth about John de Morgan's whereabouts is properly established before Stoker is implicated," I said smoothly. "Sir Hugo indicated that the official position was that John de Morgan had disappeared of his own volition."

"That *is* the official position," she said, watching me carefully. "But I smell something else afoot. Something is happening at Special Branch, and the situation is a bit hazy at present."

I gave her a narrow look. "What do you know?"

She shook her head. "Nothing."

"And you would not tell me if you did," I challenged.

Her expression was arch. "Child, my life's work has been to be the wet nurse of secrecy. I learnt concealment with my letters. Of course I would not tell you everything. However, I would suggest to you that if you can lay hands upon the means of clearing Stoker's name of any possible guilt in this matter, do so. I would not like him to be a pawn in someone else's political gamesmanship."

We were silent a long minute, watching the workmen wrestling the potted trees into place. Overhead, Stoker made swift work of the pipes, and with a great shudder of the iron framework, the blast of steam settled to a warm, gentle mist. A cheer went up from the workers, and Stoker began his descent.

"It's all so absurd," I burst out. "Even if he were suspected, Stoker couldn't possibly have done it. He has been here at Bishop's Folly," I pointed out. "I will swear to it."

She gave me a pitying look. "Do you really think you would be permitted to give evidence to that effect?"

I narrowed my eyes. "But it is the truth. I am his alibi."

She lowered her voice to a hiss. "Veronica, you are a nonentity if your father wishes it. Think. If Stoker is taken up on a murder charge, do you really think the semilegitimate daughter of the Prince of Wales would be allowed to display herself? Your very existence threatens the foundation of the monarchy. You can never take a public role."

The heat was as oppressive as a hand over my mouth, choking out my breath. "That is absurd. If it meant saving a man's life—"

"Remember Miles Ramsforth," she said. "Every trace of your involvement was scrubbed from that investigation. And it would be from this as well." I began to protest, but Lady Wellie shook her head. "Your father would hang drapes in Hades if he thought it would be good for the monarchy." She must have seen something in my face, for her tone gentled, and she put out one yellow-nailed hand to clutch mine. It was not a consolation, but at least it was an effort. "My dear girl, your father has done his best to protect you, but never forget that in doing so, he protects himself. What he does has often been at my behest. He has listened to my guidance since the cradle, and although he likes to think he is a grown man, there are times when he still harkens to my voice."

I pushed back. "He is lacking in both intelligence and judgment if he believes Stoker capable of killing in cold blood."

She shook her head slowly. "Bertie has a mulish streak. He is a German, in the end, and with all the Teutonic stubbornness that implies. Usually he is biddable as a lamb, but every once in a while I have found him to be intractable. He will become utterly dogged in his pursuit of an idea. If he decides your connection with Stoker must be made to come to an end . . ." Her voice trailed off and she did not finish the sentence. She did not have to.

"All the more reason to discover what happened to John de Morgan," I told her. "If Stoker's name is never made public in connection with the disappearance, then my father will have no reason to act against him."

She nodded slowly. "But best it were discreetly done. The longer it takes the newspapers to catch wind of this, the better."

"Sir Hugo knows we are investigating," I reminded her.

"Leave Hugo to me. I know which of his cupboards hold skeletons," she said darkly.

"Very well. Then we are agreed. Stoker and I will find the truth, and you will keep my father at bay."

I thrust out my hand.

"I can promise you nothing but my best efforts," she said by way of warning. "Bertie is capricious."

"In a fight between you and my father, I should wager upon you every time," I told her.

She smiled her crocodile's smile and shook my hand. "You will need to meet the parties concerned in order to get the lay of the land, as it were. I will send a letter of introduction to Sir Leicester Tiverton. That will get you in the door. What you do next is entirely up to you."

CHAPTER 5

That afternoon, unable to settle to our various pursuits in the Belvedere—Stoker poked idly at his rhinoceros while I was inexplicably uninterested in a tray of *Papilionidae* from Madagascar—we decided to call upon the Tivertons armed with Lady Wellie's letter of introduction. Together the hall boy George and I had compiled every one of *The Daily Harbinger*'s reports on the disappearance of John de Morgan, although I was careful not to explain my heightened interest in the Tiverton Expedition to him. We pored over the increasingly lurid tales spun by Mr. J. J. Butterworth, reading aloud the purplest of the prose.

"'Awoken from her centuries-old slumbers, the malicious Princess Ankheset has clearly claimed another victim in the hapless de Morgan,'" George read. He was slow over his consonants, finding proper pronunciation tedious, but as I had often pointed out to him, if he wished to improve himself, he must put in the effort. It was, he had confided once, his greatest wish to become a footman.

"I don't haff to speak proper to do that," he had informed me loftily. "A footman only needs to be six feet and good-lookink."

"Looking," I had corrected, emphasizing the "g." "And why stop at footman? You could be a butler or a publican or a shopkeeper if you mind your pronunciation. Or you could go to America and make your fortune as a politician. They don't much mind how their officials speak," I advised him. "The world, young George, might well be your oyster."

"I don't like oysters. They give me a green tummy," he had remarked darkly. But from that day, he had been punctilious in his drive to speak correctly. I had thought to borrow a primer from the nurseries at the Folly—his lordship's children had all learnt their letters—but George was far more attentive to his lessons if they came from the scandal sheets. The fact that he was also acquiring a thorough knowledge of the seedier side of Society troubled me not at all. The development of his moral code I left to his mother and his vicar.

He continued, reading a lengthy piece on the first Lady Tiverton, a recitation of the facts Lady Wellie had already related, ending with a brief mention of the present Lady Tiverton, who had taken up the reins of Egyptology to work in harness with her spouse. "'It is to be wondered if the current Lady Tiverton finds herself encouraged and inspired by the spirit of the late Lady Tiverton, illuminating the path of knowledge with her own inextinguishable light.'"

"What sentimental rubbish," I muttered. But I was as curious as J. J. Butterworth as to the character of the expedition's leading lady.

Along with brief sketches of each of the major players of the expedition, Mr. Butterworth's articles had provided the intelligence that they were staying at the Sudbury, a new and suitably respectable hotel on the Strand.

After George had scuttled away to his chores, Stoker and I set off on foot, preferring a brisk walk in the elements to the stuffy rigors of a cab in London traffic. The afternoon had turned foggy and damp, and the lights of the hotel glowed amber in welcome. A procession of smartly dressed people came and went, attended by hotel porters neatly attired in livery of bottle green plush trimmed in gold braid. Chilled after our walk, we waited in the lobby, tucking ourselves into a pair of wing chairs next to the fire as the letter of introduction was sent up. I had half expected the Tivertons to refuse us, but the name of Lady Wellingtonia Beauclerk opened the highest doors in the kingdom, I reminded myself with a small smile as we were shown to the suite.

The door was answered by Sir Leicester himself, beaming and full of bonhomie as he waved us inside.

"I say! This is a pleasure indeed. How long has it been since I have heard anything from Lady Wellingtonia? I rather thought she was dead," he said, turning his bright gaze from Stoker to me. "Miss Speedwell, Mr. Templeton-Vane. Welcome. Any friend of Lady Wellie's . . . You are just in time for tea and you must join us."

With that he maneuvered us into the sitting room with all the bouncing enthusiasm of a border collie, darting here and there, gathering cushions and making introductions. He was not a tall man, being only of middling height and rather broader about the waist than he might have liked. But there was power still in the heavy shoulders and arms, and his eyes were bright with a lively intelligence. His hair was abundant but closely cropped and iron grey. His beard was the same, but his brows still showed dark—black slashes against the sunburnt skin of his face, set above eyes of an indeterminate color. In all, he gave an impression of great vitality. His enthusiasms would be infectious, I realized, and his energy difficult to match.

"This is my wife, Lady Tiverton," he told us as the lady in question rose gracefully from a chair.

As Lady Wellie had suggested, she was dressed in grey, expensive and austere, the only note of color coming from the brilliant green of the winged scarab brooch pinned at her throat. Her complexion, unlike her husband's, must have been well guarded from the fierce Egyptian sun, for it was smooth and unroughened and only slightly darker than a typical Englishwoman's. Her hair was a rich black, parted severely and winged back from her brow, untouched by even a thread of silver, and I judged her to be her husband's junior by at least a quarter of a century.

Her expression was one of such calm serenity in contrast to her husband's that she might well have been a ghost. But then she smiled, a smile of such arresting sweetness that all thoughts of specters were banished. A greater change from her husband could not be imagined. If he were champagne, full of fizz threatening to escape the bottle, she was a delicate liqueur, subtle and languid. She moved to greet us, extending her hand. "Miss Speedwell. I am pleased to make your acquaintance." Her voice was low and gentle, and I wondered if she cultivated it to calm her rumbustious spouse.

"And I yours, Lady Tiverton," I said, shaking the pretty silken hand. My own was work-roughened from solvents and glues and various tools, but she was courteous enough not to flinch.

Suddenly, a creature darted from behind her skirts, snuffling enthusiastically at my hand, and Lady Tiverton laughed. "Please excuse Nut, Miss Speedwell. I am afraid her manners are not what they should be."

It was a dog, but unlike any dog I had ever seen. Of medium size, with a sleek, muscular build, it had enormous batlike ears that stood perfectly upright, giving it a quizzical expression.

"Noot?" I asked, giving the name the same inflection her mistress had.

"Yes, but spelt N-u-t," the lady told me. "She's very like the dogs painted on Egyptian tombs, don't you think? It seemed only fitting to give her an Egyptian name. Nut was the goddess of the stars. She attaches herself to whoever is nearest the fire or the biscuit barrel," she warned me with a smile.

The dog thrust its head under my palm, demanding a pat, and I obliged.

Lady Tiverton clucked her tongue and the dog turned back to her, settling itself on a cushion in front of the fire.

"I hope that you will forgive the intrusion," I began.

Lady Tiverton's calm eyes, dark as a midnight sea, widened. "Oh, you must not apologize! My husband delights in visitors," she explained fondly. Her gestures were languid as she resumed her place on the sofa while Sir Leicester bustled about, indicating chairs and ringing for tea, as unruly as his wife was unruffled.

She turned to Stoker. "Mr. Templeton-Vane, are you connected with the viscount of the same name?"

"My elder brother, my lady," he told her. "Do you know him?"

She gave a little laugh. "We do not move in such exalted circles, I am afraid. We spend all of our time either in Egypt at the digs or our home in Surrey, cataloging the finds."

"Hence the hotel," Sir Leicester said aggrievedly. "A man ought not to live in an hotel if he can possibly avoid it," he pronounced. "There is little domestic joy to be had when one is not under one's own roof."

His wife smiled. "So exacting in England, but you should see him in Egypt! Happy to live in a tent and eat his supper from a tin can."

"We were all happy to live in tents until you came along," said a disembodied voice. Stoker and I turned in our chairs to see the draperies parting. Concealed in the window embrasure was a girl—the famous Figgy, I presumed. She was, as Lady Wellie had suggested, fifteen or so, but wearing a thoroughly unbecoming dress of a shade of green that made her look like a bilious cat. The sleeves were puffed, the skirts ruffed, and the whole effect was unfortunate. She was dark, like her father, with strongly marked brows and a decided nose. Perched atop was a pair of spectacles, the lenses smudged and greasy.

As Stoker rose, she came forwards, a book clutched in her hand, and I could just see from the cover that it was one of H. Rider Haggard's more spine-tingling tales.

"My stepdaughter," Lady Tiverton murmured by way of introduction. "Iphigenia."

Her father gave her a reproachful look. "Now, Figgy, don't grumble. You know things have been much more comfortable since your stepmama took over the domestic arrangements."

The girl looked scornfully at Stoker. "Why are you standing?"

"It is considered good manners to stand when a lady enters the room," he told her gravely.

"Well, I am not a lady and I was already in the room, so it's rather silly of you," she said.

To his credit, Stoker grinned. "Quite right."

"You have a patch on your eye. Are you a pirate?"

"Nothing so glamorous," he assured her. He flipped up the patch to reveal his eye, as healthy and wholesome as the other. "I merely wear it when my eye is fatigued."

"How did you come to get those scars?" she inquired.

"From an uncordial jaguar in Amazonia."

Figgy's eyes shone with interest. "Did you kill it?"

"Regrettably, yes. But I'm afraid the fellow left me no choice."

"Did you shoot it? I would have shot it," she said stoutly.

"I was unarmed at the time," he replied, his lips twitching in amusement.

"You killed it *with your bare hands*? That is the most thrilling thing I have ever heard. Was it difficult? What did you do with the skin of it?"

Lady Tiverton interrupted with a small patient sigh. "Figgy, we were just about to have tea. I asked earlier if we might have some of those little cakes you like so much."

"Cakes?" Figgy Tiverton rolled her eyes heavenwards. "I am not a child to be bribed with cakes."

Her father gave a snort of laughter. "Not a lady, not a child! What are you, then, Fig?" He laughed uproariously at his own joke, and I conceived in that moment a thorough dislike of the man. Fifteen was a precarious age, and she wore it awkwardly. Having a stepmother as serenely unflappable as Lady Tiverton could not have helped matters, and her father was wholly insensitive.

But Stoker was not. He indicated his chair. "If you please, Miss Tiverton. I cannot sit until you do. My old nanny would hunt me down and whip me if I tried."

Figgy Tiverton's eyes rounded as she swept her gaze along the six feet of Stoker's height and across the breadth of his shoulders. "She would have to be a very strong nanny."

"She was," he told her, the corners of his mouth twitching. Something in his unlikely charm thawed her a little. She did not take his chair, but settled herself on a hassock by the fire as Stoker resumed his seat. The dog Nut lifted its head and laid it squarely upon Figgy's lap. I was glad to see at least one creature in the family liked the girl.

Tea was brought in then, and we passed a convivial quarter of an hour in drinking and eating. Sir Leicester was devoted to the cherry tarts, while Lady Tiverton toyed with a slender sandwich. From her perch in front of the fire, Figgy toasted several muffins she did not eat. Stoker discreetly helped himself to the pile, muffins drenched in butter being one of his favorite things, and I permitted myself a piece of chocolate gâteau that would have put the earl's cook to shame. One of Lady Wellie's protégés had been employed at the Sudbury as a pastry chef, and I made a note to send my compliments.

The conversation was general and pleasant, covering travel and butterflies and books, until we brushed the last crumbs from our lips just as the door opened.

"Have I missed tea?" A young gentleman with a comely face and dark ginger hair entered. He had Stoker's years but not his inches, being very slightly shorter and leaner. (I had once compared Stoker's physique to the glorious fallen angel painted by Cabanel. In contrast, this fellow was a slimly muscled Botticelli saint.) He moved with the loosely knit grace of an athlete, a fencer perhaps, and he gazed at the assembled party with a genial expression. "I didn't realize we were having a party," he told Lady Tiverton in a tone of apology. "I would have worn a nicer tie."

She gave him a motherly smile. "You look quite presentable, Patrick. Miss Speedwell, Mr. Templeton-Vane, this is Patrick Fairbrother, our expedition philologist." She completed the introductions, and Mr. Fairbrother shook my hand, bowing slightly from the neck.

"Speedwell? I just read the most interesting piece on Saharan swallowtail butterflies, rather a new discovery, if memory serves," he began. "I don't suppose you are any connection to the author?"

"Yes, I wrote it," I told him. "It was most exciting. *Papilio saharae* was only cataloged by Oberthür in 1879. I find the yellow-and-brown coloration most interesting, given the fact that it is endemic to North Africa."

"Exactly! I confess, I am no expert on lepidoptery, but your description of the creature was absolute poetry," he said. "Did you know that butterflies feature in some of the tomb decorations of the pharaohs?"

"I did not," I admitted.

"Oh, yes! Some scholars believe the motif was used as a means of illustrating the Egyptian belief in resurrection. It is an obvious parallel with the butterfly's own metamorphosis, is it not?"

"It is. What do other scholars believe?"

"That butterflies found their way onto the walls of the tombs simply because they are beautiful," he told me, his eyes never leaving my face.

I realized then that he held my hand still in his, and I withdrew it gently.

He blushed, the delectable rosy shade to which ginger-haired complexions are often prone, and swiftly made his greeting to Stoker, who returned it with cool indifference. I was interested to note Figgy regarding him with a look of adolescent loathing.

If he noticed, Mr. Fairbrother was immune. "Save me any muffins, Figgy?" he asked her cheerfully as he seated himself.

"Only one. Choke on it and die," she said, tossing the breadstuff. It landed, buttered side down, on his lap, and he shied. Figgy laughed, the first genuine expression of pleasure I had seen out of her since our arrival. Lady Tiverton pressed her lips together in a line of disapproval, but Sir Leicester merely joined in her laughter.

"Figgy, you are such a pip," he told her.

Figgy was badly spoilt, I corrected silently, but I turned instead to Mr. Fairbrother. "What, precisely, does a philologist do?" I inquired. He paused a moment to retrieve the muffin from his trousers and drop his handkerchief discreetly over the butter stain.

I knew exactly what a philologist did, but it had long been my experience that most men love nothing better than to talk about themselves, so I kept my mouth shut and my eyes wide as he launched into a lengthy explanation of his duties and fed bits of the buttered muffin to Nut, who gazed at him in rapt adoration. When he finished his little monologue, I made suitable noises of appreciation.

"How fortunate for you to be part of such a successful expedition," I told him. "Was it your first trip to Egypt?"

"It was my second, actually, and I certainly hope it was not my last," he replied.

"Then you'd better find a new digestive system," Figgy warned. "You spent half the season in the privy."

Mr. Fairbrother blushed again, but before he could react, Sir Leicester bellowed.

"Iphigenia!" Her father had at last reached his limit. He straightened in his chair, his color nearly apoplectic. "If you cannot act like a lady, you will remove yourself to your room."

"Gladly," she said, rising from her hassock. With grave courtesy, she handed the toasting fork to Stoker. "Good afternoon," she said politely, inclining her head with all the imperiousness of a duchess. The dog Nut rose and followed her, ears pricked like a crown.

"Good afternoon, Miss Tiverton," he said, rising once more to his feet and giving her a little nod of salutation.

Mr. Fairbrother kept to his chair, ducking his head and reaching for a sandwich as Lady Tiverton offered us a wan smile. "I must apologize. My stepdaughter is a trifle high-spirited at times."

"Like a purebred filly," Sir Leicester said with grudging approval. "Although I thought she would have learnt a little better to behave in company by this time."

"She only wants understanding," Lady Tiverton told her husband.

"She wants whipping," her father countered swiftly. "But I've never had the heart to do it."

"Her resentment is natural," Mr. Fairbrother said quietly. "She feels I have usurped her place, and I cannot blame her for that."

"Patrick." Sir Leicester's voice was sharp, but Fairbrother merely waved a reassuring hand.

"She feels displaced by my very presence, and why wouldn't she? You have taken me in and treated me like a son. If I were Figgy, I'd do far worse than put a frog in my bed and oil of figs in my soup."

"Did she really?" I asked.

Patrick Fairbrother's smile was wry and entirely charming. "The oil of figs, yes. I cannot prove the frog. It might have hopped in of its own accord. It was Egypt, after all."

I grinned in reply.

Sir Leicester made a sort of tutting sound. "Listen to us, running away with ourselves! You've no interest in our little family dramas. You've come to hear about the curse," he said, giving us a knowing look. He held up a hand. "I do not blame you. It is the story of the decade—of the century, perhaps! Where would you like to begin?"

He looked from Stoker to me, and I smiled sweetly. "With the disappearance of John de Morgan."

Sir Leicester's florid complexion suffused with red, but Lady Tiverton was more composed. She made a sympathetic noise. "Such a dreadful business. I am very sorry for Mrs. de Morgan. At least . . . I would like to be."

"You suspect her of aiding her husband in the theft of the diadem?" I suggested.

"Not a bit!" Sir Leicester said.

"My husband and I are not of one mind," Lady Tiverton explained.

Sir Leicester shook his head. "I will not have such stories put about," he said firmly. "We've no proof Caroline de Morgan is complicit in the theft."

Lady Tiverton's gaze rested indulgently on him. "My husband will not admit that ladies are capable of villainous acts," she said.

"But you will?" I ventured.

Her expression was serious. "I have seen enough of the world to know that women can scratch and claw and fight just as fiercely as men for what they want. Perhaps more."

"Indeed," I said. But Sir Leicester shook his head again, like a grizzled lion shaking off the buzz of an unpleasant idea.

"No, Mrs. de Morgan is worth our pity for her husband's actions, but not our suspicion," he insisted.

"You are certain, then, that John de Morgan stole the princess' diadem?" I asked.

Lady Tiverton gave a firm nod. "Of course he did." Her husband did not appear as certain. His look was distinctly uncomfortable.

"Careful, poppet. We don't want to open ourselves to libel."

Lady Tiverton's little sigh seemed tinged with exasperation, but she concealed it well. "I think you mean slander, my love. But it is difficult. We know what we believe. However, speaking it openly is, as my husband says, a dangerous thing. And the police simply do not seem to care," she added, spreading her hands. They were long and slender, unadorned save for a slim gold ring upon the fourth finger of her left hand.

"What have they told you?" I asked.

Sir Leicester puffed himself up again. "Precious little! The Dover police were less than useless. They mishandled questioning Mrs. de Morgan badly. They sent out notices to the ports, but what does that do for getting back my crown?" he demanded.

Lady Tiverton put a quelling hand to her husband's arm. "Scotland Yard seem to have given up," she said simply. "Mrs. de Morgan refuses to speak with them further, and she cannot be compelled. Of course, the Metropolitan Police cannot spare the men to watch every port. There are far worse crimes than the theft of a single jewel. Ours must seem like a very frivolous sort of crime—the loss of a crown! What is that compared to the murders and assaults they must contend with daily?"

Put like that, it seemed entirely reasonable that Scotland Yard would have thrown up their hands after a cursory investigation.

Stoker, who had remained silent during our conversation, suddenly broke in. "What about you, Mr. Fairbrother? Do you think de Morgan and his wife stole the diadem?"

Because he was startled at the abrupt inquiry, Mr. Fairbrother's hand jerked, spilling watercress into his lap. "Good Gad," he said with a rueful laugh. "That's two butter stains in a quarter of an hour. These trousers will never come clean." He lifted his head. "Apologies, ladies, for the language. As to your question, Mr. Templeton-Vane, I do not know what to think except that it is certainly incriminating that the fellow disappears at precisely the same time as the most valuable jewel in the tomb goes missing. Whether his wife aided or was his dupe cannot, in the end, matter. The fact is, John is gone and so is the diadem, and the police are doing precious little to find either of them."

Lady Tiverton broke in. "Perhaps you would like to see the diadem." She rose and went to the writing table, carrying back a portfolio. "We have a sketch of it. We would have preferred a photograph, but I am afraid Mr. de Morgan was not an experienced photographer. There were few usable plates from his work." Lady Tiverton opened the portfolio and extracted a large sheet of paper.

"Why so?" I inquired.

"Troubles with the equipment, exposed plates, missing chemicals. It's a miracle we got any plates at all," Sir Leicester said.

"To what do you attribute the troubles?" Stoker inquired.

Patrick Fairbrother spread his hands in an expressive gesture. "No one knows. But the locals said it was the handiwork of the mummy of Princess Ankheset."

"The curse," I said, taking the page from Lady Tiverton. I held it so that Stoker could examine it at the same time. The drawing was well executed, tidy and draftsmanlike, with strict attention to detail and no flourishes save a gentle wash of color where appropriate. "The Diadem of the Princess Ankheset of the Eighteenth Dynasty" was written in neat capitals at the bottom, along with the date of the find, but it was the jewel itself that demanded our attention. It was a slender crown, graceful in its sinuous curves. A circlet formed the base and an arch of gold ran from the foundation at the center of the back to the front, ending in three sculpted golden animal heads—a vulture flanked by gazelles. A series of stiff ribbons fashioned from gold hung from the circlet; along the length of one ribbon, a cartouche had been engraved, a long oval surrounding a group of hieroglyphics—the lady's name and titles, no doubt—and the whole crown was fitted with jewels. Below the drawing of the diadem, a brief paragraph described the gems as carnelian, jasper, and lapis lazuli.

"The vulture is the goddess Nekhbet, who spreads her wings over upper Egypt," Lady Tiverton explained. "While the gazelles were symbolic of Anuket, goddess of the cataracts of the Nile. Taken together, the crown symbolizes the protection of the source of the Nile, the foundation of all life in Egypt. Our princess was a very high-ranking lady indeed."

"It is spectacular," I told her truthfully.

"And priceless," Sir Leicester said, rubbing his hands fretfully. "Of all the pieces he might have taken . . ." He let his voice trail off suggestively, but I understood. All those years of digging in Egypt with halfhearted results, only to strike gold, quite literally, in the form of a princess' tomb—and then to have the most precious object taken from it. It reminded me of the time my net split just as I brought it down upon a Rajah Brooke's Birdwing in Sumatra. It was the first and only time I ever encountered one in the wild, and I mourned for it still. The blow of losing the coronet must have been a serious one to Sir Leicester, and I felt an unexpected rush of sympathy for him.

I said as much and he was silent a moment, clearly caught in a reverie. His wife gave a gentle cough, and he shook his head, recovering himself. "Ah, yes, as you say, quite a blow indeed. But not as serious as losing the mummy would have been," he added swiftly. "Nothing matters as much as the princess herself." He nodded to the closed door behind him, and Stoker and I exchanged glances.

"You have her *here*?" Stoker asked.

"I certainly do! I wouldn't even let her be shipped through a commercial line with the rest of the grave goods," he said with a touch of proprietary pride. "I brought her privately out of Egypt. She traveled with us every step of the way from Cairo to Dover, and she will not be out of my care until her sarcophagus and all her treasures are displayed next week."

He rummaged through a sheaf of papers on the blotter on his writing desk before thrusting a piece of card at us. It was an invitation to the Tiverton Exhibition at Karnak Hall on the first of March. The exhibition would feature the finds from Princess Ankheset's tomb, highlighted by the displaying of the lady's sarcophagus. A note at the bottom indicated that admittance was by invitation only.

"You are both welcome to attend," he said graciously. "We have chosen the most auspicious date for the affair—the first of March, known to ancient Egyptians as the Going Forth of Khepri, the date when the scarab god rolls forth the sun and all is reborn. It will be quite a spectacle. Once the private exhibition is finished, we shall open the collection to the public for a short while before the artifacts are to be offered for sale," he explained. "It will give the common man a chance to elevate his entertainments."

I deliberately avoided Stoker's gaze, but I suspected he was repressing laughter. Sir Leicester was the oddest mix of bombastic high spirits and good cheer. Compared to the cool serenity of his wife, he seemed an elderly schoolboy. "This exhibition will be my crowning achievement. Lady Tiverton is even writing a book upon the subject," he added with a warm look of marital pride at his wife.

She put up her hands. "Oh, no, you mustn't call it a book," she protested. "It is only a little pamphlet upon the history of the Eighteenth Dynasty, a sort of introduction to the period for those who are unfamiliar with it. It will be a modest effort at best, nothing like the scholarly books written by the first Lady Tiverton," she finished.

I held up the invitation card with a smile. "How very kind of you to invite us. I was not certain how we would be received today, given our current task, but you have been nothing but gracious, Sir Leicester."

"Current task?" Lady Tiverton asked quickly.

I held the smile as I turned to her. "Yes. You see, we are investigating the disappearance of John de Morgan."

Making a dramatic pronouncement is akin to pitching a stone into a still pond. There is silence, but the ripples are perfectly apparent.

Sir Leicester's dark gaze rested upon us, the eyes narrowed suspiciously. "Lady Wellie's letter of introduction said that you were interested in Egyptology."

"Lady Wellie's relationship with the truth is better described as a nodding acquaintance in this case," I told him. "Mr. Templeton-Vane has an interest in discovering the whereabouts of Mr. de Morgan. If anyone can ascertain the truth, he can."

"Templeton-Vane," Lady Tiverton said slowly. "I knew I recognized the name. Now I remember . . ." Her voice trailed off.

"Yes, I am also Caroline de Morgan's former husband," Stoker affirmed.

"All the more reason to take an interest in her welfare," Lady Tiverton said, giving him a consoling smile. "It is a credit to your gentlemanly instincts that you intend to learn for her what happened to her present husband."

Before I could point out that Stoker's motivations were rather more self-interested than that, he gave her ladyship a gracious nod. "As you say. But, while we may have inflicted ourselves upon you under less-than-honest pretenses, certainly you can appreciate the merit of having this little mystery cleared away."

"Little!" Patrick Fairbrother's hands were fists upon his knees. "If you can locate John de Morgan, it will be a greater find than Princess Ankheset's tomb."

Sir Leicester nodded slowly. "Yes, I have to agree with Patrick. We would like to know what became of John."

"And recover the princess' diadem," I added.

To his credit, he did not protest. "Certainly. I will not balk at the truth, Miss Speedwell. I have written off de Morgan as a common thief, and if I never see the fellow again, it will be too soon. But I would very much like to have my diadem back."

I smiled. "Then we are natural allies. If we find de Morgan, no doubt we shall find your crown. And we shall do our best to recover both," I promised him. "Now, is there anything you can add to what we have already read in the newspaper accounts?"

Sir Leicester's mouth thinned. "You've seen *The Daily Harbinger*, then? Preposterous twaddle, all of it, concocted by that blackguard J. J. Butterworth, whoever he might be. The mummy's curse indeed!"

"But the story of the curse has kept your expedition in the public eye," I pointed out. "Naturally that will drive interest in the sale of the collection."

His expression was stern. "My dear Miss Speedwell, one does not sell pieces of a collection like this for the purposes of making *money*." He bit off the last word as if it tasted bitter. I flicked a glance to Patrick Fairbrother, who was pointedly saying nothing. Sir Leicester went on. "One sells only to kindred spirits, to those who have not the opportunity to travel to Egypt to excavate, but who live and breathe antiquities as we do. The interest of the general public is something we do not court," he finished loftily.

Patrick Fairbrother ate the last of the sandwiches. "Apart from the accidents and the misfortunes we have endured, it is a thorough nuisance, this curse," he said. "It is the entire reason we left Egypt so early."

"The tale of the curse began there?" Stoker inquired.

"It shouldn't have," Lady Tiverton said quickly. "Excavations in Egypt are arduous things. There are always complications—illnesses, accidents, delays. But this particular expedition seemed to have more than its fair share. And unfortunately, the mummy itself seemed to supply a reason."

Patrick Fairbrother leant forwards. "You see, the tomb we discovered is not intact and it does not even belong to Princess Ankheset. To be strictly correct, it isn't even a tomb. It is a sliver of a cave, and nothing more. Usually Theban tombs in the Valley of the Kings are elaborate affairs, with many chambers belowground, properly excavated from the rock and highly decorated. It takes years to prepare a royal burial properly. But our lady was discovered in a very small natural cave some forty feet above the nearest ledge."

"How on earth did you manage to find her?" I asked. "It must have been like stumbling over a particularly elusive needle in an Egyptological haystack."

Sir Leicester preened a little. "I was an accomplished climber once upon a time. I still like to keep my hand in, so to speak. The cliffs around the Valley of the Kings are treacherous beasts, crumbling and unsound, but I am careful, and I do like to get a bit of exercise. I happened to be climbing in a remote area of the Valley last year, a spot no one had ever excavated before. I stumbled upon what I thought was a mere crevice in the rock. A cursory glance showed that it was actually a proper cave, albeit a very small one. It occurred to me that it was the perfect sort of place to cache a hoard of goods. I poked my nose in a few inches and found a bit of pottery, just enough to convince me I was right."

"Last year?" I asked quickly.

Lady Tiverton took up the thread of the story. "You see, each expedition is granted a *firman* or permit to dig, and it specifies where one is allowed to excavate. My husband was climbing on the very limit of the perimeter of our *firman*, so when he discovered what he thought was a possible find, naturally we said nothing at first to the authorities."

"For fear it was not within your rights to excavate," Stoker finished.

Lady Tiverton nodded. "Exactly. To all outward appearances, the impression in the rock was just a cave, but the pottery shards persuaded him that it had been put to a far more interesting use," she said, darting him a quick look of pride. "We studied the charts and maps and realized the tomb lay just outside the permitted area for us to dig. Without official permission, we would have no claim to anything we excavated in the tomb."

"So you applied for permission to dig in the area where you already knew there was a tomb?" Stoker asked.

Lady Tiverton's smile was gentle. "It sounds dreadfully underhanded, but it is common practice amongst Egyptologists. Everyone has their pet theories as to where something wonderful may be found. And everyone jockeys for permission to dig in their likeliest spots. We were terribly lucky. The tomb is located in a particularly remote *wadi* or canyon. No one else was interested, so we had no competition for a *firman*. We returned to dig this season with great hopes of what we might find."

"And you found a princess," I observed.

"By the grace of God," Sir Leicester said with fervor. "As Fairbrother said, the tomb was unfinished, the roughest sort of cave, completely lacking in decoration, and she was crammed in there like so much wool in a bag. There were grave goods from at least seven other burials as well."

"How do you account for that?" Stoker asked. "I thought Egyptian royals were buried with their own possessions."

"In theory, they were," Fairbrother explained. "Ideally, each member of the royal family would have his or her own tomb, a suite of rooms elaborately decorated and furnished with everything they would require for the afterlife. But rock-cut tombs are notoriously difficult to create. As I said, they take a long time, and unfortunately, death doesn't wait for everyone. Many royals have been discovered stuffed into someone else's tomb—rather like sharing your granny's crypt at Highgate," he finished with a grim smile.

Sir Leicester nodded thoughtfully. "Another complication was the existence of grave robbers, even in antiquity. No sooner were the tombs sealed by the mortuary priests than someone would come along and bash them open, looking for gold and despoiling the mummies. To prevent this, some mummies were removed from their tombs with as many of the grave goods as the priests could haul. They were stashed wherever space could be found."

"I have heard of such a thing," I said, recalling some vague mention of a hoard of mummies being unearthed sometime before. I mentioned it and Stoker nodded.

"Eighteen eighty-one," he said. "People were still discussing it when we were in Cairo the following year. A whole family of royal mummies had been unearthed near one of the villages in the Valley of the Kings."

"Deir el-Bahri," Lady Tiverton supplied. "Near the Necropolis of Thebes. They were discovered by a particularly accomplished clan of grave robbers from the village of Gurneh, the el-Rasul family. The fellows had been discreetly removing grave goods and selling them on the antiquities market until suspicions were raised. The cache was investigated and the entire tomb cleared immediately to put a stop to the illicit trade."

"But where did they come from?" I asked.

Sir Leicester shrugged. "No one knows. The original tombs were never discovered. But at some point, millennia ago, the priests tasked with guarding the bodies of the pharaohs feared for their safety, so they removed them. We believe the same thing happened to our little princess."

"Do you know who she was? Anything besides her name?"

We turned as one to Patrick Fairbrother. "I have deciphered every marking upon her sarcophagus, but aside from her name, there is precious little information of any use. Except the curse," he said with a slow smile.

"There is actually a curse upon the sarcophagus?" I could not conceal my amazement. I had thought it some invention of an enterprising newspaper reporter.

"Oh, yes. And rather a good one." He drew in a long breath, clearing his throat. When he spoke, he intoned slowly, in a deep, stentorian voice quite unlike his usual tones. "'Cursed be those who disturb the rest of the daughter of Isis. Death will come to the despoiler on the wings of the vulture, and Anubis shall feast upon his bones.'"

Just then a log collapsed in the fireplace, sending up a shower of sparks, and in spite of the warmth of the fire, I shivered.

At Fairbrother's pronouncement, Lady Tiverton's hand had gone to her throat, fingering the scarab brooch.

"Are you quite all right, my lady?" Stoker asked gently.

She nodded. "Yes. Quite. Only, hearing the words, spoken aloud like that, it makes it so easy to believe—"

"Rachel," her husband said, frowning slightly.

"Believe what?" I said, ignoring the baronet.

"That Anubis really has come for us," she said, her voice almost inaudible.

"What makes you think Anubis has come?" Stoker pressed.

Lady Tiverton lifted her head, leveling her sorrowful dark gaze.

"I have seen him."

CHAPTER 6

If Fairbrother's pronouncement was dramatic, Lady Tiverton's simple statement was utterly chilling. Had she wept or wailed, it would have been far easier to dismiss her words as the ravings of a madwoman. But I had seldom seen a more self-possessed lady. She spoke calmly, with perfect composure, and from the lack of surprise demonstrated by her husband and Patrick Fairbrother, it was apparent they had heard the story before.

"When did you see him?" I demanded. "Where?"

"In Egypt," she replied promptly. "I sometimes have trouble sleeping when we are excavating. It is so terribly quiet there, you see. No city traffic or muffin men or church bells to break the peace. Only that great, desolate silence, like a living thing. And then the jackals. They make quite an eerie sound when one is not accustomed to them." She gave a rueful smile. "I was brought up in Egypt, but in the bustle of Cairo, not the barren wastes of the Valley of the Kings. It is quite the eeriest spot I have ever been. When I am wakeful, I always rise and potter about, trying to do something useful. I find it makes me more inclined to sleep when I return to my bed. One night, as I fixed together a few pieces of pottery, I heard a jackal. Not uncommon, of course, but this one was very close to the expedition house. I was wondering whether I ought to rouse my husband to order the guards to shoot it. I looked out the window to see if I could determine how far away it was, and that's when I saw it—*him*," she corrected.

"Anubis?" Stoker asked gravely.

She nodded. "He was simply standing in a pool of moonlight. I could see him as clearly as if it were day—the profile of the jackal's head atop the body of the man. It was a mask of sorts, like the ancient priests would have worn. They fashioned such things out of cartonnage and wore them during sacred rites. I knew what it was, and yet I cannot describe the effect of it. It was otherworldly. His chest and legs"—she colored slightly at using the word—"were bare. He wore sandals and a sort of breastplate of beadwork with a traditional linen kilt. Really, he looked just as if he had stepped from the wall of a tomb, a funerary painting come to life," she finished.

"And you could tell nothing else about him from his physique? His mannerisms?" I asked.

"What sort of question is that?" Sir Leicester demanded. "D'ye think my wife is in the habit of seeing men prancing about half-dressed?"

"Not at all," I soothed. "I merely thought that her ladyship might have seen something familiar in the way he moved, something that might call to mind an acquaintance with a penchant for practical jokes perhaps."

"He did not move," Lady Tiverton explained. "He merely stood there in profile, perfectly still, until a bit of cloud obscured the moon. It caused a shadow to pass over him, and when the shadow disappeared, he was gone."

"Gone?" Stoker echoed.

"Without so much as a sound."

"I presume you looked for footprints?" I suggested.

Sir Leicester nodded. "Naturally. There were no traces of the fellow to be found—no stray beads dropped from his breastplate, no marks of his sandals in the dirt."

"But you believe in this apparition?" Stoker asked.

"Of course I do! If my wife says she saw it, that's good enough for me," Sir Leicester replied stoutly.

"I saw it myself," Patrick Fairbrother said quietly. "Several nights after her ladyship. It was the dark of the moon by then, so my view was not nearly as clear as hers, but there was no mistaking that profile."

Stoker steepled his fingers together thoughtfully. "Did anyone else see it?"

Fairbrother shrugged. "Dozens of people. The fellow walked right through one of the villages of workers clustered at the edge of the Valley. Whole families shuttered their doors and windows and refused to come out again until morning."

"How dramatic," I murmured.

"It was a damned nuisance, if you'll pardon my language," Sir Leicester said. "After that, not a man from fifty miles around would work our site. I had to import *fellahin* from upriver to do the job. And of course, none of them know the first thing about proper excavation work. They made a ham-fisted business of it, destroying half of what they carried out," he finished bitterly.

"That is why we were preparing to leave early," her ladyship explained. "We simply could not manage a proper excavation with untrained workers, not to my husband's standards. We decided to empty the cave to the best of our ability and call it a day."

"And there was Jonas," Fairbrother said softly, looking at his hands.

Lady Tiverton made an inarticulate sound of distress, pressing her lips together.

"Jonas?" Stoker asked.

"Jonas Fowler. The expedition director," Sir Leicester said, the words coming quite quickly. "He took sick and died. It was not unexpected. The poor fellow had a weak heart. He'd been waiting to pop off for years. Everyone knew this was his final season, but he did hope to last to the end of it." He stopped speaking, his mouth working soundlessly.

Patrick Fairbrother picked up the thread of the narrative. "Jonas was a good old sort, rough in his ways. He liked living with the workers, eating their food and so forth. We used to joke that his constitution was as stout as a donkey's. But it was a hollow jest, as it turns out. He fell ill. He was unable to rise from his bed for several days, and then his heart simply gave out."

"We hadn't the spirit to go on after that," Lady Tiverton said in a muffled voice. "And without proper workers, it all just seemed so terribly pointless."

"Of course," I assured her. "It must have been a dreadful blow."

"To Sir Leicester most of all," Mr. Fairbrother said, giving his patron a generous nod. "His friendship with Jonas was of the longest duration."

Sir Leicester seemed overcome with emotion for a moment, and I hastened to change the subject from Jonas Fowler's untimely death.

"It seems curious that a single sighting of Anubis would put off well-trained and experienced workers to begin with," I began slowly.

Her ladyship tipped her head. "Have you ever met the average Egyptian villager, Miss Speedwell?"

"I have," Stoker put in.

"Then you will understand they are unique. They might be touched by the modern world, but they are not of it. They live in the desert *wadis*, marking the seasons by the inundation of the Nile, just as their forebears have for millennia. They dwell, quite literally, amongst the bones of their ancestors. It is little wonder that they still believe, at least a little, in the ancient gods. Tell me the average English farmer would not tremble to see the Green Man in a forest glade," she finished with a smile.

"It's damned barbaric," Sir Leicester grumbled.

Her ladyship seemed to take no offense at this criticism of her countrymen. She merely gave her husband a look that was sweetly chiding.

"You only say that because they inconvenienced you," she told him. "You are the first to champion the Egyptian worker as a marvel of industry and courage."

"Well, they are not shy of a hard day's work," he said grudgingly.

I cleared my throat. "Presuming that Anubis, god of the underworld and keeper of tombs, was himself otherwise occupied, we may safely theorize that your visitor was simply a mortal man playing a prank. Now, it might have been just a bit of harmless flummery, but it threw your excavation into confusion just after you made a significant discovery. The timing of it strikes me as interesting. Can you think of anyone who might profit from your expedition being interrupted?"

"Such as John de Morgan?" Stoker offered.

"That was my thought," Sir Leicester said quickly. "And his disappearance only confirmed it. Trouble through and through, he was."

"Possibly." I clucked my tongue. "But why go to the bother of masquerading as Anubis if he planned to run away with the diadem? What purpose did it serve him?"

"To further confuse us?" Sir Leicester suggested. But he sounded doubtful, and Stoker shook his head.

"Unlikely, I should think. I wonder, do you have any professional enemies? People who might have been jealous of your find and eager to drive you away from it?"

Sir Leicester and Lady Tiverton exchanged glances with Patrick Fairbrother.

"There is one," Sir Leicester began.

Lady Tiverton touched her scarab brooch again. "We have no proof," she murmured.

"The blackguard threatened me in the lobby of Shepheard's!" her husband blustered. "Horace Stihl," he said succinctly. "This has the stink of him all over it."

"Horace Stihl, the American millionaire?" I asked.

"The same," Lady Tiverton confirmed. "He and my husband were excavation partners for many years. Last year's season was their final joint expedition."

"What caused you to part ways?" Stoker asked Sir Leicester.

The baronet shifted. "I wouldn't like to say."

"Sir Leicester," I said in my most beguiling voice, "surely you see that any information might help us understand John de Morgan's disappearance and recover your diadem? Perhaps Mr. Stihl was involved."

Lady Tiverton made a little noise of distress. "You mean to suggest that Mr. Stihl might have bribed John de Morgan to steal the diadem? And then paid him to disappear? I cannot bear to think of it. It is horrid enough to imagine that Mr. de Morgan might have stolen the jewel for his own gain, but I could understand it. He has a wife to support and limited prospects. The temptation would be too much, perhaps. But for him to succumb to conspiring with Horace Stihl . . ." She let her voice trail off, pressing a hand to her lips.

"What can you tell us about Mr. Stihl?" I prodded.

Sir Leicester exchanged glances with his wife. "As you said, he is an American and a wealthy one. Doubtless you have heard of his businesses—mining, railways, steamships. He was a millionaire twice over by the age of thirty. But what business acumen he has was acquired on the streets, as it were. He decided after he turned thirty to remedy the defects in his education, and took up the study of Egyptology. He had already established a name for himself in that field when my wife—my first wife," Sir Leicester corrected with a hasty glance at the present Lady Tiverton, "began to publish her books. He was most impressed by them and they struck up a sort of friendship. In due course, we formed a partnership and launched the joint Tiverton-Stihl Expeditions."

He fell silent then, his complexion warming, and Lady Tiverton spoke.

"Mr. Stihl was, for a very long time, a devoted friend to the Tivertons. I am sorry to say that he never entirely warmed to my presence in the family."

Sir Leicester covered her slim hand with his own beefy one. "Damned fool," he muttered.

Lady Tiverton gave him a gentle smile.

Sir Leicester continued. "His given name is Horace, but thanks to his work in Egyptology, my first wife gave him the nickname Horus after the god king. It amused him." He shook his head, his expression suddenly mulish. "For more than a decade we dug together. But at the end of last season I told him I would not partner with him again and he took it badly. He made a scene in Shepheard's, threatened me with a pistol," he said in a tone of indignation. "Americans and their guns," he muttered.

"Did you tell him about the tomb you discovered?" I asked mildly.

The baronet flushed deeply. "I did not. Horus always ridiculed my idea of anything of value being concealed in the *wadis* in that part of the Valley. He thought it a waste of time to poke about, looking for a find. But I was right," he added stubbornly. "We were discussing where to dig this year when he began nettling me about my ideas. Well, why should I tell him the truth when he was forever carping about my lack of scholarship? My flights of fancy? I did not *want* to share it with him. I wanted to dig it all up myself and then force him to acknowledge that he was wrong. So I simply told him I refused to continue the partnership." He shifted uncomfortably in his chair. "I would not give him a reason, and that is what angered him more than anything."

"And he was back in the Valley digging this season?" Stoker asked.

"He chose to dig at Amarna instead," Mr. Fairbrother corrected. "Quite a distance from our location in the Valley, but Mr. Stihl visited other friends in the area often. It made things rather awkward."

"I can imagine. But I have seen Mr. Stihl's photograph in the newspapers," Stoker countered. "He is a gentleman of advanced years. I cannot imagine him putting on the guise of Anubis and gamboling about the desert."

"Have you seen a photograph of his son?" Fairbrother asked. "Henry Stihl could do a fair impression of an Egyptian god, I would wager."

Lady Tiverton shook her head. "It is too terrible. They were our friends. It is impossible."

I offered her a thin smile. "What was it that Napoleon said, my lady? 'Impossible is a word only to be found in the dictionary of fools.'"

"Amen," said Patrick Fairbrother, raising his teacup in a toast.

We took our leave of the Tivertons, emerging from the warm elegance of the Sudbury lobby into the darkening street. Splinters of ice shone in the glow of the streetlamps, and all around us London hurried on its way, bustling through the late-afternoon gloom.

"All right," I told Stoker as I tucked the edge of my glove under my cuff. "I could feel you rumbling like a volcano in there. You did a masterful job of holding your temper, but there's no need now. Rant."

His jaw was set in a hard line. "It's that disgraceful business with the mummy. They mean to put her on display."

"Her sarcophagus only," I corrected.

"That sarcophagus is the mummy case, the inner lining of her coffin," he countered. "There would have been at least two more surrounding it and a shrine to hold the whole of it. Displaying the sarcophagus is like letting the rabble into Windsor to see the queen in her nightdress."

I ignored the reference to my grandmother and strove to grasp his point.

"Such entertainments have been fashionable for decades," I pointed out.

"Entertainments?" He turned squarely to face me, the light from the nearest streetlamp throwing his face into sharp relief. "She was a person, for God's sake! She deserves to be left in peace, not displayed like a fairground attraction for people with half a shilling to gawp at."

"Five guineas," I corrected.

"I don't care if they charge a thousand guineas and the Koh-i-Noor. It's wrong."

"You are a scientist," I reminded him. "Surely you appreciate the discoveries which may be made from examination of the princess."

"Examination, yes. By properly trained scholars under suitably respectful circumstances. This is nothing more than a carnival show, a bit of theatrical nonsense to line Sir Leicester Tiverton's pockets. The man is no better than Barnum, hawking his freaks to anyone with the price of admission."

A nut seller uncovered his brazier, setting out a pan to roast chestnuts while a passing boy jostled me a little, muttering an apology with a tug of his low tweed cap. Stoker put a hand under my elbow and guided me to the side of the pavement. I said nothing for a long moment, waiting for him to speak again.

"She was human once," he said finally. "She walked and breathed and loved people and she had a name. Ankheset. It will be inscribed on the heart scarab that someone laid upon her to protect her in the afterlife. That ought to be respected instead of letting the rabble in to paw at her. She deserves to rest in peace."

I lifted a brow. "Stoker, what a dreadful romantic you are."

He opened his mouth, but I held up a hand. "I happen to agree with you. There is something highly distasteful about the notion of the princess being displayed for the amusement of passersby." I grinned. "All the more reason to see if we can discover the whereabouts of John de Morgan and the princess' diadem. Perhaps if we return the jewel to Sir Leicester, he would be grateful enough to listen to a little persuasion upon the subject."

Stoker thought for a moment, then suddenly took my hand. "Come on. There is someone you ought to meet."

He guided me around the corner to the staff entrance of the hotel. Tearing a leaf from his pocket notebook, he scribbled a hasty note and thrust it into the hands of a waiting errand boy with a small coin. "Take that to Monsieur d'Orlande," he instructed.

We waited a few minutes, stamping our feet against the chill. Suddenly, the door opened and out rolled a warm wave of air perfumed with cinnamon and yeast and roasted meats. A man in a pristine double-breasted white coat emerged. Atop his head perched a rakish scarlet velvet beret, and he wore a slender gold signet ring upon his smallest finger.

"Revelstoke!" he called in obvious delight, his face wreathed in smiles.

Stoker grinned and the two men embraced, clapping one another hard upon the back.

"Veronica, this is Julien d'Orlande. Julien, this is Miss Speedwell."

The fellow was perhaps Stoker's age, with long, slender hands and skin the rich silken brown of *Nymphalis antiopa*, the Camberwell Beauty butterfly. He offered me a broad smile. "Mademoiselle Speedwell." His voice carried the soft seduction of a French accent, and his dark eyes were expressive.

Comprehension dawned. "You're Lady Wellie's pastry chef!" Lady Wellie had told me once of finding a post for a French protégé as the pastry chef at the Sudbury, and I was delighted to make his acquaintance.

"I am indeed," he acknowledged. "But, Revelstoke, shame on you for keeping a lady standing in the cold! You have the manners of a Corsican peasant," he added with a quick grin at Stoker. He beckoned to me. "Come into my office, where it is warm."

He escorted us inside the hotel, and it was like seeing the inner workings of a beautiful clock—so many moving pieces, so much technical chaos—and yet the front presented only a serene and orderly façade. Here, endless rooms formed a labyrinthine arrangement, each space devoted to a separate task: preparing sauces, roasting meats, baking bread. Monsieur d'Orlande explained that his responsibility was overseeing the fine pastry, the delicate confections that graced the dinner tables in the dining salon above. The simple cakes and muffins we had enjoyed at tea were prepared by his underlings, but I could see he kept a careful eye upon them as we passed through. He glanced from side to side, offering a criticism here and praise there. One young man was teasing honey ice cream from a beehive mold while another spun sugar into a gilded cloud to form a nest.

"For a *croquembouche*," Monsieur told me as I gaped. "It is our speciality."

"It is magnificent," I said, breathing in the aromas of cooked sugar and vanilla. Stoker gazed longingly at a pyramid of tiny puffs of dough that had been fried quickly and stuffed with sweet cream and dusted with sugar. Courteous people called them *beignets soufflés*, but I had also heard them called by the rather earthier epithet of *pets de nonnes* or nun's farts. Either way, the sight of their golden seductions had reduced Stoker to a wordless whimper as we passed.

"I will send a box," Monsieur d'Orlande promised. "*Pets de nonnes* for you, Stoker, but I think *langues de chat* for the enchanting Miss Speedwell," he added with a slow smile of Gallic appreciation. Cat's tongues indeed! He showed us into a small office and closed the door behind. The air here was redolent of sugar and chocolate. There were a desk and an assortment of chairs as well as an undraped window that overlooked the pastry kitchen so he could keep a close watch upon his assistants at all times. The desk was tidy, but the bookshelf empty.

"You have no cookbooks," I said, pointing to the empty shelf.

He tapped his forehead with one slim finger. "A book may be lost. A true master carries all the knowledge he requires here."

I smiled, and he brought a bottle of dark liquid from a cabinet. He retrieved a set of tiny stemmed glasses of thin crystal and poured a thimbleful of the stuff for each of us. "It is a dessert liqueur of my own invention. I flavor it with violets and hay."

It sounded like the most unpromising thing I had ever drunk, but I took a sip to be polite. Instantly, springtime burst into flower on my tongue. The hay tasted green and fresh while the sensual violet blossomed darkly beneath.

"Extraordinary!" I proclaimed.

He gave me a satisfied smile. "I think it has promise."

Stoker said nothing but held out his glass with a hopeful look. Monsieur shook his head. "No more. It is almost finished and I have yet to perfect it. When I do, I will send you an entire bottle."

"I shall hold you to that."

Monsieur d'Orlande eased back in his chair, his manner expansive. "I think you do not come here only for the samples. What service may I perform for you?"

It was a charmingly old-fashioned request, and I found myself appreciating his courtly ways. He was a Frenchman through and through, and I had always been susceptible to Gallic flourishes.

Stoker came directly to the point. "I need you to do a bit of spying."

Monsieur's brows lifted. "Not my usual occupation, but for you I will be happy to try. Upon whom am I to spy?"

"The Tiverton party," I supplied.

"Plum cakes and plain custard," he said with a touch of disapproval. "They like their puddings very English. Not for them the crisp leaves of the *mille-feuille* or the many satisfactions of a perfectly made St. Honoré. No, Sir Leicester Tiverton always wants rice pudding with prunes." He shuddered. "But the young lady, she has promise. I am told she ate a second helping of my Turkish fantasia."

"Turkish fantasia?" Stoker asked, fairly drooling.

Monsieur shrugged. "A new creation of mine based upon an old Turkish recipe. Rosewater crème caramel, very delicate, finished with lacework of gilded sugar and a garnish of candied pistachios. The Turks are masters of the subtle uses of perfume in pastry," he added.

Stoker sighed a little as Monsieur went on. "Mademoiselle Tiverton was appreciative. I think she might be persuaded to an orange-blossom tart," he said, tipping his head thoughtfully. "I shall make for her a delicate mousse of the orange blossom and glaze the bottom of the tart with bitter chocolate and garnish it with whipped sweet cream and curls of chocolate."

Stoker gave a low moan of longing at the description.

Monsieur smiled. "Naturally, as an employee of the hotel, it is forbidden for me to fraternize with the guests, but if I were to send such a delicacy to her with the compliments of the kitchen and an invitation to see how such a confection is created, she might feel compelled to accept."

"She most certainly would," I agreed. "I think the girl is lonely." I glanced out the window to where the two assistants were assembling the pastry puffs into a mountain with the sticky aid of strong caramel. "Best to send the tart up with the dark-haired one. He is by far the better looking."

Monsieur gave a laugh, a rumbling sound that began low in his belly and worked its way up. "You are a lady of original thinking, Mademoiselle Speedwell. I suspect you have French blood."

I thought of the French princesses sprinkled throughout my father's family tree. "Perhaps a bit," I murmured. "Aren't you curious as to why we are asking you to spy upon this family?"

He shrugged. "I would never question Revelstoke, my dear mademoiselle," he said simply. "I told him once, whatever service I can render him, he has only to ask. And this is the first time he has done so."

Stoker reddened, a charming blush that warmed his complexion to the tips of his ears. "Rubbish," he muttered. "But if you help us, I will consider it a personal favor."

Monsieur shook his hand. "I will send word to you as soon as I know anything of importance."

"Shall we take a greeting to Lady Wellingtonia from you?" I asked.

He smiled, baring a set of gorgeous white teeth. "No need, dear lady. I dine with her once a fortnight," he told me. "Lady Wellingtonia, like Stoker, never forgets her friends." He bowed low over my hand. "It has been a pleasure to make your acquaintance, Mademoiselle Speedwell."

"And yours, Monsieur."

Stoker gave a low growl. "If the pair of you are *quite* finished," he said, gesturing to the door.

I flashed Monsieur a parting smile, and he touched his fingertips to his lips in a gesture of farewell.

We took our leave of the Sudbury and its scented delights, emerging into the darkening chill of the February gloom. Piles of dirty snow were heaped upon each curbstone, and the odor of manure and rotting vegetables hung heavy in the air.

"London is an unlovely place in winter," I said with some vehemence. "I would trade every smoking chimney, every grey fog for one clear Alpine peak."

Stoker shuddered. "Never." He elaborated on his dislike for mountains, but my mind was wandering, flitting away to a particular Swiss meadow where I had pursued a pretty little *Parnassius apollo* and been, in my turn, pursued by my guide. I had given up the butterfly chase, surrendering instead to the pleasures of the flesh, and to this day the smell of spring grass brings back the tenderest memories. I had gone into that meadow an eager girl and emerged from it, plucking crushed edelweiss from my hair and petticoats, a self-possessed and happily experienced woman.

"Are you even listening?" Stoker was asking.

"No," I replied with perfect candor. "I was recalling my first taste of the erotic joys."

"How on earth—never mind. I ought to know better than to question the vagaries of your imagination."

"Speaking of attractive men," I said, "what a charming man Monsieur d'Orlande is."

"Yes, Julien does tend to have that effect," Stoker said in a tone as dry as the Sahara. "I have yet to meet a woman who doesn't find him enchanting. I don't know if it is the accent or the fact that he always smells like sugar."

"They are both intoxicating qualities in a man," I informed him.

I thought of the story Lady Wellingtonia had told of the first time she had encountered Monsieur d'Orlande—at the opening of the Royal Museum of Natural History. "Was he really dressed in a loincloth when you met him?" I asked.

Stoker's handsome mouth turned down. "He was. The director of the museum thought he would make a suitable addition to the display of African apes."

I remembered Lady Wellingtonia's description of what followed. The fact that Stoker had thrashed the director with his bare fists had not surprised me. The fact that Julien d'Orlande proved to be a qualified pastry chef did.

"How did he come to such a pass with all of his talents?"

Stoker shrugged. "It is not always easy for a black man to find employment, even one as talented as Julien. His family were from Martinique, accomplished chefs, all of them. His grandfather was trained by Carême and his father cooked for Napoleon III. Julien was actually born at the palace at Fontainebleau. He trained as a pastry chef and went to work for a Parisian banker who decided to spend a winter in London, overseeing some investments. He brought Julien with him so he would dine well while he was here. As luck would have it, the fellow died suddenly, leaving neither cash to pay Julien's salary nor references. Julien spoke no English then and knew no one in London. He fell on hard times, and took the job at the museum rather than face the workhouse."

I shook my head. "He is obviously an aristocrat in the kitchen. It seems astonishing that he would take such demeaning employment."

"Julien is, like all Frenchmen, eminently practical. He thought a few days of standing on display in a loincloth would be a small price to pay to earn the wages to get himself back to Paris."

"He must be grateful that you intervened," I mused.

"Grateful? He called me a horse's ass when I thrashed the museum director. We were both thrown out, and he never received the wages he had earned. I cost him a full day's pay.

"Do not make the mistake of thinking I rescued him," he warned. "Julien d'Orlande is the proverbial cat with nine lives. He would have landed quite nicely on his feet without my interference at all."

I tipped my head. "Still, I wonder how many God-fearing Englishmen walked past him and saw what they wanted him to be rather than what he is."

"What he is is a bloody genius," he told me. "And when he sends that box of pastries, I have no intention of sharing."

"It was your idea to set him to watching the Tivertons," I reminded him. "You have earned them."

We walked on, taking in bracing lungfuls of cold London air, choking only a little on the smoke and fog that thickened it. Still, it was better than cooping ourselves up like chickens in the stuffy atmosphere of a cab, and we stretched our legs, weaving in and around the traffic, dodging the piled drifts of filthy snow. Aside from brisk laps in the earl's bathing pool, it was the most exercise either of us had had for some weeks. I felt my mood rise with every step.

I first became aware of the fact that we were being followed when we paused at the corner of Oxford Street. Here the traffic changed from the commercial vehicles and cabs to the sober respectability of private conveyances as we made our way into Marylebone. The teeming pavements gave way to casual walkers in good weather; in February, only the heartiest souls were afoot. I heard the brisk clip of footsteps behind us. Pausing to fuss with the lace of my boot, I noted the footsteps stopped. I darted a glance under my arm and saw a fellow of medium height, his cap pulled low over his brow—the same fellow who had jostled me outside the Sudbury.

Instantly, he stopped to inspect a railing, pursing his lips in a soundless whistle. His affected nonchalance did not deceive me. I noticed the rapidity of his respiration, white clouds puffing into the air as he attempted to catch his breath. Stoker and I were swift walkers. No one in his right mind would have tried to keep pace with us unless he were on the hunt and we were his prey.

I stood up and gave Stoker a smile, looping my arm through his and pulling his head near mine.

"We have a pursuer."

To his credit, Stoker did not look behind. Instead he cocked an ear. "Thirty feet behind," he murmured. "Perhaps forty."

His experience as a tracker stood us in good stead. Besides listening intently to gauge our follower's pace, Stoker occasionally flicked his eyes sideways when a large expanse of window glass reflected our quarry. We continued on our way, vigilant but with every appearance of nonchalance. We paced the length of the street until at last we came to the corner that marked the boundary of Bishop's Folly. Without discussion, we turned the corner and plunged instantly into the shrubbery, forcing our way through a modest break in the foliage. We crouched on the other side, waiting, peering through the leaves of the evergreens for our pursuer.

The fellow rounded the corner at a brisk trot, no doubt fully winded by now, exhaling in great gusts. He pulled up sharply at seeing an empty street. He stopped, openmouthed in astonishment, turning his head from side to side. The hole in the shrubbery was quite low, and it was nearly impossible to find unless one knew to look for it. Our pursuer did not. He stood, his face in deep shadow, turning in a slow circle to make certain he was entirely alone.

As soon as his back was turned, Stoker launched himself through the shrubbery. I was hard upon his heels, issuing a fair impression of a Maori battle cry while Stoker preferred to attack in a rush of menacing silence. He seized the villain by the throat and lifted him clear off his feet.

The booted feet fluttered for a moment. Then one snapped forwards, connecting with a rather delicate part of Stoker's anatomy with a vigor I could only admire. Stoker gasped and opened his fist, dropping the fellow to the ground, where he landed hard upon his posterior.

"Bollocking hell!" the villain exclaimed. In the moment of shocked surprise that followed, the blackguard leapt up and charged down the street. Stoker was in no fit state to follow, but I gave chase, pounding the pavement as I ran.

I am, as anyone who has met me can attest, accounted fleet of foot. But I was hampered upon this occasion by my sex, dear reader. Could I have overtaken our miscreant and emerged the victor in our little foot-race? Certainly, were it not for one fact: I was wearing a dress. Garbed for a polite social call at teatime, I was harnessed and corseted and knotted into submission. Even the dainty heels of my boots, so fashionable when glimpsed from under the froth of my petticoat, hindered me. My prey eluded me by the simple expedient of trousers and flat boots, taking the opportunity to jump onto the back of a passing hansom and trot smartly away as I stood watching in impotent fury.

I returned to where I had left Stoker and found him gingerly attempting to stand upright, his mouth set in a grim line. He did not have to ask. My expression told him that I had been unsuccessful.

"Well, that's an unexpected development," Stoker said mildly. "I thought you were the only woman in London who wore trousers."

CHAPTER 7

I rose the next day in a state of decided satisfaction. We had scarcely begun our investigation into John de Morgan's disappearance, but we had clearly agitated someone if we were being followed. And to what purpose? Our shadowy female friend could hardly have intended violence. She had been obviously unprepared for any sort of physical confrontation. Her surprise at Stoker's attack and her instinct to flight spoke to a lack of experience. (The fact that she had temporarily incapacitated Stoker before taking to her heels was the rankest luck.) Hitching herself onto a passing hansom had been a telling move. It revealed her as being audacious and opportunistic, but we might have guessed those things by the simple act of a young woman assuming male guise to follow us.

The question was, why? Was she an agent of Caroline de Morgan, intent upon discovering the whereabouts of an errant husband? Was she a private detective, secretly engaged by Sir Leicester to recover his priceless diadem? Curiosity seeker? Subordinate of Sir Hugo Montgomerie, sent to keep a weather eye upon us?

I considered the possibilities as I made my way to the glasshouse. The heating now regulated, it was a lush paradise, the air thick with the green scent of leaves slowly unfurling themselves from slumber.

In one corner, a little apart from the warmer regions of the glasshouse, sat a tiny copse of potted hornbeams. Nestled amidst the leaves were a series of papery cocoons, bronze-brown and wrinkled like decaying nuts, all about the length of my thumb. Each was frilled with a bit of hornbeam leaf, the last meal of the bright green caterpillars before they spun the enclosure that would shelter their metamorphoses. The caterpillars—and their costly hornbeam perches—had been a gift from Stoker's eldest brother, the Viscount Templeton-Vane. They had arrived most unexpectedly with a note inviting me to the opera and signed, "Affectionately, Tiberius." I had refused the invitation, but Stoker's order to return the caterpillars to his brother had caused me to nurture them as if they were my own children. I had always scorned moths, but I had to admit that in their larval form, they had been winsome little fellows and provided me with a great deal of unexpected amusement. I had fallen into the habit of visiting them on a daily basis, eagerly awaiting the moment they would eclose and step onto the branches, damp-winged and trembling.

"Actias luna," I murmured. "Good morning to you all."

"Are you talking to the trees, miss?" George asked, emerging from the misty reaches of the glasshouse.

"Indeed not. I was greeting my collection of cocoons, George." I pointed to the little colony. "These are specimens of *Actias luna*, the luna moth. When they emerge, they will be pale green moths as big as Mr. Stoker's hand."

I spread my hands to indicate the size of a fully grown imago, and George's eyes widened.

"Do they bite?" he asked warily. Like most city children, he had an unhealthy fear of nature.

I suppressed a sigh. "They do not. *Actias luna*, in its adult form, has no mouth."

"How does it eat?"

"It doesn't," I informed him. "It only lives a week, and its purpose is purely procreative."

"Come again?"

I paused, uncertain of how extensive George's knowledge with regard to the birds and bees might be. "They exist only to make other luna moths."

He seemed satisfied with that explanation and came to the point of his errand. He brandished the newspaper, and I saw that *The Daily Harbinger* had outdone itself. The headline was larger than usual, and Stoker's name had been spelt out in all its formality, including his honorific.

"Bollocking hell," I muttered as I hurried in the direction of the Belvedere.

The first order of business was to show the article to Stoker and weather the inevitable display of temper that would follow, but as I handed over the newspaper and braced myself, he merely sat quite still and read for some minutes. When he finished, he folded the newspaper neatly and laid it aside.

"We knew it was coming," was all that he said.

He walked out of the Belvedere, and I trotted after, following him to a broad sward of lawn, where he set to work on his latest project—restoring a Montgolfier balloon. Vibrant blue and spangled with the golden emblems of Bourbon kings, it had been commissioned by Louis XVI after several other successful flights had persuaded him of the promising potential of manned flight. It was not to be. Revolution intervened and the royalist balloon had been abandoned before it had ever flown. The king had lost his head, and the balloon had been sold to a Rosemorran earl who had been passing through Paris during the Terror. It had remained at the Belvedere ever since, the wicker gondola providing a commodious bed for the dogs. But Stoker had other ideas, and he had taken to tinkering with the thing, even managing to launch it for a memorable flight above the kitchen garden that had caused the scullery maid to shriek and hide in the coal cellar for the better part of a day. His lordship was particularly enthralled with the project, giving Stoker carte blanche to order whatever supplies and materials he required for its reclamation.

As I stood in silence, Stoker busied himself sorting various ropes and lines, his time in both the navy and a traveling circus standing him in good stead as he knotted and arranged the rigging. Spread onto the frost-withered grass, the brilliant azure of the balloon was shown to splendid effect. The later Montgolfier balloons had been larger and grander, but I preferred this smaller version of the Aérostat Réveillon.

"You're making quite good progress," I told Stoker by way of greeting. "Now, if you could persuade Betony to stop using the gondola as her dog basket, you might offer balloon rides for tuppence each."

He quirked a brow but did not look up from his stitching. "In point of fact, I have already spoken to his lordship about using it as a means of illustrating the properties of flight when the museum opens. For instance—" He launched into a highly technical explanation of lift and the relative density of heated air and heaven knows what else. He broke off midsentence. "You are not listening."

"Of course I'm not," I agreed. "I am thinking about our pursuer last night and the article in the *Harbinger* this morning."

His gaze sharpened. "You believe they are connected?"

"I haven't the faintest idea," I told him truthfully. "But there are half a dozen possibilities as to the identity of our miscreant. We cannot possibly examine them all ourselves, so we must have the most current information as to the state of the investigation. We must discover who might be connected with this case and also interested in our movements and whereabouts. And since you have now been exposed as connected to this *scandale*, time is of the essence. The sooner we tear the mask from the face of this mystery, the sooner we can restore your name."

I had expected my overblown prose to raise a smile, but he gave not even the merest twitch of the lips in reply.

After a moment he nodded. "I suppose you are right. You mean to consult Mornaday?"

"He is our best option for information," I said mildly. "He is fond of me."

"He hates me," Stoker countered. "That might be enough to stopper his tongue."

"I think you underestimate my charms."

We presented ourselves at Scotland Yard and were swiftly shown to Sir Hugo's office, where we were received by Inspector Mornaday, a waggish fellow with handsome hands and merry brown eyes.

"Well, 'tis always a pleasure to see you, Miss Speedwell, and that's the truth. I wish I could say the same for your pet wolf," he said with a glance to Stoker.

"Stoker, do stop looming. You're alarming Mornaday."

Mornaday and I exchanged a grin as Stoker gave a low growl. He and Mornaday frequently brought out the worst in one another, but the inspector was clearly in too exalted a mood to be cowed by Stoker's intimidation. That his high spirits were due to Sir Hugo's absence was all too apparent. He lounged behind his superior's desk with his booted feet resting atop, hands laced behind his head. He had leapt to his feet upon our arrival, but I waved him back. He was enjoying himself far too much for me to let good manners intrude upon his pleasure.

"What service may I perform for you, my glorious Miss Speedwell?" he asked with a waggle of his brows. Mornaday's eyebrows were a gift of Nature, well shaped and more expressive than the rest of his features combined. He used them to great effect, conveying interest, curiosity, skepticism, and credibility with equal skill. With me he frequently used them to indicate passionate flirtation. How sincere he was I had yet to determine, but the question did not keep me wakeful at night.

"We have come to discuss the disappearance of John de Morgan," I replied promptly.

He shook his head. "I am afraid your timing is unfortunate. His Superiority is home abed with a nasty catarrh," he told us with an air of satisfaction. I resisted the urge to look at Stoker. We had agreed to proceed with Mornaday as if we were unaware of Sir Hugo's indisposition. Mornaday loved nothing more than feeling as if he knew more than other people, and this seemed an innocuous way to get into his good graces.

"How unfeeling you are," I remarked. "Sir Hugo is, for all his faults, a man of good principles and your mentor. I am surprised to find you taking pleasure in his ill health." I gave him a repressive glance, and he put a hand to his heart.

"Pleasure! Nothing could be further from the truth," he said, but his lips twitched.

Stoker chose that moment to ease himself onto one of the small chairs Sir Hugo kept for visitors. The writing desk was a slender Regency affair, and the matching chairs were designed for elegance rather than substance. It was only after my third or fourth interrogation that I realized they had also been selected for maximum discomfort, no doubt to encourage his visitors to keep their visits brief and their answers truthful.

The chair gave a little groan of protest at Stoker's considerable weight, and Mornaday shot him a worried glance. "Steady, old man. I shouldn't like to explain to Sir Hugo how his chair ended up a pile of splinters."

"Because you aren't actually supposed to be in here," Stoker hazarded.

Mornaday looked uncomfortable. "Well, that is a matter of debate. Sir Hugo did ask me to conduct business as usual."

"With your boots on his desk and sipping his best single malt?" I asked sweetly.

Without a word, Mornaday poured a measure of whisky for me, sliding the bottle and a glass to Stoker as an afterthought. "For your silence," he said thinly. "Now, what do you want?"

"We have questions about the Tiverton Expedition. Specifically, about the disappearance of John de Morgan, the expedition photographer."

"The expedition thief, you mean," he corrected.

I inclined my head and Stoker said nothing, sipping deeply from his glass.

Mornaday rubbed his chin thoughtfully. Like Stoker, he eschewed facial hair. Stoker had shaven off his beard during our first investigation and left it off as a matter of habit. Mornaday, I suspected, shaved closely in order to flaunt the rather adorable cleft in his chin.

"Ordinarily, the investigation would not fall under the aegis of Special Branch," Mornaday began, imitating Sir Hugo's plummy tones. "But in this case, the stature of Sir Leicester Tiverton, as well as other considerations, means that reports have been made to this office."

"What other considerations?" I asked quickly.

He gave a sharp shake of the head. "That is not for me to say."

I suppressed a sigh. "Very well. What do your reports say?"

He tipped his head in recollection. "Almost nothing. The Tiverton Expedition was enjoying its most successful season in Egypt, having secured the tomb of a previously undiscovered princess of the Eighteenth Dynasty. Unfortunately, they were beset by illness and accident, as well as the death of the expedition director, a Mr. Jonas Fowler. Fowler's death was not unexpected. He had a well-known heart condition. But the timing of his demise only added to the sensationalist stories, and rumors began to circulate of a curse placed upon the expedition by the restless spirit of the disturbed princess."

"Horsefeathers," Stoker said succinctly.

Mornaday shrugged. "I am merely repeating what the reports say. Once the suspicion of a curse took root, every incident or accident, no matter how mundane, was ascribed to its malign influence. The last victim was John de Morgan, who fell ill but recovered his strength enough to leave the dig abruptly with his wife, Caroline. At the same time de Morgan left, a priceless diadem belonging to the princess' cache of grave goods went missing."

"And you are convinced de Morgan took it?" Stoker asked.

Mornaday shrugged. "What other conclusion is there?"

"Then what about this business of his disappearance?" I asked.

"I can give you a dozen reasons, but the likeliest is to be found in the person of his wife. According to rumor, their relationship was a tempestuous one, demonstrably affectionate in good times, loudly disruptive in less good times."

"So you believe he took the diadem with an eye to financing his escape from his marriage?" I supplied.

"His marriage, a job to which he was unsuited, England—take your pick. De Morgan has been unsuccessful at most of his ventures. He has no capital of his own and has been dependent upon the generosity of others to supply him with opportunities. This was, finally, a chance for him to be his own master and rid himself of a wife who had—by some accounts—possibly become a millstone."

"Whose accounts?" Stoker asked in a quiet voice.

Mornaday roused himself to look at Stoker. "Come again?"

"Whose accounts? You say Mrs. de Morgan was a millstone around her husband's neck. Someone must have suggested it to the police. I doubt you'd have got there on your own."

Mornaday spread his hands. "It was corroborated by several members of the Tiverton Expedition. De Morgan had a temper and apparently Mrs. de Morgan gave as good as she got."

"Then why take her with him?" I asked swiftly. "If de Morgan stole the diadem to underwrite his flight, why not leave his wife in Egypt?"

"What sort of blackguard would leave his unprotected wife in a filthy foreign land?" Mornaday countered.

"Egypt," Stoker pointed out acidly, "is not filthy. It was once the cradle of civilization. I would suggest you read a book, but I am not entirely certain of your ability to do so."

Mornaday dropped his feet to the ground, half rising from his chair. Stoker did the same, and I hastened to intervene.

"Boys!" I said sharply. "There will be no brawling with your shirts on. Kindly remove your upper garments and give them into my keeping."

Both men turned to look at me, wearing identical expressions of astonishment.

Mornaday spoke first. "I beg your pardon?"

I adopted my best nanny tone—one that I had used with excellent results to bring unruly suitors to heel. "You cannot strike an opponent properly while hampered by a tight coat," I pointed out. "Or a fitted waistcoat. And white does show the blood so badly. The shirt must come off as well." I put out my hands. "Come on, then. Shirts off, both of you. Shall you fight to first blood or unconsciousness? I always think first blood is a little lacking. Let's go until one of you is entirely senseless, shall we?"

They exchanged sheepish glances and backed down, resuming their chairs and taking up their whisky glasses once more.

I looked from one to the other. "No brawling, then? How very disappointing. Where were we?"

"The de Morgan disappearance," Mornaday said promptly. "For whatever reason, de Morgan chose to return to England with his wife. They had a bad Channel crossing, and he fell ill again with the same complaint that had troubled him in Egypt. Mrs. de Morgan took her husband to lodgings in Dover, a small private hotel where the expedition had stayed on their way out to Egypt. Once there, they registered and took separate rooms. De Morgan did not wish to be disturbed and his wife slept heavily. The next morning, she awoke to find no trace of her husband or the room which he had been assigned or any of his effects. We have tracked his departure on the steamer out of Alexandria with his wife, but after that all signs of him are lost."

"You mean he might never have crossed the Channel at all," I said.

Mornaday nodded. "The trail simply vanishes. We know Mrs. de Morgan claims he crossed the Channel with her, but there is no proof. He might have boarded a ship out of Marseilles or Cherbourg for anywhere in the world, taking the Tiverton diadem with him.

"The Dover police inspector made such a blunder of questioning her that she went into hysterics and refused to answer any more questions beyond saying that she had told the truth: her husband had come with her as far as Dover and then vanished in the night. We have pursued every possible avenue of investigation, but we have nothing. Without further evidence, we are left to conjecture, and Special Branch have more important things to worry about than one stolen bit of jewelry and a cast-off wife," he added a trifle pompously.

"Why would Mrs. de Morgan make up such a fantastical story?" Stoker asked. He drained his whisky as he waited for the reply. His knuckles were white upon the glass, and I knew that for all his outward calm, he was still tamping down the embers of his temper.

"Sir Hugo thinks she is colluding with her husband, that the stories of their quarrels were exaggerated and that she means to slip quietly away and join him when the furor has died down."

He paused, an unholy gleam lighting his brown eyes. "For my part, I believe de Morgan has absconded on his own. I think he left her in France and that Mrs. de Morgan has spun this fanciful tale in order to avoid another scandal with herself in the role of abandoned wife." He spoke the last words as if tasting them, and his expression was one of cold satisfaction as he casually laid his hand on the newspaper on his desk—the latest edition of *The Daily Harbinger*.

Stoker's mouth curved into a mirthless smile. "You rotten little bas—"

I leapt up before he could finish the sentence, gripping his coattails in both fists. "Stoker, that is quite enough. Sit *down*," I ordered. I put up a hand, gesturing for Mornaday, who had risen to his feet in a defensive posture, to resume his chair as well.

"So you are acquainted with Mrs. de Morgan's marital history," I said, keeping a weather eye upon Stoker.

"I am," Mornaday said with relish. "And quite a history it is."

I gave him a cold look. "Mornaday, bearbaiting has been illegal for more than fifty years and it requires a special stick," I told him. "Behave yourself."

He had the grace to look abashed. "All right, then. Yes, we know that Caroline de Morgan once featured at the heart of a Society scandal when she sued her first husband, the Honourable Revelstoke Templeton-Vane, for divorce on the grounds of cruelty and desertion. With the tempestuous nature of her second marriage, it is possible that Mrs. de Morgan has once again been abandoned and that she finds this difficult to accept."

"You really think she is lying in order to hide the fact that she has been cast off by her husband?" I finished.

"It is as likely an explanation as her partnering with him in order to steal the diadem. It depends entirely on the character of Mrs. de Morgan," he said, turning a thoughtful eye to Stoker.

"John de Morgan left Egypt in the company of his wife and has not been seen since. Perhaps she killed him," Mornaday said flatly. I sucked in a sharp breath and he went on in a conversational tone. "After all, it wouldn't be the first time she left a man for dead."

The glass made no sound as it flew past Mornaday's head, but it shattered on the wall with the reverberating report of a gunshot.

Mornaday leapt to his feet as the door was flung open.

"Mornaday! What the devil is the matter with you, man? This is no place for brawls, and is that spirits I smell?" The man in the doorway was average in every possible way. Average height, average build, average coloring. Only his eyes, piercing and cold, were remarkable.

Mornaday swallowed tightly. "Inspector Archibond. I did not realize you were in the building."

Inspector Archibond's gaze swept from the whisky-dampened wall to the puddle on the floor. "I should think not. Clear up this mess and then get down to the mortuary. I've just had a note from Sir Hugo and he shall be away until the end of the week at least. I am to keep an eye upon his open cases until his return."

His posture was ramrod straight, but he managed to raise himself a little more stiffly. "Do you have official police business? Might I be of assistance?" he inquired in a voice that was anything but solicitous.

"They were leaving," Mornaday said swiftly.

Stoker and I rose and slipped away just as Inspector Archibond began to lecture Mornaday upon the evils of drink. Once upon the pavement, Stoker paused, his eyes skimming over the assortment of folk bent upon their daily activities. After a moment he narrowed his gaze to a woman in rusty black standing upon a soapbox and hectoring a few woebegone-looking fellows.

Stoker scribbled something into his pocket notebook, tore out the page, and handed it to the woman with a pound note. She bobbed a thank-you, bonnet plume waving, and Stoker and I turned away.

"What was that?"

"A subscription for Mornaday from the Temperance League of Greater London. I told her he was a disordered soul in need of saving from the degradation of drink."

He grinned, a shadow of his usual cheerful self, and we walked along in silence for some minutes, until Stoker stopped, not turning to look at me.

"You haven't asked about her. Not really."

"I shall not," I promised him. "When you want to tell me, you will."

Still he did not look at me, but he reached out and brushed a fingertip over my hand. It was a tiny thing, that gesture, but the whole world was contained within it—gratitude, partnership, understanding. I had taken lovers around the world, more than a score of them at last count, but Stoker was the nearest thing I had ever known to an actual partner. And I knew better than to ask him for what he could not give.

"We never told him about being followed last night," I began.

Stoker shrugged. "We are just as likely to solve the matter as he is. If we were followed once, we will most likely be again. We must be watchful for her and lay a better trap."

"Perhaps. At least we know they have exhausted all possibilities. They have given up on finding de Morgan. So long as we are prepared to stick it out, we can hardly do worse than the professionals."

"Where next?" Stoker asked as we came to a crossroads.

I considered our options. "I think it is time to meet a millionaire," I told him with a broad smile. "We are calling upon Horus Stihl."

CHAPTER 8

As befitted an American millionaire with a penchant for theatricality, Horus Stihl had booked himself and his son into the Allerdale Hotel, the most expensive lodging in London. Designed to mimic the queen's retreat at Balmoral Castle, the hotel was a neo-Gothic Scottish monstrosity complete with tartan carpets and waiters imported from the Highlands. But the food was incomparable and the modern amenities second to none.

We presented our cards to a passing porter and settled into the plaid lobby to await Mr. Stihl's pleasure, but to my delighted surprise we were summoned immediately. The porter escorted us into the hydraulic lift and we were whisked up to the Empress suite on the seventh floor.

"Mr. Stihl is most particularrrrrr," the porter observed. I narrowed my eyes at him and he grinned.

"The accent was too much, wasn't it?" he asked.

"A trifle," I said thinly. "I presume you are not really Scottish?"

"Cockney, born and bred," he said with a nod. "But I needed the work and they'll only hire haggis-eaters."

Stoker snorted, and I pressed a coin into the fellow's hand. "Just mind your r's and you will do quite nicely," I advised.

He bowed us into the suite, and I was pleased to see that here the decorators had used a modicum of restraint. The carpet was one of the more subdued tartans, and the upholstered furniture was elegantly finished in bottle green velvet. Prints of Highland scenes had been scattered about, and china bowls of heather added touches of soft purple. Above the mantel hung a picture of an indifferent deerhound looking down his nose. A fire was crackling merrily upon the hearth, and two armchairs of brown leather had been drawn near to its warmth. The whisky decanter and soda siphon were near at hand, as were the day's newspapers. The two men who occupied the chairs rose at once.

"Miss Speedwell, Mr. Templeton-Vane? Horace Stihl," said the taller of the two coming towards us, hand outstretched. I took it and he shook mine warmly, holding it in the firm friendly grasp I had so often noted amongst Americans. He was of medium height, but slim, and his wiry build coupled with a shock of white hair standing on end made him seem much taller. His brows and moustaches were snowy and luxuriant, his blue eyes bright with interest. He bore a strong resemblance to the Yankee author known as Mark Twain, and he seemed the sort of man who would always find a way to enjoy himself.

His companion was decidedly more subdued. Of a similar height to Mr. Stihl, the other man was easily half his age, with a markedly sturdier build. His demeanor was watchful and quiet, and he held a book in his hand. *A Study of Drains and Effluent Matter in the Capital Cities of Europe.*

"Henry Stihl," he said, coming forwards with obvious reluctance. He might have been the great man's son, but he bore little resemblance to him, and I wondered what kind of woman Mrs. Stihl had been. He wore clothes of obviously expensive make that had probably been well tailored, but they were so heavily creased and crumpled it was impossible to tell. His hair resembled the plumage of a disheveled porcupine, and there were ink stains upon his fingers.

"You are interested in drains, Mr. Stihl?" I asked brightly with a glance at his book.

His expression was grave. "It is a subject which ought to interest us all, I think. It is only by the application of proper engineering and sanitation methods that we can hope to halt the spread of some of the most virulent diseases that currently plague us. Your own city of London provides the most instructive study. Did you know there are entire underground rivers flowing beneath our feet at this very moment?"

I blinked at him in surprise. It is seldom that a gentleman raises the subject of sewage so early in a conversation, I reflected. His father seemed not at all shocked. He merely gave a long-suffering sigh.

"Henry," he said with firm authority. "No drains. Not now."

The young man flushed to the roots of his hair.

"Perhaps we can resume the topic at a different time," I suggested.

He gave an indifferent shrug, and I wondered if it was the fate of the Tiverton and Stihl children to be overshadowed by their charismatic fathers.

The introductions complete, Horus Stihl waved us to chairs and began the conversation with a directness that was typically American. "What can I do for you?" he asked, his expression genial but wary. No doubt the great man spent the bulk of his time fending off fortune hunters, rapscallions, and wastrels who would always linger about those with money, hoping to pick up whatever crumbs they might.

I gave him a disarming smile. "It is more a question of what we can do for you," I said.

Henry Stihl narrowed his eyes. "We are not in need of any professional service at this time," he said shortly.

His father cut him off with an abrupt gesture. "No call to be rude, boy. We must observe the form," he said with unnecessary firmness. Henry Stihl flushed again, this time retreating to his book to hide his blushes.

Horus Stihl made apologetic noises. "You must excuse the pup. Henry is determined to see villains behind every strange face. Now, what can you do for me?"

"We have come about the disappearance of John de Morgan," I told him. From the tail of my eye, I could see Henry Stihl's book slip. He caught it before it fell, his knuckles tightening to whiteness. He made a show of propping the book up, but during the ensuing conversation, he turned not a single page.

"Sad business," Horus Stihl was saying. "But nothing to do with us. We never even met the fellow."

"You had a different concession this year," I ventured. "And I understand it was de Morgan's first year digging with the Tivertons."

"That's right." Horus Stihl nodded, his extraordinary halo of white hair glowing like a nimbus about his head.

"Where did you dig?" Stoker asked.

"Amarna" came the prompt reply. "I thought I would have a go at finding ol' Akhenaten. Are you familiar with him?"

"Originally called Amenhotep IV. Eighteenth Dynasty, successor to Amenhotep III," I answered swiftly. Stoker stared at me in frank surprise. The fact that Lord Rosemorran's collection was bound to house some of the finest Egyptological works was something he should have deduced himself. I had read late into the night, giving myself as thorough a grounding in the subject as I could.

Horus Stihl gave me a look of approval and I went on. "Akhenaten founded the city of Amarna, moving the capital from Thebes and wresting power from the priests of Amun by establishing the worship of the one god, the Aten.

"The Aten was associated with the sun, was it not?" I asked.

"The sun disc," Horus Stihl said, his voice taking on a dreamy quality. "Amenhotep IV believed that the sun disc, the Aten, was the source of life. He changed his name to Akhenaten because it means the 'living spirit of Aten,' the conduit for all life in Egypt. He created a revolution, overthrowing all that had been known of culture and religion for thousands of years. He built a new capital city and commissioned art depicting himself and his family as the recipients of the favor of the Aten. Nothing like it has ever existed before or since. Imagine that," he instructed, sitting very straight, his eyes burning with fervid heat, "a single man uprooting everything his society had known with his own two hands and refashioning the world in the image of himself."

His son snorted, but when I looked, his eyes were fixed firmly on the page before him. But Horus Stihl had heard it as well.

"My son doesn't approve of Akhenaten. He views him as an iconoclast and a rebel, but I believe he was a forward thinker, a man ahead of his time."

"He changed the art and moved the capital, but he did nothing to materially alter the lives of his subjects," Stoker objected.

From behind the book came a growl of approval.

Horus Stihl smiled thinly. "He didn't have the chance. First he needed to change the court and the temples. The rest would have followed in time."

From the slender book I had unearthed on the Amarna period, I knew Akhenaten's reign had spanned at least a decade—plenty of time to have allowed him to improve the life of the average Egyptian who toiled from sunup to sundown.

But it would not do to contradict Horus Stihl, I reflected. I shifted in my seat, bringing the point of my parasol down quietly but firmly on Stoker's booted foot, pinning it in place.

"How very fascinating," I murmured, batting my lashes a little. Stihl looked from Stoker to me and stroked his lavish white moustaches.

"And of course," the millionaire continued, "he was most fortunate in his consort, the Great Royal Wife."

"Nef—what was it again?" I asked, opening my eyes very wide and deliberately stumbling over the name.

"Nefertiti," Stihl supplied promptly. "She was called the Lady of Grace and Sweet of Love, you know, among a host of other titles. She was the most honored consort in Egyptian history, and the most beautiful. It is a wonderful love story."

"Of all the sentimental rubbish," the younger Stihl burst out, tossing his book aside. "Nefertiti was a *partner*, not some bit of decoration. In the temple at Karnak, she is *clearly* shown smiting her enemies with all the powers of a pharaoh—"

"Now, hold on, son," instructed the elder, holding up a hand. "I will grant you that she was his helpmeet, but presuming that she wielded the powers of a pharaoh is just nonsense, errant nonsense."

Henry Stihl clutched at his hair with both hands. "Do you see what I have to endure?" he demanded of no one in particular. I looked to his father and saw Horus Stihl watching his son with a gleam in his eye. Their clashes were clearly a thing of long standing and an obvious source of amusement—at least to the father.

I hastened to pour oil on the troubled waters, as much to calm the son as to draw the father back to the point of our visit. "Naturally, Amarna would offer the greatest scope for your interest in Akhenaten and Nefertiti. Was it a successful season?"

Henry Stihl made a sound of disgust and returned to his book. His father was more composed. He stroked his moustaches thoughtfully. "Not particularly. We unearthed a pretty cache of pottery and excavated a pavement."

"A pavement!" muttered Henry with some feeling.

Horus Stihl ignored his son. "Ours was not nearly as productive and engaging a time as was had by the Tivertons," he remarked.

"Yes, their find was extraordinary," Stoker said smoothly.

"Too extraordinary," Henry said from behind his book.

"Indeed?" I asked, lifting my brows.

Henry did not elaborate. His father gave me an apologetic smile.

"Henry has been at school for several seasons, and last year was his first time in the field since he was a child. Our discoveries were less than scintillating, so that's why I decided to have a go at Amarna. I hoped we would find something to write home about this time, but I am sorry to say luck was not on our side. The boy is still resentful that we did not share the Tivertons' good fortune."

"But you might have," I said in a voice silken with insinuation. "I understand they were digging on a concession you had last year."

"And should have had this year!" burst out young Stihl. His eyes were blazing and a muscle in his jaw twitched furiously. "I don't know how they did it, but they secured the *firman* and cut us right out."

Something flickered behind the sharp blue eyes. "Now, son, Sir Leicester Tiverton is not the sort of man who would do a friend down in business," his father said mildly.

"And yet he did," Henry Stihl riposted with real bitterness.

"But what could have prompted such an act?" Stoker asked.

The elder Stihl shrugged. "I wish I knew."

Henry Stihl rose stiffly, clutching his book on drains. "Please excuse me," he said quietly as he fled the room.

No one spoke for a long moment. The only sound was the steady ticking of the mantel clock, a hideous thing painted with Highland scenes.

I cut my eyes at Stoker and flicked them quickly in the direction of the door. He rose. "Do excuse me, Mr. Stihl. I'm afraid I just remembered—there is a telegram I need to send."

The millionaire nodded, and Stoker took his leave, giving me a significant glance as he did so. I turned back to Mr. Stihl.

"I must apologize. Discussing the Tivertons seems to have upset young Mr. Stihl, and that was not my intention."

His smile, barely visible under the lavish white fringe of his moustaches, was tired. "I have stopped keeping count of the things that upset young Mr. Stihl."

"I believe Miss Iphigenia Tiverton is similarly prickly," I observed mildly.

His expression was one of wistful fondness. "It's a difficult thing to lose one's mother, particularly a mother as unique as Lady Tiverton."

"I understand she wrote some highly regarded works on Egyptology," I told him.

"That she did," he said, his eyes gleaming. "Lucie Ward Tiverton was a miracle of a woman. Do you know she was diagnosed with consumption at the age of nineteen? Specialists told her she would be dead within two years. She lived to be more than forty years of age, and that by the sheer force of her will. I have never known a woman who could light up a room the way she could," he said, his voice suddenly thick with emotion. The Tivertons had mentioned Horus Stihl's affection for Lucie Tiverton, but I began to wonder if his feelings had not been more significant by far.

"Is Miss Iphigenia very like her mother?"

"Lord love you, no! Lucie was sharp as Toledo steel and with eyes, great dark eyes that would look right into your heart and dare you to tell the truth. Poor Figgy takes after her father's side, both in looks and temperament. But I have high hopes she will emerge from her adolescence as a credit to the mother she has lost," he finished gallantly.

I smiled back. "Children, I am told, are both blessing and burden, long after they are grown."

"You can say that again," he replied with heartfelt emotion. "I have never understood my own boy, not from the day his mama pushed him into the world. He takes after her people, quiet bookish folk," he confided. "The Stihls were doers. They carved out a place and a name for themselves in America when you Brits were cutting the heads off your kings."

"Well, we don't make a *habit* of it," I said.

He chuckled and waved a hand. "The point is, we Stihls have got in the way of shaping our own destiny. We make our mark in the world. We take risks and damn the consequences, if you'll pardon the expression."

"I will. I am of similar bent," I assured him.

He gave me an admiring look. "The problem is, too much of that in the bloodline eventually breeds stupid."

"I beg your pardon?"

"People are like horses, Miss Speedwell. Bloodlines carry certain traits. Too much of the same kind of blood eventually breeds stupid. I had a racehorse so simple he followed a pig around because he thought they were kin. Families are the same. We Stihls are fire-in-the-blood types, always up for a challenge, never backing away from a fight. But my mother was a second cousin to my father, and that was just too much of a good thing. My younger brother was so impatient, he once deliberately burned down a house just to cook a steak. I thought if I married a woman different, someone sober and refined, it would dilute some of that Stihl bullheadedness."

"It seems to have worked," I mused. "Mr. Henry Stihl is certainly a young man of quiet tastes."

"Quiet tastes!" He snorted. "I have to pay him ten whole American dollars just to get him to go to a music hall and have a little fun. He's sober as a parson, and half as interesting. I just wish he would put the damn books down and live a little, if you'll pardon the expression," he added hastily.

"Certainly. But you are fortunate, Mr. Stihl. Your son takes an interest in your travels and excavations. Surely that is something you can share."

He shrugged. "I suppose. But the bloom has gone off the rose a bit. I had the devil's own time getting him out to Egypt this year. I don't know as he will want to go back again."

"Why?" I pried gently.

But for all his expansive habits of conversation, Horus Stihl could be close as an oyster. He gave me a bland smile. "I have bored you too long with discussions of my family. You are a sympathetic listener, Miss Speedwell."

I batted my lashes and did a few other revoltingly female things, but the moment for confidences was past. Knowing when to surrender the field, I rose.

"Thank you for seeing us, Mr. Stihl."

He took the hand I offered, holding it carefully in his own, as if it were a precious object. "The pleasure has been entirely mine, Miss Speedwell. I am only sorry I could not help with your search for Mr. de Morgan."

I paused, then seized the chance for one last desperate throw of the dice. "Mr. Stihl, if you know anything at all, I should consider it a personal favor if you would tell me. It might help us to discover the truth behind Mr. de Morgan's disappearance and offer some consolation to his grieving wife."

Horus Stihl flinched a little at the mention of a grieving wife. He was, as his son had pointed out, a sentimental man, and I had pressed ruthlessly upon that vulnerable point. But he merely shook his head.

"I wish you every success," he replied obliquely.

Defeated but determined to be gracious, I went to the door, followed closely by Mr. Stihl, who insisted upon opening it himself. "Miss Speedwell," he said, "wait here a moment." He disappeared into his bedchamber, returning a moment later with a pair of volumes bound in identical faience-blue kid. They were stamped in gold on the spines. The first was called *A Lady's Adventures upon the Nile* while the second was titled *Further Adventures of a Lady Egyptologist.* Both were authored by Lady Tiverton.

"Take them," he urged. He was quite close, and I caught the sharp spicy scent of bay rum, warmed by the skin of his freshly barbered chin.

"Mr. Stihl, I couldn't possibly," I protested.

He smiled. "She was a very dear friend, and I have many copies. It would please me greatly for you to have them."

Then, in a wholly unexpected gesture, he swept a low bow and kissed my hand. I left him then, but the brush of his silken moustaches against my fingers lingered for some time.

I collected Stoker from the lobby, where he was comfortably ensconced reading a newspaper article about the recent establishment of the National Geographic Society in Washington, DC. Without letting him finish, I tossed the newspaper aside and bore him off into the gloom.

"Blast this weather!" I muttered as we stepped from the lambent warmth of the hotel. "I would sell my virtue for a sunny day and a tropical trade wind."

To his credit, Stoker did not point out that my virtue was no longer mine to sell. Instead, he tucked my hand in the crook of his arm and guided me down the street. We proceeded from the hotel in the direction of Bishop's Folly, neither of us inclined to summon a hansom. It was frigid and mizzling, filthy weather, but the temperature had dropped from the previous day and the air was too cold to bear its usual stink of horse and rotting vegetables and coal smoke. It was sharp as a new blade, that air, and I drew in several lungfuls of it as we moved through the gathering shadows, pacing off our steps between the glowing pools of light from the streetlamps.

"So, Mr. Stihl was impervious to your charms?" he hazarded as we crossed a street behind an omnibus.

"Not entirely. He was kind enough to give me copies of Lady Tiverton's Egyptian memoirs," I told him, deliberately omitting the millionaire's kiss to my hand. "He is a child in a grown man's suit—all enthusiasm and rush and forwardness. I fancy his son is exhausted."

"And prickly as a cactus."

"He has that in common with Iphigenia Tiverton," I observed. "They should form a club. Children of obstreperous parents."

"Little wonder that Stihl and Tiverton got on so well for so many years. They are of a type."

"And even smaller wonder they eventually fell out," I added. "Both of them strike me as highly idealistic, extremely stubborn men. As soon as one of them conceived of a slight, he would nurse it to the grave. That sort always bears a grudge."

"But over what?"

I shrugged. "Egyptology, what else? Sir Leicester permitted simple avariciousness to come between him and his friend, as Mr. Henry Stihl so acutely observed. I am only surprised his father does not admit the quarrel."

"He had no other complaints?"

"None. He was quite correct in his praise of Sir Leicester's abilities—if not his probity—and he has a soft spot for Figgy, although it is not half what he felt for her mother."

Stoker nodded. "He's the sort who would have done well with daughters. All indulgent benevolence. I pity his son."

"Do you? Is it worth pitying the sole heir of a millionaire?"

Stoker snorted. "Henry Stihl will earn every penny of his inheritance, I assure you. No doubt he has totted up every slight in a ledger somewhere."

"I suspect his father has caused him a great deal of embarrassment. I further suspect that Horus Stihl is entirely unaware of the effect he has on his son. He is mystified by the boy. He clearly wishes he had some more dashing fellow for an heir."

"Thus my pity for him. I am only too familiar with the subtle vengeances of a father on the figure of a son he does not value." The words were spoken lightly, but a lifetime of slights rested in those few words. Stoker had amassed a collection of petty hatreds from his father, and he showed them to precious few.

Deliberately, I changed the subject. "So, the friendship of twenty years has foundered upon Sir Leicester's avarice in claiming the tomb for himself. Is he naturally disloyal, or do you think something else prompted him?"

Stoker was silent for some minutes as we navigated a particularly crowded thoroughfare, turning at last into a quiet residential street bordering a private square. The trees in the square had given up their leaves, the slim black branches bearing a thin coat of ice. They stirred suddenly in a gust of wind, clicking together like the finger bones of a dead man.

Stoker squeezed my hand, quite unconsciously, I thought. He spoke at last. "What if the Tivertons were short of money? Egyptology is a devilishly expensive proposition. He has a country house in Surrey, a daughter to educate and launch into Society, a wife to keep. He has kept pace for twenty years with an American millionaire, underwriting his own expeditions. What if he has gone to the well once too often?"

I tipped my head. "That would account for his desire to keep the hoard to himself. Many a greater man has sacrificed a friend for the sake of a fortune. But there is more than just money at stake."

"Fame," Stoker supplied.

"Precisely. Despite the paucity of the find, this discovery will forever be known as the crowning glory of the Tiverton Expeditions. It will be written in all the books and newspapers. Sir Leicester has secured himself a place in Egyptological history. Perhaps that is as great an inducement as money."

"Perhaps."

We walked on for several minutes more before I could steel myself for what must come next.

"We have interviewed the Tivertons and Horus Stihl," I began slowly. "We have set Lady Wellingtonia to ferreting out any Society gossip that might prove useful, and Julien d'Orlande is keeping a careful eye upon the goings-on at the Sudbury. But there is one obvious stone we have not yet overturned."

The arm beneath my fingers tensed. "I see no reason—"

I pushed on ruthlessly. "Of course you don't. You are not thinking logically. We must interview her. Caroline de Morgan is the last person to see her husband. She knows something."

"She knows nothing." His voice was harsh.

"You cannot say that for certain."

"Sir Hugo and Mornaday both said she was in hiding."

"Sir Hugo and Mornaday are, for all their gifts, merely men. They lack imagination. She is in the care of her parents."

"You don't know—"

"I do, actually." I matched his coldness with an arctic chill of my own invention. "I have confirmed that she is in London, currently residing at the home of her parents in a house in Kensington just off the Cromwell Road."

He stopped dead, wrenching his arm free. He had stopped in a shadow, but his eyes blazed through the darkness. "How in the name of bleeding Jesus do you know that?"

I felt my lip curl. "I have my methods."

It took him only a moment to work it out. "George."

"He is a most obliging fellow and quite clever. It took him only an afternoon to find the house and to confirm that she is there. We must speak with her."

A stillness settled over him, so complete, so encompassing, that I could not reach him. He had moved a thousand miles from me and yet we stood half a foot apart. I could feel the warmth thrown off by his big body in the cold air, but he was as far away and forbidding as a mountain.

"I do not wish—"

"It is not about what you wish," I cut in savagely. "Caroline de Morgan might well hold the key to her husband's disappearance and we have to clear your name. So I will see her and I will ask her whatever questions must be asked, and I will do it with you or without you."

What he said next was something so profane that no clergyman in

England would have shriven him afterwards. I waited while he expounded upon his theme, calling me every name he could conceive and a few I had never heard.

"Are you quite finished?" I asked after some minutes. I spoke the words in a tone of complete boredom, careful not to let him see that my hands were trembling.

"Quite," he said, biting off the word sharply.

"Good. There is no time like the present," I said, turning to whistle for a hansom.

CHAPTER 9

We settled into the cab, locked in our silences. Stoker and I had two forms of disagreement, violent and vocal discord or completely mute hostility. Our current disaffection manifested as the latter. I knew he was enraged at my insistence, but he was more enraged that I was right. Caroline had to be faced, and the fact that he could not avoid her galled him more than anything else about this business.

For my own part, I tried not to think about how desperately he must care about her to be so deeply affected. I had heard his tortured cries in nightmares; I knew she haunted him still. I had felt his lips on mine, moving to form the syllables of her name even as he pushed himself out of my embrace. I was grateful for it. Stoker and I were partners rather than lovers, but the blow to my *amour propre* still stung. I had forgiven him, not that he noticed. He had no memory of that aborted kiss, at least none that he had ever acknowledged by so much as a flicker of an eyelash. But he must have remembered the dreams. No man could suffer as he did and not remember when the morning came. He called her name then too, an invocation in the darkness, but she never came except as a ghost to torment him. It was a score I meant to settle with her one day, I promised myself as the hansom rattled along. I had provided the driver with the address and Stoker did not seem surprised.

"This house in Kensington," I began in a tone of marked froideur, "I take it the place has been in her family?"

"Her father purchased it," he replied after a long silence. "His family were in manufacturing in the North. Something to do with plumbing supplies. Her mother is an Honourable. She was the daughter of a baron before she married Marshwood."

"She married down," I observed. "Either she truly loved him or her people had no money."

"Very much the latter," he said in a hollow voice. He was reciting from memory and had no attachment to the words themselves, but I wanted to keep him talking. Anything to prevent him from thinking too much about what he must do once we arrived.

"So she married with an eye to using her husband's fortune to regain lost prestige."

"She tried. After they were married, she discovered that Mr. Marshwood's prospects were far less grand than she had been led to believe. She has devoted her life to pushing him into better circumstances."

"Why did they go to Egypt?"

"He accepted a minor diplomatic post. She used her father's connections to secure his appointment, but Marshwood was something of a disaster. He wasn't brought up to that sort of thing and bungled it frequently." There was a casual snobbery in Stoker's remarks. The fact that Mr. Marshwood had not been born to the ermine of aristocracy did not preclude him from being a man of talent and ability. But this was not the time to brangle with Stoker.

"Why did they come back to England?" Too late, I realized I had blundered.

He turned his head, his smile a harsh, thin line. "Because they needed to rescue their daughter from her brute of a husband."

"I apolo—"

He held up a hand. "Don't. I may forgive you for forcing me into this, but it will not be today."

The hansom rocked to a stop, and Stoker flung a coin at the driver. "Keep the change."

"That's half a crown!" the cabman protested in half-credulous joy.

"I don't bloody care," Stoker called over his shoulder as he stalked away. He mounted the steps of a stolid house, as characterless and dull as all the rest in that particular square. I followed hard upon his heels. He turned as we reached the top.

"You really have no idea what you've done, do you?" he asked. Before I could reply, he made a fist and brought it down hard upon the door.

The door was answered after a long moment by a tall, imposing butler with florid cheeks and ramrod posture. He swept us both in a long, cool glance that might have meant anything.

"Yes?" he inquired in a tone that perfectly balanced hauteur and politeness.

Stoker wordlessly produced a card from the depths of his pocket. The butler looked pained at the lack of card case and still more grieved at the condition of the card. In Stoker's pocket it had doubtless kept company with bits of string, marbles—for use as eyes in his taxidermic mounts rather than a child's playthings—paper twists of sweets, and the occasional feather collected upon his walks.

The butler placed the grubby card upon a silver salver, but it was clear from the change in his manner that he had read it and taken note of the "Honourable" preceding Stoker's name.

"Shall I direct your compliments to the master or the mistress, Mr. Templeton-Vane?" he inquired.

"Neither. I want to see Mrs. de Morgan."

The butler had been well trained. He gave a politely regretful smile. "I am sorry to say that Mrs. de Morgan is not at home to callers."

"But she *is* at home," I pressed.

The butler gave nothing away, merely inclined his head and kept his smile fixed. He moved towards us, as if to guide us back through the door. "I shall of course convey the fact of your visit to Mr. and Mrs. Marshwood," he began.

Stoker drew himself up to his full height and folded his arms over the breadth of his chest. "I am not leaving. If I cannot see Mrs. de Morgan, kindly arrange for me to see her parents."

"I regret—"

"Not yet, but you will if you don't do as I say," Stoker cut in ruthlessly. "I can smell his bloody cigar smoke from here. Go fetch him and be quick."

The butler flushed, his complexion mottled above the stiff starched white of his collar. "Now, see here—"

Although things had not yet deteriorated to fisticuffs, the altercation was loud enough to draw the master of the house from his lair. A door just off the entry opened and a short, barrel-chested man emerged, drawing furiously on his cigar.

"Bowles, what the devil—" He choked off the last word when he caught sight of Stoker. His ruddy complexion drained of color, and the cigar slipped from his lips. He caught it with a bare hand, scorching himself, and muttered a curse. He thrust the smoldering stub into his pocket and pointed a plump finger at Stoker.

"I suppose you've come to gloat."

"I have done nothing of the sort," Stoker said calmly. "In fact, I might be able to help. I need to see her."

"See her?" Mr. Marshwood's eyes rounded and he gave a harsh laugh. "Not bloody likely. Go back to whatever hell pit you crawled from and take your tart with you," he added with a jerk of his chin in my direction.

Stoker's hands clenched, but he did not raise them, nor did he move.

Instead he looked down at his former father-in-law, disdain writ clearly upon his features. "I need to see her," he repeated, clipping the words in his most aristocratic tones.

"You need to see her," Marshwood mocked in his decidedly less modulated accent. "You need to go to the devil, is what you need." He raised a hand, pointing a shaking finger at Stoker. "Remove yourself from my property and do not come back." He looked to his butler. "Throw him out bodily if he will not go of his own accord."

The butler glanced at Stoker, startled, and Mr. Marshwood grimaced. "Get the lads from the kitchen to help if you cannot manage it on your own."

With that he turned on his heel and returned to his sanctum, slamming the door behind him.

The butler stared at the closed door, then turned slowly to Stoker. He gulped audibly as he surveyed Stoker's inches.

"Perhaps we could come to an understanding," the butler began, pitching his voice low.

"What sort of understanding?" I asked, quick to seize the olive branch.

"Your companion wishes to see Mrs. de Morgan. It is impossible through the conventional methods, but Mrs. de Morgan does like a turn in the conservatory before her supper," he said with a meaningful gesture towards the back of the house. He moved a fraction nearer. "In the wall of the garden is a door. You can find your way from there. Go quietly and he need never know," he added with a lift of his brow at the closed door.

Stoker inclined his head graciously and turned to go. The butler sagged in evident relief.

"Wise man," I told him. "Blood can be devilishly hard to get out of white linen."

The butler closed the door firmly behind us, throwing the bolt instantly. Without a word, Stoker circled the property, leading me through a small mews to the back of the garden. I could just see the roofline of the conservatory, a small affair of wrought iron and glass. It was nothing to the glasshouse at Bishop's Folly, but the fogged and dripping panes meant it would be warm at least.

The street door to the garden was unlocked, and we slipped in, hurrying through the shadows until we reached the conservatory. This too was unlocked, the door giving way with a small shriek of the hinges as we entered. Whoever loved this place had a fondness for ferns, for they abounded, draping long green fronds every which way. They had been badly tended; some were browning, the edges crisp as new taffeta. Others were clearly root-bound, tendrils of white root clawing their way out of the bottoms of the pots. But the heating system worked, pumping steam through the enclosure, and a garden seat had been installed amidst the leafy greenery.

It might have been a pleasant place on a sunny day, but in the darkness of a February afternoon past sundown, it was oddly unwelcoming. Shadows shifted and stirred, raising little fingers of mist against the blackness outside, and the pipes gave low moans and the occasional shriek as they rattled about their business.

Sitting on a garden seat was a woman dressed entirely in white, her gown loose and shapeless, her body wrapped in a woolen shawl that shrouded her to the knees. Her head was bowed over a piece of needlework. Stoker stopped, his gaze fixed upon that head. It gleamed gold in the lamplight, the long tresses unbound except for a small plait around the crown of the head. Her white hands moved smoothly, setting tiny stitches in a rhythm that never varied as she hummed tunelessly.

The hair hid her face, but just then my shoe scraped against a pebble, and she looked up, breaking off her song midnote. If Stoker reacted, I did not notice it. I heard only my own sharp intake of breath as I looked for the first time upon the face of Caroline de Morgan.

I had seen her photograph, and I had thought myself prepared. I had taken note of the perfection of her bones, the graceful features which would be beautiful when age had stripped the flesh from them and wrinkled her skin. I had studied the lines of her face and figure, marking each place where Nature had favored her. The list was long. From the arch of her brows to the tips of her tapered fingers, from the curve of her swan neck to the sweet Cupid's bow of her lips, she had been created by a benevolent hand.

But what I had not realized, what no photograph could convey, was the pure perfection of her coloring. Her hair was the rich color of summer corn silk, her lashes a fraction darker. Her eyes—but what can one say about such eyes? It would need a poet to do them justice. They were some variety of light blue that would have given a sapphire envy, the irises impossibly wide with the tiniest of ebony pupils. Roses bloomed in her cheeks against a complexion so fine and white, it would have caused a snowdrop to turn away in shame.

Her hands stilled and she blinked slowly, peering into the leafy shadows. "Who is there?" she called.

Only the voice lacked perfection. It was high and light but oddly hoarse. Stoker stepped forwards and I moved in his wake on unwilling legs. I had forced my way into this meeting, and in that moment I would have sold my soul to a tinker to be anywhere else.

Stoker moved into the circle of lamplight, the warm glow settling over his features and illumining his form. Caroline de Morgan raised her face, expressionless as she gazed at her former husband.

She blinked twice in obvious puzzlement, then spoke. "Do I know you?"

Stoker opened his mouth, but not a syllable escaped him.

I moved to her, smiling a smile that cost me everything. "Good afternoon. You are Mrs. de Morgan, are you not?"

At the sound of her own name, her face puckered in confusion. She looked from me to the pile of needlework in her lap. She lifted her needle and set another stitch. "Mama says I must not tax my strength," she said slowly.

"Of course not," I told her. "May I see what you are working on?"

I moved past Stoker, for he stood as one turned to stone. I was careful not to move too close to her, for she seemed timid as a doe. Her needle trailed red silk through a large piece of white cloth, and she held it up for me to see. The cloth was uneven at the edges, a rough piece of linen that might once have been used for toweling. Patches here and there had been covered in random stitches, variations on a theme of chaos, no two sections alike. She had stitched at whim, moving from an untidy flame technique to the crooked crosses she made as I watched.

"It's very pretty," I told her. I glanced to Stoker, but still he stood, rooted to the spot, his mouth slack in shocked comprehension. I remembered then the hints we had been given about her state. Sir Hugo, Mornaday, even the Tivertons had indicated that she had succumbed to the strain of police questions regarding her husband's disappearance. Sir Hugo had blamed the Dover police for handling her roughly. Little wonder her nerve had broken under the strain.

She looked at me, that blue gaze blank as she searched my face. "Do I know you?" she repeated.

"No, Mrs. de Morgan. My name is Veronica Speedwell," I told her. I darted a glance to Stoker to urge him to come nearer, but he stood at the edge of the ferns, his hands curled into fists.

"Why have you come?" she asked me.

I hesitated, unwilling to deal as brutally with her as the police had done.

Stoker moved then, folding his arms over his chest. "Enough. You might have duped the police with your little performance, but I recognize your amateur theatricals."

She looked up at him, blinking slowly, a vacant look upon her face.

Then, with an audible sigh, she settled back in her chair, her expression entirely lucid. "What gave me away?"

"You forget I saw your Ophelia. You did the same little trick of wringing the hands," he replied with a coolness I suspected he did not feel.

The beautiful mouth did not smile, but the corners softened ever so slightly. "I did forget. Well, I mayn't have fooled you, but thankfully the men at Scotland Yard are not quite so suspicious."

"That's the stratagem, is it? Pretend to be witless so they will leave you in peace?"

Indignation flared in her gaze. "They have been monstrous to me. They think I conspired with John to steal that wretched little crown," she burst out.

"To be fair, that is only one of their theories," I corrected.

She regarded me with a distinct lack of warmth. "Revelstoke, who is your friend?"

"Miss Speedwell is my professional associate," he informed her.

She tipped her head to the side, studying me closely. "And something more, I suspect."

Stoker did not rise to the bait. "Is that all you have to say to me?"

Her lips thinned. "I suppose you want an apology."

"I think we are far beyond that," he replied. "You could carve out your own heart and offer it up on a platter and your ledger would still run red."

Her hands curled into fists. "Don't, Revelstoke. I am not proud of what I did. But neither am I as evil as you would like to believe. Malice was never my motivation."

"What a consolation that is," he said, the words sharply edged as any blade.

"You may mock me," she told him evenly. "God knows you have earned the right. But it is the truth. I intended to make you a good wife."

"Of all the lies you have ever told me, that, I think, is the most terrible," he replied. He moved again and she watched him, her expression wary.

She lifted her chin in defiance, but I saw from the quickening of the pulse at her throat that she was afraid.

He moved slowly, carefully, and she licked her lips as she watched him approach, seemingly unable to tear her gaze from him. Her fingers tightened on the needle in her hand, and I wondered how close he would have to get before she plunged it into his flesh.

He stopped just short of touching her. Without a word, he slipped to his knees before her, his face almost on a level with hers. He tipped his head back so that the light fell full upon him, exposing the scar that marked him from brow to collar.

"I thought you might like to admire another piece of your handiwork," he said, his voice low and terrible. He nodded towards the needle in her hand. "Did you want to sign it? Go on. There is nothing more you can do to hurt me now. You have already broken the man you knew, crucified every part of my humanity and left me with nothing except the ruins of what I once was. Why do you look away? Have you developed a conscience? What a burden it must be to you."

He might have gone on. He might have goaded her to plunge the needle into his flesh. He might have taunted her until she fled or broke down weeping. And I would have let him, happily, if it meant causing her pain. I had seen the disgust in her expression as she looked at the scar, the flicker of revulsion that revealed her feelings only too clearly. She regarded him and counted only the damage; I saw only the places where he had stitched himself back together. What repelled her was to me the greatest part of him. Every mark that his suffering had left upon him was a mute monument to his strength, the inhuman courage that had caused him to reject death and degradation and every evil with which he had consoled himself on the long journey back from his destruction. He had walked through hellfire and back again and she saw only the scorch marks whilst I saw the phoenix.

I hated her for that. Oh, let me be honest—I hated her for a thousand reasons! But in that moment, I hated her most of all for the fact that she had the power to hurt him still. He was on his knees before her, lowering himself to revile her, and it was that stripping bare of all his defenses that drove me to intercede. She would *not* hurt him again, I vowed.

"Did you kill your husband, Mrs. de Morgan?" I asked, my voice sharper and louder than I intended.

Instantly, their heads swiveled to me. Caroline de Morgan's mouth went slack and she gave a little cry of protest, bringing her hands up. Stoker's gaze was empty a moment. Then his eyes seemed to focus and he wrenched himself back into the present, seeing me where a moment before—but who can say what devils he conjured in his mind's eye? Was he thinking of her as she had been, an innocent bride whose altar-blessed lips he had kissed before she had left him for dead? I could not bear to think of it.

He forced himself to his feet as Caroline de Morgan addressed me, her voice cold with rage. "How dare you? That is the most monstrous suggestion."

"Is it?" I asked mildly. "Reports of the state of your marriage indicate that it was not entirely happy."

"It was—it *is*—perfectly happy," she insisted angrily. "John loves me and I love him. And if we quarrel sometimes, it is only because we are neither of us temperate. Ours is a marriage of great passion," she said, breaking off as she looked at Stoker. "I don't understand why you have come, tormenting me with questions."

"We have come because we are investigating your husband's whereabouts," I returned.

"Investigating! And who are you that you should do the business of the police?" she demanded.

"I do not feel inclined to explain our interest in the matter. But if you will not speak to the police, you ought to speak to us. Surely you wish to uncover the mystery to your husband's disappearance." I let my voice trail away suggestively.

"Surely I wish!" She mimicked my tone with sharp cruelty. "How cold you are. You can stand there and discuss the greatest tragedy of my life as dispassionately as if I had misplaced a latchkey! You are the most unnatural woman I have ever met."

The tightness in my chest eased a little. I had successfully directed her venom to me instead of Stoker, and I hoped a few moments' respite were enough to enable him to gather his dignity and his temper once more.

"You might imagine the insult to be original," I told her, baring my teeth in a smile. "You would be wrong. Now, the police seem to favor the theory that your husband stole the diadem and made away with it in order to leave his marriage and make a new start, perhaps in America. Do you have any proof that he did not?"

She gave me a look of purest loathing before her mouth curved into a mirthless smile. "Do I have proof? Yes, Miss Speedwell. I have proof that my husband loved me, proof that he would never abandon me." She put aside her needlework and rose slowly to her feet, letting the knitted shawl drop to the ground. Her figure was obviously slight, but she put her hands protectively to her thickened middle, pulling her gown taut over the ripe, rounded belly.

"There is your proof, Miss Speedwell," she said, her voice ringing in triumph. "He would never abandon his son."

We stood, the three of us, in a sort of frozen tableau. I did not look at Stoker to assess his reaction. I dared not. Before I could form a response, the door to the house was flung back and a lady entered. She had clearly just arrived, for she was still dressed for an afternoon outing, in rusty black from head to toe. The wing of a blackbird had been mounted upon her hat, and the effect when combined with her aggressive profile was one of arrested motion, a vulture preparing to take flight. I disliked her instantly, although I could not have said why apart from her appalling taste in millinery. Around her neck was some variety of weasel or stoat, dyed black to mimic mink, its bright glass bead eyes staring balefully at me as she advanced. She took in the scene with a glance, sweeping her gaze from me to Stoker and then to Caroline.

Without a word to either of us, she turned to Caroline. "You oughtn't upset yourself, my dear. Go and rest in your room until the dressing bell."

For an instant Caroline looked as if she would have liked to refuse. But she nodded. "Yes, Mama. I am quite finished here."

In spite of her thickening figure, her walk was still graceful. She did not look back. When the door had closed behind her, Mrs. Marshwood turned on us.

"Bowles described the man who had come to see her. It required little imagination to realize it must be you," she said, her tone cold as she addressed Stoker. Her mouth curled in distaste. "I am surprised to find you here, Revelstoke. I thought never to see you again."

He said nothing for a long moment, the seconds ticking past in the beat of my pulse. The woman had not acknowledged my presence, and a person of delicacy would have excused herself from what could only be a painful and private conversation. But delicacy has never been one of my failings. Stoker was my friend, and I would not give ground if there was a chance he had need of me.

He lowered his chin, and when he spoke it was in a voice of such quiet intensity, such controlled rage, that I knew he was very near to breaking something.

"You really mean to let her carry on with this ridiculous charade of being insensible? You cannot imagine the police will be put off by such a stratagem."

She shook her head, causing the blackbird's wing to tremble. "They have thus far. It is an untenable situation, and we are coping as best we can. Her husband is missing and the authorities have misused her cruelly. If they believed they could get more information from her, they would hound her night and day. At least now she is left in peace." The woman's gaze flicked to me for the first time. "I think this interview is best conducted in private."

"Anything you would say to me, I will only repeat to my associate. Miss Speedwell stays."

She curled her lip again as she took the measure of me from top to toe. "Very well, Miss Speedwell stays." She glanced about the moldering greenhouse. "I will not offer you refreshment," she told Stoker. "Nor will I ask you to make yourself comfortable. I am an old woman and I have no stomach for this business. State your purpose and be gone."

He tipped his head, his gaze glacial. "How remiss of me. Permit me to make formal introductions. Mrs. Marshwood, this is Miss Speedwell, a fellow employee of Lord Rosemorran's and my colleague. Veronica, this is Mrs. Marshwood. As you have no doubt deduced, my mother-in-law."

"Former," she corrected swiftly. "For which I thank God upon my knees."

"No more than I," he replied.

She bridled at that. "I told you to state your purpose."

Stoker said nothing, and I spoke. "Mrs. Marshwood, we are investigating the disappearance of Mr. de Morgan."

"Investigating!" she said, her lips thinning into an unpleasant smile. "Revelstoke Templeton-Vane has no place here," she said, the wing on her hat trembling in outrage.

"We might be allies," I began.

"Allies!" She gave a sharp shake of the head, nearly dislodging her fur. "That is a pretty word to use to a lady. We have no need of the help of outsiders, and even if we did, to accept aid from him, of all people—" She carried on in this vein for some time while I let my thoughts wander to the conservatory and how it might be improved.

Mrs. Marshwood continued her litany of abuse until I turned to Stoker.

"I thought she would run out of air by now, but she has rather impressive lung capacity for such an elderly person. Do you think she will come to the point anytime soon? Not that this isn't entertaining, but I really ought to get back to work. I have a delectable little *Bassaris gonerilla* that needs fixing. It is so difficult to get specimens from New Zealand, I should hate to lose this one," I remarked.

Mrs. Marshwood cut off her diatribe to fix me with a look of loathing. "You are an impertinent person, and no better than you should be, I would wager. Working with a man of such notorious reputation," she said with a shudder. "It is not respectable."

I waved a hand. "Respectability is as overrated as virginity, madam, and I have precious little use for either. Now, Stoker has done a remarkable job of holding the reins of his temper throughout your abuses, but I cannot promise he will sustain the effort. In fact, I should encourage him not to." I turned to Stoker. "Would you like me to give her a good shake? Nothing to leave a mark, just a bit of firm handling to bring her to the point."

Mrs. Marshwood's hat trembled in rage. "Odious creature!" She launched into another venomous monologue, criticizing my morals and appearance before returning to the subject of her former son-in-law's shortcomings. Stoker took it, stoically accepting every bit of abuse she heaped upon him, arms folded over his chest as he regarded his mother-in-law.

Bored with her acidulous remarks, I cut in swiftly, interrupting her in full flow.

"What do you think happened to John de Morgan?" I asked.

She blinked furiously. "What happened to him? He ran away, of course. He stole that diadem and abandoned my daughter."

"Are you certain of that?" I asked. "Mrs. de Morgan doesn't seem to think so."

Mrs. Marshwood curled her lip in distaste. "I am not answerable to you, Miss Speedwell."

I ignored the provocation. Frankly, it was not one of her better ones. "Mrs. Marshwood, do try to use a little intelligence, taxing as it may be," I instructed. "There is no proof that John de Morgan stole the diadem and abandoned his wife. No one knows what has become of him. Surely the truth, no matter how painful, would be better than this current state of affairs."

"My daughter's welfare is none of your concern," she returned.

"On that we are in complete agreement," I told her. "But the facts behind de Morgan's disappearance must be established. Your daughter cannot even be declared a legal widow without a body," I pointed out.

The old woman reared back, her thin lips suddenly bloodless. "Caroline cannot be left in a state of limbo. It is intolerable."

"Then help us discover what happened to her husband," I urged.

She said nothing, but her mouth worked furiously as she gnawed her own lips. After a moment I sighed. "Never mind, Stoker. Mrs. Marshwood will not be persuaded to see reason. Let us take our leave."

I extracted a card of my own and left it lying upon the garden seat. "You may reach us at that address should you change your mind."

She curled a lip. "I ought to lodge a complaint with the police that you have forced your way into our home uninvited. It would serve you right."

Stoker, who had moved to leave, turned back. The leafy shadows of the ferns played over his face like jagged fingers, giving him a menacing look, and when he spoke it was in a quietly terrifying voice I had never heard before.

"Before you do, think of everything you have said about me, every evil act you have attributed to me, every sin you have laid at my door.

Recite to yourself my catalog of cruelties and ask yourself if you really want to provoke me."

Mrs. Marshwood shrank back, her lips trembling. She lifted a bony finger that shook with rage and fear. "Go!"

We did not look back.

CHAPTER 10

We returned to the Belvedere in silence, and I had not even divested myself of my coat before Stoker had shed his, drawn the cork on a bottle, and splashed a hefty measure into a tooth mug.

"Stoker—" I began.

He held up the mug, sloshing the contents. "Drink with me or get the hell out," he ordered.

I held out my hand and he gave me the tooth mug, then drank straight from the bottle. He stalked up the small staircase to the snuggery on the upper floor, kicking a fossilized coprolite out of his way as he went. He flung himself into a chair while I stirred the fire and hung my hat.

Between swallows of extremely expensive single malt, he wrenched off his collar and necktie, waistcoat and cuffs, flinging them aside. I took the chair opposite, pacing my sips.

"Would it do any good to apologize?" I asked finally.

He tipped his head. "I am not one of your bloody butterflies, Veronica."

"I never thought—"

"Yes, you did." He tipped the bottle up, taking another deep draft of whisky. "You like to think you are smarter than everyone else, and the bloody hell of it is that you usually are. You like to put people into little boxes just like those bollocking moths, a pin through the thorax and pop them up on a bit of card to look at when you're bored."

I stared into the fire, saying nothing.

"You think you know me. You have me all sorted—*Homo sapiens exsolutus*. It has quite the ring, doesn't it?"

"Your Latin is filthy," I replied, keeping my tone light. "I should have said *vulneraverunt*."

He gave a mirthless laugh. "Even now you cannot be wrong. But you are. You are so unbelievably, unbearably wrong."

I nearly turned my head then. I nearly turned and told him that I did understand him; I knew he loved Caroline. He loved her with a passion that excused everything she had done to him and was not blunted. Perhaps he loved her the more for her cruelties, I reflected. It would be a sad irony if he did. How appallingly tragic to carry a torch for a woman who had abandoned him and exposed the secrets of his unkindnesses to public scrutiny. But how often do we learn to kiss the boot that kicks us?

He went on in a bitter voice. "I am glad you saw her. She is beautiful, is she not? Like an angel come to earth. That's what I thought the first time I saw her. It is the most appalling cliché, but it suits her. She is not of this earth. That is what a poet would tell you. I was shy with her. Can you imagine that? The first time I put out my hand to touch her, it shook. The hand that had killed men in battle and saved men in surgery, and it shook to touch her. What sinner would dare to touch the hem of the saint's gown?"

I let him speak, but that silence cost me dearly. Each word out of his mouth was a laceration, flaying me to the bone as he talked on, listing her perfections. And the worst of it was that he spoke the truth; she was the loveliest creature I had ever seen. Menelaus might launch a thousand ships to reclaim Helen, but the gods themselves would have quarreled over Caroline de Morgan.

"I never felt worthy of her," he said after another deep pull at the bottle. "Not once. She was so unspoilt and shy. We hardly spoke two words alone before I got down on my knees in a moonlit garden and begged her to marry me. She was too timid even to answer me for herself. She ran to her mother, who gave me the happy news. The day I married her should have been the happiest of my life, but it wasn't. Do you know why? Do you?" he demanded, reaching out a booted foot to nudge my chair. I held quite still. "Because I never really believed she was mine. I did not deserve anything so beautiful for my very own. I knew what I was—my father, my mother. My dirty little soul was just a patchwork of compromises and lies and desperate acts. Tainted from birth by other people's deceptions," he said bitterly. "But I asked and she came. She married me and I carried her off to Brazil. I thought, fool that I was, that it would be a grand romantic adventure."

He broke off, his gaze unfocused. He was not with me then, sitting in the snuggery of the Belvedere, with a cold British February outside and a warm fire within. He was tramping the jungles of Amazonia with his best friend and his beautiful bride.

I cleared my throat. "Jungles and mud and crocodiles," I said lightly. "I don't know that I much blame her for going back to England without you. I suppose it was gentlemanly of him to escort her home if she were unhappy at traveling in so wild a place."

He tipped his head, his smile cold. "My dear Veronica, you don't understand. She did not leave with him. She left me *for* him." He pierced me with his gaze. "Don't you see? I was never the one she wanted. I took her for my wife, and I thought it meant that God understood, that God forgave what I was. Just a filthy little changeling bastard. That's what my brothers called me, and they were right. I was nothing more than the product of some frantic tumbling by people who ought never to have given in to their lusts. You of all people understand that, don't you, Veronica?"

I thrust myself out of the chair. I went to the stove and took up the empty coal hod and placed it carefully next to his chair.

"You've drunk an appalling amount. If you mean to be sick, do it there. I'll not clean up after you."

I did not look behind me as I left, but his laughter followed me down the stairs and into the darkness.

The next morning I had no stomach for work. I began a dozen projects and cast them aside, furious at myself, at Caroline de Morgan, and thoroughly out of charity with Stoker. I could bear anything except his self-loathing. I was ripe for a diversion, and when the note arrived from Lady Tiverton inviting me to meet her at the Curiosity Club, I was on my feet and reaching for my hat before I finished reading.

The Curiosity Club was a unique establishment. Formally known as the Hippolyta Club, its purpose was the edification and support of women of adventure and accomplishment. Membership was strictly private and by invitation only, and I had been permitted to darken its hallowed halls only once before as a guest of Lord Rosemorran's sister. I longed to return, and even if I had not been eager for Lady Tiverton's company, the lure of the club itself would have been sufficient. The day had dawned bright with a valiant winter sun doing its best to banish the coal fog and grey clouds that scudded on the horizon. The banked snow at the edge of the pavement was grimy with soot and other unspeakable things, but now and again I caught a glimpse through a garden gate of a pristine stretch of white, glittering in the sunlight.

Almost against my will, I felt my spirits rise as I strode up the front steps of the club and rang the bell. A discreet scarlet plaque identified the club, but apart from that, it was a perfectly ordinary town house in a perfectly ordinary square. The door was opened by the portress in scarlet plush. I recognized her from my previous visit, but before I could speak, she smiled.

"Miss Speedwell. Welcome back to the Hippolyta Club."

"Thank you, Hetty." She stood back to admit me, signaling to a page to take my coat as she closed the door upon the winter chill. Inside all was crimson warmth, from the thick carpets to the blazing fireplaces in the public rooms. The walls, draped in dark red silk, were hung with assorted photographs from members' expeditions as well as sailing charts, maps, and a rare collection of memorabilia from around the world.

Over it all presided Hetty, the serene face of the Hippolyta Club. She wore a shawl wrapped elegantly around her head—a fine bit of Chinese silk in a shade of deep blue that flattered the dark color of her skin. Her eyes were dark as well, and sharply attentive to every detail of the club. She indicated the leather ledger with a smile.

"Lady Tiverton has already signed you in, Miss Speedwell. She is awaiting you in the Map Room."

I thanked her and was just turning to follow the page when Hetty called, "A moment, Miss Speedwell." She reached below the desk where she presided, bringing out an envelope of thick creamy paper sealed with a bit of scarlet wax and the emblem of the club, the letters *H* and *C* entwined in an Amazon's bow with the legend ALIS VOLAT PROPRIIS circling the perimeter. She proffered it with a grave smile.

"A message for me?" I took it, noting my name inscribed in an elegant hand in a swirl of crimson ink.

"An invitation. You have been proposed for membership to the club and this is the official notice."

My heart thudded against my ribs. "Proposed for membership? But Lady Cordelia never said—" I broke off, thinking how curious it was that the earl's sister should think of such a thing while she was stuck in Cornwall supervising the education of her brother's children.

But Hetty shook her head, setting the fringe of her turban to swinging. "It was not Lady Cordelia, although she provided the necessary second to the nomination for membership. You were put forward by Her Royal Highness, the Princess Louise."

I smiled in spite of myself. My last interview with my aunt had not been pleasant. Stoker and I had undertaken our last investigation at her behest, and she had been a less-than-appreciative beneficiary of our efforts. She had also made it clear that our association was not to continue. I would not be presented to my father, nor would she receive me publicly. But this was no little thing, I realized as I slipped the envelope into my pocket. This club was her sanctuary, and to admit me here was almost a more intimate act than introducing me to the family.

"Thank you, Hetty."

"The favor of a reply is requested within a week's time," she told me. She gestured for the page to guide me to Lady Tiverton. The Map Room was located on the ground floor, just behind the stairs, a high-ceilinged chamber that overlooked the back garden, its aspect bleak just now with the leaves stripped bare and the limbs of the trees blackened with cold. But the fire was built high and the lamps glowed warmly, casting an amber light over the walls hung with enormous maps of the known world, the British bits picked out in pink, a chain of pearly possessions girdling the waist of the world.

Pairs of deep leather chairs were scattered about the room, but Lady Tiverton had chosen a sofa, a handsome Chesterfield drawn close to the fire. A low tea table stood in front of it, and on that rested a tray of light refreshments and a bowl of chrysanthemums, the petals a rare shade of deep blue-red.

"It is pleasant, is it not?" she asked as she rose to greet me. "All the color seems to banish the grey of winter, and I feel almost warm."

She gestured for me to join her on the sofa, and I settled myself against a flame-stitched cushion. "Do you suffer from the English climate?" I asked.

She nodded. "Dreadfully. I was brought up in Egypt, you know, and every winter was spent with my mother's family. My father's people were Scots, and a winter there was not to be borne," she added with a smile. She moved to offer me some refreshment, and I took the chance to study her. She was dressed once more in grey, but this gown was fashioned of heavy velvet, only a year or two out-of-date, and she had pinned the scarab at her throat.

"Your brooch is very unusual," I told her. "And quite lovely."

One graceful hand went to the jewel. "A heart scarab," she told me. "They are buried with mummies. It is said that in the afterlife, the goddess Maat weighs the heart of the dead. If the heart is as light as her feather, the dead will be given entry into the fields of Hetep and Iaru."

"Hetep and Iaru?"

"Think of the Elysian Fields of Greek myth," she instructed.

"What happens if the heart of the dead is heavier than the feather?" I asked.

She gave a little shudder. "Then the heart of the dead will be snatched and devoured by Ammit. He is a monstrous creature with the head of a crocodile and the body of a lion."

"Monstrous indeed!"

The ghost of a smile touched her lips. "Even more when you know that Ammit's back legs are those of a hippopotamus. He is called the Gobbler because he does nothing but sit and wait to gorge himself on the hearts of the unworthy."

"What, then, is the purpose of the heart scarab?" I asked.

"It is inscribed with prayers, pleas to the heart to weigh lightly so that the dead may walk freely into the afterlife." She touched the scarab at her throat with a light fingertip. "I admired this particular piece, so my husband had it fashioned into a brooch as an engagement present."

"A generous and thoughtful gift," I said.

"A trifle ghoulish, you mean," she said with a knowing look. "But it suits me far better than more conventional jewels. It is a piece of my history, after all."

We fell silent a moment, and her ladyship kept her finger resting upon the scarab brooch, stroking the dark green stone absently.

Then she roused herself, setting a smile to her lips. "I believe congratulations are in order," she said brightly. "I understand you have been put up for membership."

"Yes. I was rather surprised, but pleasantly so."

"And with such a sponsor," she added. "Her Royal Highness has never before nominated a member. She must hold you very dear."

I made a noncommittal noise, and Lady Tiverton went on. "I hope you do not mind my inviting you without Mr. Templeton-Vane, only I find sometimes it is easier for ladies to speak without the interference of gentlemen."

Her expression was very nearly apologetic, and I gave her an encouraging look. "Do you have something to tell me? About the investigation?" I asked.

She spread her hands. "I rather hoped you would have something to tell me. The newspapers have been full of such dreadful stories—" She broke off and looked at me expectantly.

"You mean about Mr. Templeton-Vane," I supplied.

A faint touch of color rose in her cheeks. "I do not mean to suggest that he is guilty of any of the atrocities the newspapers report. In fact, having met him, I cannot imagine him guilty of any of them."

"He is not," I returned sharply.

She gentled her voice. "And it does you credit as his friend and associate that you believe him. Having spent time in proximity with the de Morgans, I can only say that I found them to be a most unusual couple."

"How so?"

She hesitated, searching for the proper words, it seemed. "If I were a painter choosing a couple to stand together in a painting, I would have selected them out of a thousand. They were striking, her with a sort of ethereal blondness and him darkly handsome. You could not help but look at them when they appeared together, they were so attractive. And they were clearly devoted in spite of their quarrels."

"Some couples seem to thrive upon conflict," I remarked mildly. Heaven knew Stoker and I were none too gentle with one another, although we were certainly not a pair in the conventional sense of the word.

Her ladyship nodded slowly. "I suppose what you say is right. My own parents were frequently quarrelsome, but a more devoted couple you cannot imagine. I could never be content with such an arrangement. I have a horror of scenes and dramatics."

I chose my words carefully. "Sir Leicester is a very energetic man," I ventured.

She smiled. "But never out of temper with me. I had the advantage of seeing him for many years in the intimacy of his first marriage. He was always kind and solicitous towards the first Lady Tiverton. I never intended to marry," she confided. "Such a thing seemed beyond possibility. When he proposed, it was the most absurd good fortune. I promised myself I would always be as serene and peaceful a helpmeet as I could. I owed him that much."

I had not expected her to be so forthcoming about her marriage, but it suddenly occurred to me in a flash of intuition that Lady Tiverton was lonely. Lady Wellie had suggested that Sir Leicester's friends had not all been accommodating of his new connection. I wondered how many friendships had been sacrificed because people could not reconcile his marriage to this tranquil and kindly woman.

I decided to trespass a little on that kindness and venture an indiscreet question or two. "You were a sort of companion to the first Lady Tiverton, were you not?"

"Indeed," she said promptly. When she spoke of her husband's first wife, she did so with real warmth. "Or, rather, a secretary companion. I attended to her correspondence, helped her to write her books."

"I understand she was ill for much of her life."

"Consumption, a dreadful way to go," she said, her eyes suddenly bleak. "It is a terrible thing to witness in a person you love, and I will own that I loved the first Lady Tiverton. She was like an elder sister to me. We shared confidences and secrets. Oh, nothing important. Just silly things. But they meant everything to me. She told me once, when she had grown very weak, that she feared most of all leaving Sir Leicester behind."

"Not her child?" I asked sharply.

She shrugged. "Lady Tiverton always said Figgy took after her, resourceful and clever. And a child whose mother has been ill for the greater part of her life is not surprised by death. Sir Leicester, however, always seemed to think the worst would never happen, that somehow she would go on forever, just as she always had. It came as the most wretched shock to him when she died."

"But you were able to console each other," I suggested, careful to keep my voice neutral.

She folded her hands together. "Impossible. He was inconsolable. I sometimes think if it weren't for the work, he might have done something terrible to himself."

The work! I felt impatient with the Tivertons, people who had made a child and seemed to give her no more thought than a stray dog.

"His daughter was not consolation enough?" I could not hide the touch of asperity in my voice.

She shrugged again. "Sir Leicester adores Figgy, but he does not always know how to handle her. Particularly now. She is at such a difficult age, half a child, half a woman. He tries to talk to her, but most often they end up in a quarrel. I have hopes she will grow out of it. I make allowances because she has lost her mother."

"And does not accept you in the role of replacement?"

She looked aghast. "I would never presume! You must understand, Figgy is like the Wards, her mother's people. They are very self-contained, very stoic. It was only because of the effects of her illness and her medications that the first Lady Tiverton ever spoke as openly to me as she did. She very much just got on with things as she had been taught, as she taught Figgy."

"As you now do," I observed.

Her lips parted, then pressed together, as if she were about to say something, then thought better of it.

"It can be a thankless and tiresome task, always being the person who holds the world together," I said gently.

Her smile was wan. "If I do not, who will? I promised the first Lady Tiverton that I would always take care of Sir Leicester. It was a deathbed vow and one I will keep until the end of my days. She knew how important the work was to him. She knew how much he needed someone to support him in his work, to look after him. That is why it is so essential that the exhibition goes forward."

"Is there a danger of its being canceled?"

Her hands were still folded neatly in her lap, but the knuckles were white, the skin stretched taut over the bone. "I fear that if the newspapers make too much of this, if there are too many more stories of the curse, that somehow it will be ruined."

"Surely the opposite will happen," I argued. "The more people talk about the curse, the more they will want to see the collection. Whoever this J. J. Butterworth is, Sir Leicester owes him a debt of gratitude. He is single-handedly providing the expedition with more press than you could ever possibly purchase."

"I suppose," she said. But her expression was doubtful. "I cannot rid myself of the fear that something else is at work here, something darker."

"You cannot mean that you believe the curse might be real?"

Her lips thinned. "I am half Egyptian, Miss Speedwell, but I assure you my education was not neglected. I know there is no such thing as a curse. Whatever is done in this world is done by the hands of men."

There was something chilling in her words, and I swallowed hard. "You fear an enemy?"

"I do not know what I fear," she burst out, the tranquil façade deserting her briefly. She drew in a deep breath, mastering herself. "Forgive me. My nerves are worked to pieces."

"And still you are one of the most composed women of my acquaintance," I told her truthfully.

"Composure that is hard-won and the result of long practice," she assured me. "I learnt long ago that when one is only half British, the other half will be blamed for every evil of temper or habit. I schooled myself in deportment so that the part of me that is Egyptian may never be held up as a pattern for degradation or vice. I became more British than any Englishwoman I knew, and still every syllable I speak, every gesture, every thought is examined by Society. I could take tea with the queen at Windsor every day and twice on Sundays and I would still not be English enough for some." She spoke without bitterness, but there was a fatigue to her resignation, and I began to understand the weight she carried with her at all times.

"Sir Leicester, I hope, appreciates the difficulties you have faced."

"Sir Leicester is blind to them," she said simply. "For all his faults, he is without bigotry, and I honor him for that. He would never register a slight because he would never inflict one."

"A noble thing, but it means you must contend alone with whatever insults you encounter."

"A small price to pay, Miss Speedwell. After all, I am content in the love of the man I esteem most in the world. Can every woman say the same?"

"I wonder if Caroline de Morgan can," I mused.

"I cannot imagine her fear, her confusion just now," she said, the knuckles turning whiter still. "Not to know what has become of her husband—I only hope that she may be provided with an answer. However painful the truth, it must be preferred to the horror of not knowing."

"And all the more necessary now," I said carefully. "Caroline de Morgan is going to have a child."

Lady Tiverton paled. "How do you know that?"

"Mr. Templeton-Vane and I called upon her yesterday. She is in seclusion with her parents, but we managed to gain entry. If I had to guess, I would say she is in her fifth month."

Lady Tiverton covered her face with her hands and said nothing. No sniffle, no sob broke the silence. Only the rhythmic ticking of the mantel clock, measuring off seconds and heartbeats.

"You did not know?" I asked.

At last Lady Tiverton lifted her head. "No. She wore her gowns rather loose, but many do in Egypt to throw off the heat. I am sorry to hear she is expecting," she said. "I cannot think that bringing a child into her present situation is at all desirable."

"I think she is happy," I said. "If her husband is dead, she has some remnant of him in his child. Of course, if he has deserted her—"

"He has not," she said flatly. "I did not know him well, but intimacy grows quickly in the field. I saw enough of him to know a little of his character, and John de Morgan loved his wife, and he loved children. His dearest wish was to become a father."

"How do you know this?" I asked.

Her voice was dull and she spoke as if she were reciting facts by rote. "At dinner one night. It was Patrick Fairbrother's birthday and I had asked the cook to make him a cake. He blew out the candles and made a wish and we fell to talking about wishes. Mr. de Morgan was seated next to me, and he confided that he hoped above all things that he and his wife would be so blessed."

"Did anyone else hear the conversation?"

"No." She fell silent again, but I could tell her thoughts were working furiously. After a long moment, she seemed to come to some sort of decision, for she rose abruptly.

"Perhaps you would like to accompany me to Karnak Hall. I must see how preparations for the exhibition are progressing, and you might enjoy a little foretaste of our efforts."

"Thank you, my lady. I would indeed."

We secured a hansom and very shortly were being whisked through the streets towards the Hall. The route took us down a major shopping street where traffic was thicker, and our pace was slowed. I did not mind, for the delay afforded us a chance to look at the gaily decorated windows of the shops. The display of a fashionable milliner caught my eye.

"Look there, my lady! A decidedly Egyptological homage," I said, nodding towards the window. A trio of hats was featured, each fashioned in a distinctive motif. One had lotus flowers and a ribbon trim printed with hieroglyphics, another was vaguely shaped like a pharaoh's headdress with lappets to frame the face, and the third was a red wicker affair surmounted by a stuffed vulture.

"That may well be the most hideous thing I have ever seen," Lady Tiverton said acidly. "And I have seen a jackal eating a cat."

I grinned. "It is dreadful. Do you suppose anyone will actually buy it?"

She shook her head. "I would hope not. Good taste ought to count for something, but I am told our expedition has generated quite a fashion for such atrocities. Heaven help us, Miss Speedwell, but we are *modish*."

In a short while we drew up in front of Karnak Hall, a modest exhibition facility of some antiquity in a street just off Leicester Square. The Hall had been built in the style of its namesake temple, the edifice set with a series of recesses, each featuring a great statue of Ramses in a different pose. The rest of the façade was painted terra-cotta to resemble the walls of the temple and decorated with fanciful Egyptological friezes. We passed between the legs of one of the Ramses to enter, and I resisted the urge to look up.

The front doors of the Hall led into a wide foyer, a sort of anteroom to the main exhibition space. Workmen were clattering about with lumber and hammers, making an unholy din, but even above the noise I could hear the outraged voice of Sir Leicester Tiverton.

"I'll thank you not to trouble me until you have something of interest to report!" he thundered. He was standing toe-to-toe with Inspector Archibond, who looked distinctly unhappy. Patrick Fairbrother stood a little apart, clearly torn about intervening in his employer's verbal brawl with a member of the Metropolitan Police.

"Certainly, Sir Leicester," Archibond said in clipped tones. "I thought only to keep you informed of the results of our investigation," he began.

"Results! What bloody results? You don't know anything. You have got no information out of Caroline de Morgan because she'll not see you. You haven't found de Morgan, and you haven't found my diadem! Until you do, you can go to—" The rest of what he said caused Lady Tiverton to intervene just as Inspector Archibond was opening his mouth, clearly bent upon expressing himself with vigor.

"My dear," Lady Tiverton said, laying her hand gently upon her husband's sleeve.

He turned to look at her, having the decency to look heartily abashed. "Oh, I did not realize you were about. You either, Miss Speedwell," he added, catching sight of me. "Apologies, ladies."

"I must add my own as well for being the cause of Sir Leicester's ill temper," Inspector Archibond said thinly.

"Not at all," I said, baring my teeth in a smile.

He turned to go but suddenly swiveled back again, eyes narrowing. "Miss Speedwell? I believe you and I have a mutual acquaintance. Did I not see you in the company of Inspector Mornaday?"

I was just trying to decide whether or not to lie to him when Sir Leicester broke in, crowing a little. "You ought to remember her name, Archibond. She will be a match for you, and no doubt about it. Miss Speedwell is investigating the disappearance of de Morgan with my diadem and I'll lay you a guinea she beats you to the mark."

"Is she, indeed," Archibond said, and it was not a question. He gave me a stern look. "I am certain I do not need to tell Miss Speedwell that this is, in fact, a police matter. Any interference on her part will be viewed as obstructive."

"Not if she finds my diadem," Sir Leicester retorted. "Good day to you, Inspector."

With that, Sir Leicester gave him his congé and Archibond departed, looking like thunder.

"Of all the impertinence!" the baronet complained, turning to his wife. "The largest vitrine arrived with a cracked glass, the nurserymen seem to think that date palms are the same as coconut palms and have delivered the latter, and there is a fault in the gaslights which simply cannot be tolerated. I am being driven to distraction, and have had no help," he finished peevishly. I thought that rather hard upon poor Mr. Fairbrother, but he merely grinned at me, ignoring Sir Leicester's ruffled temper.

Lady Tiverton gave me an imploring look. "Miss Speedwell, I wonder if you would mind touring the Hall with Mr. Fairbrother. There are a few matters I must attend to just now, and I fear they are rather pressing."

"Certainly," I told her, and she hurried off with Sir Leicester while Patrick Fairbrother smiled wryly at me.

"You chose rather a dramatic moment to make an entrance, Miss Speedwell," he said.

"Didn't I, though?"

He bent near, pitching his voice low enough that the Tivertons could not hear. "I am sorry about Sir Leicester landing you in it, though. I cannot think Inspector Archibond will take it at all well that you are involved in this investigation."

I shrugged. "He did not seem pleased, but I have a great deal of experience at infuriating gentlemen. Now, introduce me to your collection, Mr. Fairbrother, and I promise to make suitably admiring noises."

He led me into the great Hall itself, a spacious area that had been furnished with an array of vitrines and pedestals for the display of the collection. Gaslights had been fitted, as well as the newest in ventilators, shiny brass grilles that ensured a bit of fresh air even if they did spoil the impression of an Egyptian temple. A long gallery ran the length of one wall, while opposite it workmen were in the process of building a dais.

"The sarcophagus of the princess will rest there. It will be quite dramatic when they finish, and the whole of the place will be hung with banners and decorated with potted palms, very atmospheric and suggestive of ancient Egypt," he told me.

He guided me to the few vitrines that were finished, the glass polished to a sheen and the shelves lined with small goods from the find.

"We have put out only the most minor artifacts at present," he told me. "Wooden boxes, pottery bowls, that sort of thing. But there is quite a bit of jewelry, pretty beaded things, and one or two rather lovely statues."

"It will be most impressive when it is finished," I assured him.

"Nothing will be as impressive as the sarcophagus," he said. "Would you like to see it?"

"It's here? Now?" I looked around but saw nothing that resembled a coffin.

He smiled. "The princess will not be coming into the exhibition proper until just before we open to the public. For now she is locked safely away, but I have the key," he said, brandishing it.

Beneath the gallery there was a long wall hung with draperies, and behind one of these lay a corridor, neatly screened from the main part of the Hall. "These are storerooms along here, and that leads to the alley behind," he told me, nodding to a door at the end of the corridor. "We cannot be too careful with security, so we've kept the place locked tighter than the Tower of London."

He fitted the key to the lock and threw the door open with a flourish. Behind lay a darkened chamber, and he moved into it, turning up the gaslight. "There! Behold our Princess Ankheset," he instructed.

The sarcophagus was smaller than I had expected. It was crafted of gilded and painted wood, thickly decorated with hieroglyphs. At the head was the portrait of a woman's face, her gaze distant, as if she saw and heard only those things which were invisible and inaudible to mere mortals. One end of the sarcophagus was badly scorched, the ancient wood blackened by fire that had destroyed part of the cartouche, the gilded oval bearing the names and titles of the princess.

"The bitumen," he said regretfully. "Dreadfully pitchy stuff and flammable to boot. The ancient Egyptians used it sometimes to mummify animals, and there must have been an accident when our princess was being moved by the priests because her sarcophagus was badly stained with it. Not surprising when you think of how improvised the whole thing was—hauling her from a proper tomb in the middle of the night to avoid raising the interest of the thieves. It must have been a real hole-and-corner affair, very hush-hush and everyone sworn to secrecy and working by the barest torchlight. It's a wonder anything at all survived. A stray spark from a torch fell when we were shifting her out of the cave and nearly sent the whole thing up. We only just managed to save her, thank God." It was not heresy; he spoke with fervent gratitude. "Here, you can just make out the more important bits of the cartouche, her name and honorifics." He read them out to me, not quite touching the ancient wood with his finger. "And here is Anubis, guardian of the dead, protector of those who have moved to the afterlife," he added, pointing to a familiar jackal-headed figure at the bottom of the sarcophagus.

"I can see why he would make for an alarming apparition," I told him.

His face clouded a little. "It has indeed cast a shadow over our achievements."

"I am sorry for it. Our fields are very different, but I can well imagine how such cruel tricks can blunt the pleasure of your accomplishments."

"Thank you, Miss Speedwell. I am grateful for your kindness."

"And Sir Leicester's, no doubt," I mused. "It is surely a coup for so young a man to be afforded such responsibility in an expedition of this importance."

He nodded gravely. "I have indeed been the beneficiary of Sir Leicester's generosity. By all rights, I ought to have toiled away for another few years under the tutelage of someone much more experienced." He hesitated, his expression slightly abashed. "I must say, I was rather surprised when Sir Leicester handed over so much authority to me this year, but with all the difficulties with the workers and the loss of Jonas Fowler, I think he found it a bit overwhelming at times."

"He must have great faith in your abilities," I said lightly.

He grinned, a singularly charming expression. "I don't know about that," he told me, his manner self-deprecating in the most attractive fashion. "I still have much to learn about hieroglyphics and Egyptology in general."

"Did you go to school for this sort of thing?" I inquired.

"No, I did not. My formal education was a makeshift affair. My family were poor, Miss Speedwell. Genteelly so, but my mother married badly and my father abandoned his family. My sister and I were left to shift for ourselves."

"I am sorry," I began.

He held up a hand. "Don't be. As much as I hated it at the time, the vagaries of my childhood forced me to be resourceful and to appreciate what I have."

"Your mother and sister must be very proud of your success."

"My mother did not live to see it," he told me with a wistful look. "And

I do not see my sister nearly as often as I would like. But I owe her everything. She worked tirelessly to find sponsors to pay for my education, to clothe and feed me and give me the proper introductions so that I could make something of myself. Unfortunately, that sort of 'catch as catch can' education leaves much to be desired. I am constantly finding things I wish I had learnt properly in school. But Sir Leicester is patient with me. He is determined to see in me a sort of successor he can groom."

"An heir apparent," I suggested.

"Heir presumptive," he corrected with a rueful smile. "There is still Figgy."

"A somewhat thorny child."

"Who has scratched me badly enough to draw blood once or twice," he admitted. "Metaphorically speaking. She doesn't hate me quite enough to resort to physical violence. Ah, I should not jest! She does not hate me, not really. There are times when we are almost friendly. But she is wildly immature and her father's affection for me is a sore point."

"I can well imagine. But perhaps in time she will come to appreciate your finer qualities."

He blushed an enchanting rose pink to the tips of his ears. He was standing near to me—a necessity when pointing out the small figures on the sarcophagus—and he seemed suddenly to recollect it. He straightened. "Forgive me. I ought to have considered the possible impropriety of inviting you here. Most ladies would have come over with an attack of the vapors, but I suspected that you—"

He broke off suddenly, and I hastened to reassure him. "You judged, quite rightly, that I am every bit as much a scientist as a woman. I am intrigued by your work, Mr. Fairbrother. And heaven protect me from missishness!"

"You are very understanding. But still, we ought to join the others before Lady Tiverton suspects I have eloped with you to Gretna Green," he said lightly.

"Do people still do that? What a delightfully old-fashioned notion of sin you have, Mr. Fairbrother."

He locked the door carefully behind us and we rejoined the Tivertons; her ladyship appeared to have everything well in hand, including her husband. Sir Leicester's ruffled feathers had been smoothed, and he was deeply immersed in directing the workmen as to the proper installation of the dais.

Lady Tiverton broke away and hurried over to me. "I hope Patrick has been an instructive host," she said with a smile.

"Very much so. He introduced me to the Princess Ankheset. I must confess it is the first Eighteenth Dynasty sarcophagus I have seen, and I found it most impressive."

"There are better examples," Fairbrother said with a wry twist of his lips. "But we are fond of her."

Lady Tiverton gave him an appraising look. "Yes, well. I am certain that our princess will cause quite a stir. Patrick, Sir Leicester requires your assistance. There is some confusion about the decoration of the dais."

Mr. Fairbrother inclined his head to me. "Duty beckons, Miss Speedwell. Good day to you, and I hope we will see you at the exhibition."

I acknowledged that he would, and he hurried to his employer as Lady Tiverton watched, her expression inscrutable. He approached Sir Leicester, raising a calming hand, and produced a notebook from which he began to read, settling the differences between the baronet and his workmen.

"Mr. Fairbrother seems indispensable," I observed.

"Sir Leicester relies upon him," she acknowledged. "He thinks of him almost as a member of the family."

"That must be a relief, to have someone else to share the burden of the work," I said mildly.

She turned to me, her lips parted as if to speak. But she must have thought better of it, for she pressed her lips together and extended her hand. "Thank you for coming, Miss Speedwell. I am sorry to have taken you from your work, but it was very kind of you to keep me informed of the latest in your investigation."

I shook her hand. For an instant she gripped it quite tightly, and I had the oddest fancy it was the grip of a drowning woman.

"Lady Tiverton," I said, looking her in the eye. "If you have need of a friend, you may count me as one."

She smiled, but the smile did not touch her eyes. "You are very kind, Miss Speedwell."

I returned the smile and pulled on my gloves. "If you knew me better you would not make the mistake of thinking so."

I took my leave of her then, picking my way through the workmen, dodging bits of lumber and pots of paint, and out onto the pavement. I hailed a passing hansom and climbed in, giving the driver the direction of Bishop's Folly. As he sprang the horses away from the curb, a slim, boyish figure detached itself from behind a stray pile of rubbish to watch.

I twisted around in my seat just in time to see a slender white hand raised in salute.

CHAPTER 11

I had returned to the Belvedere and was hard at work on my *gonerilla* when Stoker finally appeared. The scales of the wing having been badly damaged, I had decided to remove the rest to expose the delicate tracery of the wings, leaving them transparent as a leaded window fitted with clear glass. I worked slowly, removing the scales carefully with the back of a silver fruit knife.

"Go back to bed," I told him shortly.

"I am fine," he returned in a low voice as he took a seat on his favorite camel saddle.

"You are unshaven, bloodshot, and weaving."

"You have never before objected to my whiskers, my eyes still function, and I am very nearly vertical," he said, pushing himself upright with a visible effort. "Veronica—"

"If you speak another word, I shall fling this fruit knife at your head," I told him pleasantly as I brandished the weapon in question.

"Don't be daft. You couldn't hurt a caterpillar with that," he replied. "You want something with a bit of heft. That brass cannonball, for instance," he added, nodding towards the lump of metal resting on the desk.

"Would it do any good to apologize?" he asked.

"It would not." I wrote out another card, blotting it badly. I tore it into careful pieces and wrote another, taking time to letter it perfectly.

"So we both behaved badly and we are neither of us going to make amends?"

"That," I told him calmly, "is exactly right."

"Veronica—"

"Do shut up, Stoker. I am in no mind to listen to your pathetic excuses."

He was silent a long moment. "Very well," he said quietly. "I cannot fault you for that. I can only tell you that one day I hope you will forgive me for what I said. God knows I will never forgive myself."

I hurled the fruit knife cleanly past his head, causing him to sit up suddenly. "Don't! Don't you dare feel sorry for yourself," I raged at him. "Self-pity is a gutter from which you will never arise. Do you know how hard I have worked to keep your head above the mud? But I was not the one who rescued you, you impossible fool. You were half-alive when I met you, a ruin of the man you could be. I have watched you claw your way back to life in the past months, taking an interest in your work, in your future. You have been the agent of your own resurrection, and you do not even see it. Have you no sense of your own gifts, of your own strengths? You are more blessed with natural abilities and native intelligence than any man I have ever met. You are a savage miracle, Revelstoke Templeton-Vane, knit together by the hands of Nature herself. But you cannot see it. In your mind, you are Samson shorn of his hair and Caroline has been your Delilah. Very well. Mourn what you have lost and pull down the temple on top of yourself. I will not weep for you. But neither will I watch you do it."

He stared at me in frank astonishment, his mouth open. After a long moment, he spoke, forcing the words out slowly, with obvious effort. "I hardly know what to say to that."

"Do not say anything. I do not require a response. I only wanted you to understand that I will do many things in this life, but watching you destroy yourself over Caroline de Morgan is not one of them."

I packed away my *gonerilla* with hands that were perfectly steady. "I have reading to do in my chapel, so unless you have anything of significance to add, I must beg you to excuse me."

I did not wait for a reply.

By mutual and unspoken understanding, we avoided each other for the rest of the day. Stoker worked on his balloon in the garden whilst I hid out in my little Gothic chapel, reading one of the first Lady Tiverton's books on Egyptology. It was a pleasant distraction from my bleak thoughts, and I was keenly aware of the fact that—to a disinterested observer—what I was doing might appear to be sulking.

My hand went more than once to the invitation I had been given. Membership in the Hippolyta Club was a mark of one's standing as a woman of intrepid spirit and intelligence. It meant recognition for one's achievements in fields that were too often the dominion of men. It meant regular meetings with kindred souls, and the making of friends. It meant putting down a root, slender as it was, into the soil of London. If I accepted, I should have a place of belonging, the first place I had known in the whole of my life that I had not been forced to create for myself. The idea was oddly unnerving.

I ran a finger over the seal, tracing the letters of the motto. ALIS VOLAT PROPRIIS. *She flies with her own wings.* How much easier to do that! If I refused, I should carry on as I had, keeping myself as solitary as I chose. I should be comfortable, I reflected.

After another moment's consideration, I drew a clean piece of paper towards me and began to write. The response was short—two words only. I signed and sealed it and slipped it into my pocket to give to George to put into the post.

I returned to the Belvedere after tea to find Figgy Tiverton perched atop a camel saddle feeding bits of sausage to the dogs. Nut had accompanied her and had taken a perch on Huxley's favorite pillow, looking down at him with lofty disdain.

"You ought to put up a sign," she said by way of greeting. "*Cave canem* or something. I thought you had a wolf in here." She nodded to his lordship's Caucasian sheepdog.

"Betony wouldn't hurt a hair on your head, nor would Huxley," I told her. "You'd be in far more danger from the Galápagos tortoise that roams the grounds."

"I saw it. Looks positively prehistoric."

"What brings you to see us, Miss Tiverton?" I asked as she fed more titbits to the dogs slavering devotedly at her feet.

"Us?" she asked, coloring swiftly.

"Mr. Templeton-Vane will be along in a moment. He is finishing up with his latest project."

"I saw," she said, her blush deepening. "From the windows of the house. I came to call upon Lady Wellie. She knew my mother, and it seemed courteous to pay her a visit since we were back in England." It was a feeble excuse, and I suppressed a sigh. She wasn't the first female to use any pretext to see Stoker. With her untidy hair and smeared spectacles, she looked a child still, but she was more of a woman than I suspected her father understood.

Before I could reply, Stoker entered, kicking the mud from his boots. "Miss Tiverton," he said, his voice warm with welcome. "How nice of you to call. I see you've met Bet and Huxley, and you've brought them a friend," he added, bending to scratch the hound Nut behind her tall, pointed ears.

"Oh, yes! They're lovely dogs. Is Huxley yours?"

"Or I am his," Stoker said, giving her a devastatingly handsome grin. To my relief, a day spent tinkering with his balloon seemed to have improved his temper to no end. He still looked tired and distracted, but the cold air had whipped color into his cheeks, and he was in a markedly better mood.

I turned to the pile on my desk and began to sort it as they talked. Stacks of letters and periodicals and a few grubby parcels that I put to the side. "You like dogs, then?" Stoker said. It was a thoroughly redundant question. Stoker had seen her with Nut when we first met them both, but as a conversational gambit, it was effective. Figgy brightened immediately.

"Very much. Even Nut, although she's frightfully stupid," she added with a fond look at her pet. "People think she's from Egypt because of how she looks, but Father had her shipped over from Malta. She only *looks* like the dogs in the tomb paintings. People say these Maltese hounds are descended from the Tesem. Do you know the word? It's a bit of hieratic, or do I mean hieroglyphic? In any event, the Tesem were the hunting dogs of the old pharaohs, a sort of greyhound."

"You seem to know quite a lot about ancient Egypt," he told her. I picked up the lion's tooth I used for a paper knife and slit open an envelope with vigor.

She colored furiously. "I don't, not really. Not compared to my mother. She was a scholar of Egyptology, you know."

She fell silent then, her lips pressed tightly together. I skimmed the letter—a request for a certain species of hairy moth—and filed it into a pigeonhole. I moved on to an unwholesome-looking parcel wrapped in brown paper. It was addressed to me but lacked a postmark—no doubt a specimen from yet another collector wanting to see his name on a placard in the Rosemorran museum when the thing was finally complete. I pushed it aside and picked up the latest edition of *The Daily Harbinger* instead.

"May I offer you some refreshment, Miss Tiverton?" Stoker asked.

She shook her head. "I had tea with Lady Wellie, and she stuffed me with all sorts of buns and cakes. In fact, I have overstayed already. My stepmother will be wondering where I am. And I shall have to make up some story or other." She slid down from the camel saddle, and Stoker was there to assist her, putting a steadying hand to her shoulder. "Oh, thank you," she said, blushing again.

I interrupted ruthlessly. "We made the acquaintance of some friends of yours recently—Mr. Horus Stihl and his son, Henry."

She rolled her eyes but said nothing.

Figgy wandered to a bell jar covering a particularly ghoulish display. "What is that?" she demanded.

"A hand of glory," Stoker told her. "They were all the rage amongst thieves a century or two ago. It was thought that if a housebreaker carried one, it would cast a spell of slumber over the entire household and he would be able to carry out his work unmolested."

Figgy warily eyed the atrocity. "What is it made of?"

"A human hand," I told her with some brutality. "Hacked from the body of a condemned criminal and dipped in tallow. The idea is that you light the fingers to serve as a lamp when you are bent upon thievery."

She gave it a scornful wave of dismissal. "I've seen things *heaps* nastier than that. My mama once found a mummy case with a person still inside."

"You have attended an unrolling?" Stoker asked.

"There was nothing to unroll. As soon as the lid came off, the poor old thing just fell to dust. He was badly embalmed, you see. He ought to have had a full forty days of immersion in the natron salts of lower Egypt—" She launched into a highly technical explanation of mummification that included all the nastier bits of pulling brain matter out of the nostril cavity and embalming the internal organs, which she related with what I could only think was an unhealthy relish. But Stoker seemed to enjoy it immensely, and I returned to my newspaper while they exchanged disgusting stories.

At length, the clock in the corner—stolen from the tsarist court in Bulgaria—chimed the hour, and Figgy jumped up with a start.

"Heavens, is that the time? I must dash."

I flicked a glance over the top of my newspaper. "Oh, leaving so soon? Good-bye, then, Miss Tiverton." I waved a casual hand as I went back to my reading.

Stoker was frowning at her. "Your parents do not know you are about in the city on your own?"

Figgy hastened to explain. "I know that sounds terribly cloak-and-dagger, but it isn't like that. Father's just stupidly strict sometimes. He does not understand the modern young woman. He thinks I am twelve!" she burst out. "He is perfectly content for me to roam to my heart's content in Egypt, but here he is so bothered by the dangers of the city, he hardly lets me take a step without an escort. I had a difficult time slipping out to come here today. They shall probably make a terrible fuss when I go back," she finished darkly.

"Have you given him reason to be afraid?" I asked coolly. Stoker made a noise of disapproval, but the girl nodded.

"The last time we were in London he discovered I had been skipping my drawing and French lessons in favor of meetings."

"Meetings?" I asked. "You mean, assignations?"

"Heavens, no! Political meetings. I am a suffragist," she told us proudly. "And if I were permitted to vote, I should vote Liberal. That is what galls him the most. He's the most appalling Tory."

"Show me an aristocrat who isn't," I murmured.

Stoker bristled. "I resent that."

"You are the exception that proves the rule," I told him by way of consolation. "Miss Tiverton, darkness has fallen. Wait a moment and we will send the hall boy to hail a cab."

She looked as if she would have liked to protest, but she shrugged. "Very well," she said ungraciously. We followed her out, and no sooner had we emerged from the Belvedere than Figgy gave a cry of shock, staggering back and raising a shaking finger. Stoker and I stared to where she pointed, exchanging a quick glance of mutual astonishment, for there, framed between a pair of trees in the distance, backed by a tall stand of shrubs and wrapped in wisps of fog, was the terrible figure of the great god Anubis himself.

He was bared to the waist, kilted in a pleated linen garment and wearing a heavy collar of gold and precious stones. His feet were shod in gilded leather sandals, and his head was—even now I can barely bring myself to recall the horror of the great black jackal head that tipped ever so slightly, the nose coming forwards as if he were sniffing out his prey.

Paralyzed in shock, we watched as he raised an accusing hand to Figgy, pointing to her heart. The girl shrieked in terror, covering her face with her hands. A nicer pair of people might have attended the poor child, but niceness has never been one of my virtues, and Stoker was already launching himself towards the little clearing. I followed hard upon his heels, urging him to still greater speed. Stoker held his fists high, and I had already extracted a sharpened hatpin, but we needn't have bothered.

The garden was entirely empty.

Stoker inspected the shrubbery, cursing lavishly. "A hole has been cut, just large enough for a man to fit through and giving directly onto the street. If he had a conveyance waiting, he will be well on his way by now." He thrust his head through the hole and emerged a moment later like Alice from Wonderland. "As I suspected, the street is empty."

"It was cleverly done," I observed. "The grounds are poorly lit here. He must have realized that we would be shocked into inaction upon first seeing him. That delay purchased him a few precious seconds to retreat through the shrubbery and into a waiting carriage. Still, he would have to be a quick and athletic sort of man." I hesitated. "If it *was* a man."

Stoker's look was pure scorn. "Do not even suggest it," he warned me.

"What? That this was an actual visitation by Anubis? Stranger things have happened, my dear Stoker."

"They bloody well have not. You call yourself a scientist," he said, trailing off with a sound of disgust. In an effort to prove me wrong, he scoured the ground where the figure had stood, hoping for what? A glimmering sequin or a lost jewel? But there was nothing.

"Stoker, do give it up. You'll not even find a footprint. The ground is too hard."

"There must be *some* trace of the devil," he grumbled.

"Well, we shall not find it in the freezing darkness. Now, come along. We ought to look to Figgy."

"Figgy! Blast, I forgot the child," he said, hurrying back to where we had left her. She was standing perfectly still, clutching Nut and staring after us with enormous eyes.

"Well?" she asked sharply. "Did you catch him?"

"We did not," I told her. "But I have to wonder why the Lord of the Underworld would disport himself in a Marylebone garden, particularly in these temperatures."

Her look was scathing. "You oughtn't mock what you do not understand," she intoned darkly.

"I understand that someone is playing a malicious trick," I returned with some tartness.

Stoker stepped forwards. "Come along, Miss Tiverton. I will see you back to the Sudbury myself."

"Oh, thank you. I'm most awfully grateful," she said, turning a shining face to Stoker. I did not bother to tell them good-bye. I retreated to the Belvedere and worked steadily until Stoker returned nearly an hour later.

"Finished with your errand of mercy?" I asked.

"I wonder sometimes if you use a whetstone on that tongue or if it is naturally sharp."

He flicked through his correspondence while I plucked a dusty, decaying African Map butterfly free and dropped it into the wastepaper basket. Unfortunate, I thought, as the African Map—*Cyrestis camillus*—was a winsome fellow with dashing stripes. I made a note to find his lordship a replacement of suitable quality.

"What do you make of our supernatural visitation?" Stoker asked. "And no more entertaining the possibility that we have actually seen Anubis. I don't believe in such rubbish, and neither do you."

I sat back in my chair, pondering. "A prank, as I told Figgy. Something designed to get our attention."

"But why?" he persisted. "What purpose could be served in trotting Anubis through our garden?"

"I can think of one," I told him, slanting him a meaningful look.

It took him a moment to comprehend. "Veronica, no. I cannot believe that child would do something so devious."

"She is the strangest mixture of woman and child," I observed. "And it would not be the first time a girl has resorted to theatrics to get the attention of a man she finds attractive."

He flushed. "Don't be feeble. Figgy is a *girl*."

"On the cusp of womanhood," I insisted. "She is not too young to conceive a passion for a man some years her senior."

"Even if that were so, and I am *not* conceding that it is," he warned, "how would she secure an accomplice to play the part of the god?"

I shrugged. "Figgy is resourceful," I told him, repeating what Lady Tiverton had revealed to me earlier in the day.

"I refuse to believe it," he said flatly.

"Now who is being unscientific?" I said mildly. I turned back to my collection of Madagascar butterflies.

"I wonder what she really came for," Stoker mused.

I stared at him a long moment, marveling that any man that enticing could really be so free of vanity. "I daresay we shall know in time," I told him.

• • •

The next morning I awoke in a foul temper, no doubt exacerbated by the fact that I had stayed up far too late, smoking my little Turkish cigarettes and thinking. I finished the first volume of Lady Tiverton's memoirs and embarked upon the second, but I remembered little of what I read. The books were engaging and well written, full of both scholarly observations and pithy witticisms. There were even photographs taken on some of her travels, but the images always blurred into Caroline de Morgan's triumphant face as she told us she was expecting a child.

Throwing off my blankets after a poor night's sleep, I washed and dressed and was surprised to find Stoker already hard at work in the Belvedere, stripping the rotten sawdust from the inside of his moldering platypus as he recited verses from "The Eve of St. Agnes." He maintained that Keats had written a poem for every possible mood, and whenever he resorted to "The Eve of St. Agnes," I knew he was in need of strenuous diversion. He had just got to a rather saucy passage when I interrupted him.

"That thing looks positively feral," I observed.

"It shan't when I've finished," he replied mildly.

I spied the latest copy of *The Daily Harbinger* set neatly to the side. From the blaring headlines, I could tell that J. J. Butterworth had once more scooped his rivals.

ANUBIS WALKS IN LONDON

I made a moue of disgust. "How the devil did Butterworth discover that?" I demanded from no one in particular.

Stoker dug the broken bits of a glass eyeball from his platypus and dropped them to the floor. "The old god was spotted near the Strand last night."

I lifted my brows. "The Strand? Near the Sudbury Hotel, you mean. It sounds as if our god paid a visit after he left us."

"Not exactly in turn," he corrected. "Note the time. Anubis was spotted by the hotel at almost exactly the same time as we saw him here. There are two Anubises. Would one call them 'Anubi'?"

"That isn't possible," I pointed out repressively. "He cannot be in two places at once."

"Unless he actually *is* a god. I believe you wished to entertain that possibility last night."

I sighed and refused to rise to the bait. "So, we have a pair of tricksters assuming the guise of an Egyptian god and running about town." I tipped my head thoughtfully as I considered the lavish headline. "I could almost suspect J. J. Butterworth himself of taking a hand in this, were it not for the fact that we saw Anubis with our own eyes."

Stoker paused, considering. "He still could be behind it. There are no photographs, only statements from eyewitnesses who wished not to be named. Butterworth might have made the whole thing up as a diversion from the fact that he was actually here, playing in the dressing-up box himself."

"But to what purpose? Flitting about the city in the guise of Anubis is certainly a way to heighten interest in the curse and sell newspapers, I suppose."

"A likely motivation for a reporter," he said, returning to his platypus. "The story of his visitation will spread. The public will go mad to see the treasures the Tivertons have unearthed. Furthermore, I should like to point out, you have wronged Figgy Tiverton. Clearly she did not engineer the apparition here in order to spend time with me," he added with a triumphant smile.

I gave in with bad grace. "Very well. I suppose I was a trifle . . ." I groped for a word.

"Unsporting," Stoker supplied. Our eyes met, and for an instant, I felt a rekindling of that strange something which made us alike, that quicksilver understanding that flowed between us.

I picked up the newspaper and turned to read below the fold. The sight of those bold black letters chilled my marrow. "Stoker, this is monstrous—" I began.

"It is what we expected." There was an air of resignation about him that I could not like.

"It as good as accuses you of John de Morgan's murder," I raged. "Does that not upset you?"

He shrugged one muscular shoulder. "To what purpose? I have my work and my friends, few though they may be. The rest of the world may think what it likes."

"They may not believe these lies," I cut in. "Calumnies! The rankest atrocities," I began, warming to my theme.

He cocked his head, a small, tired smile playing about his mouth.

"What is so amusing?" I demanded.

"You. Has it never occurred to you to wonder if I actually do have an alibi for the time de Morgan disappeared? It wouldn't take long, you know. A few hours to Dover to dispatch him, a few hours back. We haven't always been in each other's company. I might have done it."

He spoke with a casually jocular air, but beneath it I felt the desperation of the question. *Do you believe in me?*

"After all," he went on in the same maddeningly calm voice, "I have killed a man. You know that, but you don't know how or why. Perhaps I am what they say I am. The word 'monster' was used. How do you know they are wrong?"

"Because we are the same," I burst out. "You are not the only one of us with bloodied hands and a death on your conscience," I reminded him, not bothering to disguise my anger. "Why must you do this? Why must you test me?"

The tight muscle in his jaw relaxed into slackness. "I did not think to test you."

"Yes, you did. You do it every time you find yourself in danger of relying too much upon me, or hadn't you noticed? You are so afraid of depending upon another soul that you will burn down your own house rather than risk someone else doing it. You are so determined to believe that your wounds make you less than human that you think yourself a monster when others are merely men. And whatever this bond that is between us, whatever this thing is that makes us akin to one another, you do not trust it. Because you do not trust yourself. But I am tired of the games, Stoker. And I am tired of your little monstrosities when I have atrocities of my own to account for."

With that I returned to my work and said nothing more, waiting for him to walk away.

He returned to his platypus and I scraped away at my little *gonerilla* for a while, letting the scales fall away and exposing the crystalline wing beneath. It was exacting, tiresome work, and I found my mind wandering as my hands stayed busy. I turned over all that I had thought of the previous night, carefully pursuing each line of thought out and back again. Stoker stayed at his platypus, pulling bits of it free until sawdust filled the air and the floor was littered with unpleasant bits of fur and padding. Knowing he would be considering our next move as well, I let him destroy it until we stopped for elevenses, at which point he paused in his work and came to stand behind me, wiping the worst of the grime from his hands and face.

"Most people do not realize it is the scales that give a butterfly wing its color," I told him in a calm voice. "If you strip them off, the wing is clear as water, and the filaments between look like the leading of glass windows. Perhaps I should scale a wing or two for display purposes."

"Veronica." He had uttered my name a thousand times, but never before had it sounded like prayer. "There are things I should tell you."

I paused in the scraping of the wing, not quite trusting my hands to stay steady enough.

"I am listening."

"I do not know where to begin. And this is not the time." He thrust his filthy hands through his hair, powdering the dark locks with cobwebs and dust. "We must go to Dover."

I looked up, blinking. "I beg your pardon?"

"Dover. It is where de Morgan disappeared. I am convinced that she is telling the truth and that he crossed from Calais with her. That means whatever happened to him, it happened in Dover."

She. He never said her name, I realized. I had never heard him say it except moaned in his sleep and on that singular occasion when he had moaned it against my skin, his breath mingled with mine. Even now he could not bear to speak it.

I set a smile on my lips. "An excellent notion. Very sensible. I will pack a bag. If we leave on the train directly after luncheon we will be there in time for supper."

He opened his mouth as if expecting me to say something more. I gave him a long, coolly assessing look. "You cannot possibly board a train looking like that. They will take you for a vagrant. Go and wash yourself."

CHAPTER 12

He said nothing until we were safely aboard the train to Dover carrying a small carpetbag each. George the hall boy had been slipped a copper to feed Huxley, and I had scribbled a note to Lord Rosemorran to let him know we would be away for a night. I gave the vague impression that we were on the trail of an addition for his collection, and there was little danger his lordship would think otherwise. He never read *The Daily Harbinger.* Lady Wellie did, and that caused a chain reaction of thoughts I did not much like.

"Do you think it possible that Lady Wellie was the one who gave information to the newspaper?" I asked as the chimney pots of London gave way to the back gardens of suburban villas.

Stoker shrugged. "Possible. But so is everyone else we have spoken to with regard to this business. Sir Hugo, Mornaday, the Tivertons, the Stihls, the Marshwoods, Julien. Any one of them might have let the story out."

"For what purpose?" I demanded. He made a gesture as if to dismiss the question, then seemed to think better of it.

"As we have already noted, the Tivertons may not like the stories, but they will drive attendance at their exhibition and increase demand for their antiquities. Sir Hugo and Mornaday have their own dastardly political games with Special Branch, and Lady Wellie's motives are known only to her. She would confound the serpent in Eden."

"Truly," I agreed. "What of the Stihls?"

He shrugged. "They could have decided that making the story public would discredit the Tivertons somehow and throw a shadow over their grand exhibition. Julien could have done it solely for money, the Marshwoods to see me tarred and feathered in the court of public opinion again."

"Surely you do not really suspect Julien," I protested.

His smile was feeble but real. "No. I include him only for the sake of thoroughness."

"Besides," I went on, "those might be motivations to speak to a reporter, but none are strong enough to provide a motive to kill John de Morgan."

"No, only mine," he said, then lifted a hasty hand. "I am not wallowing in self-pity. I merely note it for the purpose of argument."

"Good," I said, putting out a hand for the pocket notebook he always carried. "Now, let us put it all down logically from the beginning. . . ."

Due to the vagaries of travel in winter through the countryside—snow on the line, an errant cow—we arrived early in the evening at our destination. We had filled pages in his notebook with our conjectures, but nothing seemed to fit. Who was our female pursuer and why was she shadowing us? Who played the part of Anubis—both at Bishop's Folly and outside the Sudbury—and was it merely to create excitement or did he have some more sinister purpose in mind? In the end, I flung the notebook from the window in a moment of pique, an action for which I atoned by purchasing a replacement at the station upon our arrival—an inferior replacement, Stoker noted with some degree of injury.

I ignored him and proceeded to the nearest porter to inquire as to the whereabouts of the Victoria Hotel. It was a few steps down a narrow street, a nondescript house in a nondescript street overlooked by the looming bulk of Dover Castle. Only a demure sign posted on the front indicated its status as a lodging house. VICTORIA HOTEL. MRS. R. D. GIDDONS, PROPRIETRESS. Stoker and I stood upon the pavement, taking in our surroundings.

"It would not be my first choice if I were Sir Leicester Tiverton," he observed.

"It is certainly nothing like the Sudbury for elegance," I agreed.

A sharp rap brought the sound of shuffling footsteps, and the door was thrown back by a slender, pinch-faced maid.

"We would like rooms," Stoker began.

"A room," I corrected swiftly as I trod on his foot. "My husband and I are very tired from our journey."

The girl shrugged and stepped back to let us enter, gesturing vaguely towards the front parlor. "Wait here, if you please. I shall fetch Mrs. Giddons."

We proceeded into the parlor, and the little maid bobbed her head, closing the door behind her. The room was stuffed with the kind of uncomfortable upright furniture that people save too long to buy and enjoy too little when they do. An array of indifferent watercolors was hung on the walls, and every corner was filled with either an aspidistra or a malnourished fig tree.

"Don't stand still for too long," I told him helpfully. "The mistress of the house might drape you with an antimacassar."

He snorted but said nothing as he peered at a bookcase full of dusty sermons. A little brass rack upon the mantel held the proprietress' cards and I plucked one free, testing its quality. The paper was rather thin and the ink slightly inferior. The proprietress' name, Rebecca F. Giddons, was prefaced with the honorific "Mrs.," but I suspected from the absence of a man's name anywhere about, she had taken it as a courtesy title. Most cooks did so in order to preserve authority over their staffs, a single woman having little prestige, and it seemed hoteliers were likewise hobbled by a solitary marital status. It was maddening that a woman in business for herself should have to resort to such stratagems, but I did not blame her.

"I apologize if I took you by surprise with my request for a single room," I began. "Registering as a married couple is the only way to avoid arousing comment."

He flicked me a preoccupied glance. "What's that? Oh, good thinking. Best not to use our real names either."

"I shall make a note of it," I said in a dry voice. We were left alone only a moment more before the door opened and a lady entered. She wore a stiff gown of black bombazine and a vague smile. Her hair, once no doubt a bright auburn, had faded a little, and the beginnings of lines had etched themselves at the corners of a pair of watchful fox-brown eyes. The maid trotted obediently behind, awaiting instructions.

"Good evening," she said. "I apologize for the delay. I am Mrs. Giddons, the proprietress of the hotel. I understand you wish a room for the night?"

"If you please," Stoker said, taking the lead.

"Certainly. Dinner is included in the price and will be served here in the parlor," Mrs. Giddons told him. She went to a table draped in a starched cloth and opened the register resting atop it. She held out a pen to Stoker. "Your signature, sir?"

Stoker took the pen and made a lazy scrawl on the page. The proprietress peered at it.

"Lord and Lady Templeton-Vane," she pronounced, her spine stiffening a little at the title. "An honor indeed," she murmured. She straightened and turned to the girl, whose eyes had gone very wide. "Take his lordship's bag—and her ladyship's—up to the Chinese Room." She turned back to us. "Our largest and most comfortable accommodation," she said with a regal nod of the head.

Something in her manner struck me as disingenuous. A touch of mockery, perhaps? Stoker and I certainly made an unlikely pair of aristocrats. We doubtless looked like exactly what we were—an unmarried couple bent upon some illicit activity. How was the proprietress to know we were bent upon sleuthing instead of fornication?

The girl scuttled out with our bags, and Mrs. Giddons turned to us. "If you would care to make yourselves comfortable, dinner will be served shortly."

She withdrew from the parlor, leaving us alone with the aspidistras, their heads bent together in leafy conversation. "This place gives me the cold shivers," Stoker said flatly.

"I know. Was it wise of you to give your brother's name?" I asked.

He shrugged. "Tiberius always enjoys playing a part in an intrigue, no matter how small." I was surprised. He seldom spoke of his brothers, and Tiberius—in his role as head of the family—was the Templeton-Vane who riled Stoker the most. "Besides," he added with a smile, "we have almost no baggage, and you have no lady's maid. I am quite certain our hostess suspects the worst of us already."

In a very few minutes, the thin little maid crept in to poke up the fire and lay a table. We seated ourselves and suffered through a succession of grim courses. Indifferent fish, inedible stew, and a chicken of such antiquity I feared it would be of interest only to scholars of ancient history.

"I have apples in my bag," I murmured to Stoker when a particularly nasty dish of creamed turnips was placed before us.

He waited until the maid had scuttled out again to reply. "I shall go you one better—I have smoked oysters and a capon."

I toasted his ingenuity—the wine was surprisingly good, although it had clearly been watered—and after we poked at the dried-up remnants of a vile rice pudding, Mrs. Giddons appeared to inquire about the dinner.

"Was everything to your liking?" she asked, her brow furrowed in concern.

"Perfectly satisfactory," Stoker lied.

"You are perhaps kinder than you are honest, my lord." A sudden smile brightened her features. "I am sorry to say that we have lost our cook and the meal was a meager one. Not at all our best effort," she said, her voice trailing off. She produced a bottle. "But I have brought a special treat by way of compensation—my homemade turnip wine!"

I looked longingly at the dregs of the French burgundy I had just finished.

"Turnip wine?" Stoker asked in a faint voice.

"Yes, yes." Mrs. Giddons went to a cupboard and extracted two slim crystal goblets. "My very best," she said, somewhat shyly. She uncapped the dark green bottle and poured out a murky fluid, handing us each a glass filled to the brim. The aroma was vegetal, and I resisted the urge to wrinkle my nose.

"You must tell me what you think," she said, turning expectantly to Stoker.

I moved a little to the side, ostensibly to study a print of Dover Castle hanging upon the wall.

Behind me I heard Stoker take a deep sniff and then down his glass in a gulp. Mrs. Giddons gave a little gasp of delight. "Oh, I do like to see a gentleman enjoy his spirits," she said, her voice suddenly girlish. "Another glass, my lord?"

"I really shouldn't," Stoker replied, choking only a little.

"Nonsense! A gentleman of your inches can hold his liquor," she told him. While she played the coquette, pouring out another full glass and explaining the fermenting process at length, I took the opportunity to tip my glass into the nearest aspidistra.

"Oh, my lady," she said, suddenly glimpsing my empty goblet, "you must have another."

I thrust the glass behind my back. "I am afraid I couldn't possibly, Mrs. Giddons."

She gave me a narrow look and her manner was suddenly aggrieved.

"Well, I only meant to be friendly, I'm sure," she said. "I will send Daisy to show you to your room."

She swept out, taking her vile concoction with her, but not before she had stared at Stoker so pointedly he gulped down his second glass to mollify her.

"I think you have wounded her feelings," he said.

"Better her feelings than my digestion," I remarked. "You will regret drinking that." At that moment, Daisy appeared and guided us up the stairs to the Chinese Room, taking her leave after Stoker pressed a coin into her palm.

The room was papered in pale green with furniture of light bamboo and an iron bedstead. A few prints of vaguely Eastern style and a single piece of cheap porcelain in the shape of a pagoda were the concessions to the name.

"This could not have been John de Morgan's room," I said quietly. "According to Sir Hugo, he was given a back room and it was papered in forget-me-nots with a green carpet. This must have been Caroline's accommodation."

"No doubt," he said, ferreting in his bag for his victuals.

"Don't you mean to investigate?" I demanded.

"Not yet," he said, calmly tearing the leg from a roasted capon. "There's no point creeping about until we know the proprietress and that sad little maid have retired for the night."

I fretted at the delay, but he was correct. He held out a capon leg and I took it, grateful for the sustenance. We stripped the bird completely and threw the bones out the window. There was a narrow yard with a few outbuildings—the washhouse and other more necessary conveniences, I realized. A low fence separated the yard from the neighbor's, and I could see washing still pegged out on the line in spite of the late hour. The garments flapped, ghostlike, in the darkness, and I gave an involuntary shudder, turning back as Stoker peeled the apples, slicing the skin off in a single luscious red strip which likewise went out the window. We followed that with hard biscuits and a healthy nip of aguardiente, that potent South American liquor, from my flask.

While we ate, we waited, listening to the sounds of the household settling in for the night. They retired early, closing up shutters and bolting doors before ten o'clock.

"Provincial hours," I observed. Stoker nodded, and we waited another hour before we dared to emerge from our room. We moved on stocking feet over the threadbare carpet until we reached the door of the back bedroom. I extracted a pin from my hair, but before I could apply it, Stoker reached out and turned the knob. It gave easily in his hand, and he looked back at me with a shrug. We slipped inside and closed the door behind us, breathing heavily.

The draperies were closed tightly, admitting no moonlight, and it took several minutes before our eyes adjusted enough that Stoker could extract his case of vestas and strike one. The flame leapt to life, a tiny thing in the pressing blackness of that room, but a welcome sight. He applied it to a lamp on the mantelpiece, and I hurried to lay a pillow across the threshold, blocking the glow from anyone who might venture upstairs.

Our preparations in hand, we surveyed the room. It was like any other accommodation in any other third-rate hotel: impersonal and immutable, waiting for its next inhabitant. A thousand travelers could come and go, but they would never leave an impression on this place. It was home to none.

I examined the contents of the night table, but there was only a tract of improving literature in the slim bamboo piece and a bit of spilled face powder from a lady's powder box.

Stoker looked through the bookshelf, reporting that there was nothing to be found there, although he shook each book carefully and ruffled the leaves of the pages. Together we went over the clothespress and the washstand, looking for hidden compartments and searching the drawers until at last we sat back, defeated.

"There is no proof to Caroline's story," I said in a low whisper. "Nothing to indicate that John de Morgan was ever here."

"What did you expect?" Stoker demanded. "The police searched the place thoroughly and found nothing."

"Heaven help us if we are not better observers than the police," I retorted. "We are scientists, trained in the art of observation," I reminded him. "So what do we observe here?"

He sighed, clearly tired of the endeavor. But he gathered up his resolve and answered anyway.

"The room fits with the rest of the hotel, cheap furnishings bought in sets to make themes," he said, trailing off slowly as he looked around. "Except that this room *doesn't* fit, does it?" He rose and moved from piece to piece. "The clothespress is mahogany, German in style, while the night table is a flimsy bamboo affair. The chair is striped yellow velvet with a vaguely Oriental pattern, clearly from the Chinese Room, but the bedcover and wallpaper are blue. This room wasn't furnished like the others—it is a hotchpotch of styles and colors, as if—"

"As if they decorated it in a tearing hurry, taking pieces from the other rooms," I finished.

We stood in silence, each of us training an observer's eye on the surroundings. Almost without being aware of what I was doing, I moved to the corner where the edge of the wallpaper had not quite been stuck down. I picked at it with a fingernail, prying up the corner with a gasp.

Behind the blue wallpaper was another paper, dark green with large roses.

"Exactly the wallpaper Sir Hugo said Caroline de Morgan described," I said.

Stoker examined it closely, pulling more of the paper free. After a long moment, he sat back on his haunches. "She was telling the truth, then. John was here. And he disappeared."

"You don't know that," I argued. "We can only say for certain that

Caroline saw this wallpaper at some point. She went to John's room. She might have observed it while she sat with him." But even as I said the words, I knew they were ridiculous. Stoker was right; Caroline de Morgan had come to this hotel with her husband and he had disappeared, all traces of his presence papered over like the walls in this room.

"It is oppressive," I said, thrusting myself to my feet. "I cannot breathe in here."

Stoker took a twist of paper from his pocket and extracted the sweets within. He sucked them for a few minutes, then took one out and rubbed it over the exposed wallpaper. He then pressed down the new paper, sticking them together as best he could to hide our vandalism.

"No point in tipping our hand," he said grimly. "We will go back to London tomorrow and tell them to come back and search again."

I had no such intention. To begin with, Sir Hugo would be difficult to persuade, given that the Marshwoods had threatened legal action, and I had little hope that Mornaday would prove any more amenable. But that was an argument for another time, I thought in happy anticipation.

We retired to our room, neither of us undressing. We even kept our boots on, arranging ourselves decorously atop the coverlet as we waited for morning. We had shared sleeping accommodations before, so the situation was nothing new to us, but I was keenly aware of him that night, lying inches away in the darkness. It was a long time before I slept, but when I did, I slept heavily and I dreamt I wandered in a dark wood. I was chasing something through the trees, a figure flitting in white. Moonlight shone on her gilded hair, and I realized it was Caroline de Morgan, showing herself and then darting behind a tree, elusive as she encouraged me to chase her, laughing every time I stumbled. My hands were bloody from falling and my face had been scratched by thorns, and I could hardly breathe, I had run so far. There was a stitch in my side, and I stopped, putting my hand to a tree for balance. Suddenly, the top of the tree erupted into flames, and as I looked about in horror, I saw that the entire forest was alight.

I jerked awake, coughing and gasping for air. I sucked in great heaving breaths, but there was no relief, only choking, strangulating smoke, and I opened my eyes to see the room was full of it.

"Stoker!" I shoved hard, but he did not move, and I wondered if, lying closer to the door, he had breathed more of the foul stuff than I. I put my hands and feet flat against his back and thrust him off the bed. He landed hard upon the floor, but gave only a muffled groan. I pulled up his eyelids, but his eyes were rolled back into his head and he made no response. He was breathing normally, though, and I realized then that his trouble was not the choking clouds of smoke. He had been drugged.

I rummaged in his pockets for one of his enormous scarlet handkerchiefs and took it to the washstand, wetting it and wringing it out before tying it loosely over his mouth and nose. I fixed my own dampened handkerchief about my face and took stock of our situation.

I went to the window, but the room overlooked a short flight of stone steps. If I could maneuver Stoker to the window, I could do nothing more than shove him out; he would doubtless break his back on one of the stone treads. Neither could I climb out and leave him as I went for help; the fire would no doubt move too quickly for that. There was only one thing to be done.

How, you may wonder, did I—a woman of diminutive inches and slender build—manage to rescue a man of Stoker's prodigious size from a burning building?

Reader, I carried him.

CHAPTER 13

With every bit of strength I possessed, I hauled Stoker onto my back, draping his torso over my own and letting his legs drag behind as we made our way down the stairs. I saw no one, heard no alarm, but I made no effort to see to Mrs. Giddons. The woman could be burnt to cinders for all I cared. I had no doubt the source of Stoker's indisposition had been something slipped into the turnip wine. Only my distaste for the stuff had kept me from suffering the same fate—unconsciousness and oblivion as fire raged around us.

The front door was open, no doubt to facilitate Mrs. Giddons' flight, but I turned and went the opposite direction. The parlor was fully engulfed, and the smoke stung my eyes as the conflagration raged, hot tongues of flame lapping at Stoker's booted feet. With one last burst of effort, I reached the back of the house and opened the door, gulping in great heaving breaths of cold air. The sudden rush of it fed the fire, sending sparks heavenwards as I hauled Stoker down the short flight of stone steps and across the yard. It was the work of a moment to force open the door of the washhouse and see him settled there. I yanked the handkerchief from his face and tore off my own, taking several deep, shuddering breaths before I crept out, rounding the side of the house, careful to keep to the shadows. I could hear the bells then, summoning the fire brigade, and from the glow of the inferno I could see Mrs. Giddons and Daisy huddled on the pavement amidst a consoling horde of neighbors.

The fire brigade appeared, leather buckets in hand, fitting hoses and herding back the spectators. I could hear the chief of them asking Mrs. Giddons if everyone was out.

She shook her head. "No. I have two guests, in the Chinese Bedroom in the front. I tried everything to wake them, but they must already have been overcome by the smoke." She broke off, pressing her hands to her mouth and doing a very good impression of a woman in distress.

My suspicions confirmed, I slipped back the way I had come. It took a good deal of effort and some rather nasty methods, but Stoker was eventually roused.

"What the devil is that smell?" he demanded in a thick voice.

"Burnt hair," I told him.

"Why did you burn your hair?"

"I didn't." I explained as briefly as I could. When I had finished, I settled myself next to a gap in the washhouse wall, keeping an eye upon the proceedings as Stoker slipped back into sleep. Now that I had satisfied myself that he had suffered no permanent damage from the sedative, the simplest course of action was to let him sleep it off. I certainly could carry him no further, and attempting to do so would only attract unwelcome attention. Far better to stay where we were, tucked securely away in a spot no one would think to look, and slip away in the morning. In due course, the fire brigade had finished its work, saving the structure, although the interior had been burnt to ash. Members of the brigade and neighbors milled about for some time, but the cold eventually drove them inside, and things grew quiet. I occupied myself with surveying the washhouse. I had sat down hard upon something sharply pointed, and after a gingerly inspection, I discovered the culprit—a shard of pottery. It was terra-cotta, marked with a curious painted symbol in ochre. A careful hunt produced a single silver sequin and a tiny piece of some material I could not identify but of a dazzling blue color with a high sheen. I pocketed the little collection and settled myself again upon the packed-earth floor. It would be an uncomfortable night but by no means the worst I had known.

We had left our coats behind, but by the expedient of huddling together, we retained sufficient body heat to pass the night in reasonable comfort. It was just getting on for seven in the morning when Stoker roused himself, rubbing his eyes and putting a hand to his doubtless aching head.

"What in the name of bleeding Jesus happened?"

"What do you remember?" I asked, smoothing my hair into some semblance of order and neatening my disordered clothes.

"Precious little. I thought I saw a fire and I had the oddest sensation of being carried."

"You were. I'm sorry to say, you were drugged, no doubt in that vile turnip wine. Then our hostess appears to have set fire to the hotel, fully intending to roast us in our beds."

Stoker swore then, something fluently profane, and I knew he was well on the way to recovery.

"How well do you feel?" I asked.

"Well enough to get the hell out of here and back to London," he said with some feeling. He glanced around, taking in our surroundings. "Not that I am entirely certain of where 'here' is," he temporized. As soon as he was capable of standing, I used our dampened handkerchiefs to wipe the soot from our faces and we slid out of the washhouse.

"A handy washhouse in the yard of the Victoria Hotel," I informed him. "I thought it best to let you sleep off the effects of the drug, and we have no coats. A washhouse was the warmest solution I could devise."

"Or a police station?" he suggested. "It is not beyond the realm of possibility that we could inform the authorities of Mrs. Giddons' murderous ways, Veronica."

"Out of the question," I told him in a brisk voice. "Let her worry when the fire brigade do not find a pair of nicely crisped corpses."

"But—"

I held up a hand. "Stoker, you are in no fit state to argue. Now, I have little doubt we could have eventually prevailed upon the Dover police to believe us, but at what price? We are an unmarried couple, masquerading as a lord and his wife, no doubt bent upon the purposes of prurient exercise. At least that is what they will assume. And that is the *best* of what they might assume about us. Do not forget, you are implicated in the possible murder of a man who disappeared from the very hotel where we stayed. Does that not seem the slightest bit suspicious to you?"

He gave me an unhappy look. "Well, if you put it that way . . ."

"I do." I rose and put out a hand. "Now, let us be off."

We arrived at the train station just as the first train was preparing to depart. If our wrinkled clothes and lack of appropriate outer garments raised questions, no one was rude enough to voice them directly. In a few hours' time, we were back in London and settled at the Belvedere, washed, dressed, and demolishing the most enormous breakfast Cook could provide. The dangers through which we had passed added spice to our repast. Were eggs ever so fresh, toast ever so crisp, ham ever so sweet?

I had just helped myself to a second plate—Stoker was on his third, his appetite suffering nothing from his ordeal—when George appeared, the latest copy of *The Daily Harbinger* tucked under his arm.

"Good morning, miss, Mr. Stoker," he said, proffering the newspaper in exchange for a piece of bacon. I turned to the newspaper, preparing myself for the worst. No doubt J. J. Butterworth had embellished the tales of Stoker's misdeeds to egregious new depths.

George took a second piece of bacon, tearing it into bits for the dogs. "I was sorry to hear about your brother, sir," he said to Stoker.

Stoker looked up from his eggs. "What about him? And which one?" he asked, but even before I looked at the newspaper, I knew.

"Oh," I said faintly. I turned the newspaper so that the headline faced Stoker.

VISCOUNT FEARED DEAD WITH MISTRESS IN DOVER FIRE

"Bloody bollocking hell," he said, dropping his fork.

"Exactly," I replied.

The fact that Tiberius, Viscount Templeton-Vane, waited until after breakfast to pay a call was indicative of his native courtesy. He did not bother to announce himself at the main door of Bishop's Folly, but proceeded directly to the Belvedere and entered without knocking. He was, as ever, beautifully dressed, with a knack for elegant tailoring that Stoker would never achieve. They were of a similar height and build—although his lordship was several years the senior—and their features were strongly marked by Nature in the same mold. As they were half brothers, their coloring varied. Stoker's hair was black as only the baseborn son of a Welshman's can be, and his eyes rather violently blue. His lordship was somewhat less arresting on first sight, with brown eyes and hair. But it took only a brief second glance to appreciate the silken wave of his locks and the mischievous gleam in the depths of those smoke-dark eyes.

The mischief was not in evidence this morning. The viscount wore instead an expression of nearly implacable fury, damped down to a finely honed coldness that was perfectly calibrated to the situation at hand.

"Miss Speedwell, Revelstoke," he said by way of greeting. He did not remove his gloves or his hat, a clear indication that he meant this to be a call of the most formal variety.

"My lord," I said, rising from the remains of the meal we had just finished. "I am afraid you have caught us over a late breakfast. Might I offer you some tea?"

He held up a hand. "I require nothing, my dear Miss Speedwell, except an explanation." His gaze fell to the newspaper upon the table. With a thin, cold smile, he seated himself upon the camel saddle we kept for visitors and looked from me to his brother expectantly.

Stoker sighed. "The fault is mine," he began.

"I have no doubt of that," the viscount replied.

I stepped forwards. "Now, see here. That is not entirely true. I am just as involved in this investigation as you are."

"Ah!" His lordship raised a brow into a perfectly pointed Gothic arch. "One of your little investigations. I might have guessed."

"We were pursuing a line of inquiry in Dover and it became necessary to check into an hotel. Naturally, we could not use our own names," I told him. "Think of the scandal if we registered as an unmarried couple."

His lordship opened his mouth, but it was my turn to cut him off. "I promise you that nothing happened, apart from the proprietress trying to murder us."

His handsome mouth went slack in genuine astonishment. "Is this true? Your lives were in danger?"

"Yes," Stoker said quietly. "I'd have been burnt to ash if Veronica hadn't awoken."

The viscount's brow winged upwards again. "Indeed?"

I sighed. "We shared a room, but I can assure you that no one's honor was compromised."

His expression turned mocking. "Shall I demand that you make an honest man of my brother?"

"There is no call for that," I promised him. "He was a perfect gentleman in every regard."

A slow smile spread over the viscount's features as his eyes met mine. "I always said he was a fool," he said softly.

I grinned, and Stoker cleared his throat. "Pardon me for pointing it out, but I thought you were here to castigate us. If you mean to rant, do it and get out. I have things to do."

The viscount held my gaze a moment longer, then looked—reluctantly, it seemed—to his brother. "Very well. I am a man of the world, Revelstoke. Your little peccadillo is hardly going to harm my reputation. I am glad the pair of you escaped harm. How *did* you escape harm?" he asked.

Stoker flushed a little. "Miss Speedwell carried me."

His lordship's mouth twitched, but he shook his head. "No, I will not laugh at it. But I vow, I will enjoy the thought of it for the rest of my life." He turned to me. "I congratulate you, Miss Speedwell, on your presence of mind as well as your coolness in a crisis."

I acknowledged the compliment with a gracious inclination of the head.

"For God's sake," Stoker muttered.

The viscount looked from Stoker to me. "I think, as you have taken my name in vain, I might at least know what you are about." I saw no point in prevarication, so I pointed to the newspaper.

"The Tiverton story. The disappearance of John de Morgan."

He raised his brows suggestively. "Indeed? I should have thought you would be first on the list of possible suspects, Revelstoke."

"Thank you for the vote of confidence," Stoker returned with equal hauteur.

"Although," his lordship went on, "I would expect rather less theatrical window dressing if you were involved. A nice clean beating or a knife to the throat. Those would be far more your style."

Stoker rolled his eyes heavenwards but refused to rise to the bait. I turned to the viscount. "Do you know the Tivertons?" I inquired.

"I have not had the doubtful pleasure of making their acquaintance."

"Doubtful?"

He shrugged. "Sir Leicester is an excitable little monkey of a man, although I hear his second wife is unobjectionable and his first wife was an absolute paragon."

"From whom have you heard that?"

"From one of her most devoted admirers," he informed us. "Horace Stihl."

"You know Horace Stihl?" Stoker demanded.

"My dear fellow, I do have a social life, and it does occasionally include befriending Americans. I'm considered eccentric for it. We share an interest in art and have on occasion crossed swords at the auction houses. Ours is a casual connection, nothing more."

"What can you tell us about him?"

The viscount stroked his chin thoughtfully. "He outbid me at auction for a charming little Fragonard. I have never forgiven him, although we do occasionally meet for dinner. He is devilishly shrewd. Oddly, he is also frightfully romantic, a sentimentalist, and you know I have no time for such things."

"Are you so unmoved by sentiment?" I asked.

"Sentiment is for children, and Horace Stihl is nothing so much as an overgrown child when it comes to matters of the heart."

"And you, of course, are entirely lacking in such an organ," Stoker said nastily.

The viscount clucked his tongue. "If that was meant to be an insult, you will have to try harder, dear fellow. I pride myself on my detachment, save where my interests are stirred," he added with a significant look at me. "But if you are inquiring about his character, I have found him trustworthy. Once or twice he has put me in the way of a piece he knew I particularly wanted and might have bid for himself."

"You do not think him underhanded?"

"No more so than any other successful man and probably a good deal less."

His lordship rose smoothly. "Well, I have satisfied myself that you are both in good health. I will send a telegram to the Dover police informing them that I am alive and well in London and completely mystified as to who might have been masquerading as me."

Stoker gave him a grudging nod. "Thank you, Tiberius. That is uncommonly decent of you."

The viscount bowed over my hand. "I am an uncommonly decent fellow." He rose and bent to my ear, his lips very nearly brushing my skin. "Although I should like more than ever to be indecent with you, my dear Miss Speedwell," he murmured just loudly enough for me to hear. Before I could reply, he stepped back and raised his voice. "How are your little lunas fairing?"

"Very well. They should emerge from the cocoons any day now. Would you like me to let you know when they have eclosed? You should get to see them fly, after all."

"I would be delighted."

He turned to go, then paused and turned back almost as an afterthought. "Oh, and while I deplore the habit of keeping score amongst one's friends and relations, I think it best if the pair of you remember how very accommodating I have been under the circumstances."

Stoker gave him a baleful look. "Meaning?"

The viscount smiled, baring strong white teeth in a wolfish smile. "Meaning that one of these days I might well have circumstances of my own which require your accommodation. I shall expect to be able to call in this favor."

Stoker opened his mouth—no doubt to say something entirely rude—but I forestalled him.

"We shall be at your disposal, my lord."

"I am counting upon it, Miss Speedwell."

"Why on earth did you promise him that we would help him?" Stoker demanded when he had gone.

I shrugged. "I like him."

Stoker gave me a narrow look. "Of course you do. He is handsome and charming and a lord."

"Those are the least interesting of his qualities," I told him. "His lordship is also complicated and unpredictable, with some very intriguing hobbies."

"I give up," Stoker told me.

We applied ourselves to our work then, Stoker making good progress on his platypus and my *gonerilla* at last being revealed in all her exquisite nudity. We had just finished when the afternoon edition of the newspaper was delivered.

I was not surprised to find my world once again upended by the headline. It had become so common an occurrence that I would have been shocked if J. J. Butterworth had found anything else to write about.

MUMMY'S CURSE STRIKES AGAIN

Stoker glimpsed the headline over my shoulder. "What fresh deviltry has happened now?" he demanded. I showed him the article, a lurid piece about the sightings of Anubis in the city.

"Which brings us back to the question, who is playing Anubis? And do not start with any more of that nonsense about spectral visitations," he warned.

I pulled a face. "I told you, I was merely entertaining possibilities. Think of it as an intellectual exercise. In this case, I quite agree with you that Occam's razor is appropriate. The simplest explanation is the likeliest."

"And the simplest explanation is that someone connected with the Tiverton case is going around haunting people in the guise of Anubis."

"More than one Anubis, thanks to his appearance at the Sudbury," I reminded him. "But it is most logical to take them one at a time. The figure, whoever he might be, has appeared in Egypt, here in Marylebone, and in the Strand. Now, to suspects. The form was undoubtedly male, which lets out Lady Tiverton and Figgy. We are left with Horus and Henry Stihl, Patrick Fairbrother, and Sir Leicester Tiverton as the most obvious choices."

Stoker snorted. "Stihl the Younger and Fairbrother I will grant you, but Sir Leicester? And Horus Stihl? They are aged."

I primmed my mouth. "I think you will concede my expertise on the subject of the male form," I said sedately. "I can assure you that while both of those gentlemen are of advancing years, they would both strip admirably. Like our Anubis, Sir Leicester has broad shoulders, and if you took away Mr. Stihl's lavish white hair and moustaches, you would find him significantly younger than you think. He moves with a certain allure," I finished, thinking pleasurably on his silken moustaches upon my fingers.

Stoker snapped his fingers in front of my face. "*If* you can tear yourself away from your salacious woolgathering, I would like to point out that you have forgot another man who deserves to be a suspect."

"Oh?"

Stoker paused, clearly relishing the moment. "First, the reporter for *The Daily Harbinger*. The fellow is making a name for himself out of all this drivel. It seems at least possible that he is behind some of the more outlandish aspects."

I nodded. “Well-done,” I acknowledged. “That is certainly plausible. And I have one more name to add to the list of possible villains.”

He quirked up a brow in inquiry, but I held the moment, heightening the anticipation.

“Well?” he demanded. “Who else might be wearing the guise of Anubis?”

“The man who began it all,” I told him. “John de Morgan himself.”

CHAPTER 14

We argued for the better part of an hour. "You cannot be serious," he said more than once.

"As the grave," I replied. "All we know for certain is that de Morgan disappeared. We do not know where he is at present. Nor do we know what has become of him."

"I think it is bloody well obvious he met with foul play in that *hole* of a hotel," he returned hotly. "The changes to the room prove that."

"The changes to the room are theatrical window dressing. What was the point of them? To confuse and upset Caroline de Morgan. Or to give the appearance of upsetting her," I added as an afterthought.

"You still think she might be in league with John," he said sharply.

"I think it possible. She has been clever and devious enough to pretend she is having a mental collapse in order to avoid more questions by the police investigators. Consider, she left Egypt with her husband and turned up in Dover, hysterically claiming he has vanished. Has she been detained? Arrested for his murder? No. She has simply been handed over to the care of her parents. In time she will be forgot, and what then? With no body and no evidence against her, she will fade from notoriety. She can go where she likes, perhaps to meet up with him, perhaps to sell the jewel herself if she has betrayed him."

He looked at me for a long, inscrutable moment. "You are as good as accusing her of her husband's murder. At the very least you think her capable of conspiring with him. At worst, you think her a potential murderess."

"A potential murderess carrying a child," I said thoughtfully. "That does complicate matters. But that diadem would go a very long way towards supporting her and her infant if she made her escape from England."

He said nothing more. I turned to the rest of the post, leaving him with his thoughts.

There was the usual assortment of bills and circulars, letters and journals, and I collected everything in a basket to sort later. I took supper alone in my Gothic chapel, relishing my solitude.

Once I had eaten, I went to the Roman temple, where his lordship had installed the latest accomplishments in the plumbing arts. The wash in my own facilities had been insufficient after our Dover adventures, I decided. I needed a proper scrubbing from head to toe and all the attendant relaxation. In the temple were three plunge pools of varying temperatures as well as a soaking tub and a shower bath, the last of which I made full use of in order to scrub myself free of the lingering traces of soot. I returned to my little Gothic chapel to smoke and think over the case. I had supplemented my wardrobe with bits and pieces from the collection in the Belvedere, and my current dressing gown was a rather splendid and tattered robe from the Chinese imperial opera. It was scarlet silk, heavily fringed and embroidered, and I wore it belted at the waist, my hair loose as I sat before the fire to dry it.

Fatigued from our adventures in Dover, I slept, waking far later the next morning than was my custom. Still dressed in my robe of China silk, I perused the rest of the post as I brushed my hair, sorting the letters and bills from the periodicals. At length, all that remained was the parcel I had noted the day before our departure—plainly wrapped and lacking a postmark. I tossed the brown wrapping paper aside to find a pasteboard box of the most common variety. Within it, nestled carefully on a bed of excelsior, was another box, this one of brass worked with Egyptian motifs. I turned it over, but could find no significant markings, no note to identify the sender.

With a sigh, I put it aside and thrust my feet into slippers. Stoker was still sunk deeply into sleep, sprawled over the width of his bed like a starfish. His coverlet had slipped to his hips, revealing chest and belly, both admirably muscled, molded by the benevolent hand of Nature into a form so alluring, it would have given Michelangelo pause to sculpt it. I poked one delectable shoulder.

He growled and put a pillow over his head. "Go away."

"There has been a development in the case," I told him.

"I don't care if Queen Victoria herself has confessed to killing John de Morgan in Trafalgar Square. I need sleep."

"You need to get out of that bed," I countered. He growled again, and I reached for the coverlet, twitching it down another six inches to bare his iliac furrows. With a howl of outraged modesty, he bolted to a sitting position, hauling the coverlet up to his collarbone.

"Veronica, have some decency. You very nearly exposed my . . . *erm* . . ."

"Yes, I have seen your *erm* before, if you will recall. And you've nothing to be shy about. It's quite impressive."

He blushed furiously and yanked the coverlet up until only his eyebrows were visible. "My *erm* is mine to show when I wish, not for your prurient gawping when it suits you. What do you want?"

"I want you to come to my pavilion. I have something to show you. Whether you come naked or not is entirely your affair," I told him.

I hurried back to my pavilion to dress—the thin China silk robe was little comfort against the February chill—and stoked up the fire. Stoker was five minutes behind, still buttoning his shirt when he arrived.

"This bloody well better be worth it," he rasped.

I handed him the box. "From an anonymous party."

He scrutinized it carefully. "And you think it contains a threat?"

"Remember what happened the last time we received an anonymous box in the post?" I prodded.

He grinned. During our previous investigation we had received a clue in the form of a body part that had been carelessly left in the Belvedere until one of the dogs ate it.

Stoker was many things but stupid he was not. He turned the box away from us and opened it from behind. As soon as the lid was opened, a cobra sprang out, launching some six or seven feet across the room before coming to rest on my bed. It fell behind, landing with a *thud* upon the floor. Together we flattened ourselves, peering under the bed.

"It isn't moving," I told him. "Do you think it died from inanition whilst confined in the box?"

He took a closer look, then dove under the bed, emerging with the serpent clasped in one fist. "It didn't die because it was never alive. It was knit," he told me, tossing the thing in an easy arc.

I caught it reflexively. The surface was cheap wool, rough and inelegant, nothing like the smooth warmth of an actual snakeskin. "Shabby thing, isn't he?"

Stoker pointed to the embellishment of the hood and a peculiar dark mark upon the face. "It's got the teardrop marking under the eye. Someone went to a good deal of trouble to make us think, at least for an instant, that it was real."

"Pity they wasted the effort. I presume you have seen the thing in the wild?"

"And mounted dozens. Every army man who serves in the East brings one of the beastly things home, but they have often been badly done and I have to take them apart and rebuild them." He cocked his head curiously. "Where did you become acquainted with them?"

"A particularly memorable interlude at a marketplace in Madagascar. It is an incident I do not recall with especial fondness," I told him. "Where do we think this fellow came from?"

"I presume you have examined the wrappings?"

"No postmark. It was with the rest of the letters the day before yesterday."

"Which delivery?" he asked, narrowing his eyes.

"The one that was sitting on my desk when Figgy Tiverton was here," I said, keeping my voice carefully neutral. I needn't have bothered. He did not trouble to mask his outrage.

"Of all the vile insinuations! That shy and delightful girl," he began.

"You only think she is delightful because she worships you," I countered.

"She most certainly does *not*," he cut in sharply.

I held up a hand. "I am too fatigued for false modesty, Stoker. You have a peculiar effect upon the fair sex—we may agree upon that. And Miss Tiverton is merely the latest in a long line of females who have succumbed to your charms."

He was not mollified. "There is no possible way that Figgy Tiverton is responsible for that," he said, pointing to the woolen snake in my hand. He brandished the box at me. "There is a spring in here to launch the thing at an unsuspecting recipient. It has *fangs*. It was designed to provoke a response of sheer terror."

We fell silent. Then Stoker raised a point that had not occurred to me.

"The box was delivered the day before we went to Dover," he began. "It was intended as a threat of some sort."

"It failed spectacularly," I replied with some relish.

"But only because you have the sensitivity of a Russian boar," he pointed out. "Most women would have fainted or flailed at such a thing."

I opened my mouth, but he held up a quelling hand. "I know. You are not most women. It was intended as a compliment."

I sat a little straighter. "But why was it directed to me? You are engaged in the investigation as well. Why not put both our names on the parcel?"

Stoker gave me an inscrutable look. "Because whoever sent it—and I do not concede for a moment that it was Miss Tiverton—expected hysterics, no doubt with an eye to encouraging you to drop the investigation."

"How very curious. You wouldn't drop the investigation for such a silly reason. Why should I?"

"Most people are incapable of understanding a woman like you," he said simply. "You defy comprehension."

"That might be the nicest thing you have ever said to me." Being brushed with the black wings of death had done wonders for his temper. He was still prone to lapsing into silence, but his natural vitality had begun to assert itself once more.

"The timing raises another point," he went on. "If the box was intended as a warning and we did not heed it, then whoever wants us to leave John de Morgan in peace might attempt more drastic measures."

He removed the box from my hand. "Therefore, we must take the battle to them."

"'Them'? To whom? We don't know our enemy," I pointed out.

He shrugged. "Our movements are being observed, at least upon occasion. Otherwise, our little adventure in Dover would never have happened."

"You think it was a deliberate attempt on our lives and not a spontaneous act born of desperation?"

"Unlikely. It might have been purest coincidence that the hotel just happened to burn down the night we were there, but I don't like coincidences. I suspect the proprietress was put wise to our investigation and instructed to eliminate the evidence of John de Morgan's disappearance. The fact that we were there at the same time would have been two very tidy birds slain with a single stone—no corroboration for Caroline's story and no meddlesome sleuths determined to ask uncomfortable questions."

I nodded. "And somehow I do not like Mrs. Giddons for a mastermind. She is clearly answerable to someone, but whom?"

"That is what we need to discover. Go and put on a hat," he instructed. "We are bound for the Sudbury."

I am seldom inclined to do as I am told, but with Stoker's decisiveness came a resurgence of both his energy and his resolve, and I gave way with good grace, buttoning on my black astrakhan coat. My spirits were even more buoyed by the addition of a new hat—a fetching beaver top hat embellished with a cluster of lush red velvet roses and a length of black veiling tucked atop the rolled brim. The day was fine, at least as fine as may be expected in the killing fogs of February, and as we set off for the Sudbury even Stoker seemed jaunty. He wore his eye patch, and his normally tumbled locks were even more windblown than usual. He made no effort to subdue them, but merely clapped on a low, slouching hat purchased off a gaucho in the Argentine. The wide brim shadowed his face, giving him a menacing air, and as he enjoyed nothing better than frightening the timid, he set a brisk pace as we walked.

We arrived at the Sudbury in good order. Julien d'Orlande was presiding over the first service of the luncheon hour, supervising the appearance of every tray before it was carried up to the waiting guests. He adjusted a bit of crystallized mint on a plate of ices, nodding as if bestowing a benediction. He gestured for us to wait in his office and joined us as soon as he was able, flicking an invisible bit of lint from his immaculate coat as he did so.

"Hello, my friends. Please, make yourselves comfortable. I have arranged for some refreshments," he said, ushering in one of his staff, who carried a tray laden with tiny glasses of sharp blackberry cordial and another with a plate of tiny tarts shaped like quatrefoils and filled with sweetened almond-scented cream and topped with candied cherries.

Stoker sighed in rapture as he sank his teeth into the pastry. Then he gave a frankly indecent moan while I looked inquiringly to Monsieur d'Orlande.

"We have come about the Tivertons," I began.

"Mademoiselle Speedwell!" he said in a tone of lamentation. "What am I to do with you? I am an artist, and yet you think only of business." His expression was gently chiding, and he nodded once towards the pastry before me. "Eat that. Savor it. And then we will talk."

I did as he bade me, letting the crisp pastry melt on my tongue. He watched me narrowly, assessing my enjoyment of his arts, and I made the appropriate noises of appreciation. When I had swallowed the last delectable crumb, I settled back in my chair, folding my hands on my lap for good measure.

Julien threw his head back and laughed. "Like a schoolgirl. But you liked it?"

"It was heaven," I told him. Stoker nodded emphatically, his cheeks bulging with cream.

Julien accepted the praise as no more than his due. "I have worked for fifteen years to perfect that recipe. It is not yet what it can be, but it is better than it was."

"Will it ever be perfect?" I wondered.

"No," he told me with a smile. "Nothing in life is. But, my dear mademoiselle, life is not about achievement. It is about the effort. If one takes pleasure in every step, one enjoys the whole journey." His eyes were twinkling, and I realized he might well be the most contented person of my acquaintance.

"You wish to know about the Tivertons," he said, pulling a face. "They are dull beyond belief. Typically English! Milk puddings and boiled chickens." He glanced at the window overlooking his domain and flicked a finger. Instantly, a subordinate appeared, his attitude one of reverence as he approached the master. Julien gave him a careless look. "Ask Mademoiselle Birdie to come."

The fellow bobbed a head and vanished, reappearing almost instantaneously with a tiny, buxom brunette whose lavish curves were barely confined by the crisp lines of her chambermaid's uniform. Her curls were covered by a starched white cap, but they threatened to escape, and her lips were a trifle too pink to owe their color to nature rather than art.

She was a luscious-looking girl, but she had eyes only for the pastry chef. "Monsieur d'Orlande?" she asked breathlessly.

He introduced us briefly. "Miss Speedwell, Mr. Templeton-Vane, this is Birdie, the chambermaid who attends the Tivertons. Birdie, you will speak frankly to Miss Speedwell and Mr. Templeton-Vane," he instructed. "Whatever questions they put to you, you will answer."

She nodded, her eyes round and bright with the devotion of an acolyte. "Oh, yes, Monsieur!"

"Good girl," he said, his voice practically a purr. "Now, I regret to say that Mademoiselle Tiverton has resisted the charms of my pastries. She does not send her compliments, no matter what delicacies I prepare. I have learnt nothing."

I felt a rush of disappointment which must have been visible, for he lifted a quelling finger. "But I have perfect faith in Mademoiselle Birdie. My little *oiseau*, you have watched the Tiverton girl for me. What have you discovered?"

Birdie was eager to tell. "She's bored silly, Monsieur. Those parents of hers keep her on a short leash, they do. She doesn't go to shops or entertainments. She keeps to her room, reading her books—always sensational novels like Rider Haggard's."

Monsieur d'Orlande spread his hands in a thoroughly Gallic gesture.

"If she wants adventure, I would recommend to her Dumas, but that is neither here nor there."

"Does she have visitors?" Stoker asked.

The girl gave him a lingering look, paying homage to his attractions, but in the end she shrugged. Her attention was firmly fixed upon Julien. "Who would visit the little Tiverton? She is bored, I tell you. She goes out to walk the dog, and that is all. No callers, no going to the shops or entertainments. She talks to me sometimes, but I don't like to tell her about my life."

"Why not?" I asked.

Birdie tipped her head. "It sounds peculiar to say I feel sorry for her, miss, but I do. That father of hers is supposed to be so rich and high-and-mighty, but what good does it do her? I have three sisters and I have a laugh with every one of them. I go to the museums on my day off or the shops. I have friends and interests and a proper life. What does she have besides her dreary books and her dull papier-mâché?"

Stoker and I looked at one another, and a smile of sheer delight spread over his features. "Did you say papier-mâché?"

She glanced at Julien, who nodded his encouragement. "Yes, sir. Although why that should interest anyone, I cannot imagine. It is a pastime for children! But she is always asking me for newspaper, and there the poor girl sits in her room, making fruits and vegetables and ghastly heads out of whatever I can find her. It is most peculiar."

"On the contrary," I told her. "It is the most interesting thing in the world right now."

"I'm sure I don't know why," she began, but Julien lifted a brow.

"My little flower, who are we to judge the pleasures of others? We are responsible only for our own," he murmured.

She gave a breathy little sigh, and I flicked a glance to Stoker, who shrugged.

"Is there anything else you can tell us about the Tivertons?" he asked the girl.

She tipped her head, putting the tip of her tongue between her teeth as she thought. "Nothing that comes to mind, sir."

"Very well. If you think of anything else, you'll be sure to tell Monsieur d'Orlande directly, yes?"

She beamed ecstatically at Julien. "Of course."

She sketched a brief curtsy in our direction as Julien rose to walk her to the door. "You've done very well, my dove. Perhaps later you will come back and I will make for you a *religieuse*," he promised.

"Oh, what is that?" she asked, eyes wide with anticipation.

"It is the French word for 'nun,'" he told her. "But we will speak no more of chastity."

She gave a low giggle, and he closed the door behind her, turning back to us as he smoothed the velvet of his cap. I suppressed a smile, but Stoker looked at him reproachfully.

"She is half your age," he pointed out.

Julien d'Orlande lifted his hands in a perfectly Gallic gesture. "Who am I to quibble with the demands of Venus?"

"Mercury, more like, if you aren't careful," Stoker muttered.

"Stoker!" I said sharply. "Kindly do not make reference to the treatment of venereal diseases in polite company."

"I wouldn't exactly call Julien *polite*," he protested, but he said nothing more. I rose and gave Julien my hand.

"Forgive him. He's been out of sorts lately."

Julien's handsome mouth curved into a conspiratorial smile. "Really? How can you tell?"

We shared a laugh as Stoker regarded us sourly. Julien bent over my hand. "Ah, this sweet blossom of a hand! How I hate to relinquish it," he said, stroking it gently.

"Relinquish it or swallow your own teeth," Stoker told him in a pleasant tone laced with steel.

Julien shook his head. "Mademoiselle, does he often threaten violence in your gentle presence?"

"More than you would expect," I told him. "And he has even, upon one notable occasion, stabbed me. But since I am responsible for his being shot a few months ago, I am inclined to overlook his moods."

Julien straightened, clearly startled as he turned to Stoker. "You *stabbed* her?" he demanded.

Stoker looked mightily affronted. "Not deliberately! I would only ever stab Veronica on accident."

"Quite," I said, giving him a fond smile. "You are, for all your sins, Stoker, a gentleman."

We bade a befuddled Julien farewell and made our way through the Sudbury kitchens, emerging onto the pavement.

"I do wish you wouldn't tell people I stabbed you," Stoker protested.

"But you did," I pointed out. "I still have the scar."

"You bloody well do not! I stitched you up more prettily than the Bayeux Tapestry. Furthermore—" He was just warming to his theme when I stopped him with a hand to his chest. I may have applied rather more force than I intended, for he rocked backwards, stumbling into a coal hauler, and it was some several seconds before he disentangled himself and brushed off the coal dust.

"Veronica, what the devil are you about?" he demanded.

I grabbed his hand and towed him towards the corner, taking the precaution of pausing to peep around the building before emerging into view. "Look there," I instructed, jerking my chin.

Some little distance ahead, Figgy Tiverton was walking Nut.

"So? We know the girl walks the dog," he said in some irritation as he excavated a lump of coal from his pocket.

"Look at who Figgy is following," I ordered.

Forty or fifty yards ahead of Figgy walked a slender figure with a graceful, distinctive step.

"Lady Tiverton," Stoker said softly, catching the scent of an intrigue.

"Exactly. Now, why would young Figgy follow her stepmother without making her presence known?"

Without bothering to wait for a reply, I moved to follow Figgy. Stoker's hand clamped to my arm stayed me. "What do you mean to do?"

"Trail them, of course." I glanced at him, all six feet of distinctly male Revelstoke Templeton-Vane. He was dressed conventionally enough, in a town suit and proper shoes rather than his usual breeches and boots. But his hair was long, his hat was Bohemian, and his ears glinted with the gold of the loops threaded through each lobe. He looked like nothing so much as an Elizabethan privateer, and he would certainly attract attention just when we needed to be unremarkable. I pointed this out, to which he made a few rather sharp and somewhat nasty observations of his own—I believe the phrase "Roman prostitute" was bandied about with regard to my hat—and then I pulled down the veil on my hat, covering my face.

"Stay here," I hissed without bothering to wait for the inevitable protest. I slipped into the stream of foot traffic upon the Strand, following Figgy following her stepmother. It was easy enough to keep the child in view. She wore a sailor hat with a particularly lurid shade of yellow for the bow, and Nut kept darting in and out of the pedestrians, causing a bit of jolly havoc wherever she went.

Ahead of us, Lady Tiverton walked with purpose, looking neither left nor right. We followed her as she crossed a street—Nut nearly expiring under the hooves of a passing tram team—and turned several corners before her ladyship reached her destination. She entered a narrow stone building with a jaunty blue-striped awning. Figgy hesitated when she came to the building, then continued on, looking behind her once or twice with a doubtful expression.

I darted into a bookshop, browsing the volumes in the window as I kept a weather eye upon the street. After several minutes, Lady Tiverton emerged, carrying a parcel marked with the name of the business, Caswell and Co. Linen Drapers. I counted to thirty before stepping from the bookshop, but I needn't have bothered. I had assumed Figgy had carried on down the street, but this was a miscalculation. Just as I stepped from the bookshop, she passed, so close I nearly trod on Nut's paw. But the dog paid me no attention. Instead, she was straining at the lead, whining and lunging until the slim bit of leather slipped from Figgy's hands.

Without warning the dog dashed across the street, narrowly avoiding a streetcar and launching herself into the air. At the last moment Stoker caught her, holding her at arm's length as she squirmed in delight, lavishing licks to his face.

Figgy, with a cry of alarm, followed. I was not near enough to hear what Stoker said, but he must have spun her some tale, for she let him take Nut's lead in hand, setting the dog carefully onto her feet again. With great courtesy, Stoker offered his arm, and the girl took it, her blush apparent from across the street. They turned in the direction of the Sudbury, and I watched them go in frank irritation until I saw Stoker take his lead hand and flick a sign at me behind his back. It was a brisk gesture in the direction of the blue awning, and I understood instantly what he intended.

I entered the shop and waited to be attended to. A few minutes' skillful conversation extracted the information I wanted. By way of showing my appreciation, I made a purchase of my own from the clerk and returned to the Sudbury to collect Stoker.

He fell into step with me as I passed the hotel. "What did you learn?" he asked softly as we made our way to the Folly.

"Nothing of real importance and this case begins to task me. I am in need of physical exertion to clear my mental processes," I told him. I made my way directly to the Roman temple, where the plunge pool was located. Stoker was polite enough to wait until I had stripped off my clothes and paddled vigorously for some minutes before presenting himself. Too small for proper exercise, the plunge pool nonetheless provided an excellent opportunity for exercising the limbs, and I was rather deliciously invigorated by the time I emerged. With enormous delicacy, Stoker kept his back to me until I had wrapped myself in a Turkish robe I had left hanging in the bathhouse. Although mindful of my modesty—of which I had none, but it was sweet of him to think so—in contrast to his earlier mood, Stoker was perfectly heedless of his. He dropped his clothing with the nonchalance of Adam stalking through Eden without a fig leaf and slipped into the pool, crossing it several times with masterful strokes as I combed through my hair.

When he was finished, he swam to the edge, his dark head as sleek as a seal's. He folded his arms on the warmed tile, resting his chin as he gave me a long look.

"All right. Reveal all, I beg you."

I primmed my mouth in the manner of a student preparing a recitation. "At quarter past two this afternoon, Lady Tiverton entered the establishment of Caswell and Co., linen drapers, where she proceeded to purchase—wait for the shocking revelation, I beg you—handkerchiefs."

"Handkerchiefs? All that cloak-and-dagger nonsense from Figgy about following her stepmother and for handkerchiefs? How do you know?"

"A very helpful clerk was only too happy to reveal that they enjoyed Lady Tiverton's custom there. She chose very sober handkerchiefs woven with a narrow band of black at the edge."

"Half-mourning," he mused.

"We were told that she still observed mourning for the first Lady Tiverton. We have never seen her in a color other than grey," I agreed. "I don't approve of the current fashion for ostentatious grief, but I must applaud her loyalty. Her affection for her predecessor strikes me as thoroughly sincere."

"And yet Figgy is suspicious enough of her to track her like a bloodhound upon the most innocent of errands," Stoker said. "To what end?"

We fell silent a moment, contemplating that question. I formed my own theory, and the more I considered it, the more I liked it.

"What?" Stoker demanded. "You're thinking something. I can always tell from the unholy light in your eyes when an idea strikes you."

"One should not hypothesize without enough information," I reminded him.

He gave me a stern look, one that was slightly mitigated by his current state of near nudity. "Kindly do not lecture me on scientific method. Now, speak, woman."

"Very well. It simply occurred to me that much of the colorful prose spilling from the pen of Mr. J. J. Butterworth is markedly detailed. Perhaps too markedly for someone outside the expedition."

He was quick to seize the idea. "You think someone inside the expedition is feeding the blackguard information? *Figgy?*"

I shrugged. "Why not? We have already observed that she is a decidedly odd mix of child and adult. She is adventuresome enough to gad about town on her own. Why could she not have decided to supply the loathsome Butterworth with grist for his mill?"

"To what end?" Stoker argued. "The stories are upsetting to her father, whom she clearly adores."

"Adores and deplores," I reminded him. "Theirs is a prickly relationship. She might not mind upsetting him a trifle if it means distressing her stepmother. And the stories *do* vex Lady Tiverton. Besides which, you are overlooking the most obvious motivation. Members of the press have been known to remunerate their sources."

"Not scrupulous ones," Stoker pointed out.

"Does Mr. J. J. Butterworth strike you as particularly encumbered with such burdens as scruples?"

"Not especially," he admitted. He shook his head. "I still cannot believe the girl would stoop so low."

"I have a more thorough understanding of my own sex than you do," I said kindly. "I know the horrors of which we are capable."

"I have a little experience of that myself," he reminded me dryly.

"Yes, but you think such monstrosities are an aberration. In your generous heart of hearts, you still believe we are good and gentle and everything men are not. You are, in short, my dear fellow, entirely too romantical about the crueler sex."

He did not argue.

Abruptly, he flattened his palms on the tile and pushed, levering himself straight out of the water and onto the floor, like Poseidon rising from the deep. Rivulets of water cascaded from his body, shimmering over the taut muscles. A truly gracious woman would have looked away.

Our exercises concluded, we returned to the Belvedere in our dressing gowns to collect the evening post before returning to our respective abodes to prepare for dinner. As I put out my hand to the door, Stoker's fingers clamped about my wrist. Without a word he nodded, and I saw that it was ajar. I never shrank from confrontation, but I was hardly dressed for battle, I reflected ruefully. I stepped back and let him take the lead as I worked a sharpened hairpin out of my Psyche knot purely as a precaution.

We stepped inside, edging on silent feet towards the glow of light from the lamp that sat upon my desk. I was perfectly certain I had blown it out when I had finished my work, and we advanced as one, Stoker's hands clasped into loose fists, my hairpin at the ready.

We paused behind a handy caryatid, exchanged glances, and silently mouthed a count of three before springing out from the shadows.

CHAPTER 15

In the bedlam that erupted, I soon realized three things: 1. Our visitor was not bent upon harming us. 2. Our visitor was Mrs. Marshwood. 3. She was not actually being strangulated by a weasel in spite of her shriek and the fur at her throat. It was meant to be decorative.

She recovered herself quickly, putting a hand to her heart and fixing us with a repressive look. "How dare you come upon me like ruffians!" she demanded. "Is this any way to greet a caller?" Without waiting for a reply, she jerked her chin towards the enameled stove that formed the center of our little sitting area. "She is waiting for you. I tried to talk her out of this, but she insisted. I fear no good can come of it."

Caroline de Morgan was seated before the stove in a porter's chair that had once graced Versailles. The silk brocade was shattered, the gilt wood splintered, but there was a suggestion of former glory about it. The lady herself was wrapped in a heavy coat of moldering sables, no doubt a precaution against the chilly weather in her expectant state.

I looked at Stoker. "I am surprised the two of you don't get on better. You both have such a fondness for dead animals."

Caroline de Morgan raised her head and fixed me with a defiant stare. "If that is your idea of a cordial greeting, I will take my leave now."

I bared my teeth in a smile. "Do close the door firmly behind you. There's such a draft otherwise."

She curled a lip. "My business is not with you. I have come to speak to *him*." She gestured vaguely towards Stoker with a stick, and he heaved a sigh.

"I think we have said all that needs saying," he began.

She flapped her hand, startling the dogs. They had both taken refuge behind a cradle—a curious piece fashioned of half a tortoiseshell set in silver. They huddled behind the cradle, peering over the edge from safety. Cowards.

"There have been new developments," she informed us. "Can you not even bring yourself to offer the barest courtesies?" she demanded.

"Tea?" Stoker asked sweetly. "Coffee? Hemlock?"

She opened her mouth—no doubt to blast him—and I held up a hand. "That is enough from both of you. Yes, Mrs. de Morgan, I realize you came to speak with Stoker, but he is incapable of common courtesy in your presence. You bring out the worst in him. In his defense, I suspect you would drive the pope himself to strong drink. Now, I give you my word that Stoker will not poison you, but I encourage you to keep your remarks brief and to the point. What do you want?"

She did not like my taking charge of the situation, but if they were going to behave like recalcitrant schoolchildren, I was certainly capable of playing the nursery governess. She gave me a mutinous look and gestured towards a small carpetbag at her feet. "This is the only piece of baggage I brought out of Egypt. I want you to have it."

"Why?" Stoker demanded.

"Because someone wants it," she said darkly. "When I arrived from Dover, there was an attempt to take it from me at the train station. I thought nothing of it at the time. I presumed it was a common thief. The city is *full* of such blackguards," she said, clearly preparing to give vent to her feelings on crime in the capital.

I cut her off swiftly. "There must have been a new attempt to take it. What happened?"

She gave me a look of grudging approval. "You have a brain at least. I will give you that. Someone broke into our house last night—specifically, they broke into my rooms."

"Did you apprehend the fellow?" Stoker asked.

Her expression was sour. "We did not, thanks to the ham-fisted foolery of that imbecile butler. He tripped over a rug and was knocked completely senseless. Poor Papa nearly had an apoplexy fighting the thief off."

Stoker lifted a skeptical brow. "Mr. Marshwood fought off a housebreaker?"

"Well, not so much fought him off as surprised him," she amended.

"How do you know the housebreaker intended to steal the carpetbag?" I asked.

"Because it was in his hand! Papa surprised him and he dropped it as he fled."

"Did he get a look at the fellow?" Stoker inquired.

"Papa is not in the habit of consorting with thieves," she returned acidly. "Such a person is naturally beneath his notice."

Stoker rolled his eyes at such snobbery, but I took a more patient tack. "Do you believe you are in some sort of danger if you keep the bag on the premises?"

"How should I know?" she demanded. "But I will not have a repeat of it. Heaven knows what the villain will try next."

Stoker folded his arms over the breadth of his chest and cocked his head. There was an unholy light in his eyes. "If you truly believe you are in danger, you ought to hand that over to the Metropolitan Police."

"The Metropolitan Police are a collection of fools and half-wits," she said, her sables trembling in scorn. "They still believe I am quite possibly involved in a conspiracy with my husband. There is not a gentleman amongst them."

"And you think to find one here?" Stoker challenged with a grim smile.

She narrowed her eyes. "For all your sins, Revelstoke, and *they are legion*, you are a gentleman born and bred. You will not desert a lady in distress. It would be a violation of eight hundred years of breeding."

"I wonder how much it cost you to admit that," he said softly.

She glared at him, and I moved once more to pour oil upon troubled waters. "Leave it with us, Mrs. de Morgan."

"I don't think so," Stoker said in a dangerously even voice.

Caroline de Morgan and I turned as one woman to stare at him. "Stoker," I began.

"I am not inclined to offer my assistance."

"Of course you aren't," I said in a reasonable tone, "but that shouldn't stop you from doing it. If there have been two attempts to recover the bag, there might be something significant about it—" I broke off. "How stupid of me. Of course there is something significant."

Stoker flicked me an approving glance. "You begin to understand her. There is something she has not told us."

Caroline de Morgan opened her mouth, then snapped it shut as a tide of furious color rose in her cheeks. "Very well," she managed finally. She thrust the bag at me, and I handed it to Stoker.

He opened it far enough that we could peer inside. There were the usual items one might expect from a woman traveling abroad. A few toilet articles, a change of linen, a soiled shirtwaist. There was a romantic novel of the most torrid variety—something I should not have expected from Caroline de Morgan. These Stoker put to the side, revealing an apparently empty bag. I gave him a querying glance, but he had already anticipated my question. With a conjuror's quickness, he lifted out a false bottom. Beneath it nestled a pasteboard box, and I went to stand next to him as he opened it.

On a bed of plain cotton wool lay the diadem of Princess Ankheset.

The homely little nest did nothing to detract from its beauty. The sinuous lines, the glow of the gold, the glimmer of the jewels. I could well imagine the princess of the Eighteenth Dynasty settling the slender crown onto her oiled black braids, lifting her chin imperiously.

Caroline de Morgan said nothing, but her gaze was mutinous as she watched us survey the little crown.

"You have had this the whole time," I said, unable to keep the accusation from my tone.

"I did not know the diadem was there," she said quickly. "I did not travel with jewels and had no reason to open the hidden compartment. It was not until this morning when I was thinking about the attempt last night to steal it that I wondered—"

"If John really was a thief," Stoker finished flatly.

"If John took that diadem, he had his reasons," she insisted. "And I want to know what they were."

"Isn't it obvious?" I asked gently. "Apart from the mummy, this is the centerpiece of the Tiverton find. It is worth a great deal of money."

Her glance to me was scornful. "John would not have *stolen* it," she swore.

"Very true," Stoker said with quiet malice. "After all, John de Morgan never took anything that didn't belong to him."

She gasped as if he had struck her. Then a slow, cruel smile spread over her face. "How vicious you are. I never imagined the depths to which you could sink."

"Didn't you? You're the one who told the world what I was. Are you now so surprised to find proof of it?"

She stepped closer, raising herself to her full height. "You will do this for me, Revelstoke."

"And how do you mean to compel me?" he asked, his voice curiously detached.

"I know what happened last year. You did not even realize I saw, did you? But you thrashed John in plain sight of me. I can describe every filthy blow in sickening detail. I can tell the whole story and make certain everyone knows you are John's greatest enemy. I wonder, will your life stand up to scrutiny a second time?" She flicked a glance to me. "Won't your association with *her* prove interesting fodder for the newspapers? What exactly do you get up to here?" she demanded, spreading her hands wide to encompass the chaos of the Belvedere. "I call in broad daylight to find the pair of you not even respectably dressed. You're flushed and damp, the pair of you," she went on, dropping insinuation into every syllable. "What have you been doing with yourselves? I will make certain the newspapers ask. And you know what journalists are, Revelstoke. Once they catch scent of the game, they will stop at nothing to run you to earth. You survived the last time. Do you really want to expose Miss Speedwell to their ugly tricks?"

She stopped, her color high with triumph, and I realized with a sickening jolt to my stomach that she was actually enjoying herself. Something about torturing him *pleased* her. She was the sort of woman who would pluck the wings from a butterfly and smile as she did so.

"Do you really think your own behavior could stand up to scrutiny?" Stoker asked. "I could tell them the truth, you know. I could tell them that I found you in John's tent. Three months my wife and yet you had your thighs around another man's waist. Shall I tell them that?"

Caroline de Morgan's knuckles turned white as she gripped the chair so hard I thought the wood would break under her grasp. "You lie," she gasped, but the words were empty. She did not mean them. Something in his quiet litany of the facts had broken her resolve.

"Do I lie?" he asked softly. "Am I lying if I tell them that when a jaguar attacked me in the jungle, you and John left me for dead? Am I lying when I say that you knew the truth and still you peddled your filthy fabrications to anyone who would listen? You painted me a brute and a monster, and all the while you knew what you were, didn't you?"

She opened her mouth, but Stoker's quiet voice cut across her, forcing her to silence. "For the longest time, I did not understand you, but I do now. You did what you must, didn't you? You told the only story you could, because to tell the truth meant admitting that you are a monster. You married me for money and a name, but your vows were a lie from the moment you spoke them. You wanted John. You loved John. But you could not stomach the notion of marrying a poor man, a man like your father and brothers. You wanted security more than anything and you sold your soul to get it. But you couldn't face up to what you had done. Why? Did some flicker of guilt kindle in your soul? I suspect not. I suspect it was John who was remorseful about what the pair of you did to me. It didn't matter in the end. You both told the same story, the only story you could tell, that you left me because I was brutal to you." She made a low moan of protest, but he spoke on, silencing her with his litany of accusations. "I wonder sometimes if you took John just to prove that you could. He hated you at first. Did you know that? He warned me off marrying you, said I would regret it. Curious, isn't it, how right he was? I have had a lot of time to think of things as they were then. Do you know how many sleepless nights you can pass in a year? Two? Three? There isn't a night I close my eyes that I don't think of the mistakes I have made and the tragedies I have wrought with my own two hands. But they are nothing compared to what you have done."

Her mouth worked furiously, but she did not attempt to speak. I think she understood by then that the dam had broken and Stoker would have his say, come the devil himself.

"It took me a long time to understand why John told me not to marry you. I thought he was jealous that I had found someone and he had not. It's because he already knew what you were, didn't he? He was so unhappy those last few months. That's why I wanted to take him to Amazonia. I thought he would recover something of himself, but that wouldn't have been possible, would it? He was already in love with a woman who did not deserve him, but he could not bear to tell me the truth about you. Still, he was wiser than I was. He knew you for what you were and he loved you anyway. I loved only the illusion, the mirror face you chose to show me. I wonder which of us I pity more."

A silent angry tear slid down her cheek. She did not brush it away. She wore it instead like a badge, defiantly, letting it run into the collar of her coat, wetting the fur.

"I won't make the mistake of thinking that tear is for me," he said, each word weighted with pain. "They are crocodile tears and I do not believe them. I seem to recall John has an uncle, a baronet with a tidy fortune and a line of dead sons. Tell me, with John missing, who will inherit when that uncle dies? If the child you carry is a son, you will have control of it—the estate, the money. Quite a pretty packet. And you don't even need John, do you? You are wed, so any child born to the marriage is legally his. As long as that baby is healthy and male, whoever controls the child controls the fortune. Tell me I am wrong."

With each word, she had lowered her head, beaten down by the weight of his accusations. But at his command, she flung her head up, defiance kindling in her eyes. "What of it? Do you think to sit in judgment of *me*, Revelstoke? What do you know of being a woman? Of suffering the whole of your life for the mistakes the men in your family have made? My father, my brothers, my husband—over and over the same story, letting everything slip through their fingers through what? Carelessness? Stupidity? Women, horses, bad investments, gambling. A thousand excuses, but it all comes back to the same thing: your sex is weak," she said, fairly spitting the words. "It is always down to us to make of life what we can, to recover from your mistakes and to carry on. Yes. I want the de Morgan fortune.

I admit it. We are very nearly destitute, and my child's inheritance is the only thing standing between us and ruin. I will do whatever I must to secure it. I will have a son, and I will take what is mine. Does that make me a monster? It makes me a survivor," she spat.

Before Stoker could speak, I moved to take the diadem out of his hands. They were tightening into fists around the crown, and already I could see the box bending. I replaced the lid and set the box to the side. I repacked the carpetbag and handed it to Caroline de Morgan.

"Your property, Mrs. de Morgan. We will keep the crown, and we will discover what happened to your husband. Not because of your feeble attempt at blackmail but because it is the right thing to do. I am certain that motivation is foreign to you, but you will have to accept it."

She darted a look at Stoker. "Is that all? Are you going to set your lapdog on me?"

I stepped between them just as Stoker moved. "You enjoy your games, Mrs. de Morgan. That much is obvious. And baiting Stoker obviously gives you tremendous pleasure. But let me make one thing perfectly clear: so long as I draw breath, you will not hurt him again."

She gave me a thin smile, drawing her sables about her with an imperious air. "And who are you to stop me?"

"I am the woman who knows twenty ways to kill you and all of them with pain," I told her with an answering smile. "Now, take your carpetbag and your decaying mother and leave. If you come here again, I will not be answerable for my actions."

She pointed to the crown and her hand was steady. "Judge me however you like. I care not. Just find my husband. I know you will not refuse me, no matter what has passed before. Your honor will not permit it." Her lip curled as she looked at Stoker. "As I said, your sex is weak. If my unborn child were Miss Speedwell's enemy, she would cut its throat in the cradle. We are the daughters of Hera, Miss Speedwell. It is what keeps us alive. I will see myself out."

It was not until the door slammed behind her that the dogs brought their heads above the edge of the cradle.

I did not look at him. I went instead up to the snuggery and poured a glass of aguardiente, a double measure, and drank it off. I poured another and handed it to him as he appeared at the top of the stairs. He drank his slowly, holding the bitterness on his tongue.

"You are forty kinds of a fool," I said finally. "I cannot believe that you loved such a creature, that you, with all your gifts, could have been blinded by beauty to so much malice."

"Believe it," he replied simply.

I poured a second measure of aguardiente for myself and another for him. He stared into the little cup as a Gypsy scrying his fortune. Then he gave a laugh, bitter and mirthless.

"What?" I demanded. "You cannot be drunk yet. You've scarcely begun."

"She is right, you know. All this time, all that has happened, and she still knows me better than anyone because she knows what I endured without a word. All that public humiliation, the agony of my name being dragged through the mud, never to be clean again. She was right to call me weak."

"What does she know?" I sipped at the aguardiente, warming my belly with the fire of it.

He shook his head and looked at me with eyes that seemed to have seen a thousand years.

"Everything the newspapers printed about me," he said in a hollow voice. "The beatings and the mistreatment. It's all lies. I never touched a hair of her head."

"Stoker, I never thought you really visited violence upon your wife. It is not in your nature to bring harm to the innocent."

"The innocent. God, to think of her in those terms! But she was innocent, at least where I was concerned."

He broke off, giving me a level look.

"You mean, you did not—"

"Never."

"But she was your wife."

"She played the part of the coy maiden well during our courtship. She never let me so much as kiss her. I pressed her hand and thought myself privileged. When our wedding night came, I took her into my arms to kiss her and she began to tremble. I did not mind. I was no virgin, but I was scared, so frightened of hurting her. I thought we could be terrified together. And that's when she told me she could not."

"She refused you?"

"Categorically. And she made it clear that she was not prepared to be a wife to me in the fullest sense of the word—ever."

I thought of him as he must have been then, before life and time and pain had changed him. He must have been so handsome it hurt to look at him, offering his heart to her. And she had twisted it in her hands, mangling it as a child will break a toy. Hatred, hot and violent and satisfying, coursed through my veins, drumming a rhythm in my head.

"You might have annulled her," I said in a voice I did not recognize.

He looked surprised. "It never occurred to me. I was prepared not to have her body if it meant I could have her heart. That, she pretended to give. She was affectionate and sweet, and I thought she meant it. I believed that over time I could bring her to share my bed if only I was patient enough, kind enough. I did not yet realize she refused me her maidenhead because she could not bear the touch of my hands upon her. And all because I was not John."

He laughed, that peculiar unhappy sound that twisted my guts. "What kind of fool loses his wife to his best friend?"

"You weren't a fool," I said slowly. "You were in love with her."

He looked at me in surprise. "In love with her? It seems impossible now, but I thought so. I thought it was love, but I was so very wrong. I have never known love, at least not until—"

He broke off sharply and took a swift drink. My heart thudded against my ribs, and I was conscious of a single thought. *Not like this.*

I changed the subject with brutal haste.

"Why did she marry you if she was in love with John de Morgan?"

He waved an impatient hand. "He was poor and his prospects were worse. Her parents would have permitted the match, but Caroline tortured him. She mocked his poverty and teased and tormented him. I thought it was silly banter, the games a comely girl will play with a suitor she does not mean to have. I excused her cruelty at the time, but it ought to have warned me. I ought to have seen her for what she was." He passed a hand over his face. "God help me, I did. I did see the cruelty in her and I mistook it for a game. I never realized she meant it. I thought her wild and dangerous and exciting. And she was exactly what my parents wanted for me—beautiful and accomplished. She danced like an angel and spoke good French and that was supposed to be enough. But John knew."

"What were his feelings?"

He spread his hands helplessly. "I don't even know. He said almost nothing about her except that feeble attempt to talk me out of marrying her. I even joked that he was jealous, and he laughed with me. I ought to have seen he was half-sick with longing for her. They could not be within twenty feet of each other or they quarreled. I was so naïve," he said, taking up the cup to drain it. "I thought they merely needed time to get to know one another better. It was important to me, I told them, that they become friends. I insisted upon the Amazonian trip as a means to bring them closer together."

He curled one lip in disgust. "Do you have any idea how much I have hated myself?"

"For what?"

"For all of it. For falling for her machinations and marrying her when I could not see her for what she was. For not understanding her or myself. For not pushing John to tell me what was really in his heart." He paused. "Did you ever read mythology when you were a child?"

"Insatiably."

"So did I. I was always affected by those couples who seemed destined for one another. Eurydice and Orpheus. Hero and Leander. Pyramus and Thisbe. I thought at some point in my life, I would have a great love like that, a woman fashioned by the gods just for me, as I had been made just for her, that we would find each other. I always believed she was waiting for me. But I did not wait for her. I married a base metal when the gods had promised me gold." He gave a great sigh that seemed to empty him from the soul.

"How did John come to marry her in the end? If he knew her true character?"

His expression was bereft. "Because she got into his soul, and there is no cure for a man when a woman does that. She seduced him on the expedition, caught him in a moment of weakness, and when they were discovered and I was halfway to death's door, they would have had only one way out then—they had to paint me as vicious a devil as they could. It was the only chance they had to salvage their life together. They sacrificed me to purchase a future, and I know what that cost John. He sold every last scrap of his self-respect when he did that to me. That is why he stood still and let me beat him when we finally came face-to-face. Every blow I landed drew blood, and never once did he lift a finger to stop me." His mouth twisted at the memory. "And when I had knocked him to the ground and you could hardly see his face for the blood, do you know what he did? The bastard smiled at me. He raised his hand in forgiveness and he smiled at me. And I turned on my heel and walked away. I left him, bleeding into the gutter, without a backwards glance."

He put aside the cup. "So now you know the worst of me, Veronica. It isn't that I killed a man in Brazil or bought prostitutes or spent my youth in a thousand debaucheries. It is that my greatest pleasure in life has been beating a man nearly to death because he took what I loved. We are not supposed to rejoice in the pain of others, but it feeds me. Every time I think of him, taking what ought to have been mine—my wife, my name—and paying for it with his heart's blood, I am glad of it."

"There are those who would tell you to give up such bitterness," I told him. "That kind of hatred will only poison you from within."

He gave me a cold smile. "Do not fear for me, Veronica. The devil takes care of his own."

It was Stoker's idea for me to wear the diadem to the Tiverton reception at Karnak Hall that evening.

"You must be joking," I told him flatly. "It does not suit what I am wearing." I had donned my best evening gown, a severely cut violet satin that flattered my figure and the color of my eyes. Innocent of the usual furbelows and embellishments, it boasted neither ruffles nor rosettes, only a graceful fall of fabric from a gently gathered bustle and a precise, almost military sharpness to the pin tucks.

Stoker regarded me from the top of my neatly coiled hair to the tip of my purple evening slippers. He canted his head, studying my appearance with the critical eye of an artist.

"I rather think it will do. The gown is quite plain, and you have no jewels. Against that witch black hair of yours, the coronet will show to good effect."

"I cannot simply appear wearing the crown of Princess Ankheset," I protested. "In the first place, it is stolen property that must be returned to the Tivertons."

"They won't mind," he said dismissively. "No doubt the newspapers will have sent representatives, and seeing it displayed on the head of a beautiful woman will garner them inches in the press."

I ignored the compliment; it was not intended as such. Stoker was a scientist and merely made observations. If he thought me beautiful, it was only because of an accidental arrangement of proportions and features over which I had no control and could claim no credit.

"I am not supposed to be making a spectacle of myself in the press, or had you forgot? My family won't like it."

"Your family can hang for all I care," he said succinctly.

"Save your republican notions," I warned him. "We cannot possibly explain this to the satisfaction of the Tivertons."

"Leave that to me," he replied with the assurance of a man whose blood ran blue. "Besides, you are overlooking one important factor. If you appear wearing the diadem, we have the element of surprise. We already suspect Figgy and Lady Tiverton separately of some mischief. We can observe their reactions."

I hesitated. The scheme, while theatrical in the extreme, did appeal to me. While I pondered, Stoker reached out and slipped half a dozen pins from my hair.

"That took the better part of an hour!" I protested. He ignored me entirely and busied himself redressing my hair until it tumbled about my shoulders, only the front half of it winged back, baring my temples. He lifted the diadem from its cotton nest, carefully settling it onto my hair. It fitted low on the brow, circling my head, and might have been a trifle too large but for the pinned locks that filled it snugly. He smoothed the slim golden ribbons, drawing one along either side of my face to frame it, and letting the others trail down the back, mingling with the tresses he had freed.

He stepped back to observe his handiwork, scrutinizing from every angle. "It will do," he pronounced finally. He handed me a mirror—a chinoiserie piece from a collection once belonging to Catherine the Great—and awaited my verdict. The violet of the gown highlighted the blue of the lapis and the purple of the plummy agates while the carnelians blazed orange fire with incendiary contrast. The effect was startling, and from the collarbone up, I looked quite unlike a modern Victorian woman.

"I suppose you are right," I told him with more reluctance than I felt. "Let us bait a mousetrap and I shall be the cheese."

CHAPTER 16

The hansom drew up to the curb in front of Karnak Hall, and I marveled at the difference a few days had made. The atmosphere was positively electric as carriages arrived, dispensing the great and the good dressed in their finest. Several of the ladies sported Egyptian-themed jewels or gowns, and I realized my diadem might not occasion as much discussion as Stoker and I had expected.

The Metropolitan Police were in evidence as well. Caped bobbies strolled past, their uniforms smart, their buttons shined to brilliance, no doubt in honor of the expected arrival of the Prince of Wales. A few members of Special Branch milled about the crowd, keeping themselves discreetly at the edge of the gathering. I caught a brief glimpse of Mornaday, deep in conversation behind a potted palm. Ever the flirt, he had managed to find a slender young woman to dally with, although his expression was serious. I could not see hers, for her back was turned, but I was not surprised Mornaday had singled her out. He had an unfashionable partiality to ginger hair, I recollected with a smile. Stoker and I proceeded into the Hall in search of our hosts.

Sir Leicester and Lady Tiverton were in the lobby, greeting guests as they arrived. The baronet was dressed in traditional evening wear, and his lady wore a silk gown of dove grey, unremarkable except for her own quiet grace and a spectacular necklace of Egyptian design. Her complexion was paler than I had seen it yet, with soft plum shadows beneath each eye. Her hand was laid upon her husband's sleeve, the fingers curled protectively. She looked up as we approached, the first to see us, and gave a little gasp.

The noise drew the attention of her husband. Sir Leicester swiveled his head like an owl, his gaze moving instantly to the diadem.

"Miss Speedwell!" he exclaimed, his eyes fairly popping from their sockets.

I fixed a bright smile. "I thought you would be pleased to see we have recovered it."

"'Pleased' is not the word," he began.

Stoker stepped up to my elbow. "We hoped that you would be so pleased you would overlook my gaucherie in persuading Miss Speedwell to wear it. A little joke," he finished.

Sir Leicester eyed the diadem. "I don't know." He hesitated. "It is, of course, a very valuable and ancient artifact."

Before Stoker could reply, Patrick Fairbrother approached looking harried. "Sir Leicester, I am sorry, but there is some question about the lighting of the dais when the sarcophagus is revealed, and I did not like to decide—" He broke off as he caught sight of the diadem. "I say, Miss Speedwell, is that—can it be—"

"It is," I replied, putting a tentative fingertip to the vulture hovering just above my brow.

"But where—how did you recover it? Have you found John de Morgan?" Lady Tiverton asked anxiously.

"We have not," Stoker told her. "And we are happy to disclose how we happened to gain possession of the diadem, but not now. You have guests to whom you must attend. I presume this *is* the coronet that went missing when de Morgan disappeared?" He raised his brows, surveying the small group of Egyptologists.

"Most assuredly," Sir Leicester pronounced. He looked at Stoker. "I am still not persuaded that letting Miss Speedwell wear it is the soundest proposition."

"Oh, but, sir," Fairbrother broke in. "Forgive me, but I think it a most excellent notion." He glanced over his shoulder towards the collection. "We did not anticipate its recovery, so we have no suitable vitrine for its display. The best we could do is jostle it in amidst the pots and canopic jars, and that hardly seems fitting. Far better to let it be shown to such superb effect upon the head of a lovely woman," he finished, bowing slightly.

His patron sighed. "I suppose you are right, Patrick." He turned to his wife. "What say you, my dear?"

She smiled. "Miss Speedwell looks quite magnificent. I think it could not be displayed half so well in any other fashion."

Sir Leicester nodded slowly. "All right, then. Miss Speedwell, I suppose I need not impress upon you the enormity of the responsibility you have taken on. You bear the weight of antiquity upon your head."

I murmured something suitable and turned to Lady Tiverton. "The crown is certainly remarkable, but your own jewel is very nearly as fine," I said, nodding to the thickly beaded collar at her throat.

"Do you like it, Miss Speedwell?" she asked, touching the necklace with a tentative fingertip. "It is a pectoral piece once belonging to Princess Ankheset." She pitched her voice low. "My husband excavated it. It is a point of pride with him, and it is in tribute to Sir Leicester that I wear it, although I must confess I feel unworthy."

He caught the last of her statement and patted her hand. "None of that," he said firmly. "It becomes you."

"And no doubt will further excite interest in the treasures you have brought out of Egypt," Stoker said with calculated blandness.

"Indeed, sir, indeed," Sir Leicester agreed. He adopted a confiding tone. "I understand Figgy came to see you. I hope she didn't make a nuisance of herself."

"Not at all," I said. "She was calling upon Lady Wellingtonia and was interested in our work at the Belvedere. She is welcome at any time."

"I am glad to hear it." Before he could reply further, Lady Tiverton gestured towards the decor of the Hall.

"Was it not the greatest stroke of luck that we were able to secure this hall to display the finds? The setting is most atmospheric, is it not?"

The interior of the Hall was much the same as the outside, all Egyptological paintings and terra-cotta-colored walls. Here and there potted palms gave the impression of the out-of-doors, and the carpet was the color of stone.

"Most atmospheric," I agreed.

"Naturally, we have attempted to improve the decorations," she added, indicating the long linen banners hung at the main doorway into the Hall. "Poor Mr. Fairbrother only just finished supervising the hanging of the banners before the doors were opened." The banners were decorated with the cartouche of Princess Ankheset and images of lotus flowers and gods, all rendered in gilt paint and brilliant reds and ochres and blacks.

"I could almost fancy myself in ancient Egypt," I said, nodding to Mr. Fairbrother.

He smiled down at me. "Your praise is more than I deserve, but I will accept it with pleasure."

"The banners are lovely, Mr. Fairbrother," I assured him.

"They were devilishly difficult to install," he said, bending his head close to mine. "I had to strip to the waist and climb like an athlete to get them into place. I only wish you had been here to see it."

With a rush of pleasure, I realized Patrick Fairbrother was flirting with me. I tipped my head and made good use of my lashes. "I regret that I was not," I said in a low voice.

He grinned at me. "Come and see the exhibition," he urged. "It really is quite astonishing." Stoker had fallen into conversation with Sir Leicester, and Lady Tiverton was welcoming another party, so I accepted the arm that Patrick Fairbrother offered. He guided me through the doorway into the expanse of the Hall itself. I stood on the threshold for a moment, dazzled by the brilliant blue gleam of faience, the warm glow of the gold. "Magnificent, isn't it?" His breath stirred the slender gold ribbon at my ear.

"Entirely magnificent," I said in perfect honesty. Like the foyer, the inner Hall had been furnished with potted palms and hung with linen banners to conjure a scene out of ancient Egypt. With Fairbrother as my guide, I was introduced to the Tiverton collection. He pointed out simple things, like gilded wooden chairs and screens, noting the workmanship and explaining the symbols. But his real enthusiasm was for the jewels—startlingly bright beaded strings in delectable colors: carnelian red, lapis blue, jade green, and everywhere the burnished brilliance of gold. He showed me a tiny gazelle, poised midleap, and a set of hair combs fashioned with such delicacy they would have suited only a royal head.

"But here is the piece that made me think instantly of you," he said, pointing to a necklace that had been displayed outside of any case, hung almost carelessly upon the neck of a pottery vase. It was a slender strand of beads, rather short so that it must fit close at the base of the throat, and composed of alternating materials, gold and lapis. From the center, a single charm depended, a graceful butterfly, its lapis wings unfurled, the delicate veins marked with fine threads of gold.

"Remember what I told you about butterflies in the tombs of the pharaohs," he said in a low voice. "Resurrection and beauty."

"Exquisite," I breathed. I put out a fingertip as if to touch the cartouche, but he grabbed my hand.

"Miss Speedwell, you mustn't," he cautioned with a smile. "Look, but do not touch."

As if to ensure my compliance, he kept my hand clasped in his as I admired the necklace. After a long moment, he stopped a passing waiter to secure two glasses of champagne. "It has cost us much to bring these treasures out of Egypt, but tonight is our triumph. Drink a toast with me, Miss Speedwell."

"Very well. What are we toasting?" I asked, accepting the glass.

"To unexpected adventures," he said, holding my gaze as he touched his glass to mine.

"To Princess Ankheset," I added, gesturing to the draperies which concealed the sarcophagus on the dais. "May she rest in peace."

He smiled a wary smile. "You do not approve of the public display of the coffin?"

I shrugged. "Not exactly. I understand the need for knowledge, but perhaps in a more private venue, for scholars only," I suggested. "Rather less of a fairground attraction."

The smile warmed. "Well, perhaps you have a point," he began.

Suddenly, something brushed my leg, and I moved quickly to the side, pressing myself inadvertently against Mr. Fairbrother's muscular form.

"It's only Nut," he said, coaxing the dog out from behind my skirts. "But I shall thank her for that," he added with a meaningful glance.

Lady Tiverton approached then, her expression slightly harried. "Patrick, I'm afraid Nut will make a nuisance of herself. Figgy was supposed to keep her close at hand, but she must have forgot." I had glimpsed Figgy darting behind the dais as her stepmother approached, her expression mulish. She was dressed in a youthful frock of yellow dimity, a dreadful color on her, and she had spent the better part of the evening skulking behind the potted palms, staring balefully at the crowd. Parties, it seemed, were not her favorite diversion.

Fairbrother downed the rest of his champagne in one swallow and took the dog by the collar. "Come along, little brute," he said with some fondness. "Let's go and find you a chicken to eat."

"Thank you," Lady Tiverton called after him. She gave me a small smile. "I am sorry to have interrupted," she began in a faltering voice.

"There was nothing to interrupt. Mr. Fairbrother was simply being hospitable," I assured her.

"I apologize if Nut alarmed you. She's a dear, really, but she can be terribly excitable, and Figgy will forget to look after her." She touched me lightly on the arm. "About her visit, I do hope she did not make a nuisance of herself."

Poor Figgy! I thought. Little wonder the child felt suffocated if her call had already occasioned such interest. I repeated what I had told Sir Leicester, and Lady Tiverton nodded.

"She scarcely knows Lady Wellingtonia. Calling upon her was merely a pretext." She hesitated, then darted a glance to where Stoker was still in conversation, his manly form shown to advantage in the stark perfection of his evening clothes, his expression serious. In spite of his untamable hair and his earrings, he looked like a master of creation. "He is a difficult man to ignore, and Figgy is an imaginative creature," she said, leaving the statement hanging in the air.

"You need have no fear, my lady. Miss Tiverton is as safe with Stoker as with a monk. His manners may be occasionally rough, but he is every inch a gentleman, cradle-born."

The grave eyes rounded in horror. "Miss Speedwell, you must not think for a moment I meant to suggest otherwise. No, no. The lack of propriety would originate with Figgy. I am fond of my stepdaughter," she said in a rueful voice. "But it has been difficult to be a true mother to her. She has resisted my efforts. She does not confide in me."

"Perhaps if she were a little more at liberty," I suggested.

"But how can one give liberty to a child so ill equipped for it?" she asked gently. "She is clever, like the Wards, but in temperament, she is not like her mother. The first Lady Tiverton was a scholar, very lively and merry, but serious about her interests. As Figgy has matured, I have begun to worry about her. She has demonstrated a certain wildness of temper, an intractable will of her own. It tasks her father greatly," she confided. "We do not know exactly what to do with her."

If it tasked her father, he had only himself to blame, I reflected. Figgy was nothing less than his spitting image in this regard. "Have you considered educating her?" I asked. "She is not unintelligent. Perhaps she just needs a bit of schooling to get her out of the habit of being useless."

Her eyes took on a shuttered expression. "She longs to go to school, but my husband cannot bear to be parted from her. He is a devoted father," she said with a touch of defensiveness.

"I am certain of it," I told her. "But perhaps for her own good, he might be persuaded to let her go."

She spread her hands. "I am sometimes at a loss, I do not mind telling you. He does not discipline her as he ought, and I cannot. A stepmother must naturally tread softly."

"I think," I said slowly, "that Figgy will make her own way in the end."

Lady Tiverton roused herself. "I must beg your pardon, Miss Speedwell! What must you think of me? Prattling on about our family troubles in such a fashion?"

Before I could make a suitable response, Sir Leicester mounted the dais in front of the curtains screening the sarcophagus of the Princess Ankheset.

"Pray, silence, friends!" he called. The dull roar of the assembled crowd fell to a muted buzz. Sir Leicester went on. "I am no great maker of speeches," he began. "But I must welcome you all here to Karnak Hall upon this grand occasion." He went on to talk about the expedition, glossing over the difficulties and heaping praise upon the members of his team. He recounted the thrill of discovering the cave for the first time, the slender crevice in the rock which was to answer the hopes of a lifetime for him.

He spoke briefly of Jonas Fowler, the late expedition director, and not at all of John de Morgan. Instead he lifted his glass and said, in ringing tones, "She has lain in silence and in dignity for millennia, but tonight I give you, with all her treasures, the Princess Ankheset!"

The crowd responded, glasses lifted high. "Princess Ankheset!" Lady Tiverton went to her husband then to share in receiving the accolades of the guests, while I drifted off. Stoker was nowhere to be found, doubtless following a trail of his own, and I allowed myself to be caught up in admiration of the finds. I was particularly taken with a set of sandals made of beaten gold, thin as a sheet of paper. Grouped with them was a set of twenty hollow golden pieces, shaped like thimbles but much longer, and clearly meant to cover the ends of the fingers and toes.

"They look devilishly uncomfortable, don't you think?" asked a young woman who appeared at my side. Instantly, I recognized her as the person who had been in close conversation with Inspector Mornaday upon our arrival. Unlike the other ladies who had come in their finest evening gowns, wearing jewels to rival the princess', this lady was quietly dressed in a sober gown of dark blue. Her hair was reddish and coiled in a heavy, serviceable knot at the nape of her neck. A governess or companion attached to one of the more illustrious guests?

"I should think them uncomfortable in the extreme," I agreed.

"Well, perhaps it is worth it to suffer a little to be a princess." She peered into the case for a moment, then slanted me a curious look. "I find it odd that Sir Leicester did not mention the mummy's curse with regard to the death of Jonas Fowler, don't you? Nor the disappearance of John de Morgan."

I shrugged. "No doubt he wished the attention to be fixed on the success of the expedition, not sensationalist superstition."

"I should think misplacing a staff photographer and a priceless diadem would be something more than a superstition. And to lose the expedition director in such a dramatic fashion . . ." She let her voice trail off suggestively, cocking her head to scrutinize the coronet on my head. "Half the women here are wearing Egyptian jewelry, but I rather think yours is something special," she said, giving me a narrow look as she extracted a slender notebook and pencil from her pocket. "Would you care to make a statement for the press?" My mind whipped back to the shadowy pavement outside Bishop's Folly.

"You! You were the woman who followed us," I hissed.

She grinned broadly and thrust out her hand. "I do not believe we have met. J. J. Butterworth. I said, would you care to make a statement, Miss Speedwell?"

I ignored the hand. "I most certainly would not. Does Sir Leicester know that you are here?"

She tipped her head. "Not precisely. He issued an invitation to my newspaper and it happened to fall into my hands."

"You mean you stole it."

She shrugged one slim shoulder. "A woman must make her own opportunities in this world, don't you agree?"

"If I did, would I find it in print?"

She laughed outright. "I think, under other circumstances, Miss Speedwell, we might be friends."

"I should sooner befriend a barracuda," I told her evenly. "And let us be perfectly clear with one another. I despise you and the dirty little fictions you concoct. And if you print one word about Revelstoke Templeton-Vane that is not true—"

She held up a hand. "I know. You will sue me for libel."

"My dear Miss Butterworth, there will be nothing left to sue when I have finished with you."

To her credit, she was still smiling when she walked away, head held high. I stood for a moment, staring after her and seething at Mornaday's duplicity. Having seen them together outside, I had little doubt he was the one feeding information to her like a mother bird dropping tasty morsels into the waiting beak of a chick. At least I could remove any suspicion from Figgy on that score, I thought darkly. I spotted Stoker in the crowd and wove a circuitous path towards him, eager to get him away before Miss Butterworth noticed him.

Suddenly, a voice, distinctly American, rang out through the Hall.

"Well, goodness me, but isn't this a sight!" All eyes turned to the doorway where Horus Stihl stood, hands on hips, surveying the room. His son, Henry, stood awkwardly behind him, as disheveled in his evening suit as he had been in his more casual clothes.

Sir Leicester broke from a group of guests, striding towards his former partner as a hush fell over the assembly. Henry, looking distinctly miserable, slipped to the edge of the displays, nearly flattening himself behind a potted palm in his desire to be invisible. I sympathized with him. His father had the heightened color and bright-eyed mischief of a seasoned provocateur, and Sir Leicester was not the sort of man to back down from a fight. He approached Horus Stihl as a bull will charge a red flag, not surprising, considering their last encounter had ended in threats of violence from a distinctly enraged Stihl.

"What do you mean in coming here?" Sir Leicester demanded.

Mr. Stihl touched the band of black crepe pinned to his arm. "I came to offer my condolences," he said with a touch of reproof. "I worked with Jonas many a year, and it seemed only fitting to pay tribute to his last expedition."

Sir Leicester purpled a little. "Oh, em. Of course, of course. Rotten business."

"Indeed." They stood, Sir Leicester squared off as if to prevent Mr. Stihl from entering further. Mr. Stihl indicated the displays. "I see you are still going ahead with the exhibition."

"Naturally," Sir Leicester said, puffing out his chest. "It is what Fowler would have wanted."

"He would at that," Mr. Stihl agreed. His tactic of aggressive agreeability seemed to have thrown Sir Leicester off his stride. With nothing but perfect politeness and gentility from the American, the baronet could not very well throw a scene without appearing churlish. They seemed to be at an impasse until Mr. Stihl noticed Lady Tiverton and bowed.

"My lady," he said with a courtly gesture.

Her eyes were enormous, wide and unblinking. "Mr. Stihl. This is unexpected," she said, her normally low voice even softer than usual.

Mr. Stihl smiled thinly. "As was Jonas Fowler's sad demise."

"Hardly. The fellow had a heart condition, as you well remember," Sir Leicester added sharply.

"Certainly. Why, I remember one time he took a fright at a jackal roaming too close to the camp. It howled so loudly you'd have thought it was carrying off a human soul. Poor old Jonas turned white as a sheet and collapsed. But I expected he'd have years left in him. Years," he said, stressing the word. "Still, not much a man can do against a mummy's curse, is there?"

It was masterfully done. The Tivertons could speak publicly neither for nor against the curse. They might privately deplore it, but the story was driving sales, and Sir Leicester gave every impression of a shrewd businessman who would press every advantage.

He pressed his lips together as Mr. Stihl went on. "Yes, that curse is a curious thing. From the mummy of Princess Ankheset, you say?"

"Yes. She was left in a cave in a remote *wadi* with some of her grave goods," said Patrick Fairbrother as he approached. "You can see her cartouche for yourself," he added, throwing back the curtain in front of the sarcophagus with a flourish.

Taking this as an invitation, Mr. Stihl stepped neatly around Sir Leicester. He peered at the sarcophagus, stroking his moustaches thoughtfully. "Very interesting," he said quietly. "So, this is your princess," he added, touching the scorched and gilded wood with a fingertip.

Sir Leicester hurried to put himself between Horus Stihl and his beloved princess. "It is. She is not to be disturbed."

"I shouldn't dream of it," Stihl said, giving Sir Leicester a long speculative glance.

Something in that glance angered him, for the baronet curled his hands into fists. "This exhibition will be the making of the Tiverton name. It will go down in the annals of Egyptology, and you will be nothing more than a footnote," he said through clenched teeth.

Lady Tiverton started, her hand to her throat, but Mr. Stihl merely smiled. "Do not trouble yourself, my lady. I understand your husband very well. Better than anyone, I daresay." He turned to Sir Leicester. "Don't fuss. I did not come to make a scene," he said with every appearance of sincerity. "I simply wanted to see the collection for myself, and I knew better than to expect a proper invitation since we are not as close as once we were."

The shot hit home, for Sir Leicester flushed and his hands unknotted themselves. "Of course. Look around, if you must. Have some champagne. I must attend to my guests. The Prince of Wales is expected shortly."

He stalked off, followed by Lady Tiverton. I stood rooted to the spot, hardly feeling Stoker's hand where it gripped my arm. "Steady," he murmured into my ear. "We can leave now if you like."

I turned to him, my chest burning with some unnamed emotion. "And miss seeing my father? I would not dream of it."

Before he could reply, Horus Stihl had caught sight of us and made his way over. "Miss Speedwell, Mr. Templeton-Vane," he said, inclining his head. "This is quite the to-do."

"The collection is fascinating," Stoker told him. "Although I had rather see more art and less in the way of domestic goods."

Mr. Stihl waved a hand. "Doesn't much matter, son. If it came out of an Egyptian tomb, it's of interest. I could sell a dirty flowerpot if I said it belonged to Amenhotep," he said absently. His eye had been caught by the diadem. "Why, Miss Speedwell. What have we here?"

"Just a little something belonging to the Princess Ankheset," I told him. "Do you like it?"

He looked closely, taking in the crown from the animal figures on the top to the incised cartouche about the base. I could smell the bay rum of his shaving lotion, and he was near enough that I could see the precise line of whiskers at the edge of his moustaches. His breath was oddly cool against my cheek, and just as I began to grow very aware of his scrutiny, he stepped back. "Lovely" was all that he said.

He looked around. "I don't suppose there is anything stronger than champagne on offer?" he asked in a hopeful voice.

"I have aguardiente in a flask," I confessed.

He grinned. "Miss Speedwell, you are a woman after my own heart. I have been married three times, but I am becoming quite determined to make it four."

Stoker rolled his eyes at the raillery and hailed a passing waiter. "Can you find a glass of whisky for Mr. Stihl?"

The waiter bobbed obediently and Horus Stihl favored Stoker with a smile. "Bless you, son. A man can handle only so much fizz before he floats plumb away." The waiter reappeared almost instantly, proffering the promised glass. Horus Stihl took it with a gallant gesture in my direction. "To your very good health, my dear Miss Speedwell."

At that moment the Hall was plunged into darkness, each gas mantle failing simultaneously as a low, unearthly moan filled the air.

There were excited murmurings in the crowd as people speculated that the theatrics were simply part of the evening's entertainment, but it was apparent from the Tivertons' reactions this was not so. Lady Tiverton gasped and her husband sputtered in the blackness.

"By God! D'ye know what I've paid for this place? I'll have the proprietor up for fraud, I will. This is intolerable—"

A light flared up in the musicians' gallery, a torch held high in the grip of a figure that stepped from the shadows. It was Anubis, the jackal god, dressed much as we had seen him last with a low linen kilt and a breastplate. We were paralyzed with horror and shock as he stepped to the edge of the gallery, raising his torch towards us. He motioned to Sir Leicester. He said nothing, and it was this silence that was more chilling than any threat could have been. He merely stood, pointing an accusatory finger at the baronet. Then the torch went out and once more the Hall was plunged into blackness.

For a long moment it seemed no one moved, but then everything happened at once. Sir Leicester gave a low moan, Lady Tiverton's composure broke on a sob, and I felt a rough hand snatch the diadem from my head.

I cried out and thrust my hands in front of me, trying to grab my attacker, but my fingers closed on empty air. Stoker struck a vesta and the little flame flared to life, illuminating the scene immediately around us. Sir Leicester looked stricken while Lady Tiverton started towards him, her lips pale with shock. He caught her to him in a desperate embrace, a drowning man clinging to his bulwark. There was no sign of the thief who had wrenched the coronet from me. Patrick Fairbrother looked utterly stunned as he stared blankly in the direction of the gallery. Horus Stihl, still clutching his glass of whisky, had his gaze fixed upon Sir Leicester, his expression inscrutable as Figgy collapsed with a wail into Stoker's arms just as the vesta sputtered out.

I do not know how long we remained in darkness—a few seconds only, although it seemed far longer—but the lights blazed on again, the gas mantles flickering once more to life. Lady Tiverton thrust herself from her husband's embrace. "Figgy!" she cried. Patrick Fairbrother's expression was grim.

Sir Leicester took in the sight of Stoker, his arms full of Figgy, and began to bluster. "Here, now, sir—"

"She swooned, Sir Leicester. She wants a burnt feather or perhaps just a stout slap," I offered, lifting my hand. "Shall I?" At that, Figgy moaned and fluttered her eyes.

Grasping my skirts in both hands, I made for the gallery, cursing the delay that Figgy's swoon had caused. I glanced behind me only once to see her clinging to Stoker—no doubt begging him not to endanger himself—but I did not wait to see. It took a moment to find the stairs; concealed behind a bit of paneling in the corridor, they were narrow and dark, and I hurtled up them as quickly as I dared.

The gallery, as I had feared, was empty. Stoker joined me a moment later, swiveling his head around as he peered into the shadows.

"Which way?" he demanded.

I spied a bit of paneling not quite flush with the others. "There!" The door was held in place with a flimsy lock, but Stoker put his shoulder to the panel and splintered it with a single thrust. Not waiting for him, I vaulted over the broken remains of the door and into the darkness beyond. Another narrow staircase wound up from the gallery and in the distance I could just make out the glimmer of a light.

"I hear footsteps," I called back to Stoker, not bothering to lower my voice. Anubis, whoever the devil might be, must have heard the commotion when Stoker broke through the door. He would know we were in pursuit.

Stoker close behind, I charged up the staircase and into a series of narrow passages little better than catwalks. Each ended in another staircase that brought us still higher, climbing ever upwards into the eaves of the building. We pushed on, following the dim glow of the lantern bobbing ahead. But Anubis had the advantage of us. He was familiar with the intricate passages, and by locking two more doors on the way, he gained valuable time as we were forced to pause and light vestas as Stoker battered down the narrow panels.

"You would think he'd have deduced that we are not to be stopped," I muttered at the last of the locked doors.

Stoker set his shoulder to it and gave a single brutal lunge, knocking it off its hinges. "He needn't stop us," he said grimly. "He need only slow us down."

The point was a valid one. No sooner had we burst into the last of the passages than we saw the figure of Anubis at the end of a long corridor, vanishing behind a door. We gave chase, wrenching open the door to find that it concealed a staircase.

"Bollocking hell," Stoker muttered. "He is doubling back and heading downstairs. We ought to have divided our efforts."

"Too late for that now," I reminded him as we hurtled down the stairs. This staircase ended in the corridor outside the storerooms, and we emerged into the corridor with no sign of Anubis—only the door to the alley, still swinging on its hinges, provided a clue. We charged after, shouting for police, but none replied.

"Where the devil are they?" I demanded.

"On the front pavement waiting for the bloody prince," Stoker replied as we emerged into the empty alleyway. He swore lavishly as we turned from side to side, looking for any clue as to where Anubis had fled.

"There!" I cried. Just visible in the shadows was the lid of the sewer, askew. From it, a faint light emanated, growing dimmer and dimmer with each second.

"Like a rat," he said grimly. There was neither time nor inclination for discussion. We lifted off the iron disk and stared down into the stinking underbelly of London. Directly beneath us was a narrow vertical passage leading to a sort of underground chamber some twelve feet below the street.

Stoker looked at me across the fetid hole. "Ladies first."

I gathered up my satin skirts and dropped into the opening, finding footholds on the slippery rungs of the iron staples set into the brick wall of the passage. When I reached the bottom, I put out one tentative toe. My evening slipper was instantly swallowed by the swirling brown water which flowed, ankle-deep, beneath the great city above. This was one of the legendary underground rivers of London, paved over earlier in the century to enclose the stinking open flow of sewage and halt the spread of disease. The water still flowed here, carrying refuse from the furthest reaches of town to Father Thames himself. I suspected the water was deeper than usual, for the melting snows from the storms would have raised the river, and the water gushing past us was cold and fast.

I glanced down the length of the chamber and saw a glow at the far end. I signaled up to Stoker and he swung down, skipping two or three staples at a time until he reached my side.

"We need light," I told him. "Have you your vestas?"

He shook his head. "Too dangerous. There are pockets of flammable gases down here. A spark could set off an explosion."

"But Anubis—" I began.

"Is welcome to take his own chances," Stoker said grimly. "We will navigate by his light and hope if it does blow up it doesn't take us with it."

I pointed to the fading glow. "That way."

We made our way to the end of the chamber, unspeakable things floating past our legs as we walked. The odor was beyond belief, a living thing that curled into us, noxious and corrupting. Where Anubis had disappeared, the chamber narrowed to a tunnel, scarcely higher than my head, and Stoker bent double as we entered. Far ahead I detected a gleam of light and I could hear the flow of fast water. There was the rush of wind, marginally less foul than that of the chamber.

We followed the little nimbus of light like a terrible star for a long while, so long that I lost all bearing, all concept of time in that dreadful netherworld. Anubis pushed forwards, no doubt out of desperation, for fear of discovery can drive one to do the incomprehensible. Still, we followed, driving him on like hounds upon a fox. The tunnels narrowed in places until I could barely fit through them; I dared not look behind to see how Stoker managed. In other spots, they opened into great stinking chambers, large as a ballroom, with high vaulted ceilings soaring overhead. And everywhere, the endless stench of filth and the bright, knowing eyes of rats watching us from the shadows.

Still Anubis pushed on, and still we followed until we turned down one of the labyrinthine passages after him and the light went out with the abruptness of a death. One moment we had the fitful consolation of it, glimmering vaguely ahead, and the next it was gone.

Bereft of illumination, we were blinded until our eyes adjusted. High above, a grille gave on to the night sky, admitting starlight and a fitful moon. It cast an eerie glow over the aqueous world, nightmarish and bleak. I could make out Stoker's silhouette, a tall black shadow, but nothing more.

"Bastard," he said with feeling.

"Where could he have gone?" I demanded.

"Up and out," Stoker told me flatly. "He must have seized the chance to nip up one of the ladders and let himself out, taking the light with him."

"Then we must do the same," I said. I put a hand out to grasp the lowest of the staples embedded in the wall, but I turned too quickly, or the muck attached to the base of my slipper had grown too thick, for suddenly my feet were swept out from under me and I was flailing, falling, flat upon my back and caught by the current. I was carried away, borne aloft on that fetid, stinking water.

"Veronica!" Stoker's voice cut through the impossible, endless night of that forsaken place.

"I'm here!" I cried. But I could not begin to compute where "here" was. There was no proper light, no marker by which I could gain my bearings. Only that river, carrying me away, as implacable as the Styx. The rush of it filled my ears, and after a moment I was conscious of it growing louder, ever louder, and I realized with horror that I was approaching a sort of confluence. We had seen passages like this already, places where one set of tunnels debouched into another. Sometimes, when the tunnels narrowed, it caused a great increase in the velocity of the water. In others, where the tunnels were of differing heights, it caused a sort of hideous waterfall, an unnatural cataract with falls of thirty feet in some places. The closer I was borne, the louder the water pounded, and I knew then where I was bound. I would be carried over the edge of the tunnel and off one of these precipitous drops into the hell depths below. The fall itself would at least maim. If I were lucky it would kill me quickly. I reached for purchase on the filth-slimed walls, but my nails scrabbled against the brick, breaking but never catching. My feet could not support me against the onslaught of that water, and I took as deep a breath as I dared and said one word as I was launched free of the tunnel and out into the open air of the chamber beyond.

I waited for the sensation of falling, but it did not come. Instead, there was a moment of phenomenal weightlessness as I floated, light as a butterfly hovering over a blossom. And then the feeling of a hand, strong as iron, banding about my wrist before the pain rocketed through my arm and my shoulder was wrenched nearly from its socket. My body slammed into the wall below, but I did not fall. I looked up and saw Stoker's face surrounded by a nimbus of light.

"Good God, am I dead? I cannot be, for surely you are no angel," I murmured.

"Anubis left his lantern, you daft woman," Stoker grumbled. "Now, steel yourself. I am going to pull you up."

He was flat upon his belly in that grotesque place, covered from head to toe in filth, but he was the most beautiful sight I had ever seen. He hauled me to safety like so much cargo, shifting me about with more regard for speed than comfort. But when I arose over the lip of the tunnel, I heard his muttered thanks to a deity in which he did not believe. I saw too the leg he had locked through the iron staple on the wall to anchor him as he dove for me, and I knew he would be bruised to the bone. I said nothing of my own hurts, merely gave him a determined smile and plucked a dead rat from my bedraggled hair.

I pointed to the tunnel looming just overhead. "He must have made his escape there. Let us follow."

Just then the moonlight from the grille above shifted. There was a scraping noise, and the glow of a lantern being thrust into the narrow shaft. "I say, what the devil are you doing down there?" an autocratic voice demanded. "Come out at once."

Our eyes dazzled by the sudden light, we peered up into the face of Sir Hugo Montgomerie.

CHAPTER 17

Sir Hugo put his hand out to assist me but suddenly reeled back, either at the sight or the smell. It was impossible to say which was the more off-putting.

"I suppose it's too much to ask why the pair of you were galloping about the sewers," he said politely.

"We were in pursuit of the miscreant masquerading as Anubis," I told him loftily. "Which is more than you can say for any of your lot." He applied a handkerchief to his nose, perhaps as much in defense against our odiferousness as his ailment.

"You ought not to be out in this chill when you are still suffering from a cold," I told him as I was wrapped in a blanket by a nameless bobby.

"I am recovered," Sir Hugo said, stepping sharply backwards. "Might I suggest a change of clothing, Miss Speedwell? And do not attempt to launder the garments you are wearing. Burn them."

I pulled a face but obligingly stepped some distance away. "How did you find us?" I called.

He pointed behind him, and to my astonishment I saw the looming façade of Karnak Hall. "You mean the bloody villain led us in a *circle*?" I cried. All that filthy water, the stench that sat in my nostrils, and it had all been for nothing.

Sir Hugo smiled kindly. "My men discovered the cover was ajar only after the fellow made use of this means of escape. He left his Anubis mask behind—but there are no clues to be found there. He seems to have led you on a merry chase," he added.

"And thanks to your interference," Inspector Archibond said as he approached, "the villain has escaped justice."

"Really?" Stoker asked. "I would argue that we were the only ones in pursuit and we very nearly captured him."

Archibond whirled on him. "I have a good mind to charge you with interfering in police business!"

"There will be no charges," Sir Hugo said quietly.

Archibond glowered as much as he dared at his superior. "Sir, I really must insist—"

Sir Hugo's aristocratic brows lifted, and Archibond, realizing his lèse majesté, hastened to make amends. "That is to say, I strongly believe charges are in order."

"A policeman is not interested in beliefs, Archibond. Only facts. And the fact is that this matter is now Mornaday's purview."

Archibond's mouth went slack. "Mornaday! Really, sir, with such a high-profile case, it seems highly irregular to put such an unreliable, unorthodox detective in charge."

"Taking my name in vain, sir?" Mornaday sauntered up, wearing an air of barely suppressed jubilation, hands thrust into his pockets.

Archibond turned on him with a feral growl. "Take your hands out of your pockets! I told you to leave this investigation alone," he began.

"Yes, you did, sir. And I ignored orders, for which I am prepared to be reprimanded. But since His Royal Highness found the whole incident jolly entertaining and asked for me personally, I doubt too much will find its way into my official record," he said, his merry brown eyes twinkling.

Archibond, at a loss for words, stalked away, muttering under his breath.

I scarcely noticed when he left. Stoker put a quiet hand to my shoulder, intuiting my thoughts.

Sir Hugo gave us a long, meaningful look. "Go back to Bishop's Folly and change. You would not like to be seen in your present condition, I am certain."

He inclined his head the barest inch, and I saw *him* then. Standing just outside his carriage, surrounded by a knot of people. The carriage was marked with his badge, the trio of white plumes, the ostrich feathers that were the unique emblem of the Prince of Wales. He was not a tall man, my father. I judged him some five feet eight inches or thereabouts. His features were unremarkable, although I could see from his smile and the brightness of his eyes that he must have had great charm. Without knowing him for a prince, one might have made the mistake of thinking him a prosperous man of business. But he was a prince, and that made all the difference. The unmistakable glamour of royalty drew one's attention, as a sun will draw planets into its orbit. He did not look my way. I pulled the blanket, sodden with sewer water, more tightly about me.

Sir Hugo tactfully turned away and began issuing orders.

"I think we have all made an enemy in Inspector Archibond," I observed, turning deliberately to Mornaday.

"None more than me," Mornaday said cheerfully.

Stoker, as wet and filthy as I, moved aside to accept a blanket offered by one of the policemen. I took the opportunity to speak quietly to Mornaday.

"Does Sir Hugo know that you were the source for J. J. Butterworth's exclusive information?"

He flushed deeply to the roots of his hair. "I think he suspects. How did you know?"

I shrugged. "Caroline Templeton-Vane left Society after her divorce.

Few people knew she married John de Morgan, and those who did would not have made the connection between him and Stoker. There were only a handful of people who might have shared that information with Miss Butterworth, and once I met her, I realized you were the likeliest. You have always had a keen appreciation for attractive young women," I added meaningfully.

He flushed again. "It is not like that," he insisted. "Archibond has been trying to push his way to the top ever since he arrived. He's the Home Secretary's godson. With Sir Hugo ill, it was his best chance to shove me out of the way and undercut Sir Hugo's authority. He thought if he could solve the case, it would pave the way for him to be made head of Special Branch. I could not let that happen. I used Miss Butterworth to keep stirring the pot, hoping her stories would shake loose some vital clue. I hoped someone would get nervous enough to trip up and I would be there when it happened. But with Archibond keeping me occupied with mundane work, I couldn't be on hand. Miss Butterworth suggested that she make herself useful as a sort of reconnaissance agent, keeping an eye upon all the principals in the case."

"And in return you fed her information about Stoker, tethering him to the post like a scapegoat," I accused.

He held up his hands. "I know I ought to be sorry for that, but you cannot blame me. The fellow monopolizes the only woman I truly care about." He gave me an intent stare and I smiled in spite of myself.

"Mornaday, you are a liar and an opportunist, but you have done your best for Sir Hugo, and I am inclined to believe that it is better to dance with the devil you know."

"In that case, I will tell you something for free," he said, jerking his chin in the direction of the Hall. "Sir Leicester Tiverton has suffered an apoplexy."

I turned just in time to see Sir Leicester borne out of the Hall upon a stretcher, insensible, his color high. Lady Tiverton was at his side, clutching his hand, and Patrick Fairbrother hurried after, his expression grim.

"Stoker," I said, calling his attention to the little drama playing out before us.

"I am not surprised. The whole affair must have been a dreadful shock," he remarked. Just then Horus Stihl emerged from the Hall, followed hard upon his heels by Henry. Both looked subdued, and they made no movement to follow the Tivertons, going directly to their own carriage and departing with all speed.

Last of all came Figgy, following slowly, nearly forgot in all the commotion, staring after her stricken parent with an inscrutable expression. At the last moment, Lady Tiverton turned back, beckoning to her in the crowd and guiding the girl into their conveyance.

Stoker touched my shoulder. "I think we ought to go. Sir Hugo has arranged transportation for us." He gestured the long way around, a path that would take us behind the prince's carriage and keep us to the shadows.

"I do not think so," I told him. I clasped the blanket around me as if it were a court robe and lifted my head. "Pardon me," I said to the nearest courtier. "Make way if you please. I am passing."

Seeing my bedraggled appearance, the little crowd parted, murmuring and tittering. I looked neither right nor left, but as I crossed the pavement, I felt my father's gaze resting upon me. We did not speak; we did not even lock eyes. But I forced him to notice me. It was enough for the moment.

At Sir Hugo's insistence, we were driven home, but even his generosity would not extend to the use of his carriage in our present condition. We were given the use of the Black Maria, being carried away like common criminals. But it was quick, and we were soon deposited at Bishop's Folly. In all the confusion, no one noticed the missing diadem—at least none of the Tivertons. Stoker, however, was rather more attentive to detail. He looked once at my bare head and muttered a curse under his breath.

"I know," I murmured in reply. "But if it is any consolation, I blame you entirely. This was your idea."

"Of all the bloody—"

I interrupted him then to relate what I had learnt about Mornaday and the identity of our mysterious pursuer. His response, to my astonishment, was a hearty laugh.

"You think it amusing that we overlooked so obvious a possibility as J. J. Butterworth being our enigmatic female?" I challenged as we alighted and made our way to the Belvedere. A nightcap seemed in order.

"I think it amusing that she was bold enough to come to the Tivertons' reception without a personal invitation. What does she look like in a skirt?" he asked in a thoughtful voice.

"Tall, as you might well remember. Hair with an unfortunate ginger tendency. Horns. Pitchfork. Pointed tail—just as one might expect."

"You did not warm to our new acquaintance?"

"I find her despicable."

"Curious. I should have thought you would feel an affinity to a sister trying to make it in the world on her own," he teased.

"She is no sister of mine."

I had taken up the bottle of aguardiente to pour a nightcap, but I hesitated, my hand wrapped around its neck.

"I should very much like a drink," I told Stoker. "But if I spend another second in proximity to you, I believe I shall asphyxiate."

I retired that night in a sullen mood. It took three plunges in the heated pool and an entire cake of soap before I felt clean again. We had not captured Anubis in the act; we had found nothing suspicious in Lady

Tiverton's actions; and I had lost the Ankheset diadem—a fact I was reluctant to share with the Tivertons, particularly now that Sir Leicester had apparently suffered an apoplexy.

"Cheer up," Stoker told me grimly. "Perhaps he will die and you won't have to confess it."

I had shut the door on him then, hard enough to rattle the hinges. I am usually an excellent sleeper. My ability to take my rest no matter how insalubrious the circumstances—along with a sound stomach and excellent legs—accounts for the success of my travels through varied and demanding parts of the world. I slept little that night. Something evaded me, some fact I could not grasp. It danced out of reach, as insubstantial as a will-o'-the-wisp, and the harder I chased, the more elusive it proved. It was not until morning dawned that I realized what it was.

I had, as was my custom, taken up a book to read when I found sleep elusive. It happened that one of Lady Tiverton's volumes was near at hand, and I flipped the pages idly, moving from her lavish descriptions of expedition life to the little pen-and-ink drawings she had included. One in particular caught my attention, and I sat bolt upright in bed, staring at the slender black lines. It was not until I was certain that I rose and washed, dressing with my usual attention to neatness, before running Stoker to ground in the Belvedere. He was stripping rotting sawdust from the inside of his decaying white rhinoceros mount when I found him. His head was stuck deep inside the cavity, and I knocked on the side of the animal to get his attention.

"Horus Stihl stole the diadem," I announced without preamble.

"I know." His voice echoed from within the beast.

"How the devil did you know?" I demanded.

"I realized it after I retired last night—the thing that I had noticed when the lights went out. There was a sudden waft of bay rum. That was when Stihl put out his hand to snatch the diadem."

I thumped the rhinoceros hide with a fist and went to my desk. "Braggart," I muttered as I flicked through the morning's correspondence. I worked until Stoker saw fit to emerge, shaking the moldering sawdust from his hair.

"It does not matter," he told me. He threw one leg casually over the camel saddle, perching atop the leather contraption like a lord of creation. "You cannot accuse an American millionaire of theft without proof."

"But if he has the diadem in his possession—"

He held up a filthy hand, the palm streaked with glue and paint and God only knew what else. "Veronica. If you had caught him red-handed, we might have made something of it, and even then it would have been a Sisyphean task. Without that, we have nothing."

"We have an obligation to recover the diadem. We were in possession of it when it went missing," I argued. "Besides which, I know something you most assuredly do not. I know the identity of Anubis."

I showed him the drawing done by the first Lady Tiverton, and he grinned in spite of himself. "Of all the devilish—"

"Exactly. Now you know why I believe with the proper pressure, we can bring Horus Stihl to reveal all."

"You really mean to take on a man of Horus Stihl's stature and influence? Do you know what sort of trouble you're courting?"

"Courting?" I gave him a scornful look. "I married it long ago. Come, now, Stoker. As our favorite detective, Arcadia Brown, would say to her faithful Garvin, 'Excelsior!'"

Unfortunately, Lord Rosemorran arrived before we could depart. He appeared in the Belvedere, waving a bit of metal overhead and exciting the dogs until we could hardly hear ourselves think over the bedlam.

"How nice to see you, my lord," I shouted. "Have you come to inspect the progress on the collection? I've got a rather nice set of *Nymphalidae* that have just arrived this week from the estate of the Duke of Shrewsbury."

He gave me a vague smile. "Always happy to see your pretty little winged things, Miss Speedwell, but today, *today* we are about flight! Stoker, I have just received the last part of the Aérostat Réveillon! Come and see. We must fit it at once." He bustled out again, and Stoker flicked me an apologetic smile. There was no remedy. *Whoever holds the purse strings pulls the puppet strings,* I reflected grimly.

While Stoker spent the better part of the day engaged in tinkering with the mechanisms of the balloon, I applied myself to the *Nymphalidae*. Ordinarily, the sight of their gorgeous jewel-bright wings would have enthralled me, and the differences between imagoes would have provided me with hours of delighted study. But not this day. Instead, I fretted away every minute, cursing the seconds that ticked past as events unfolded without us. I sent to the Sudbury for word of Sir Leicester's condition and satisfied myself that he was in no imminent danger.

At length, just after teatime, the ripe curve of the balloon began to fill and Stoker appeared, streaked with glue and other assorted substances which he made a hasty attempt to repair before we set off for the Allerdale Hotel.

I dressed carefully for our visit to Horus Stihl, donning my working costume. It was an ensemble of my own design, and I was rather proud of it. A pair of slim dark trousers and a shirtwaist formed the base of it. Atop that I buttoned a jacket fitted with half a dozen pockets of various sizes and a long skirt whose clever arrangement of buttons permitted me to wear it modestly or looped up out of the way. Flat boots which laced to the knee and a broad flat-brimmed hat fastened with sharpened pins completed the ensemble. I tucked a knife into my boot for good measure, which Stoker found distinctly unnecessary. We argued all the way to the Allerdale Hotel.

"We are not going there for a fight," he reminded me. "We have only a theory that Horus Stihl is involved, but no proof."

"Then we will get it."

"And you think bearding him in his den is the way to get it?"

I slanted him a smile. "Never underestimate the element of surprise."

At the Allerdale, Horus Stihl opened the door himself with an anxious look. "How is Leicester? He's not—" He broke off, his mouth working furiously.

"We have not come from Sir Leicester, but the last we heard, he is resting comfortably," I assured him.

Something stiff in his manner eased. "Well, I do not wish him well, but neither do I wish ill luck upon him," he said. "Come in."

We entered the sitting room of his suite to find Henry Stihl pacing before the hearth and Figgy Tiverton huddled in a chair.

"Miss Tiverton, this is an unexpected pleasure," I said, a trifle acidly. "We know that you fashioned the mask of Anubis." To my astonishment, she burst into tears, weeping incomprehensibly into her sleeve. Stoker took out one of his enormous red handkerchiefs, but before he could offer it, Henry took out his own, a sturdy piece of plain cambric marked with his monogram in solid block letters. Figgy took it and squeezed his hand gratefully.

Horus gave us a speaking look. "I am afraid you have just arrived in the midst of a confession of sorts, but damn me if I can make any sense of it. Pardon my language, Miss Speedwell," he said hastily.

"I think we can help with that," I told him. We settled ourselves and I began to speak. "Figgy, you needn't talk. Nor you, Mr. Stihl," I said to Henry. "Mr. Templeton-Vane and I have worked out most of it. You, Mr. Stihl, played the part of Anubis, stripping to the waist and donning the kilt of the ancient Egyptian, a costume supplied no doubt by your own extensive travels in that country."

He opened his mouth to protest, but I produced the drawing done by the first Lady Tiverton. "A winsome little sketch, don't you think?" I asked gently. "Miss Iphigenia Tiverton and her childhood companion, Henry Stihl, playing at one of their favorite games, Egyptian gods. Figgy is dressed as Isis, and you, Mr. Stihl, are dressed as Anubis. Lady Tiverton wrote at length about your pastimes, your inseparable friendship, how you were always together, forever covering for one another when your occasional peccadilloes came home to roost. I found it curious that her account did not tally with what either of you told me about your relationship. You both indicated you had not been in contact for some time. Now, that in itself is not suspicious. Childhood friends often fall out of touch. But why lie about any present connection unless you were up to something you did not want anyone to guess? It doesn't take a great deal of imagination to suppose that on the strength of your long friendship, Miss Tiverton was able to persuade you to don a similar costume once more."

He looked to Figgy, holding her glance with his own. He reached out a fingertip and she lifted hers to touch it. "We swore an oath as children," he said in a dull voice. "We cut open our fingers and held them together so the blood would mix. That made us belong to each other, for life, we said. Whenever one of us needed the other, no matter how long it had been, no matter the situation, we would be there."

His expression was slightly abashed, as if he were ashamed to be caught out as having played such childish games, but his father regarded him with warmth.

"That's a mighty loyal thing, son," he said, his lips tight with emotion.

Henry rolled his eyes. "Oh, for heaven's sake! It was just a silly game from when we were infants. But Figgy needed me and I could not let her down," he said. His father put out a hand to Henry's shoulder. Henry rolled his eyes again but did not shrug him off.

"You wore garments you had collected upon your travels in Egypt, but your souvenirs wouldn't have extended to something as curious as the head of Anubis, so Miss Tiverton fashioned one, using her skills with papier-mâché to create the great jackal head for you to wear," Stoker supplied, picking up the thread easily. "I imagine it had to be papier-mâché in order to make it light enough to wear, a modern-day interpretation of the cartonnage used by the ancients." Henry nodded his head miserably. "You are to be commended, Miss Tiverton," Stoker said. "I cannot think that such a thing would be easy to sculpt, particularly on the first try."

His gaze and voice were gentle, but Figgy erupted into a fresh bout of weeping.

"It wasn't her first try," Henry said with grim resolve. "She made one earlier, back in Egypt. For Patrick Fairbrother."

"For what purpose?" I demanded.

"The same as mine—to masquerade as the god," he told us. His hand dropped absently to Figgy's shoulder. "Her father asked her to do it. He spun her some cock-and-bull story about native superstition and how the workers were getting restless. He told her they would settle down if they feared Anubis, so Patrick was to stalk around a bit and wave his arms and put the fear of the old gods into them. She did as he asked."

"Of course she did," Stoker said. She raised her tearstained face and looked to him.

"I should have refused," she whispered.

"Few of us can resist the persuasions of a beloved parent," he told her.

"So Fairbrother wore the first mask to frighten the workers," I prodded.

"He said they were out of hand, giving trouble, and he wanted to hire new men from upriver, but that it would cause all sorts of problems if he simply let them all go. But if they were frightened away, then they would leave of their own accord and he would be free to take on whoever he liked. It made *sense* at the time," she insisted.

"Of course it did," Stoker soothed. "But if your father and Fairbrother were behind the tricks in Egypt, why repeat them here? Why turn the tables on them?"

Figgy's expression was mulish. "Because I wanted to give Patrick a fright. He continued masquerading as Anubis here in London in order to prop up the story of a curse. He pretends to think it's ridiculous, but he really *wants* people to believe it. I overheard him say it would bring heaps more attention to the exhibition if people believe in that nonsense. He's *awful*," she said, her voice nearly breaking. "I hate him. He's always played up to Papa, acting like he's a member of the family, and he's not. He's hired help," she said, fairly spitting the word. "And I know he is up to something with *her*."

She could not bring herself to say the name, but I knew precisely whom she meant. "Your stepmother? What makes you think so?"

"I saw her one day, coming out of Patrick's room. She was perfectly furtive. She would have seen me, only I was reading behind the curtains and she never noticed I was there."

"There might be an innocent explanation," I began.

"I think not," she replied in a lofty tone. "She is up to something nefarious."

"Is that why you followed her to the linen draper?" I asked with some asperity. "To witness for yourself the perfidy of a lady purchasing her own handkerchiefs?"

"Oh!" Two spots of bright color rose in her cheeks. "You are *horrid*," she told me. "I don't care if you don't believe me. I never expected you would."

She said nothing more, but set her mouth in a stubborn line and folded her arms over her chest.

"We deduced that Figgy was behind the sculpting of the mask when we learnt of her skills at papier-mâché," I told Horus Stihl. "But we did not know the identity of her partner in the masquerade until I found the sketch her mother made when they were children and read her account of their fast friendship."

"Indeed," Stihl said faintly. "Until Henry went away to school, they were always together, every dig. Scrambling over rocks, pretending to run their own excavations. They painted on rocks and made their own tombs, even made their own mummies out of papier-mâché when they learnt about cartonnage."

"And you knew what they were doing," Stoker said. "You knew Henry was masquerading in London as Anubis and that he was doing it with Figgy's help."

Stihl held up a hand. "I most certainly did not. I might have had a suspicion, but knowing and suspecting are two different things. I don't ask questions if I think the answer is something I don't want to know, Mr. Templeton-Vane."

I turned to Henry. "I am rather curious how you managed to assume the disguise so quickly last night? And then resume your own clothes with such haste?"

He had the grace to flush deeply. "Figgy made certain one of the storerooms was open for me. She hid the costume in there and kept my own clothes waiting for me."

"And the head was dropped next to the sewers so that you shouldn't be caught with it. No doubt Figgy was able to give you detailed information about Karnak Hall. And your interest in the drains of London made an excellent cover for your study of the sewers surrounding the Hall. No one would connect quiet Henry Stihl with his fondness for all things hygiene with a god disappearing beneath the city," Stoker supplied. "Very clever."

"It wasn't," Henry said miserably. "It was a stupid thing to do, and you and Miss Speedwell might have been badly hurt. I'm dreadfully sorry."

"But we did not come merely to accuse Henry Stihl of masquerading as Anubis," I said, turning a stern eye to his father. I held out my hand. "The diadem, if you please."

He sighed and went to the mantel. The rather hideous painting of the deerhound swung open at a touch. Behind it was a small wall safe, neatly fitted and thoroughly discreet.

"The latest in hotel security," Stihl the elder told us as he turned the knob to the left and then the right. "Most establishments insist that guests send their jewels and money down to the manager to be held in the main vault, but the Allerdale is a mite more luxurious than that. Private safes in every room," he said, opening the small steel door with obvious satisfaction. He withdrew a bundle of white linen, and as he approached, I realized what it was.

"You wrapped it in your shirt?"

He gave me an apologetic smile. "It is all I had to hand, Miss Speedwell. Besides, I could have wrapped this coronet in rags and it wouldn't have done it any harm."

"Because it is so intrinsically valuable?" I asked.

"No," he replied with a grim look as he thrust it into my hands. "Because it is a fake."

CHAPTER 18

"I beg your pardon?" I blinked, looking from the American millionaire to the heap of gold resting in my hands. "A fake?"

"Yes, indeed. A clever one, but a fake nonetheless. I realized it as soon as I saw the cartouche. There is an error in the hieroglyphics."

Figgy looked to him in confusion. "But that is the crown of Princess Ankheset. It was taken from her tomb."

"No, it wasn't," Stoker said, working it out. "Or, rather, it was taken from the cave your father was excavating but only because he put it there first."

"I don't understand," she said stubbornly.

"My God," Henry Stihl breathed, putting a hand to her shoulder. "He faked the expedition."

"That was why Patrick Fairbrother was tasked with scaring away the local workers. Those men would have known the goods did not come from the tomb. That is also why he chose to quarrel with you, Mr. Stihl," I said, turning to the elder Stihl. "You were partners, but he knew you would not stand for such a deception. He found the perfect site for the scheme in his remote cave, but it was located in your concession. He had to force you out of the partnership in order to carry out his plan."

"No!" Figgy wailed. But from the sudden collapse of her shoulders, I realized she knew the truth.

"Tell me, Mr. Stihl," I said. "Why did you quarrel with Sir Leicester?"

He hesitated, then burst out, "I suppose it can do no harm to tell you now. He insulted my son," he told us, raising his chin. "And no man gets away with calling my boy names."

"What provoked him to do that?" I pressed.

Henry Stihl sighed, coloring as he stared at the toes of his shoes. "I confronted him about breaking off the partnership with my father. It bothered Father something terrible, and I was angry, really angry. So I went to Sir Leicester and told him it was an ungentlemanly thing to abandon a partner of so many years without a good reason. I called him a blackguard and told him he didn't deserve to have Father for a partner. I oughtn't to have done it," he finished miserably.

"Of course you ought to have," his father countered swiftly. "You put your neck out for one of your own, and that's what Stihls do." His chest seemed to swell a little as he regarded his son. "But Leicester didn't see it that way. He stopped me in the lobby at Shepheard's and had his say, calling my boy all kinds of names, and I got tired of listening. So I pulled out my revolver to persuade him I meant business when I told him to hush. The newspapers got hold of the story and made it out like I was threatening him. I didn't bother to correct them. I just wanted the whole sorry mess to go away."

Figgy's head shot up and she looked at Henry. "But why did you never tell me?"

"Because if I had, I would have had to tell you exactly what your father said to me when I spoke with him, and those words are not befitting of a gentleman," he said with quiet dignity. "It would have grieved you to know exactly what happened. Far better to think that our fathers had just fallen out over the concession."

"Henry," she said, coloring furiously. "We've been friends forever. You're awfully stupid if you think I wouldn't believe you."

He blinked in surprise behind his spectacles, looking like a beleaguered owl, but Stoker and I exchanged knowing glances. Figgy might protest, but her loyalty to her father was still paramount. She had a child's hero worship for the man, and I pitied her the day she would find his feet were—like all men's—made of clay.

After all the revelations of Henry's derring-do, Horus Stihl was looking at his son with something like admiration. "I am rather surprised to find you had it in you, son. There is a bit of Stihl in your spine after all," he added with a grin.

Henry rolled his eyes. "Of all the errant nonsense—"

I held up a hand. "Perhaps you could sort that out later. We are trying to piece together a conspiracy. Sir Leicester secured the concession in Egypt with the intention of salting the site—that is, filling the tomb with fake artifacts he could pretend to excavate and later sell on to unsuspecting collectors. But how could he have got fake antiquities past the Egyptian authorities?" I wondered. "Surely they would have known he was smuggling out forgeries."

"Not if he gave them authentic items," Horus Stihl said thoughtfully. "That is how I would do it if I were to concoct such a plan."

"Pa!" Henry Stihl's tone was one of reproach.

"I said *if*," his father pointed out. "Leicester, like all excavators, has a substantial collection of his own. He could carry it out to Egypt in the guise of excavation equipment—household goods and so forth—and when the authorities came calling, he could just hand those pieces over and pretend they had been hauled from the cave. Even if the authorities were suspicious, they would have been satisfied with a bribe of any half-decent artifacts."

"So Sir Leicester secures the empty tomb, carries out to Egypt the necessary artifacts to fool the authorities, and purchases cheap fakes to be shipped home in place of the grave goods he never actually excavated. But to do this, he must have the cooperation of the workers," I pointed out.

"Men not from the area, so they will be far less likely to report him. Enter Patrick Fairbrother in the guise of Anubis," Stoker said. "And whatever usual hazards befall an expedition—illness, accident—they will be chalked up to the malign influence of an offended god, another clever stroke to buy the silence of his workers."

"And if there are not enough hazards to persuade them, such things can easily be arranged," I added. "A little arsenic in the teapot can go quite a long way towards conjuring illness. Jonas Fowler died, after all. And John de Morgan was unwell for much of the dig season. Perhaps their misfortunes were helped along by a malicious hand."

"But John de Morgan finding the crown and determining it was a fake was something they did not anticipate," Stoker pointed out.

Horus Stihl rubbed his chin thoughtfully. "His experience with Egyptology was limited. He wouldn't have known from looking at the diadem that it was fake. Only an expert philologist would have seen the mistake in the inscription. No, I suspect he saw the diadem before it was supposed to have been 'discovered' in the tomb. When it was presented as a great find, he would have realized at once what had happened and taken steps to expose them."

"When he left with the diadem, it must have been a brutal blow to the conspirators," I said, carefully avoiding Sir Leicester's name so as not to set Figgy off again. "They had to act in order to prevent him from exposing their plot. John de Morgan had to die, and his death would be attributed to the curse of the mummy."

Horus Stihl broke in with a frown. "It all makes perfect sense until that point. We know he went as far as the hotel in Dover, but no further. How could anyone anticipate where he would go and arrange for his disappearance so thoroughly that his room vanished as well?"

"That, we have yet to discover," I told him. "But there is one more little mystery I think we might be able to clear up now." I brought out the box with its knitted cobra and demonstrated the mechanism for the Stihls. "Your handiwork, I think, Figgy?"

"Yes, all right, then," she said, a trifle sullenly. "I didn't trust you. So many strange things had gone on. I felt horrible, so alone and confused. I didn't understand anything of what was happening. And then the pair of you appeared, and I thought you might somehow be connected. I decided to investigate you a little myself. I went to see Lady Wellie and she said all sorts of nice things about you, which almost made me decide not to leave the box, but I already had it in my pocket, and I thought if you got a good fright, it might shake things up a bit." She broke off, but no fresh weeping ensued. Poor Figgy.

"And you thought to shake things up even more by having Henry dress up and play Anubis—is that it?" Stoker asked her.

She nodded. "No one tells me anything," she said, her chin taking a suddenly stubborn cast. "They treat me like I'm a child, but I'm not. I even tried following Patrick one night, but all he did was visit a house in Kensington off the Cromwell Road. So I met Henry in secret and asked him to help me."

Stoker flicked a glance my way but said nothing. Figgy did not know what she had seen, but the visit to the Marshwoods was significant. It meant that Fairbrother had at the very least broken into Caroline's rooms in an attempt to recover the diadem. I thought of Birdie's observation that Figgy had gone out only to walk the dog and realized how much she had actually accomplished in those stolen moments.

"And I was happy to," Henry said, his manner stalwart. He was every inch the young St. George, willing to slay the dragon for a maiden. And yet I rather suspected that Figgy had taken a more active role than any helpless maiden. If she hadn't had breasts, she might have played Anubis herself, I decided. It was Henry's physique that dictated his part. There might be Stihl in his spine, but there was good mettle in hers.

"What now?" Horus demanded.

"We have to find proof," Stoker said flatly. "And we must determine the extent of the conspiracy. We believe there are three conspirators, Sir Leicester, Lady Tiverton, and Patrick Fairbrother. But we do not know who is the mastermind."

"She is," Figgy fairly spat. "My father would not be so evil or so clever as to devise such a scheme. And Patrick is thick as a plank. This is *her* doing."

"Then we must find the proof," Stoker repeated.

Figgy shook her head. "You won't. She is too clever!" she insisted.

Horus patted her hand. "Don't carry on so, Figgy. We will make certain your father is not implicated if he is an innocent man."

I resisted the urge to roll my eyes. Innocent man! When he had carried out at least the scheme to defraud the entire Egyptological community and possibly had conspired to commit murder. But Mr. Stihl had clearly cast himself in the role of surrogate father to Figgy, and was relishing his chance to manage the situation.

"Now, in the morning, I will hire the very best Pinkertons I can find—or whatever they have in London that is the equivalent to them," he began.

Henry rose. "No, you won't. Every second counts. Now that Sir Leicester has been taken ill—through my actions, actions I will have to live with the rest of my life," he added with such an air of noble suffering, it would have done credit to Achilles, "I will find the necessary proof to bring this plot to an end before anyone else is harmed."

He stood tall, his shoulders squared, his jaw firm, his eyes shining, and in that moment I saw his father overcome with emotion. If Henry intended his little display to have a similar effect on Figgy, he was sadly disappointed. She merely huffed out a sigh of irritation while Horus Stihl clasped his son to his manly bosom and choked out a few words of praise.

He stepped back and reached into his pocket for a revolver. "Here, son. You will need this."

Henry Stihl blanched, and Stoker reached for the weapon, pocketing it easily. "Thank you, Mr. Stihl. It might come in handy at that."

Horus looked to me. "I apologize, Miss Speedwell," he said in a jocular tone. "I am afraid I do not have a firearm to spare."

I bared my teeth in a smile. "Do not worry yourself, Mr. Stihl. Miss Speedwell does not need one."

CHAPTER 19

We arrived at Karnak Hall after a considerable delay. Mr. Stihl promised to escort Figgy back to the Sudbury, and I was not surprised. He was quite solicitous of her, and Henry Stihl parted from her with a lingering tender look. I had little doubt that whatever the conclusion of our perilous adventure, Figgy would land amongst friends.

The Hall was in shadow when we arrived, and we took full advantage of the dark streets, slipping around to the alley behind. As we turned into the narrow passage, we heard a sudden scuttling.

"Rats!" I pronounced, but the only creature to emerge was of the two-legged variety. A slim young man with a very white bottom hurried past, hoisting his trousers and muttering curses under his breath. A woman who made her living from the nocturnal arts stepped out from behind a discarded crate, blinking in the lamplight.

"Hello, ducks," she said cordially. "Tuppence each against the wall," she said, jerking her chin at the shadows.

"Good evening," Stoker replied. "We are not in need of your services, but I do hope we have not cost you that gentleman's fees."

She grinned and opened her palm, revealing a coin. "Always get the money up front," she said sagely. "What business have you got here unless it's my sort of business?" she demanded.

"We are in need of a pair of sharp eyes," I told her, pressing another coin into her hand. "Go to the end of the street, and if you see a bobby coming, whistle or sing a little tune."

She nodded and warbled a few bars of a popular tune.

"'Elsie from Chelsea'?" I asked.

"Fitting. Elsie's my name," she replied with a wink.

Stoker thanked her and turned to the back door of Karnak Hall, kneeling down as Henry Stihl raised the lamp. Elsie took a lingering look at Stoker's backside and the hard length of his thighs before leaning near me with a conspiratorial leer.

"I said tuppence, but if he wants a go, make it a florin."

I raised a brow. "You have just raised your prices by a factor of twelve," I noted.

She grinned again. "I reckon a fellow that good-looking has had his share for free. It might make a change for him to pay well for it."

Stoker smothered a laugh and removed a set of slender metal tools from his pocket and set to work.

"You know how to pick locks?" Henry demanded.

Stoker shrugged. "I am an experienced surgeon and a taxidermist, lad. Nimble fingers have a number of uses."

Elsie made a noise that could only be rendered as "Ooh-er."

I pressed another coin into her hand. "Have this instead. A peg of gin will keep you warmer than he will. I am afraid he is shy."

Stoker snorted as the woman pocketed the coin. She tipped her plumed cap. "Pity, but truth be told, I'd rather have a peg o' gin in any event. Thank you kindly, missus. I'll keep an eye at the end of the alley, then."

"You're a good soul, Elsie."

She guffawed. "Don't you believe it, missus. But I'm not as bad as some."

With that she went on her way, picking a path over lettuce leaves and puddles with the grace of a duchess.

"I rather like her," I said to no one in particular.

With a jaunty nod, she headed down the street, positioning herself at the end of the alley as she tucked the evening's earnings away in a pocket beneath her petticoat.

Henry Stihl turned to me, his eyes wide. "Was that a fallen woman?"

"I should rather call her an entrepreneur," I told him seriously.

We chatted for some minutes while Stoker worked, sharing a frank exchange of views on the state of the current prostitution laws and comparing them with those of ancient Egypt. Young Mr. Stihl was informative—rather too much so. I suspected him of having an unhealthy preoccupation with ladies of limited virtue. But before I could provide him with a lecture upon the subject, Stoker interrupted.

"I am in," Stoker called softly.

Henry stared at him in frank admiration. "You must teach me how to do that," he said.

"No time," I answered, pushing him after Stoker into the darkened building. I paused to wave to Elsie, who returned the gesture, moving briskly off into the night as we pulled the door closed behind us.

Deserted, the lavish lamps extinguished, Karnak Hall was an atmospheric place. The very air seemed expectant, and I was deeply conscious of the eyes watching us—painted sculpted eyes of every description peering out from the vitrines as we passed from shadow to shadow. The light from the single lantern scarcely penetrated the gloom, but it was enough to illuminate Henry Stihl's white face.

"Steady, Mr. Stihl," I said softly.

He nodded once, squaring his shoulders. He was a stalwart fellow, young Henry Stihl, and I hoped his nerve would not desert him.

The dais was empty now, the princess' sarcophagus having been moved.

"She'll be in the storage room," I told Stoker, motioning for him to follow. I led the way to the corridor where I had first encountered her. The door, not surprisingly, was locked, but Stoker bent once more to employ his larcenous talents, and we were soon inside. The sarcophagus rested on trestles, its surface glimmering in the fitful light. Next to it, propped against the wall, stood a sturdy wooden packing crate spilling forth a heap of excelsior, its lid askew. I stooped to read the label affixed to one of the boards.

"This is the sarcophagus crate. The label on it says that the mummy case came through Dover," I told Stoker, not even daring to voice the rest of my suspicion.

I did not have to. With that curious sort of telepathy that we shared upon occasion, Stoker intuited my thoughts. He sighed and stripped off his coat. "I will find a crowbar," he said.

"What is it?" Henry asked in mystification.

I gave him a pitying look. "I suggest you take out your handkerchief, Mr. Stihl, and tie it, bandit-fashion, about your nose. This is not going to be pleasant."

"What isn't?" he demanded. "What have you found?"

Stoker reappeared, tool in hand, and applied himself. It took considerable effort, and in the end Henry and I both had to throw our weight against the lid of the sarcophagus to help budge it. When we did, a noxious odor rolled out, and Henry reeled away, gagging like a cat.

"Good God! What is that terrible smell?" he asked between heaves into one of the potted palms.

"That," I said simply, "is what is left of John de Morgan."

I had not considered what it might mean to Stoker to uncover the remains of his former best friend, and there was no time to consider it after. "Well," I pronounced, "this is all the proof we need. We will go directly to the Metropolitan Police and tell them what we have discovered. Surely that will be enough."

Just as Mr. Stihl collected his composure, there was a sharp intake of breath from the doorway. We turned as one to see Patrick Fairbrother standing there, a lamp held high in his hand. How grotesque the scene must have appeared to him! We had set our lantern on the floor, and the shadows it cast onto the ceiling were enormous. We stood crowded around the mummy case, its lid askew, and the odor of John de Morgan's decomposing corpse filling the air. Without a word, he backed away, throwing the door shut.

Before we could spring into action, we heard the sound of a key in the lock.

"Hell and damnation," Stoker swore. He turned to me. "I believe we have just lost the element of surprise."

"What now?" Henry Stihl asked, his eyes rounded. "Can you pick the lock?"

Stoker gave him a kindly smile. "Rather pointless from this side."

I eyed the ventilator high in the wall. "That is the only way. A boost, if you please, Stoker."

He set his foot on a crate, providing me with the sturdy length of his thigh as a perch. I mounted it, pushing myself to my full height until my fingertips reached the grate covering the ventilator. I wrenched it free. "Catch, if you will, Mr. Stihl."

Young Henry caught it, watching in rapt fascination as Stoker hoisted me higher, pushing firmly on my posterior as I inserted myself into the passage of the ventilator.

"Is there sufficient room, Miss Speedwell?" Henry called.

"Perfectly. It is so capacious, I might just set up housekeeping," I called, more out of bravado than truth. If I am honest, the space was narrow enough to cause my chest to tighten uncomfortably. The passage itself was not so small as to constrict me, but the feeling of imperfect liberty was alarming. I had little experience of caves—butterfly hunting, of necessity, takes place in meadows—but I was not certain a familiarity with enclosed spaces would help. Only resolve and discipline would carry the day, I reflected.

I put my head down and crawled, as quickly as I could manage, wedging myself through a bend in the shaft until a lacy pattern of light showed that I had come to another cover. I punched it hard, dropping it to the floor below, and hesitated. If it led to another locked storeroom, I would be no better off and indeed worse, for I would be separated from my companions with no means of communicating with them. But every second's lead Patrick Fairbrother had upon us was another second lost.

I turned myself, with a great deal of trouble and fluent swearing, until my feet were above the ventilator. With a murmured prayer, I kicked hard, forcing it loose. I dropped through the opening, clasping the edge of it as my body dangled free. A quick glance revealed I was in the corridor and Patrick Fairbrother was nowhere to be seen. I dropped to my feet, hurrying to the storeroom where Stoker and Henry were still imprisoned.

"I am free," I called.

"I presume the devil has taken the key," Stoker replied, his casual drawl muffled by the stout door.

"Yes, and I don't suggest you try to batter your way free. This door is proper oak, nothing like those flimsy things upstairs."

"I have already made that observation," he countered. "Now, take out two hairpins and I will explain to you exactly what to do next."

The process was not so straightforward as either of us would have liked. Stoker's instructions were hampered by the sound-smothering quality of the door, and it was several minutes before we realized that his directions were transposed in my hands.

"Of all the wool-headed, cotton-witted stupidity," he grumbled. "Of *course* you ought to have reversed the instructions."

"It might have behooved you to mention that sooner," I countered icily. "And perhaps you could be a trifle more gracious when I am in the process of a rescue."

With that, I set myself once more to the task of liberation, and within a considerably longer period than I would have preferred, the lock yielded.

"At last," Stoker said, brushing the dust from his sleeves with studied nonchalance.

"Quiet, or I shall bolt you back in." Our eyes locked. "To the Sudbury?" I asked.

"Where else?"

Unfortunately, it was the time of day when the streets are most mightily clogged with traffic, hansoms and hackneys jostling with dray wagons and omnibuses as the population of London moves hither and thither. We attempted for some time to hail a cab, but in the end we were forced to make our way on foot, arriving at the Sudbury breathless and in some disarray.

Lady Tiverton opened the door of the suite, her expression grim. "Thank God you've come," she said fervently. "Help us, I beg you." Figgy stood behind her, pale and distraught.

"Where is Patrick Fairbrother?" I demanded. "He is responsible for the death of John de Morgan and we mean to see justice done."

"Then you must hurry," Lady Tiverton said.

"You have to do something about Father!" Figgy burst out. "He's gone mad!"

"He has not gone mad," Lady Tiverton corrected with some severity. "But he is not himself."

"What has happened? We cannot help if we don't know exactly what's gone on," Stoker told her calmly.

She made an effort to compose herself. She turned to her stepdaughter. "Figgy, ring for tea, please."

"I don't want bloody tea!" Figgy yelled, stamping her foot.

"Iphigenia," her stepmother said in a commanding tone I had never heard her use before. "You will control yourself and be useful or I will slap you. Hysterics will solve nothing. Tea. Now."

To my astonishment, Figgy obeyed. Henry hurried after her, and that left Stoker and me to learn what we could.

"Figgy has told me some of what has passed, and I know she suspects me of complicity in this plot. I can tell you that nothing could be further from the truth. I only today learnt the full extent of what has been happening when my husband and Patrick nearly came to blows not an hour ago in this very room. They have gone to the country house, to Surrey," she said, clasping her hands together. "I believe something terrible is going to happen."

"To which of them?" Stoker asked shrewdly.

She flinched. "To my husband. He is not a criminal. He is not hard," she protested. "Patrick will harm him. Right now Sir Leicester believes he has Patrick in his power, but I know Patrick will find a way to turn the tables on him."

"Fairbrother means to double-cross him?" Stoker suggested.

"That's what Sir Leicester believes," she said, her lips tightening. "They were equal partners in the scheme, but my husband has come to think that Patrick means to cheat him of his share."

"Why does he believe that?" Stoker asked.

"I went to Patrick's room," she said, forcing the words through stiff lips. "I searched his things and among his papers I found a ticket on a steamship leaving tomorrow. He means to go to South America, the Argentine. I also found a packet of powder," she added, her dark eyes enormous in her face. "I think it might be a poison of some sort. Heaven only knows what he did—or means to do—with it."

I turned to Stoker and mouthed the words "Jonas Fowler?" He gave a single sharp nod of the head.

Lady Tiverton went on. "I took the ticket and the packet to my husband to persuade him that Patrick was working against him, to show him what Patrick really was. I told him we could confront Patrick together, force him to give up his share and go quietly without making a scandal, but Sir Leicester would not hear of it. He left his sickbed and took a revolver to force Patrick to go with him to Surrey."

"Why Surrey?" I inquired.

"Tiverton Hall is my husband's country house in Surrey. That is where the rest of the artifacts are being kept, the ones they intend to sell," she explained swiftly. "Sir Leicester thinks the inventory may have been cleared away and he wants to see for himself. You must stop him before he does something rash!"

"We will pursue them," Stoker promised.

"But they left on the last train," she said, spreading her hands. "There is not another until morning."

"Oh, for God's sake," I muttered. "We are no rescue mission! On this investigation, we have already been half-drowned, very nearly burnt to death, and almost suffocated in a sewer."

A sudden movement in the doorway caught my attention.

"Please," Figgy begged, tears springing to her eyes as she came forwards. "You must help. He is my father."

Her voice broke on the last syllable, and I knew better than to fight. Stoker could resist many things, but a desolate girl trying to save her father from himself was not one of them.

"Very well," I consoled her. "We will do something. But what? Hired carriage?"

"Horses will never beat the train," Stoker said, stroking his chin thoughtfully. "But I know something that will."

I stared at the Montgolfier balloon. "You must be joking."

"I am not," Stoker said with maddening calm. "It is ready to fly. I meant to take it up and test it again this week in any event. And it is our only chance to reach the Tiverton house tonight. We even have the wind on our side, and that is miracle enough."

I looked to Henry Stihl, who had blanched to marble-white in the moonlight.

I sighed. "Come on, then. If we are to die, let us do it like men, and Englishmen at that."

We decided to bring Henry because he knew the whereabouts of the Tiverton country estate, and Figgy's desperate pleading had roused Lady Wellie to action. She turned every able-bodied male servant at Bishop's Folly out of bed and directed them with all the august authority of her namesake, ordering them to follow Stoker as if he were leading a charge. While the men assembled, Stoker and I hastily dressed in our warmest garments, precaution against the chill of aeronautic flight. Over the top of my costume, I wrapped a shawl, tucking the ends firmly into my belt, and Stoker unearthed an unlikely bit of bearskin for Henry Stihl to wear like a cloak.

Once we were kitted, Stoker organized the workers into groups to man the ropes and smooth the envelope of the balloon. He climbed into the gondola, directing Henry and me where to stand so that the weight would be evenly distributed with the clever addition of appropriately positioned sandbags. Stoker and Henry fired up the brazier themselves, pouring coal into it until slowly, almost imperceptibly at first, the balloon began to fill. The silk moved slowly, coming to life as the air moved into its great lung, drawing in the warmth that would cause it to lift. I watched, gripping my hands together in suppressed excitement as it grew, rising and rounding until it rose above the treetops, a grand spectacle of a balloon emblazoned with the ciphers of a long-dead king, a ghost of Versailles rising above the heart of Marylebone.

The gondola stood expectantly on the grass, quivering in anticipation, and I climbed into the basket with Stoker and Henry. At a signal from Stoker, the lads on the ground let go of the ropes and the basket rose, slowly and gracefully as a dancer. The fellows below waved their caps and cheered and Lady Wellie waved her walking stick. Next to her, Figgy did not move, her pale face upturned to watch us as we drifted away. Stoker made a few adjustments and we were turned towards the south.

Cruising above the sleeping city, we sailed noiselessly through the night sky, to the river and past the Houses of Parliament. The face of the Great Westminster Clock glowed white in its golden tower, and high above it hung the Ayrton Light, its green glitter proclaiming that Parliament was still sitting. We sailed past it, silent as a ghost in the clear star-flung night.

Over the River Thames and above the south bank, we glided until we came at last to the countryside, a vast stretch of darkness rippling below. It was punctuated here and there with shimmering dots of the firefly lights of a town, but for the most part, all was quiet and dark, rural England tucked peacefully into bed on a late-winter night. The air was bitterly cold, and I was grateful for the warmth of the brazier. The chill of the February air gave us good lift, and occasionally, Stoker and Henry paused in their frenetic feeding of the brazier to watch as England unfurled below us, illuminated by the gentle glow of the full moon behind us. From time to time the air in the balloon would cool, causing us to drop suddenly, and my stomach would swoop within me, creating a rush of exhilaration like that of riding a fast horse or standing on the deck of a boat with full-bellied sails. I loved every minute of that strange adventure, and more than once I looked across to find Stoker grinning at me in the hellfire of the brazier. I smiled back at him, reveling in our new adventure.

Poor Henry Stihl did not fare quite so well. The unaccustomed motion of the flight drove him to lean over the side of the gondola more than once, emptying the contents of his stomach with audible groans.

"This is lunacy," he moaned. "The wildest of goose chases! How can we possibly hope to find them?"

"Courage, Mr. Stihl!" I said, passing him the flask of aguardiente to bolster his nerve. He took it and swallowed deeply, gasping and spluttering as he passed it back. For a moment I thought he would succumb to his fright, but he rallied, and I believed then that his father would be proud of him. The odds that we would spy them in the dark serenity of that March night were incalculable, but I have always enjoyed uncommonly good fortune at the most unlikely of times. Through some means—divine providence? Luck? Stoker's earnest efforts?—we at last spotted the train below us, speeding through the countryside, the engine exhaling great puffs of steam. I thought of Patrick Fairbrother and Sir Leicester Tiverton and the confrontation to come. Would either of them welcome us? Would we bring deliverance? Or destruction?

"There!" Henry cried, pointing to a bend in a narrow river. "My God, I cannot believe it, but just there, where the river turns back on itself. That is Tiverton Hall. Where the moonlight is showing a broad, flat bit of ground is a lawn in the front, and you can land there."

Stoker did as Henry directed, maneuvering the balloon to the boundary of the trees that marched to the edge of the manicured lawns. He intended for us to skim gently down, as easily as a butterfly alights on a branch, but our luck did not hold. The balloon had other ideas.

The gondola came down with a precipitous drop, the treetops rushing up at us at dizzying speed.

"Up, Stoker!" I urged.

"For God's sake, I'm trying," he said through gritted teeth, tinkering with the brazier to send more heat into the envelope. But it was too late.

There followed a series of sickening shudders as the gondola cracked its way through the canopy, breaking branches on its way down. Broken limbs clawed the sides of the basket, reaching, grasping, as we hurtled down, down, down, faster and faster. I braced myself for the inevitable crash, and with a sickening *thud*, we jolted to a stop. The balloon had been snagged upon the trees and we dangled there in the gondola, like so much ripe fruit, some forty feet above the ground.

Henry peeped over the edge of the basket and gave a low moan of anguish. Stoker immediately tossed one of the guy ropes out and grunted with satisfaction when it fell just short of the ground.

"We shall have to climb for it," he announced.

Henry made a sound of protest, but just then the basket slid a little as the wind rocked the trees. I patted his shoulder. "Never mind. It's best if you don't look down. And if you break a leg, Stoker can always put you down. He's got the revolver, after all."

Henry gave me a look of purest loathing, and I shrugged at Stoker. But the goad worked. Without further ado, Henry put his leg over the side of the basket, grasping the rope in what must have been nerveless fingers. I did not watch. But the sudden snapping of a branch and a *thud* followed by a groan of pain were eloquent.

I peered down into the darkness. "Mr. Stihl! I say, Mr. Stihl, are you quite all right?"

"I believe I have broken my arm," he called, in a voice very unlike his usual.

"Well, that is unfortunate," I observed.

"Your turn," Stoker said.

"I think not," I replied in indignation. "I am lighter. I should remain behind since the gondola is unstable and might topple at any moment. I stand a better chance of surviving a fall than you do."

His expression was inscrutable. "I am, for all intents and purposes, captain of this endeavor. If anyone is going down with the ship, it is I. Now, get down that rope before I toss you out."

He advanced upon me as if to make good on his threat, and I vaulted over the edge of the gondola, gripping the rope with my hands and tightening my legs around it. I lowered myself in a steady rhythm, ignoring the creaks and groans of protest from the branches above. They were holding the balloon, but barely.

My boot tips hovered above the ground and I dropped from the rope to find Henry staring at me in frank admiration even as he clutched his arm to his chest. "Where did you learn to climb like that?" he demanded.

"On vines in Costa Rica. The best butterfly habitats are notoriously inaccessible. Do you require medical assistance, Mr. Stihl?" I asked.

He shook his head manfully. "No. I can manage." He struggled to sit, then to stand. His broken arm was folded like a bird's wing against his chest.

I removed my shawl and knotted it tightly about his neck, forming a snug cradle for his injured limb. "There you are," I pronounced. "And mind you see that shawl gets back to me. It is my favorite."

He nodded, smiling weakly as I lifted my face to call, "Come on, then, Stoker. We haven't all night."

Stoker appeared over the edge of the basket and wound one leg about the rope, gripping it with the expert technique of a man who has spent years aboard Her Majesty's ships as a naval officer. His weight, greater than mine or Henry's—and possibly both together—caused the gondola to tip perilously. The branches holding the balloon cracked, and the ominous sound of ripping silk shredded the night.

"Faster," I urged under my breath. He moved fluidly, unhurried. He was still more than thirty feet from the ground, and a drop from there could kill him. But he would do far better without distraction from below, so I restricted my comments to muttering under my breath.

There was a long, slow sound, like a seamstress ripping calico, then a breathless pause. Stoker looked up, and before I could shout a warning, the last of the branches broke with a crack so loud it sounded like a cannon shot. Stoker, the rope, the basket, the balloon, all came tumbling to the ground in a rush of wicker and silk, landing with an audible *thud* that shook the earth.

"Stoker!"

I could not see him, for the balloon had landed in a riot of destruction. It took a moment for the silk to settle, and the silence was ominous. Suddenly, the pile gave a great heave, and Stoker emerged, crawling free of the debris. He coughed heavily, clutching his side.

"You've no doubt broken a rib," I scolded. "You ought to have descended before the balloon had a chance to tear."

He looked up at me, wheezing heavily, and I realized he was laughing. "It is no more than cracked, you virago. Good God, a man could die and you would scold him for making a mess on the carpet. Never change, Veronica."

"I shouldn't dream of it," I promised him. "Although what I am to do with a pair of wounded combatants, I cannot begin to think. Perhaps you should give me the revolver after all," I suggested brightly.

"Not bloody likely," Stoker muttered. I helped him to his feet and saw the grimace of pain he tried to suppress. I did not fuss. We had a mission, and he would not thank me to distract him from it with talk of broken bones and bandages.

"They have just entered the house!" Henry called in a hoarse whisper.

Following Henry's lead, we crept near to Tiverton Hall. It might, at one time, have been a pretty Tudor manor, but the gardens had been left untended and the building itself showed signs of neglect. Sir Leicester had obviously poured every spare penny into his Egyptological expeditions, and we had cause to be grateful: a lack of proper security meant no watchman and no dog to stop us.

As we moved near to the house, we saw a progression of lights as Sir Leicester and his captive moved through. At first a distant glow, the golden nimbus of a lamp grew brighter as they came to the back. We could hear Sir Leicester's voice raised as he berated Fairbrother, giving vent to his temper.

We paused only a moment in the shadow of a shrubbery to get our bearings. The bushes led us up to the edge of a French window, undraped. Through the glass we could see Fairbrother, sitting in a chair, his expression wary as he kept his eye upon Sir Leicester and the lethal black revolver in his hand.

To my astonishment, Stoker rose slowly from the shadow of the shrubbery, openly approaching the window.

"What are you doing?" Henry asked in a high voice.

"If we surprise him, he may shoot," Stoker explained. "Better to give him a moment to accustom himself to the idea that he has visitors."

He did not bother to lower his voice, and Fairbrother's instant glance in the direction of the window drew Sir Leicester's attention. He started from the chair and Sir Leicester waved him back, menacing him with the revolver as Stoker slowly opened the door, followed hard by me, Henry Stihl bringing up the rear reluctantly.

"What the devil are you lot doing here?" Sir Leicester demanded, all traces of good humor vanished.

"We came at Lady Tiverton's insistence," Stoker replied calmly. "She is rather afraid you might do something foolish." He deliberately circled to the left while I moved to the right, dividing Sir Leicester's focus.

The baronet was not to be so easily deceived. He jerked the revolver from one of us to the other. "No. Stand together," he ordered.

"Surely you do not mean to shoot us," I said plainly. "It is far too late for that. The game is up. Much better for you to take the consequences like a man."

His ruddy complexion was florid. "Consequences? Of what? Letting myself be duped by this, this blackguard?" he demanded, turning the gun once more upon Fairbrother.

"That's a bit rough, don't you think?" Fairbrother asked in a casual tone of voice. "We did agree to this scheme together, after all. You were perfectly happy to undertake it when we began."

"Happy? How could I be happy when you were always there, goading me to do more, to risk more? I wanted only to make a little money, but you have taken a harmless little business dealing and made it something grotesque. It is your fault that I have risked my honor," he lamented.

Any sympathy I might have had for the man was fast evaporating. He seemed far more concerned for his own name than for John de Morgan's life. But I could well imagine Patrick Fairbrother nudging him to the precipice of these crimes, then tipping him gently over the edge. I was thoroughly annoyed at myself for ever thinking him charming—and not a little chagrined that I had failed to consider him earlier in the role of the mastermind of this pernicious plot. I did not like to think that a sturdy pair of shoulders and a handsome smile might have compromised my judgment, so I dismissed the thought at once and turned my attention to provoking a confession.

"You arranged John de Morgan's death at the hotel in Dover, did you not?" I asked Fairbrother softly. "It was to be the culmination of the mummy's curse, proof along with the appearance of Anubis that the expedition had discovered something unique in all of Egyptology. Tell me how you managed it. I presume you had some connection to the hotel's proprietress."

"His sister," Sir Leicester supplied, leveling the revolver at Fairbrother's chest.

Fairbrother's eyes cut sharply to me, but he was careful to keep his voice casual, perhaps sensing that we were all that stood between him and the angry baronet. "Yes. Rebecca Giddons is my sister."

"Rebecca *F.* Giddons," I mouthed at Stoker as Fairbrother went on.

"Her hotel was failing, so when I took the position with Sir Leicester, I arranged for the expedition to stay with her. I thought she would benefit from it."

"She did," Stoker remarked. "So much that she felt obliged to help you when you conspired to remove John de Morgan. He gave you the perfect opportunity to kill two birds, if you will pardon the expression, with one stone. He found the diadem while you were digging, and when you pretended to discover it in the tomb, he realized what you were doing. He became a threat to your scheme and he had to be eliminated."

I looked at Fairbrother. "Redecorating the room was a particularly cruel touch. I suppose it bothered you not at all to think that you might drive Mrs. de Morgan mad with such a trick."

"She had to be discredited," Fairbrother said slowly. "If her story was plausible, the authorities would ask too many questions. But if she told a thoroughly unbelievable story, then she would be written off as a madwoman."

"And with John de Morgan ostensibly at large, no one could prove that *he* was not responsible if the fakery ever came to light. You eliminated a witness and established a scapegoat at a single stroke," Stoker said. "All to hide what you were doing—creating a fake Egyptological find where none existed."

"How do you know that?" Sir Leicester demanded, his color rising hotly.

"Something Horus Stihl said," I told him. "That he could sell a clay flowerpot so long as he could persuade someone it belonged to Amenhotep. That is precisely what you were doing, wasn't it? You pretended to find an incomplete grave complete with a mummy. That gave the find a certain cachet, and the notion of a curse prevented people from asking too many questions or becoming too suspicious when the body count began to grow. In the meantime, you would exhibit your treasures and then sell them privately for astronomical sums. Cheap reproductions, netting you a fortune."

"Did you even bother to put the goods into the grave?" Stoker asked. "No, wait. We already know the answer to that, don't we, Veronica?" He directed the baronet's attention to me just long enough to move himself forwards an inch. "You didn't. That's why you needed workers from upriver—strangers who wouldn't talk in the Valley villages, giving away your secret. You paid off the Egyptian authorities with a few real artifacts from earlier expeditions. It meant sacrificing your own collection, but that would be a small price to pay for the fortune you stood to make from the sale of the Exhibition. You could charge astronomical prices and no one would blink at paying them."

I continued the narrative, turning an accusing eye upon Sir Leicester. "The only item you needed to produce, with theatrical flourish, was the sarcophagus—a mummy case you had already purchased, one you damaged by fire when the bitumen went up in flames. Easy enough to add a few inscriptions, particularly with a pet philologist to hand," I said, nodding at Fairbrother.

Sir Leicester started to protest, but Fairbrother let out a gusty sigh. "Oh, for God's sake, Sir Leicester, we've had it. They have put all the pieces together and they know enough to hang us both."

"Hang us!" The revolver in Sir Leicester's hand jumped wildly. "I shall not hang! I am no murderer!"

Fairbrother's mouth twisted into a grotesque smile. "Do you think that matters? Do you think your title is going to save you when the story gets out? If you aren't hanged, you're disgraced, ruined forever. Unless I swear that you murdered Jonas Fowler," he said, a cunning expression creeping over his face.

"But I did no such thing!" Sir Leicester protested.

Fairbrother shrugged. "Can you prove it? There was no post-mortem," he pointed out. "Jonas died of heart failure after gastric trouble—a common thing when a man has been poisoned with arsenic. And there is a tidy packet of arsenic powder currently in your lady's possession. She cannot prove she took it from my room, can she? I shall say she took it from yours. If you lay the blame for de Morgan's murder on me, I shall lay blame for Fowler's on you."

"But you cannot," the baronet said, his voice thick with rage. His complexion was empurpled, and I wondered if he was about to have a second apoplexy.

"I can," Fairbrother told him slowly. "And I will unless you agree here and now to take the blame for the planning of this endeavor. If neither of us admit to involvement in de Morgan's death, they cannot hang either one. We will spend our lives in prison, but we will live."

Sir Leicester looked frantically from Fairbrother to the rest of us. Stoker inched closer again, but Sir Leicester brandished the gun. "Back. You must stay back. I need to think," he said, jabbing the weapon in Stoker's direction.

"It is all right, Sir Leicester," I said soothingly. "You do not need to decide anything now. Give us the gun, and let us take Fairbrother in to the authorities. They will know best what to do."

Sir Leicester looked confused. Beads of perspiration sprang out, beading the edge of his hairline. He panted a little, as if struggling to get his breath.

"Sir Leicester," Henry said gently. "You do not look well. Perhaps we ought to summon a doctor."

The word galvanized Sir Leicester. "No," he said, holding up the gun with renewed vigor. "No. He is trying to manipulate me, but I will not have it. I know the truth, and the truth is that I would never have embarked upon this road were it not for him and he intended to cheat me of my share. He means to flee to the Argentine, leaving me to clear up the mess. He has a ticket on a ship leaving tomorrow. Did you know that?" he demanded. "After all the sins we have committed, he means to add treachery to the list. But now he has been caught in his own web. He will lie and twist and connive and he will go free. They will believe him because he is clever and I am not. Every evil that I have done has been at his instigation. And now I will atone for it," he said.

He lifted his chin with a quiet, desperate resolution.

"No!" I cried. But of course it was too late.

Before any of us could act, he lifted the gun and fired once.

Patrick Fairbrother made no sound. He merely widened his eyes in astonishment, looked down to the crimson stain blossoming across his chest like a terrible flower. He fell to the floor in silence. A second shot followed hard upon the first as Sir Leicester Tiverton pressed the revolver to the soft flesh just under his chin and pulled the trigger.

CHAPTER 20

The suicide of the baronet and the murder of his expedition philologist only heightened the allure of the mummy's curse. Far from explaining away the tragic events as rational actions by a cruel conspiracy, *The Daily Harbinger* maintained that only the malign influence of a vengeful mummy could have driven Sir Leicester and Fairbrother to such desperate acts. It was nonsense, of course, but J. J. Butterworth's lurid prose did its work. Even knowing many of the artifacts to be fake, the public flocked to the Tiverton Exhibition at Karnak Hall in astonishing numbers.

A few days after our desperate flight into Surrey, we met Lady Tiverton at the Curiosity Club at her invitation. She was dressed in black now, and she seemed to have aged as she came forward to greet us. She was heavily veiled to avoid attracting attention, but she needn't have bothered. The members of the club took care of their own.

"Thank you for meeting me," she began.

We started in her direction, but Hetty, the portress, came out from behind her desk, stopping in front of Stoker with a firm step.

"I am sorry, sir, but the Hippolyta Club does not permit gentlemen to enter."

Stoker cocked his head and Lady Tiverton threw back her veil. "It is my fault, Hetty. I forgot the rules against gentlemen guests. I do not suppose you might bend them just this once?"

Hetty surveyed Stoker from head to toe and gave a grudging nod. "Gentlemen may be admitted in extraordinary circumstances, but only to the Parley Room on the ground floor and only for twenty-nine minutes."

Stoker grinned. "That is terribly specific."

"That, sir, is the rule. Stay a second longer, and I will come myself to escort you out," she told him sternly.

He inclined his head and trotted meekly behind as she showed us to the Parley Room. She pointedly turned an hourglass on the mantel and left it, sands slipping downwards as she took her leave, shutting the door firmly behind.

"I am surprised that you want to see us," I told Lady Tiverton. "We failed in our endeavor."

Her lips curved, but I would not have called it a smile. No smile was ever so sad. "You tried, Miss Speedwell. You tried to save him, and so did I. But he involved himself in the plot, and in the end the responsibility for its dreadful conclusion must lie with him." Her grave dark eyes looked from me to Stoker and back again. "I know Figgy believed I betrayed her father with Patrick, but it is not true. I loved my husband very much, and I take my vows seriously. Including the vow I made to the first Lady Tiverton to take care of Sir Leicester to the end of his life."

"She saw you coming out of Fairbrother's room and misconstrued it. That was the first time you went looking for evidence against him, wasn't it?" Stoker asked with a gentleness I had seldom heard him use.

She nodded. "That was when I found the letter from his sister confirming that John de Morgan had been dealt with." She gave a little shudder and collected herself with a visible effort. "Forgive me. I want to talk about this. I want to hear it all said aloud. Just this once, and then I never want to speak of it again." She took a deep breath and began to speak.

"I knew from the beginning of the season that something was amiss, but I could not say who was the author of the mischief. At first it seemed like nothing more than silly tricks—de Morgan's camera plates damaged, the sightings of Anubis. Destructive and demoralizing, but not malevolent. And then Jonas Fowler died, and I did not know what to think. He was ill. He had been for several years, and the demands of excavation life are strenuous. I did not want to believe that anyone might have hastened his death."

"Do you believe it now?" he asked.

She spread her hands. Her wedding ring caught the light. She would wear it always, I was certain. "The chemist's envelope I found in Patrick's room. There was only a trace of powder left in it, and no way to tell what it might have been. I do not want to believe he might have—even now—" She broke off, covering her mouth.

"It was arsenic," I told her gently. "He admitted it just before his death. But he would not confess to using it on Jonas Fowler. In fact, he was prepared to swear the packet belonged to you and that you had a hand in Mr. Fowler's death. But with no post-mortem . . ." I let the sentence trail off.

She was silent, clearly struggling with strong emotion. After a moment she composed herself.

"So we will never know if poor Jonas was the first of his victims. Perhaps it is best. I like to think Jonas died as he lived, giving all of himself to the adopted country he loved. Let him rest in peace." I had my own thoughts upon the subject. The fact that Fairbrother had been so willing to arrange John de Morgan's death when it suited him made it clear he would not have balked at easing Jonas Fowler's passage into the next world. But if he had, Fairbrother had paid for his crimes, and Lady Tiverton needed no fresh horrors.

She paused again, and when she began to speak, she sounded older, resigned to the burden of grief she would carry to the end of her days. "I have seen evil, and it wears a smiling face. I liked him when he first came to us," she said, her expression soft with reminiscence. "I realized soon after our marriage that Sir Leicester and I were not to be blessed with children. But he liked young people. It made him feel youthful to have them around. I encouraged Patrick. I thought he showed great promise, and over time they became close. So close that when Sir Leicester discovered the cave last year, it was to Patrick that he confided his find, and not to me."

"And Patrick who suggested the use to which it might profitably be put?" I suggested.

She nodded. "I think so. It is not the sort of plot Sir Leicester would have contrived on his own. It took planning, audacity. Certainly my husband was audacious, but methodical he was not. Someone had to arrange for the faked antiquities to be made and shipped out of Egypt, and someone had to arrange for them to be received in Dover and sent on to the house in Surrey."

"Fairbrother's sister," Stoker said. "We made her acquaintance."

"She was the one who murdered John de Morgan," Lady Tiverton said. "On his orders. Her letter revealed that he had sent very specific instructions as to how the deed was to be done. She complied. She was his willing accomplice in every way, and I can only imagine the hold he must have had over her to force her to do such terrible things."

I remembered Mrs. Giddons and her cold-blooded treatment of Stoker and of me, and I smiled thinly. "I do not think Mrs. Giddons requires much persuasion. She and her brother are two of a kind." He had spoken to me of her once and with real affection—the self-sacrificing sister who had done everything to make certain her beloved brother was given every opportunity. She had not even scrupled at murder to ensure his success.

Lady Tiverton nodded. "Her letter indicated that he was the one who schemed to spirit away the body in the sarcophagus, knowing the authorities would never look inside. Mrs. Giddons had only to store the corpse in her washhouse for a few days until we arrived from Egypt.

Patrick did the rest. He put John's remains in the sarcophagus and we brought it with us, never knowing."

"All that talk of a mummy and it never existed," I murmured. "Princess Ankheset was a fiction from start to finish, just a few faked hieroglyphs on a mummy case and a diadem."

"It was an audacious plan," Lady Tiverton said, her voice tight. "It might have worked."

We were silent a moment before I raised the subject of Patrick Fairbrother again. "It was his idea to redecorate the room, was it not? In order to confuse and terrify Caroline de Morgan. No one would believe her story because she would sound mad, and with de Morgan gone under mysterious circumstances, the easiest explanation was that he had stolen the diadem for his own gain."

She nodded. "It was monstrous. The police say that Mrs. Giddons has disappeared from Dover. They have no idea of where she has gone, but they are quite certain she has quitted the country."

"A wanted murderess? No doubt she has put as much distance between England and herself as possible," Stoker agreed. "And her brother has paid for his crimes."

I thought of Patrick Fairbrother, the clever, grasping young scholar with the charming smile and the winsome ways. I was not often slow to suspect evil in a man who was capable of it; my life had, upon occasion, depended upon my ability to tell villainy from virtue. I should not soon forget my failure here.

"Yes, he has paid—as has my husband," Lady Tiverton said with some bitterness. "Poor, foolish Leicester."

"What drove him to it?" I asked. "He was a man who had every advantage."

"Money," she said simply. "The first Lady Tiverton divided her fortune evenly between her husband and her child. Sir Leicester ran through his half. Egyptology is a messy and expensive business," she added with a rueful smile. "He thought that one great find would make his name, and he was right. If he had discovered a tomb of note, he would have made a fortune. As it was, he intended to sell worthless trinkets for enormous sums to amateurs who would not know the difference."

"But you did," I observed. "What raised your suspicions?"

"The sarcophagus," she said promptly. "It was the one thing he could not afford to fake. With a genuine mummy case, the rest of the find would have received far less scrutiny. He took a sarcophagus that he had purchased some years ago and, with Patrick's help, contrived to make it appear authentic to the Princess Ankheset. I did not recognize it at first because of the alterations, but something troubled me about it. Eventually I thought to compare the Princess Ankheset's sarcophagus to a photograph the first Lady Tiverton had in her collection of the pieces Sir Leicester had bought. The parts that were not altered or damaged in the fire were a perfect match."

"And the fire was a deliberate attempt to damage the sarcophagus and make it untraceable," I deduced.

She nodded. "A bit of bitumen and the fire damage covered up the places where they were unable to change the previous inscriptions. They thought it would be enough, but I suspect I would not have been the only one to realize the fraud in time."

"What of the beautiful pectoral piece you wore to the reception? The one Sir Leicester claimed to have excavated?"

"Worthless," she said briskly. "Except as a conversation piece."

"And the diadem of the princess?" Stoker asked.

"A modern forgery. Not worth anything more than the weight of the gold and the gems."

"About the diadem," I began. She held up a hand.

"Mr. Stihl has kindly returned it. I have sent it back to him to keep in trust for Figgy. It is not worth a tremendous amount, but it is something."

I blinked at her in surprise. "In trust for Figgy?"

Her smile was thin. "My husband was superstitious about things like wills. He only ever made one, during his first marriage. As the previous Lady Tiverton was wealthy in her own right, he provided only a token amount for his widow. The provisions for Figgy remain unchanged. In the event of his death, Figgy is to be given into the care of Horace Stihl, along with the management of her inheritance. I could possibly make a case in court, but such a thing would be doubtful at best and terribly expensive. I am content to accept the situation as it is."

"But you are her stepmother," Stoker argued. "You ought to have charge of the girl."

She shook her head. "Figgy blames me for too much of what has happened."

"That is unjust," he told her.

"The young are often unjust. But in time I hope she will come to see that I am not the villainess she believed. I did everything in my power to save my husband from ruin. Instead I caused it."

"How?" Stoker asked.

"I gave my husband the steamship ticket I found in Patrick's room. That was what drove him to rise from his sickbed and go to confront him. He found Patrick in the action of preparing to flee."

"It was his own choice to take matters into his own hands," Stoker reminded her gently. "He might have turned Fairbrother over to the authorities."

"For murder, yes. And confessed himself as a fraud, dragging his family name through the mud, condemning his daughter to a lifetime of whispers. No, bless him. He tried to spare her that. But, as I said, my husband was not much of a thinker."

She rose and extended her hand to each of us in turn. "I am leaving for Egypt just as soon as I can make the arrangements. I do not believe we will meet again."

We emerged from the Parley Room with six minutes to spare. Hetty gave Stoker a close look as we walked past, and he tipped his hat to her.

"Miss Speedwell," she called. "A moment." She emerged from behind the desk holding a vellum portfolio. "We received your acceptance. You will be inducted at the next formal meeting, in a fortnight's time. Here is the information for new members. It is confidential."

I took the heavy vellum portfolio. I glanced at the wall where the photographs of the members were hung. Past and present they were arranged, a gallery of women of accomplishment, women of stalwart spirit and indomitable courage. And in spite of my misgivings, I knew I had found a home.

Just at the end there was a small empty spot, not prominent, tucked just beneath the stairs.

"Right there," I told Hetty.

"Pardon, Miss Speedwell?"

"That is where I want my photograph to hang."

She grinned. "Welcome to the Curiosity Club, Miss Speedwell."

The next afternoon Lady Wellie invited us to tea to hear the final report of what she insisted upon calling the Tiverton Case.

"Poor Messy Lessy," she said as she added a hefty measure of whisky to her tea. Stoker had cried off on the grounds that he was attempting repairs to the Aérostat Réveillon, but I suspected it would be futile. His lordship had taken one look at the wagonload of splintered wicker and torn taffeta and turned away in despair. Still, Stoker felt obligated to try, and so he was busy stitching and gluing and weaving under the earl's watchful eye.

"What is to become of Figgy?" Lady Wellie asked.

"School," I told her promptly. We had spent the previous evening dining at the Allerdale Hotel in Mr. Stihl's suite, discussing the situation. At my urging, Mr. Stihl enrolled Figgy in the Laidlaw-Upton Academy for Young Ladies, a unique establishment in Colorado founded to nurture the "gumption" of unusual young women. It was no secret that he harbored a hope that one day she would make up her mind to marry young Henry, but I encouraged her to give it ten years and travel the world at least twice before taking such a drastic step. She thanked me for my advice with a reluctant handshake. To Stoker she entrusted Nut, the hound, explaining that she could not take him to America and that the animal could ask for no better place than at Stoker's side. It took a concerted effort and all my strength to pry Figgy off Stoker when she went to hug him good-bye, but at last she was removed from his person and we were allowed to get on with our evening.

Lady Wellie nodded as I related the story. "It will be the making of her. She might look like a Tiverton, but she's a Ward, and if she's anything like her mother, she will show it now. Adversity builds character," she finished briskly. "Speaking of one's parents, this arrived today."

She handed over a small box of black kid stamped on the top with a trio of distinctive feathers.

"Are those—"

"Yes. His feathers. Open it."

I did as she bade me. Inside, nestled on a bed of oyster satin, was the slender strand of beads from the Tiverton Exhibition. The blue lapis butterfly dangled from the bottom, poised as if to fly away. I did not touch it.

Lady Wellie spoke first. "It is one of the few pieces that are genuine. Don't worry—he paid for it, the going rate."

"Why?" I asked in a voice unlike my own.

"Who can say?" she replied with a shrug. "There was no note with it, only the instruction to see it delivered into your hands. Take whatever meaning you like from it."

I closed the box. "And if I do not take it at all?"

"That is also your choice," she acknowledged. "But do not close the door entirely, Veronica."

"He has closed it upon me often enough," I countered quickly. Too quickly. She gave me a pitying smile.

"Do not ever let your pride dictate your principles, child."

I put the box into my pocket and took up the teapot. "I think you need a fresh cup," I said. And when I poured, my hand was steady.

I left Lady Wellie and made my way to the Belvedere, lost in thought, and had reached my desk before I realized I was not alone.

"Good afternoon, Mrs. de Morgan. I am afraid Stoker is busy with his work, but I can send someone to find him for you, if you like."

She gave me a coolly appraising look. "I do not want to speak to him. I came to see you."

"Whatever for?"

"Because you are the one who found John." Her voice broke on his name. "I can bury him decently, and that is worth something at least."

"I am sorry for your loss," I told her.

"My loss?" Her eyes were bleak. "What do you know of loss? Have you ever been in love? Not calf love, Miss Speedwell. I mean proper love, the kind that is not sweet or tender but burns in your bones and tears you in two. That is what I felt for John. We fought like devils, but that was our way. No one understood that when we quarreled we felt alive. God, how I shall miss the savagery of our life together. He was not a good man, but he was good to me." I thought then of all they had destroyed between them, and my blood ran hot through my temples.

"Perhaps you should use that as an epitaph," I suggested.

"You despise me, Miss Speedwell, but you do not even know me," she said, curling a scornful lip.

"But I do know you. I have always known you. You belong to that contemptible breed of female who will forever look at what she has been denied rather than what she has been given. What gift has Nature refused you? You were born under a faery star! Beauty, breeding, good health, native intelligence—these were yours from birth, but what gratitude have you ever expressed for them? None. You rise from your bed every day on two strong legs and can think only to complain that someone once spoke harshly to you. You had parents who reared you gently, but you scorn them for being poor—you who have lived abroad and seen real want. Tell me, Mrs. de Morgan, when you were in Egypt, did you ever look at a woman laboring in the fields and understand that it was the merest accident of a kind Providence that you were not born to toil your life away? Have you ever looked a starving beggar in the eye and thought that the privileges you enjoy are nothing more than a whim of the cosmos? You are Fortune's darling, beloved of the gods, blessed with every advantage, but you are blind and deaf to your endowments. You have ease and comfort, but you do not live. You merely exist because you appreciate nothing. Waken, Mrs. de Morgan, or else you will slumber your life away."

She rose. "You think you are clever, Miss Speedwell. You think you are so much smarter than I am. But I will tell you something you ought to know. You have befriended a dangerous man. Revelstoke has killed a man. Think about that. He has taken those useful talented hands of his and used them to crush the life out of someone. That should make the marrow in your bones run cold. How can you stand to be near him now that you know he has taken a life?" she demanded, her eyes cruel in her triumph.

I moved closer to her, giving her a slow smile, a tiger's smile. "Because, Mrs. de Morgan, I have taken two."

The day after Caroline de Morgan's visit, I went into the glasshouse to find that my luna moths had emerged. They had broken free from their dark little prisons, pushing forth on damp silken wings. As I watched in rapt wonder, they spread them slowly, drying them as they flapped back and forth. They were pale green with long, elegant hind wings and markings like eyes that seemed to watch me as I studied them. They were large, each exceeding the length of my hand. One by one they rose from their branches, testing themselves as they lifted into the warm, humid air of the glasshouse, attempting their freedom for the first time. Each silken wing was edged in cerise, and the antennae were frilled and golden, frivolous little embellishments that danced above their bodies.

"They've eclosed," Stoker observed, coming to stand behind me. I nodded, marveling as the last moth flitted off in amorous pursuit of a mate.

"I received word this morning. John de Morgan's child was born last night, well before its time. A girl," he said quietly. "That, no doubt, came as a nasty shock to her mother."

"And Caroline? How is she?"

"Well enough, although the child may not survive."

"If she does, I am glad she is a girl. Her mother will have no claim upon the de Morgan money," I said with a touch of asperity.

"No. She will have to leave off her machinations for now. As soon as they are able, they mean to move to the country."

I turned, but his face gave nothing away. Did it pain him to speak of her? Still he did not say her name, had never willingly said it in front of me.

And suddenly the words I had never planned to speak fell from my lips.

"Why do you never say her name? I have only once heard you speak the word 'Caroline.' Does she torment you so much?"

His expression was one of astonishment. Then he smiled. "No. I do not say it because I never called her that except upon one occasion—on our wedding night, just before she refused me her bed. I kissed her and called her by her given name. It was, I believed then, the happiest moment of my life, one perfect golden moment before it all went to hell."

I turned away. That was what it meant, then, the invoking of her name when he was drugged and half-delirious and his mouth was on mine. He was remembering not the woman who had come before, but the promise of happiness he had glimpsed once and never thought to know again.

I cleared my throat and brushed aside a stray leaf. He stood in front of me, very close. He reached out, putting a fingertip to the pendant at my throat. "A handsome little butterfly. I don't remember seeing this before."

"It is new," I told him. There would be time enough to explain. He went on, still touching the lapis butterfly, his knuckles just grazing the skin of my chest.

"The case has been put to rest now. John is buried, and whatever was left of my reputation has been salvaged," he said, his voice oddly soft. "Thank you for that. You fight harder for me than you would ever do for yourself. Why?"

"Because there is no power on earth that could make me abandon our friendship. There is no deed you could confess so dark that it would make me forsake you. You said of us once that we were quicksilver and the rest of the world mud. We are alike, shaped by Nature in the same mold, and whatever that signifies, it means that to spurn each other would be to spit in the face of whatever deity has seen fit to bring us together. We are the same, and to leave you would be to leave myself. Make of that what you will."

I turned away to watch my lunas rising and swooping amidst the iron lacework overhead.

Hunting butterflies requires an oblique approach. If one charges them directly, they flit away, mapping a mazy, elusive path until they disappear from sight with a final flap of jeweled, defiant wings. But if one is cunning and careful, it is possible to approach them so subtly they do not realize you are upon them until the net descends. The trick is to move with them, parallel but not intersecting, guiding them gently to a suitable landing spot where they can be captured without injury. The timing is all. Hurry them and they will bolt. Dawdle and they will dart away after some tasty sip of nectar. It requires patience, skill, and resolve—qualities I had in abundance and which Stoker would give me ample opportunity to exercise.

I turned back to him, words that I thought never to say to any man rising to my lips.

At that moment a voice hailed us from just beyond the little grove of hornbeams. I closed my mouth and stepped away.

"Miss Speedwell? I received your message. Have the little devils finally emerged?" It was the viscount, with impeccable manners and deplorable timing.

"Good morning, my lord," I called brightly. "Stoker and I are just admiring them now."

"Oh, is my brother with you?" the viscount asked, pushing his way through the foliage.

"Yes," Stoker told him, coming to stand behind me, his hand grazing my waist. "I am."

ACKNOWLEDGMENTS

It is an honor and pleasure to be able to share my gratitude to the following:

For welcoming Veronica with open arms and giving her a truly fine home, the lovely people at Berkley with special recognition of Craig Burke, Loren Jaggers, Claire Zion, Sarah Blumenstock, Roxanne Jones, Sara-Jayne Poletti, and Kara Welsh. Tremendous thanks to the art department for their inspired work and to the sales, marketing, editorial, and publicity teams. I will forever be indebted to Ellen Edwards for seeing the potential in Veronica.

For polishing Veronica with such tact and consideration, my truly superb copy editor, Penina Lopez.

For nearly twenty years of guidance, business acumen, advice, and friendship, my agent, Pam Hopkins.

For friendship, support, and many kindnesses, Blake Leyers, Benjamin Dreyer, Ali Trotta, Joshilyn Jackson, Ariel Lawhon, Delilah Dawson, Rhys Bowen, Alan Bradley, Duchess Goldblatt, Helen Ellis, Susan Elia MacNeal, Lauren Willig, Nathan Dunbar, Stephanie Graves, Holly Faur, and Carin Thumm.

For all the heavy lifting of the practical work, the team at Writerspace and my assistant, Jomie Wilding.

For taking Veronica to their hearts and sharing their enthusiasm, booksellers, reviewers, bloggers, and readers.

For love, patience, and willingness to run errands, my family.

For everything, for always, my husband.

A TREACHEROUS CURSE

A VERONICA SPEEDWELL MYSTERY

Deanna Raybourn

QUESTIONS FOR DISCUSSION

1. Stoker and Veronica are clearly drawn to each other and share a special connection. What do you think is the most significant issue keeping them apart, and do you think it's valid?

2. Veronica's relationship with the royal family is complicated. Do you think they should acknowledge her? What problems would this present?

3. In lieu of a typical family, Veronica is creating a "found" family. Which characters would you consider to be members of this family? What roles do they play?

4. Stoker feels strongly that the mummy of Princess Ankheset should not be publicly exhibited and that even the ancient dead should rest in peace. Do you agree? Why or why not?

5. Veronica's character is inspired by actual Victorian explorers such as Margaret Fountaine and Isabella Bird. How do these women differ from the stereotypical Victorian lady?

6. Two of the new characters introduced in this book are Julien d'Orlande and J. J. Butterworth. How do they fit into Veronica and Stoker's world? What roles might they play in future books?

7. The Tivertons are a blended family with complicated relationships. How does Sir Leicester's connection with his protégé Patrick Fairbrother stoke Figgy Tiverton's resentment? How successful is Lady Tiverton in her self-appointed role as peacemaker?

8. Stoker's former wife, Caroline de Morgan, plays a significant role in the story. How would you characterize her relationship with Stoker? How has her remarriage to John de Morgan changed her life?

9. Veronica is invited to join the Hippolyta Club, an organization dedicated to exceptional women. How does the club's motto—*Alis volat propriis* (She flies with her own wings)—apply to Veronica?

10. What do you think the ending suggests about Veronica's future?

London, March 1888

"What the devil do you mean, you're leaving?" Stoker demanded. He surveyed the half-packed carpetbag on my bed as I folded in a spare shirtwaist and *Magalhães's Guide to Portuguese Lepidoptery.* It was a weightier volume than one might expect, featuring an appendix devoted to the butterflies of Madeira and certain flamboyant moths found only in the Azores.

"Precisely what I said. I am packing. When I have packed, I will leave this place and board a train for the coast. There I will leave the train and get onto a boat and when it stops at Madeira, I will have arrived." My tone was frankly waspish. I had dreaded telling Stoker of my plans, expecting some sort of mild explosion at the notion that I had at last secured an expedition, however minor, to which he was not invited. Instead, he had adopted an attitude of Arctic hauteur. I blamed his aristocratic upbringing for that. And his nose. It is very easy to look down on someone with a nose that would have done a Roman emperor justice. But I could not entirely blame him. As natural historians, we had balked at our enforced stay in London, each of us longing for the open seas, skies that stretched to forever, horizons that beckoned us with spice-scented winds. Instead, we had found ourselves employed by the Earl of Rosemorran to catalog his family's extensive collections—interesting and modestly profitable work that stunted the soul if endured for too long. One could count only so many stuffed marmosets before the spirit rebelled. The notion that I was to escape our genial confinement whilst he labored on would have tested the noblest character, and Stoker, like me, bore a healthy streak of self-interest.

"At Madeira?" he asked.

"At Madeira," I replied firmly.

He folded his arms over the breadth of his chest. "And might one inquire as to the expected duration of this expedition?"

"One might, but one would be disappointed with the reply. I have not yet formulated my plans, but I expect to be away for some months. Perhaps until the autumn."

"Until the autumn," he said, drawing out the words slowly.

"Yes. Look for me in the season of mists and mellow fruitfulness," I instructed, with a feeble attempt at a smile. But even a nod to his beloved Keats did not soften his austere expression.

"And you mean to go alone."

"Not at all," I told him as I tucked a large pot of cold cream of roses into my bag. "Lady Cordelia and I shall travel together."

He gave a snort of laughter that was distinctly lacking in amusement. "Lady Cordelia. You know her only experience with shipboard life is the Channel steamer, do you not? Her notion of rough travel is not taking the second footman. And I do not even like to *think* of what Sidonie will have to say on the matter."

I winced at the mention of Lady Cordelia's snippy French lady's maid. "She will not be coming."

His mouth fell agape and he dropped the pose of icy disdain. "Veronica, you cannot be serious. I know you long to shake the fogs of London out of your clothes as much as I do, but dragging Lady Cordelia to some benighted island in the middle of the Atlantic makes no sense at all. You might as well haul her to the North Pole."

"I should never attempt a polar expedition," I assured him with a lightness I did not feel. "There are no butterflies to be found there."

He gripped my shoulders, his thumbs just brushing the tops of my collarbones. "If this is because of what I said earlier today," he began, "what I *almost* said—"

I raised a hand. "Of course not." It was a pathetic attempt at a lie. The truth was that both of us, in an unguarded moment, had very nearly given voice to sentiments we had no business declaring. I could still feel the pressure of his hand, burning like a brand at my waist, as his breath stirred the lock of hair pinned behind my ear, warm and impulsive words trembling on my lips. Had his brother, the Viscount Templeton-Vane, not interrupted us . . .

But no. That line of thought does not bear consideration. The point is quite simply that we *were* interrupted, and as soon as the viscount left, I had taken tea tête-à-tête with Lady Cordelia, Lord Rosemorran's sister and a good friend to both Stoker and me. By the time we had shared the last muffin between us, we had decided upon a course of action that we knew would surprise and quite possibly annoy the men in our lives. Lord Rosemorran had behaved with his characteristic good-natured vagueness, offering money to fund the venture and raising objections only when he realized his sister's absence would mean taking care of his own children.

"Call one of the aunts to help you," Lady C. instructed with unaccustomed ruthlessness. "I am thoroughly exhausted and a holiday is just what I require."

Lord Rosemorran gave in at once, but Stoker was being bloody-minded as usual, not least because so much hung between us, unsaid but thickening the air until I thought I would never again draw an easy breath.

"It is quite for the best," I said, forcing the last of my shirtwaists into the bag. "This business with the Tiverton Expedition has been demanding. A little peace and quiet to recover from it will do us both a world of good."

On the surface, it was a tolerable excuse. The investigation we had just concluded* had been harrowing in the extreme, entailing all manner of reckless adventures as well as a few bodily injuries. But Stoker and I throve on such endeavors, matching each other in our acts of derring-do. No, it was not physical exhaustion that drove me from the temperate shores of England, gentle reader. It was the recent entanglement with Stoker's former wife, Caroline de Morgan, a fiend in petticoats who had very nearly destroyed him with her machinations. I longed to repay her in kind. But I had learnt long ago that revenge is a fruitless pursuit, and so I left Caroline to the fates, trusting she would see her just deserts in time. Stoker was my concern—specifically the powerful emotions he stirred within me and what, precisely, I was going to do about them. It seemed impossible to assess them with the cool and dispassionate eye of a scientist whilst we were so often together. After all, a proper examination of a butterfly did not take place in the field; one captured the specimen and took it away to regard it carefully, holding it up to the light and accepting its flaws as well as its beauties. So I meant to do with my feelings for Stoker, although that intention was certainly not one I meant to share with him. Knowing how deeply he had been wounded by Caroline, I could have no hand in hurting him further.

Luckily for me, Lady Cordelia had been desperate, insistent upon leaving right away, and I seized upon her invitation with alacrity, determined to make my escape without revealing our purposes, even to Stoker.

"I daresay I will have nothing more interesting to write about than

---

* *A Treacherous Curse*

butterflies, so do not be surprised if I am a poor correspondent," I warned him. "You needn't trouble to write if it bores you. I am sure you will have far more interesting activities to occupy your time. I am sorry if it leaves you in a bit of a lurch with the collections," I finished, buckling the carpetbag.

"I will manage quite well alone," he replied as he turned away, his expression carefully blank. "I always have."

As he no doubt intended, Stoker's parting words haunted me for the better part of six months. Madeira was beautiful, lush and fragrant and offering tremendous opportunities for my work as a lepidopterist. But more times than I cared to admit, whilst hotly in pursuit of a sweet little *Lampides boeticus* flapping lazily in a flower-scented breeze, I paused, letting the net drop uselessly to my side. Articles for the various publications to which I contributed went unwritten, my pen resting in a stilled hand while my mind roamed free. Every time, my thoughts went to him, like pigeons darting home to roost. And every time, I wrenched them away, never permitting myself to think too long of him for the same reason a child learns not to hold her hand too close to a flame.

In the summer, when the late-blooming jacaranda poured the honeyed musk of its perfume over the island, it was necessary—for various reasons I shall not detail here—to call in the doctor to attend both Lady Cordelia and me. By the time we had regained our strength, half a year had passed and our thoughts turned to England once more. Long afternoons had been spent upon the veranda of our rented villa as we rested like basking lizards in the sun. We were both slimmer than we had been when we set out. Lady Cordelia's pale milk skin had gathered a cinnamon dusting of freckles in spite of her veils and broad brims, but I had tossed my hat aside, turning my face up to the golden rays.

"You look the picture of health," she told me as we boarded the boat in the port of Funchal. "No one would ever imagine you had been under a doctor's care."

I plucked at the loose waist of my traveling suit. "You think not? I am skin and bone, and you are little better. But some good Devonshire cream and plates of English roast beef will see us right again," I assured her.

Absently, she linked her arm with mine. "Do you think they have missed us?"

"The frequency of their letters would suggest so." Frequency was not quite the word. Every mail ship had brought fresh correspondence. The earl and his children had written regularly to Lady Cordelia, and I had received my share of the post as well. Colleagues in lepidoptery had much to say, and there were weekly letters from Lord Templeton-Vane, Stoker's elder brother. He wrote in a casual, conversational style of current affairs and common interests, and as the months passed, we became better friends than we had been before.

And from Stoker? Not a single word. Not one line, scribbled on a grubby postcard. Not a postscript scrawled on one of his brother's letters. Nothing but silence, eloquent and rebuking. I was conscious of a profound and thoroughly irrational sense of injury. I had made it clear to him that I did not intend to write letters and expected none. And yet. Every post that arrived with no missive from him was a taunt, speaking his anger as eloquently as any words might have done. I had sowed the seed of this quarrel, I reminded myself sternly; I could not now complain that I did not like the fruit it bore.

And as I stood arm in arm with Lady Cordelia on the deck of the ship bearing us home, I wondered precisely what sort of welcome I could expect.

"What in the name of seven hells do you mean you want to 'borrow' Miss Speedwell? She's not an umbrella, for God's sake," Stoker grumbled to his eldest brother as the viscount entered our workroom.

(Such comments often comprised the bulk of Stoker's conversation; I had learnt to ignore them.) "Besides which, she has only been home for two days. I very much doubt she has even unpacked."

Lord Templeton-Vane bared his teeth in what a stupid person might have mistaken for a smile. "Stoker, how delightful to see you. I hadn't noticed you behind that water buffalo's backside. Perfecting your trade, no doubt," he mused as he looked from the moldering buffalo trophy to the pile of rotten sawdust Stoker was busy extracting. As a natural historian, Stoker's lot was often the restoration of thoroughly foul specimens of the taxidermic arts. The backside of a water buffalo was far from the worst place I had seen Stoker's head.

His lordship clicked his tongue as he gave Stoker a dismissive glance. "Besides which, I hardly think Miss Speedwell requires assistance in arranging her affairs." He lingered on the last word just a heartbeat too long. The viscount had a gift for silken suggestions, and I suppressed a sigh of irritation that he had exercised it just then. Stoker and I had scarcely spoken since my return, exchanging cool greetings and meaningless chatter about our work. But I had hopes of a thaw, provided the viscount did not scupper the possibility.

I looked up from the tray of *Nymphalidae* I was sorting and gave them both a repressive stare. "I am not your nanny, but if required, I will put either of you over my knee," I warned them.

Stoker, who topped me by half a foot and some forty pounds, pulled a face. His brother's response was slightly salacious. He lifted an exquisite brow and sighed. "One could only wish," he murmured.

I ignored that remark and brushed off my hands, putting my butterflies aside. "My lord," I said to the viscount, "before you explain further, perhaps we might have a little refreshment."

His lordship looked pained. "I abhor tea parties," he protested.

It was my turn to snort. "Not that sort of tea." With Stoker's grudging consent, I retrieved a bottle of his best single malt and poured out a measure for each of us. We settled in and I studied my companions. In certain respects, they could not have been more different, yet in others they were startlingly similar. They shared the fine bone structure of their mother: from high cheekbones and determined jaws to elegant hands, they were alike. It was in coloring and musculature that they varied. While his lordship was sleek as an otter, Stoker's muscles, honed by his long years of work as a natural historian and explorer, were heavier and altogether more impressive. He made good use of them as he worked on the mounts that would form the basis of the Rosemorran Collection. Whilst we sorted the family's accumulated treasures from centuries of travel, the earl had given us the use of the Belvedere, the grand freestanding ballroom on his Marylebone estate, as well as living quarters, modest salaries, and a few other perquisites such as entertaining visitors when we chose.

Stoker, as it happened, was not entirely pleased with our current caller. His relationship with his eldest brother was difficult at the best of times, and it was apparent from his lordship's expression of feline forbearance that he was rather less inclined than usual to tolerate Stoker's bad temper. Stoker, for his part, was determined to play the hedgehog, snarling with his prickles out.

The viscount gestured expansively towards the specimen Stoker had been stitching when he arrived. "Why don't you go and play with your buffalo? I have business with Miss Speedwell."

Stoker curled his lip and I hastened to intervene before bloodshed broke out. "Poorly played, my lord. You know that Stoker and I are colleagues and friends. Anything you have to say to me can be said freely in front of him." I had hoped this little demonstration of loyalty would settle Stoker's hackles, but his mood did not change.

The viscount's expression turned gently mocking. "Colleagues and friends! How very tepid," he said blandly. He took a deep draft of his whisky while Stoker and I studiously avoided looking at one another. Our investigative pursuits, invariably dangerous and thoroughly enjoyable, had drawn us together, forcing a trust neither of us entirely welcomed. We were solitary creatures, Stoker and I, but we had discovered a mutual understanding beyond anything we had shared with others. What would become of it, I could not say. In spite of six months' distance, I still thought often of that last significant meeting, when words had hung unspoken but understood in the air. I had alternately cursed and congratulated myself on my narrow escape from possible domesticity—a fate I regarded as less desirable than a lengthy bout of bubonic plague. I had been so near to making declarations that could not be undone, offering promises I was not certain I could keep. My vow never to be relegated to the roles of wife and mother had been tested during a moment of vulnerability. Stoker was the only man I knew who could have weakened my resolve, but it would have been a mistake, I insisted to myself. I was not made for a life of ordinary pursuits, and it would take an extraordinary man to live with me on my terms. It was a point of pride with me that I hunted men with the same alacrity and skill that I hunted butterflies. Only one sort of permanent trophy interested me—and that had wings. Men were a joy to sample, but a mate would be a complication I could not abide. At least, this is what I told myself, and it was perhaps this elusiveness that made me all the more attractive to the opposite sex.

His lordship included. He was lavishly lascivious in his praise, his conversation usually peppered with deliciously outrageous comments. I never took him seriously, but Stoker took him *too* seriously, and that was the root of their current lack of sympathy with one another. Like stags, they frequently locked horns, and although neither would admit it, I suspected they enjoyed their battles far more than they did the civil affections they shared with their other brothers.

Stoker was glowering at the viscount, who held up a hand, the signet ring of the Templeton-Vanes gleaming upon his left hand. "Peace, brother mine. I can feel you cursing me."

"And yet still you breathe," Stoker said mildly. "I must not be doing it right."

I rolled my eyes heavenwards. "Stoker, behave or remove yourself, I beg you. I still do not know the purpose of his lordship's call."

"I do not require a reason except that of admiration," his lordship said with practiced smoothness. Stoker made a growling noise low in his throat while his brother carried on, pretending not to hear. "I missed you during your sojourn abroad, my dear. And, as it happens, I do have business. Well, business for you, dear lady, but pleasure for me."

"Go on," I urged.

"Tell me, Miss Speedwell, in all your travels around this beautiful blue orb of ours, have you ever encountered the Romilly Glasswing butterfly?"

"*Oleria romillia?* Certainly not. It was as elusive as Rajah Brooke's Birdwing and twice as valuable. It is unfortunately now extinct. I have only ever seen one preserved specimen in a private collection and it was in dreadful condition."

The viscount held up a hand. "Not entirely extinct, as it happens."

My heart began to thump solidly within my chest as a warm flush rose to my cheeks. "What do you mean?"

"I mean that there are still specimens in the wild. Do you know the origins of the name?"

I recited the facts as promptly and accurately as a schoolgirl at her favorite lesson. "*Oleria romillia* was named for Euphrosyne Romilly, one of the greatest lepidopterists in our nation's history. She founded the West Country Aurelian Society, the foremost body of butterfly hunters in Britain until it merged with the Royal Society of Aurelian Studies in 1852. She discovered this particular glasswing on the coast of Cornwall."

"*Off* the coast of Cornwall," the viscount corrected. "As it happens, the Romillys own an island there, St. Maddern, just out from the little port town of Pencarron."

"A tidal island?" I asked. "Like St. Michael's Mount?" The Mount was one of Cornwall's most famous attractions, rising out of the sea in a shaft of grey stone, reaching ever upwards from its narrow foundation. On sunny days it was overrun with parties of picnickers and seaside tourists and other undesirables.

The viscount shook his head. "Not precisely. St. Michael's is accessible on foot via a causeway, whilst St. Maddern's Isle is a little further out to sea and significantly larger than the Mount. There are extensive gardens as well as a village, farms, a few shops, a quarry, even an inn for the occasional traveler seeking solitude and peace. It is a unique place, with all sorts of legends and faery stories, none of which interest me in the slightest, so I cannot recall them. What I do recall is that the Romilly Glasswing makes its home upon this island, and nowhere else in the world. And this has been an excellent year for them. They have appeared in record numbers, I am told, and they dot the island like so many flowers."

I caught my breath, my lips parted as if anticipating a kiss. Nothing left me in such a heightened state of expectancy as the thought of finding a butterfly I had never before seen in the wild. And glasswings! The most unique of all the butterflies, they traveled on wings as transparent as Cinderella's slipper. Ordinary butterflies derive their color from scales, infinitesimally small and carrying all the colors of the rainbow within them, reflecting back the jewel tones associated with the most magnificent butterflies. Moths and more restrained specimens of butterfly have scales with softly powdered hues, but the most arresting sight is by far the butterfly without any scales at all. The wings of these butterflies are crystalline in their clearness, patterned only with narrow black veins like the leaded glass of a cathedral window, the thinnest of membranes stretching between them. It seems impossible that they can fly, but they do, like shards of glass borne upon the wind. Their unique wings make them delicate and elusive, and the Romilly Glasswing was the most delicate and elusive of all. The largest of the glasswings, an adult Romilly could span a man's hand if he were lucky enough to catch one. I lusted for them as I had lusted for little else in my life. But it was no use to me.

I forced a smile to my lips. "How kind of you to share this information," I said in a toneless voice. "But I no longer hunt, my lord. My specimens from Madeira were all gathered after their natural demise. I have lost the drive to thrust a pin into the heart of a living creature. My efforts are directed towards the vivarium that Lord Rosemorran is graciously permitting me to develop on the estate."

Once the derelict wreck of a grand freestanding glasshouse, the vivarium had been my own pet project, undertaken at Stoker's suggestion. While he tinkered happily with bits of fur and bone and sawdust, I had been permitted to stock the restored structure with exotic trees and the larvae of a number of specimens. I had nurtured them carefully as any mother, bringing several species to life in my bejeweled little world.

"You should know that better than anyone," I reminded the viscount. "You were kind enough to send me a grove of hornbeams and luna moths to feast upon them."

The viscount crossed one long leg over the other, smoothing the crease in his trousers. "I remember it well. You gave me quite the education upon the subject of the luna moth. What was it you said? That they have no mouths because they exist only to reproduce? One is not certain whether to regard them with envy or pity."

He arched a brow at me and I gave him a quelling look. "Precisely," I told him, my voice crisp. "And while I am glad to hear the Romilly Glasswing is not extinct, I must leave its pursuit to others."

The words pained me. I had only within the last year discovered in myself a reluctance to carry on my life's work as I had always known it. The pursuit of the butterfly had given my existence meaning and pleasure, but it had dried up for reasons I did not entirely understand. Madeira had been a test, after a fashion, a short expedition to test my mettle. And I had failed to conquer my reluctance to kill. The few inadequate specimens

I had brought back had made the entire affair pointless and I could not justify further expeditions if I had no better expectations than the results I had achieved there. It chilled me to think that I might never strike out again, net in hand, for foreign climes and exotic lands. The notion of being forever immured in Britain, this too often grey and sodden isle, was more than I could bear. So I did not think of it. I pushed the thought away whenever it occurred, but it had crept back over and over again as our ship had neared England, returning me to the complacent little life I had built within these walls. It teased the edge of my consciousness as I drifted off to sleep each night, that little demanding voice from a place that longed for adventure. *What if this is all there is?*

Stoker grasped his lordship's meaning before I did. "Tiberius does not mean you to hunt them," he said quietly. "He has found you larvae. For the vivarium."

I smothered a moan of longing. "Have you?" I demanded.

His lordship laughed, a low and throaty chuckle of pure amusement. "My dear Miss Speedwell, how you delight me. I have indeed secured permission from the current owner of St. Maddern's Isle, Malcolm Romilly, for you to take a certain number of larvae for your collection. While not a lepidopterist himself, he is an ardent protector of every bit of flora and fauna unique to his island, and he believes that if the glasswing is to survive, there must be a population elsewhere as a sort of insurance policy."

My mind raced with the possibilities. "What do they eat?"

The viscount shrugged. "Some shrub whose name escapes me, but Malcolm did say that you might take a number of the plants with you in order to make the transition to London as painless as possible for the little devils. Now, I am bound for St. Maddern's Isle for a house party to which Malcolm has invited me. It seems only natural that we should combine our purposes and I should escort you to the castle."

"What a splendid notion," Stoker put in smoothly. "We should love to go."

"Stoker," the viscount said firmly, "you are not invited to the castle."

"Castle!" I exclaimed. "Is it really so grand as that?"

His lordship favored me with one of his enigmatic smiles. "It is small, as castles go, but it is at least interesting. Lots of hidden passages and dungeons and that sort of thing."

"What of ghosts?" I demanded archly. "I won't go unless there is a proper ghost."

The viscount's eyes widened in a flash of something like alarm before he recovered himself. "I can promise you all manner of adventures," he said.

I could scarcely breathe for excitement. Stoker gave me a long look as he drained the last of his whisky, put down his glass, and walked silently back to his buffalo.

His brother leaned closer, pitching his voice low. "Someone is not very pleased with us."

"Someone can mind his own business," I said fiercely. "I am going to St. Maddern's Isle."

"Excellent," said Lord Templeton-Vane, his feline smile firmly in place. "Most excellent indeed."

Author photo © Sigmon Taylor Photography

Deanna Raybourn is the author of the award-winning, *New York Times* bestselling Lady Julia Grey series, currently in development for television; the *USA Today* bestselling Veronica Speedwell Mysteries (*A Curious Beginning, A Perilous Undertaking, A Treacherous Curse*); and several stand-alone novels. She lives in Virginia with her family.

CONNECT ONLINE

deannaraybourn.com
facebook.com/deannaraybournauthor
twitter.com/deannaraybourn
pinterest.com/deannaraybourn
instagram.com/deannaraybourn